THE
BOBBY-SOXER

Books by Hortense Calisher

NOVELS

FALSE ENTRY
TEXTURES OF LIFE
JOURNAL FROM ELLIPSIA
THE NEW YORKERS
QUEENIE
STANDARD DREAMING
EAGLE EYE
ON KEEPING WOMEN
MYSTERIES OF MOTION
THE BOBBY-SOXER

NOVELLAS AND SHORT STORIES

IN THE ABSENCE OF ANGELS
TALE FOR THE MIRROR
EXTREME MAGIC
THE RAILWAY POLICE and THE LAST TROLLEY RIDE
THE COLLECTED STORIES OF HORTENSE CALISHER
SARATOGA, HOT

AUTOBIOGRAPHY

HERSELF

THE
BOBBY-SOXER

HORTENSE CALISHER

Doubleday & Company, Inc.
Garden City, New York
1986

Library of Congress Cataloging-in-Publication Data
Calisher, Hortense.
The bobby-soxer.
I. Title.
PS3553.A4B6   1986   813'.54   85-16039
ISBN 0-385-18426-3

PART ONE

"Craig Towle's married a bobby-soxer," my father said, the evening before my mother left him.

My mother never hushed him when he made remarks about real life, whether or not he made them at the dinner table. For one thing, since he was a lawyer, the harsher points of existence often impinged on him in the way of business, where she could not hope to constrict him or follow him. For another, we lived on one of those streets where the existence of, well, real life, could not hope to be concealed.

It was a street that we younger ones already knew was going to be enshrined in our memories, even if our high school teacher and the movies hadn't already told us so. Although we were not in the Middle West of Middle America but in a New Jersey town just off the rim of commuting New York, and our wide street, not Main Street but one of a half-dozen comfortably like it, had no elms, still its maples were large and almost overarching, and the houses were mostly frame. Because of a certain fraying at one end where the factory workers—carpets, furniture, nothing untidy—had their houses, we would never be the estate section, but we were what was called "well set back." We seemed farther from Jersey's farmtowns now than from the city, but front lawns were pretty large and backyards sometimes surprisingly so. The word "garden" was still for vegetables, though we took magazines that dealt only in the ornamental kind and some of the women were inclining that way. In summer, when all down the evening street every father or elder son made a precise arc with the waterhose—girls did not yet—we knew very well what we were and that somebody should be painting us.

I had already tried that particular scene, in a three-by-four canvas now embarrassing me in my paternal grandmother's back parlor. Though her house and ours had much the same conformation, we had made the double parlor into a living room, where such a local scene would not have suited, and I did not want it there, an awkward testimony to all I hadn't got into it. What that canvas had taught me was that although I lived on a street that prided itself as the height of convention, all its under-layers were perfectly clear to everybody—and my brush had not known how to make this evident. Yet I knew quite well how the street's situation had come about, what with three generations working on it.

Did Mrs. Denby, down at the corner, who no longer slept with her husband and shared her elder daughter's bedroom, really hope to conceal this fact by switching back the best bedspread for the benefit of Sunday drop-ins? Or in her heart of hearts did she know that my younger brother, forever underfoot in her house with his bosom pal, her Pat, would one day innocently reveal the pattern of her life to us? Our own family position, with my long-widowed grandmother still in a house of her own instead of having to come to us, was uncomfortably plain to my friend Phoebe, who lived with hers at the neighborhood's border, in one of the four-room factory cottages. Yet my gran did not live separate only because she had the money to do so. All my mother's women friends, who had to cope with her Southern-belle-gone-slop housekeeping whenever our barn of a place was "opened" for some local function, thought they knew why. As well as that a lawyer whose wife had no live-in maid must not be doing well. While Phoebe's gran, a nurse who had at one time hired out to wrap the dead for a living, knew what had on one occasion appeared in a medical book hopefully not accessible to my family's immediate public (and only fully disclosed to me later): that our gran's youngest sister and lifetime legacy, already in long skirts when my grandfather had moved the family here, and later a large-fingered, noble-nosed lady revered all the way from her charities to her cookie jar as "Aunt Leo," had been physically part man.

We sound unmodern. We were not, even as things go now. Drinks served on those summer porches were cocktails, or at least beer, and there were other signs that we saw looming ahead. We were no longer quite a neighborhood. Too many of the men now had city business connections. The women sometimes had little time-chipping jobs "in town"—our downtown. And the tree-shade was going down.

But as a street we were still what I thought my father meant when he spoke of a business deal as an open-and-shut proposition. Front doors and back, to be crept out of or slammed, windows and porches naked or enclosed, washlines to be ashamed of and love-nest paths between, and the garage door in front of which Denby could be found dead drunk. Plus those candlelit dining rooms that, quite without meaning to, showed the permanent presence of indigent relatives. Or the dark house next door to us, with only a single light on for show, whose blind owners, Mr. and Mrs. Evams, taught the classics in braille for free.

We were simply a group of houses able to be still in control of our connections, three generations of those, however we managed them. Wherever there was a peccadillo, or a virtue, somebody was getting at the root of it. In my painting, I hadn't been able to get that going yet. I had the spirit to do it, but unlike at the Evamses', the blind couple next door, it didn't yet show.

Actually, my father was doing well at the time, but had a mistress in the city who kept us poorer than we ought to have been, in more ways than one. As the saying goes, I "never knew." What is never? Why else was I always measuring?

But that night at the dinner table we could all gossip in a way, if each of us privately. As my father's voice perhaps said, his other woman was of a decent age for a man of his years, and Towle's was not. My mother, who like half the women in town had been in love with Craig Towle since he returned, but unlike them had been successful with him, would have noted this. As for me, if I had a special interest—which my parents' glances now recorded—how could I be blamed? I too was a bobby-soxer.

Craig Towle was everybody's business right out, and what a relief that was. Though very modest about his life since leaving town, he was our native son. Born not twenty blocks away from our house, he had attended my school, though few of the elders on our block had known him, for he had had the luck, as some now saw it, both to be born at the frayed end of our street, and to win a scholarship away from it. A craggy man in his forties with a hospitable face, he didn't seem to mind that we knew even more about him than the newspapers did, for though as the papers said, he might have come back to his roots because he had to, we also knew from him that he hadn't done so until when, divorced, with two children at a Pennsylvania boarding school conveniently nearby, and at far too loose ends for a man of his superior meditations, he had reflected that he still owned a house here, never lived in since his parents' time and now aged into the charming. For unlike our own gawky verandahs and bays, the factory workers' homes, though small, had mostly been of ancient stone or brick, with blistered early-glass panes, wide-board floors and pine rather than hard oak, and if very run-down, cobbled walks.

We in turn didn't mind if he was here to get another play out of us, even if he didn't know that yet. On that score we seem to me now to have been more sophisticated than he. We were proud that, whatever he had become since, he had done it entirely out of what he had started with: us—a few blocks down. We couldn't understand why the newspapers thought he should feel guilty about reporting on his own people, even if he had risen above them. Many of our elders had read his plays in the library. Some had even gone to the theater to check on them, even if they never usually did that sort of thing. If he was supposed to know more than anyone else about our class habits, our moody lower-middle to middle-middle aspirations, and our whole country's sad money based nostalgias—then so did we. Also, though we didn't see him very often, he and we had our contacts, and for a man who could express himself better than most of us he didn't seem to be taking things down in any nasty way, or even to be listening too hard. Not any harder, that is, than us. As Mr. Evams, our blind expert on that, and also a real theatergoer, said keenly to my father: "Towle may allot us a murder or two more than we think we have, or deserve. But certainly no more sex."

So there was no criticism of a professional sort, so to speak, from us.

"He's a man of ideas," Gilbert, our neighbor on the other side, said. As one who had been through all the philosophies allied to the restaurant trade, Gilbert was that himself. "Ideas come to all of us unannounced. But to him more so than to most people. And in his own way. Sure, now he's back in the place he got famous on. That could be a mistake. Maybe we'll correct his viewpoint for him, more than he likes."

I could see my father thought Gilbert was planning to. But Gilbert's own trade made for quick summings-up. "Some people fester about what he's going to say next. About them especially. That's nonsense. One of these days, like an idea—we'll just come to him. The he'll put us all together, like a seven-course dinner." What Gilbert had his eye on, he said, was the property. "Theatrical?" my father said, for Gilbert was getting rich. "No—the Towle house." Towle now and then came alone to the restaurant, Gilbert said, and that was where you could see how a mind worked, even with very little talk. For one thing, he hated what the newspapers said about his being here. Once stuffed a whole Sunday *Post* into a wastebasket, from which the waitress had retrieved it, because of cigarettes of course. "Whatever he does do on us," Gilbert said, "once he's looked us in the eye he'll find an excuse to move out of here. For good."

"Towle gets out of the restaurant without talking to Gilbert?"

my father said when Gilbert had gone. "Wonder how he manages it."

My mother, eating chocolates, had not replied.

Towle and the other town wives? They were either home-birds making crepe-paper costumes for the children at the proper intervals, or else loud, leftover office girls with too much Saturday night flair. Even their husbands could scarcely have imagined anything between them and that "classic-looking man," as he came to be called fraternally in the husbands' own banks and garages and hardware stores. Very friendly he could be, too, but otherwise only seen walking his dogs or his weekending children. A man who whatever he wanted would go out of town for it, the town humbly thought, and indeed Towle was often gone. We assumed from the first that we wouldn't be enough for him in any real-life way. Yet, why then, I wondered, had he had to come back to us to check up?

As my mother said when I asked this, "He's learned to live fast. Now he wants to remember how it is to live slow,"—in the same moment offering me her Whitman Sampler box. She was always generous with what she called her vice, but I had no taste for it. What I wanted were the remarks that came with our chocolate-fests. So I would take a piece, to be as polite as her Southern manners had taught me to be, and I suppose, as circuitous. Whitman's were not her favorites, but the best the drugstore stocked. My father supplied her also from a Hungarian shop in the city, or once in a while a red satin three-decker box from a place called Rosemarie, which she accepted with a special smile. These, I assumed, were his atonement boxes, and cheap at the price. The mistress had probably got another whopping coat or ring; surely she must take full advantage of her position. So did my mother.

All this I knew without being told straight out, though she would not have lied. We handled it peripherally. If she somewhat later remarked that she didn't care for fur coats or was glad she already had her family jewelry—two modest necklaces of pearl and garnet, a pendant and a cameo—I could suspect why.

How she actually knew what the mistress might have got, or even had found out there was one—and possibly who—was her concern, though she wouldn't have spied. Even if she hadn't been too "social smart," as she called her Carolina shrewdness, she was too indolent. "I like to indle," she would say, claiming her origin for both the word and the deed. "If the ladies want to sweep out my corners when they come to borrow the house for an occasion—well and good." She was fond of these double phrases. Many people are, but she taught me to listen for the meaning of even the simplest. She really did like to lie on a sofa, read novels, and eat her nut cremes and truffles, even if the novels got short shrift in lieu of her own ruminations. Though these were never offered, people grew to know she had them.

"You went to school with Craig Towle's divorced wife, didn't you?" Gilbert asked my mother on another evening on our porch. "What was she like?"

"Yes, we were at school together," my mother said. Seated as always well back of the elders, I wondered if he felt she had corrected him. People who had gone to boarding school said they "were at" instead of "went to," it seemed. My mother, who had been a day pupil in such a school, in the New England town to which her father had been sent north as branch manager of the mill in his hometown, was the only person of that class of education any of us knew. It was agreed that she did not presume on it, but there it was, accounting for what people said was her style—though I didn't think it did. My mother's style lay in always going ahead with what she wanted to do, which she always saw clearly; it was just lucky she was so relaxed she didn't want to do too much.

"His wife's name was Venice," she said now. "Because she had been conceived there, though her people were from Boston, mostly. Her father didn't have to work, but he did. She said the men in her family generally hung around Harvard. We thought they were professors. She didn't like to say they were trustees. Which was nice of her. I went home with her once. They were required to speak Italian at one meal, French at the next, and as

far back as during World War I there had been a scandal because
the family had refused to intern its Fraülein. Venice was best at
Italian, because of her name. They had a retarded cousin living
with them, a boy who looked like a frog, to whom they were very
kind. They were very kind to me when it was found I knew
nothing about sailing, though we were down at the shore.
Dorchester, their summer place. Venice's daddy let me wind
things on their sloop. Even at the shore her mother had a bulletin board in the bedroom, on which she wrote her causes and the
times for them. Venice said the board back home was even bigger. The beachhouse was very plain, but commodious."

"Commodious" was one of my mother's words. I never heard
anybody else use it in conversation.

"What's a Froylein?" I asked.

"Governess. German." My mother laughed. "I asked that too.
Back then."

"And what did you do, when they spoke those languages you
didn't know?"

"I listened," my mother said pointedly. "Like you back
there."

My father, nearest me, reached over to pat my hand. I always
listened from the rear, he said—like him. He thought I would
likely be a lawyer because of that. I was no painter, he said. He
was right. But I was no lawyer either.

"Why didn't they switch to English?" I said. "If they were so
kind."

My mother hesitated. That is, she poured more coffee for
everyone, and tea for the blind Evamses, whose sense of direction coffee confused. It was a chilly September night, late for
porches. No one among us drank liquor on Monday nights. "I
think I was a cause," she sighed.

The whole porch tittered. The house was real messy just then;
that's why we kept to the porch. But our neighbors on either side
never failed to come for their Mondays, an off night, as they
called it, when Mr. Evams kept no classes, my father never
stayed over in the city, and Gilbert closed the restaurant.

"For God's sake," Gilbert's wife, Luray, said, "the way you tease us fish. You Southerners. What did she look like? Craig Towle's wife."

"Venice? Why, she was tall and rangy. Taller than—than most of the boys. Long hair she never cut, and real crisp features. Fine legs, though she never wore heels. Parties with boys—she simply piled up the hair and wore family earrings. You know the type."

Luray wouldn't, as everybody on the porch knew; still, my mother wasn't being mean. If she was circuitous she always gave full measure. She also had a way of talking like whoever she was talking to. It was said that Craig Towle had the same.

Now—Luray was a sexy talker. A big brassy-hair with a brass tongue, she was vulgar in the warm way that made people think she was soft-hearted, but my mother was of the opinion that Luray might be too busy to be, always changing her waistline as she was, and improving her diamonds, and heading the committees my mother would never join. "A looker? You didn't say."

"Oh yes I did, Luray. Blond eyebrows. No breasts."

"Class," Gilbert said instantly. "And the boy from Cobble Row fell for it." He was from there himself, but he hadn't done the same.

"Nerts—" his wife said, "listen to what she's telling us. Those flat-chested kind, they can't get enough of it. That's what happened. Maybe on that sloop."

My father coughed; the Evamses rose to go. Blind people are delicate in their tastes. Whenever I went next door to learn braille, as I did to enlarge my horizon, I was always very careful to wash, Mrs. Evams having told me how uncomfortable their sharpened other senses could make them, in company.

Luray got up too. She had her Flower & Fruit luncheon to benefit the hospital, the next day. Though she spread herself on her charitableness, we knew Gilbert charged the committee full price. All the women were crazy for Craig Towle, and ever since Luray had rescheduled their meetings to coincide with his regular day in there after driving his children back to school, the restaurant had never had so many reservations for Tuesday lunch. My mother could meet him too, Luray said, or next best to it, for he always nodded politely to all—if she just wasn't so un-community-minded.

"Nevertheless, they got divorced, he and his Venice," my father said, joining all at the porch railing. He was against divorce. So must my mother be, though I had never heard her say. "By mutual consent, I understand. And no property settlement. On either side."

"Class," Gilbert muttered.

My mother turned to him. "Maybe she was a woman of ideas, Gilbert. Her family dealt in them."

No one had caught on that my mother had started to say that Venice had been taller than Craig Towle was. Weeks back, when he had come to see us, I had been home upstairs, comfortably in bed for the first hours of my period, not sick, but on my mother's advice cosseting the rhythm of it, settling in to being a woman in the right way. I suspected I was being taught her own rhythm as well, but felt able to correct myself when necessary, meanwhile alternately copying a small Tiepolo drawing and sketching a bowl of real ivy, while enjoying the cool of the newly laundered blanket cover, the smell of wax and all the extraordinary couthness of our house. Over the past months there had been bad rows about the condition of our furniture, descended to my father when he married, and my grandmother, who blamed him, had been having a housekeeper sent in.

My father was in the city, with the lady. Perhaps she had no furniture, only pillows. Although in the city he played squash, a sissy game I had heard him twitted for when he and I went to the hardware store where our townsmen hung out on Saturday mornings, I thought of him always as seated in one of our high-backed chairs, his tanned face and thick white hair, not so premature as it once had been, sticking out over the top. He was taller than Craig Towle, and handsomer, as I was about to find out. Whenever I was tomboyish, rebelling against my periods, it was clear even to me that I was taking after him, though at the moment I was only five foot eight, and unaware that one day, when past eighteen and in full growth, I would be able to look him in the eye. That would be a day. Today would be another. One gathers them in later, the days that tot up.

"Honey—" my mother called, "can you come down?" Though she was not an affected woman, all the street had a company voice. "Mr. Craig Towle is here. He's come from grandmother's." How quick she was. She always prepared me well.

I slipped out of my housecoat, jammed into my new plaid skirt and white saddle-shoes, and went bed-woozily down the stairs, my flesh heavy and sensitive. Perhaps that's why I learned so much. I'll be brief about that, while admiring the fact. In one's forties, where I am now, reflection begins to drag the pace of learning down.

Briefly: my mother was in one of the wandlike dresses her home dressmaker down South still copied from *Vogue* and sent up to her, the dream-client whose measurements always stayed the same. Though she was slim enough to let waistlines rise and fall as they might, this dress winningly had none, and she had just been trying it on, in one of those lonely, self-gathering intervals when women do that. She was in luck therefore, for drop-in company. She had truly not expected him, at least not that night. But these intervals I speak of, when women try on and try on, rousting out the wardrobe of their expectations, do not come without reason. She and Craig Towle had met before. I had been called down in part to be duenna—though I think now that my mother herself may not yet have known this.

Craig Towle's brown-eyed, pleasantly hooked face was hospitable, yes, but to facts more than to persons. When you are truly genial yet truly remote, then you are hard. I could see no trace of the Pennsylvania miners he was said to come from before his more recent forebears had descended to factory furniture, neither the Polack Catholic mother nor his father's Scots. When you see a face that much on its own, take it as a sign, or a warning, of what may not be bad but is extra. When there is no trace. This she had no time to tell me.

He was too short for my romances at the moment, but his scrutiny was like a well that pulled on you, making you eager to find your own face in the depths down there. Women would cast themselves hopefully in; apparently, even my mother's ninety-year-old mother-in-law had succumbed. He had gone to her, my father's mother, as to the patrician of the town's lore, and already knew of our six-month feud. He said he had also met my young brother in her house. No doubt our grandmother had introduced my brother as "My son-and-his-wife's-reconciliation child"—a habit she refused to drop, though my parents had never really been parted.

"The little devil—" my mother said. Her smile was luminous, not only with motherhood. "We thought Tim was sleeping overnight with Pat Denby. So that's where he goes. Well, he'll learn there not to kick the furniture."

So had I, and had hated that house for it. All families have these divided allegiances—and in my brother and me ours has two differing historians.

"He sits there entranced," Craig Towle said—and turning to me: "I saw your painting." He had asked whose it was and was interested to hear now that I already knew in what way it was bad. I saw he would not forget that, nor my brother either; we would be ready in his head like old shrapnel, until some needed surgery got us out. As for my mother, he had indeed really wanted to talk with her about his wife Venice, as soon as he heard the two had been schoolmates. I went back up the stairs then. Their glow, which they would soon begin to explore, was already visible. Perhaps I had seen it because he had been sitting in my father's chair.

Upstairs, I tried to decode this jumble of the perhaps and the happened, which was so much deeper than gossip, but I could not. I was not old enough to want to be a well—and I see now that I have not been brief. The scene would never again be that pure. Reflection had entered in. But without it I wouldn't have sensed what I had. It came through that wooziness and cell-breakage going on inside me. He too had a process whereby he sloughed things off. Mine, just beginning, had been alerted, though to what, I could not phrase, as I do now. Craig Towle found his privacy in women. They were the privacy he took on the sly. From now on, I thought, he had no power over me, even no charm, now that I had seen how it worked. For even a young girl could see that his process never would stop.

After that day I wasn't to see him again for a year of the three he stayed on in the town. He telephoned her at first; later she telephoned him, neither hiding the fact nor obtruding it. But after some weeks, I one day said to her: "Why do they, why do all the women call him Craig Towle, never just Craig?" Even she did it, when she had to mention his name.

She smiled uncertainly. She really didn't know, hadn't noted, and now never would. Women such as she had to find their public in their lovers, and he was already that.

Now back to us at large.

Shortly after that day, my grandmother, majestic on the arm of my eleven-year-old brother—as if, though he had no license to drive her limousine, he could still squire her—came to visit us, to break the feud and, we thought at first, to check on the house-cleaning. Standards had already gone down; my mother relaxed servants, too. But the high fervor in my grandmother's age-mas-culinized cheeks had to be otherwise explained, and shortly was. It was "Craig" this, "Craig" that; she had come back to us in order to talk of him. "He brings me out in the world."

They had gone first to one of those "nasty" big New Jersey restaurants where they serve you steak and lobster on one plate, then to several others, increasingly better and farther afield, that she wouldn't further identify. Though she was no recluse, there had never been any question of our taking her out anywhere. Her house was where you went when asked—family being no guaran-tee—to large, discriminatory dinner parties, where the conven-tions of her youth were rolled out one after the other, on a par with her silver chafing dishes. She would avoid senility to her end, at one hundred and four, by refusing it her house. But still it was a shock to my father, whom she had derisively called "Sir" since his majority, to hear his past ninety-year-old mother say of a man younger than he: "He and I have a relationship."

My brother had gone with them to some of the restaurants. What did they talk about? For that was surely what they would have done, my grandmother plucking at the discreetly flowered skirts that humanized her old bones, in order to sink the more lightly into that soothing depth across the table. My brother would not tell me. Years later, Pat Denby did. My brother had been sat at a small table apart. "Towle had him sent a fake Manhattan with a cherry in it. There was no disliking Towle. But Tim never heard a thing."

In payment perhaps, if not apology, Craig Towle one day took my brother to a restaurant along with Towle's other children, a pleasant act, if not the man-to-man talk my brother had hoped for. Craig Towle had not chanced to tell my mother about this, but there was nothing strange about that, though years later, hearing of it, she was surprised. We all of us, the town too, were continually surprised by the number of people here Craig Towle knew personally, and it would seem exclusively—though one always forgot this, they said, when his face fronted yours, one shoulder politely aslant. He had even been to the blind Evamses'. "He has a hard face, but a good one," Mrs. Evams, who had been allowed to feel it, reported. Her husband said: "He listens abstractly. He could almost be blind.

We had all humbly and correctly diagnosed Towle's relationship to each of us, but it would seem that our own gossip, in which all roads and all nerves were interconnected, had kept us from really taking the man as a whole into our consciousness.

As was never clearer than the night my father brought down his own house with his soon verified report of the bobby-soxer, Craig Towle had a larger life.

And now we had heard that larger-life echo, in our own house. "—married a bobby-soxer" my father said.

Before supper that very evening, my father had given my

mother a gold bangle, very handsome, but as she and I had already exchanged in a glance, too heavy for our tastes. Some fathers never gave to the mother without giving to the daughters too, but neither he nor I would have cared for that—wanting not to dilute what he had it in him to give to her alone. The bracelet was one of those whose embossing seems to spell a name but doesn't. I felt it would never spell hers.

A rose silk shade shaped like the Taj Mahal hung over our dining-room table. There were several of those around town, meant to soften the harsh outlines of the day. What ours did was to influence for life my idea of dinner conversation. Under the lamp's cast, I could chew the gristle of some heartache and appear only to be concentrating, or my brother could creep to table with his latest secret safe in those daylight-blue eyes which could not otherwise hold back. My mother, who never stooped to hide anything of value, merely indled more quietly. My father, who conducted his life on some theorem apart from us, seemed neither to need that light nor to notice it. Men are not as subject to home shadow.

"A—bobby-soxer?" my mother said. She might have been asking what that was, though I sat before her, in the new penny-in-the-slot leather loafers which had overtaken saddle shoes, and ankle socks. I was seeing how even the Taj Mahal could not hide the dark red shock of life-surprise.

My father reached out to grasp the wrist with the bangle on it. He was a man who liked to see that houses, and the lives of those in them, kept themselves up, and that night I wondered if he wasn't helping her at this, under the rose radiance of the dining-room lamp. I wasn't sure why they stayed together, but I wasn't one of those children popularly held to be afflicted by fears of impermanence. I always knew they would continue as a pair.

Nevertheless, she and I left for Greensboro the next morning. Once a winter she and I went to see her parents, now removed from the small manor farm which had been my maternal grandmother's inheritance to a tiny white town house, where I was able to learn the real etymology of indling, or the temperament, and how breakfast on a tray could still be managed for all, even on a small pension, if you still had an in-coming black. Up North, my mother had simply kept the temperament. That winter, although we had come on such short notice, we would stay longer than we ever had. "What with one thing or another—" my mother phoned or wrote my father back home—though she never said precisely what, we would not return again until well through spring.

On the train down there, she was restless; she had forgotten her chocs, she said. That alone would have shown the power of the distress under her neat suit, toque, and fur. But I had picked up a box on my way to the car. Father of course had driven us to the station.

"Honey, I'm so touched," she said to me, once we were in the train. "You have the memory of a Southerner."

"And we can buy chocolate bars from the vendor who comes through," I said, basso with responsibility and praise. "Soon as

we get beyond Philadelphia they still have them. Vendors." I was
already remembering what you had to remember if I was to be as
my mother had said. Napkin-rings all round, not just for babies.
Bibs on the babies. Parties with old ladies at them. If the babies
and the small children were there also, a "dawky"—a word my
mother said I was not to say, would be there to take care of
them. Whether or not I said it, the girl would be there. My
other grandmother, a fine contrast to my severe Jersey one,
would feed us up "as if our livers are to be made into pâté," my
grandfather would say, proud. After that, his free-to-coarse
speech would be curbed, at least at table. The women loved to.
We two would have a round of obligations, attending to which
we would acquire the fierce, if temporary local opinions which
made it easier. Any eccentricities I had, if interesting and not
too troublesome, would be praised as individuality. In return, I
would have to drawl, not cross my knees in company, and giggle
when there were boys. Compared to Phoebe Wetmore's brother
Bill, they would still be boys.

"Have a choc," she said.

I took one, careful as always to take the nougat she didn't
much like, though when she caught me at it she would make me
take a truffle creme, not suspecting, I thought proudly, that I
didn't care which.

She took one of the pink bonbons she usually left till last—
often saying they melted on the tongue like leisure itself. The
train made our wrists brush. She was wearing the gold bangle.

"Very distinguished—" she said, "twenty-two carat. Not eighteen." Might this mean the mistress was given the eighteen-
carat stuff? But was that the only reason she was wearing it? She
rarely wore her own good jewelry, substituting the odd little bits
of Bakelite now known as Art Deco. She only liked to have the
other by. She caught my eye. "Your Greensboro grandmother
will be pleased to see this. It will make up for our not having a
maid."

We munched, while the last pig-towns of Jersey raced backward, unable to hold us. I would miss them, yet still be full of

new delight. Father would miss us too. But he had New York.
And the lady.

"I think—I think he gave it to you—for you." This was daring.

She sat up. "Why?"

Because of the bobby-soxer. But, looking at my own legs, the
accordion-pleated skirt, the whole outfit—I found I couldn't say
it to her. "Because—you're you." And that was true, too. We
never lied.

She sat too formally straight for the fields of smashed cars and
other rusted iron we now were passing. She even closed the
chocolate box. "Tell me. Do you think—you know too much?"

That depended. Had she noticed last year in Greensboro that
I no longer giggled at men—even at uncles? Did she know that
Bill Wetmore no longer regarded me as merely his kid sister's
friend? Or that when we lay upstairs in the loft of the old out-
building, once a hayloft, that now served them for garage, while
he spoke of his great-grand-uncle, the Beaux Arts sculptor he
meant to emulate, and I of the painter I wanted to be in spite of
absolutely no background for it—that we had no longer merely
nestled? Or that I had stopped going there altogether, the day
after Phoebe, who had only a grandmother to inform her, had
told me what she said no one else but them knew—that my
mother visited Craig Towle in his nearby house? To tell me had
seemed for a minute still friendship, if misguided, or—in the
arcanum of what the Wetmores already knew about us—even an
ever deferent old-town function. Until Phoebe had added, lip
retracted, "Maybe these days, for what both of you come down
here for, she could give you a lift."

"Take your time," my mother said. "Or don't answer at all.
Or not yet."

I thought of all I knew because of her—which was what she
was asking. How, at the rare times we went to New York as a
family, I lost myself in fancy on the side streets of where I meant
someday to paint all streets, and to be the mistress as well of
somebody who had no wife. How, in the very scene we lived in, I

would never have sensed the layers of things, even to the small, severe still-life judgments between truffle and nougat. Or to the way the lip retracts in jealousy, even on an otherwise nice young girl. Without my mother, I would never have had the hayloft courage to do what I had done with Bill Wetmore, which I did not regret then, and do not now. Even at this moment, she was teaching me the difference between fast and slow.

If the parents don't burden us, they cannot teach us. I didn't know that yet, but I answered, and joyously.

"Never. I can never know too much."

She smiled. That's my girl. She whispered it really, bowing her head. "Your father would not agree."

Though I was desperately fond of him, here he seemed an intrusion. I did not mind that he thought as he did. Though I would never fault her, he was the brake. Because of him, I had an inkling I would one day do as she had: I would marry well.

But at the moment, her mention of him confused me. Was she running away from him, or from Craig Towle?

Perhaps she saw my state. Her way was to confuse me further, but always one step ahead. "Would you like to know something I know about you?"

If she saw my scare, she also saw I was ready. To be told I was illegitimate? Or destined to suffer a rare hereditary disease? No —this she would have managed to let me know. But suppose she had seen that I was not going to be able to do what I thought I was fitted for?

Anyway, she put her arm around me, which was rare enough to be valuable. Under her pushed-back cuff I saw that she was wearing another bracelet entirely, a broader flash of torqued silver, the purest, worked with many angled forms of onyx and jade —what must surely be the lustrous Paris progenitor of her Bakelite.

We both looked at it, hung there at my shoulder. "Came last week," she said. "I can't send it back. That would be bad taste. And they'll have only that small mailbox out there." So did we. But out there always meant the old town. I could see the mail-

boxes, the Towle one not too far down the lane from the
Wetmore's. And the bobby-soxer, going to it. *"Bracelets,"* my
mother said, squeezing her eyes shut. She opened them. "Here
—why don't you wear it." She quirked at me. "Forgive me, but
on you they won't know it's real." She put it on me, kissing the
wrist she clasped it on.

"Is that it?" I said. "What you know about me."

"Why, darling." Her face crumpled. So had mine. "No,
never," she said. "Never." I thought I heard an echo. "Never"
always made one. She put her lips to my ear. Lovely lips—I
never saw them retract. I hear her whisper. "I know—that you
really don't like chocolate."

Then we embraced, as the train and we flung ourselves forward onto the long green fields.

We came home that spring much refreshed. Down there I could be smart without having to show it; unlike up North, you could just use it in your daily life. My mother, languid toward new dresses, had been admonished on her duty to the dressmaker— "We owe it to Miss DeVore." Obligation was different from convention; fewer people—often nobody—could be blamed, either for expense or offense. Gossip, open and catty, was so polite you could mistake it for lessons in etiquette. I learned once again how my mother had come to be as she was, when we talked to my father on the phone, as of course we did—with everybody in the house listening. I tried to be as knowledgeable about him— knowledge is charity—but with him that was not the same. I wanted him to be a mystery so that I could still love him. For the sake of them both, I succeeded in losing the silver bracelet, but Greensboro, furnished with two systems of vigilance, one black, one white, unfortunately restored it to me. Nevertheless, when we came home I was not wearing it. Neither was she wearing the gold one, but that was mere impatience with the object itself. My mother was still a woman with two mysteries in her head.

The difference that spring was that now my mother would be doubly alone. Father's mistress was very ill, and in his loyalty— which stretched vainly, like too short an elastic, between the two

households, finally took precedence. He slept in the city, spending all his spare time at the hospital. Meanwhile, I was going to a
junior college in our neighborhood, in lieu of the real college for
which I was eligible but deemed too young. Later, I could be a
transfer, perhaps next year.

It struck me that my family was beginning to make too many
substitutes for the real, but in any case I wouldn't be around
home very much. Next term my brother, in spite of the demo-
cratic influence of the Denbys, or perhaps because of it—Denby
Senior now drank openly inside the garage door, never closing it
or sleeping in the house—was slated for boarding school, if he
could get a scholarship.

For it seemed that my father's mother, though utterly willing,
could not pay for him as planned. In a snit over her suddenly
terminated "relationship"—since though the Craig Towles at
the end of their extended honeymoon, applied to see her, she
would not receive his "juvenile wife"—my grandmother, revert-
ing to her customary chain of command, money, had suddenly
invested in what promised to bring her a fine return in her one
hundredth year but meanwhile left her short of ready cash—
which my father must now supply.

This was the end of the first year of Craig Towle.

The evening my father was to come back to deal with all this,
the train station was brilliantly lit for a town rally over what
some posters cried as KEEP OUT URBAN SPRAWL and others as
DON'T BE A BEDROOM SUBURB.

"Seems a developer has been sighted on the horizon," Gilbert
said, nodding to my mother and me on the platform. Some forty
miles away there was talk of a convention center. "The protesters will naturally want to call attention to us." He and Luray,
there to pick up an important woman speaker for tomorrow's
luncheon meeting, wouldn't object to a little sprawl; at least
there then might be station-cabs.

One of the circle of protesters filing up and down stopped to
comment: "Yeah, to bring 'em straight to your restaurant," but

it was all quite genial; everyone knew everyone else, and the banner carriers might well end up at Gilbert's for coffee, although having less than a full meal there was now discouraged. My mother and I had not known the town was threatened. We came so seldom here, as was clear from other platform glances. To my father, these seemed to say, our house was already a bedroom suburb.

"He coming to pay the old lady's taxes?" Gilbert said. "Saw in the paper her house is up for them." I saw Luray give him a nudge. "If he's pressed, we might work something out. Leave the old lady occupancy till she goes."

"Oh, lovely," my mother said lightly, down-home artifice still with her, "but who's to say she'll ever go?" Though we didn't want grandmother's house for ourselves, I could tell she was what Greensboro called "spit furious." Her eyes were fixed on the track.

"Men who see him on the train," she murmured, "simply don't know the pressure he's under." That was true. Not bluff and hearty, but tanned and white-crested, he would spring down from the train steps, the first one off, his glance going straight to us, from the larger life. To us awaiting him.

As I watched that image form in me, I could not believe what it was telling me. No, the resemblance to Towle must lie elsewhere; the two men themselves were not like. I was studying freshman logic, "applied logic," as it was called, and carefully I now did that. The resemblance, then, must be in the situation, in my mother—and in me, if I didn't watch out—in that we would stand by, and wait.

"*When* he's on the train," Luray said.

He wasn't. The woman was dead.

But of course we waited until the train emptied, Gilbert and Luray passing us with their guest, who I saw with my new perspective was merely a person who had spoken at the college some time back, to a very scratch audience. All the other fathers, three or four, were picked off by their waiting wives. The train heaved off, leaving the rally still circling. In the pre-autumn air with the faintly seen hills beyond adding what intensity they could, the protesters did not want to give up their own small opera. Each was swinging a Coleman lantern. So it was that my mother and I first saw Craig Towle's bobby-soxer, in that jockeying light.

Almost all the town knew of her was that she traveled in a pack of other young people, all much alike. In the eight months since her marriage that visiting pack had come and gone, come and gone—this mournful repetition being our street's. Who could live so, here? That rhythm—the open cars swirling the streets, the housekeepers coming and going, the weekend rousings and the weekday dearth—must surely come to a stop someday—and for such a crowd, a stop meant disaster. Craig Towle was now and then seen among them. How did he look—bewildered, lost? No, he never looks that. Pleased—if a little remote? Well—he always looks that.

As for his own rhythm, he came and went, which was different. We, the town, had almost got used to him—a loss of distinction on both sides. Which the town was prepared to forgive him for, even if necessary to take him back altogether. There was now a school among us, however, which held that we were what he would ultimately reject, once he found out, like many a foolish man before him, that with a young wife one often gets the young crowd as well.

The difficulty was how to tell, out of all those coltish girls who seemed to be studying how to be wild, yet how never to be caught in any garb except neat-collared sweaters of subtle weave and skirts mostly of yellow or gentian blue—which was the wife?

"A lack of differentiation—" Mr. Evams, to whom I once described them, said. "Yes, at first it's attractive." He pinched my fingers, which are large for braille. "Now, I would know you anywhere." Some of the blind smile generally; to do so over particulars is rarer. Mrs. Evams did neither. "Oh, I don't know —" she said. "So many of the girls are now over six feet, like you. In the elevator at Lord & Taylor I am often quite overwhelmed by their breathing down."

I don't go on about my size; my generation of girls didn't, and doesn't. If many of us look more like our fathers than needed, mine did me well enough. To have one's first boyfriend an admiring sculptor also helps. Rather, as that ruff-headed bunch of Towle's visitors rumpled off the first car of the train in their huge varicolored sweaters, it was my mother who moved back, though some of the girls were as small as she. She was wearing just her tan windbreaker and slacks and her one beautiful slouch hat, but only the middle-aged kept themselves that perfectly matched.

On my part, I saw that over the summer this laughing sleek vanguard, as it came toward me, had made the leap I had only half achieved; they were collegiate now. Though still a pack of a certain sort, their eyes were long with knowledge of the best books proffered, and perhaps slighted, but in an atmosphere of all the socially proper oratorios being sung. A girl went by me, with bones no better than mine but in outline all icy confidence. One by one they sallied past us, some with leonine hair and some doll-prim, but I could never attain that insolently loping air. They were youth in full cry; I was merely young. I had thought myself libertarian. They were liberty. My mother pulled her hat farther over her eyes.

Craig Towle was coming by on the arm of a girl. As the photographers there for the rally snapped his picture—that was the way it looked. Otherwise, he was the same. She was almost as tall as me, but frailer. They kept on going. He was on the other side of her and may not have seen us. Or, a slouch hat is easier to look away from than a face. A lantern caught the girl's face, and I recognized her—the pale silver-blonde I had talked to once in the bookstore, admiring meanwhile the arrogant poise of her ballet-slippered foot, parked on the second shelf, adhering to a scale of freedom we outsize ones ought to allow ourselves more. I would have known she was one of the young crowd around Craig Towle just by that foot. I'd been looking for a course book, which she'd handed me; she'd had it once and despised it too. Are you through college?—I'd asked and she'd shaken her head, reserved but still friendly.

Nice, isn't she, the bookshop owner said afterward. Was she

ever, I'd said from a certain sadness. I missed Phoebe. I could
use a friend. Out of town, at a real college maybe, this girl might
have been one.

Now, the reverse thought occurred to me—that I could have
been hers. Maybe it was in the way she flinched from our lights,
or in the haltered way she walked with him, in her long skirt. She
was wearing what were one day to be called granny-skirts and
identified with war, drugs, and Woodstock, but at the same time
with family and farm, the mode being calico drab if you were
communal, but stretching to ochre velvets if you saw yourself in
a Tom Jones romance. Or so in later years my brother, who these
days is formally said to teach history, would point out.

"They spent the summer in England, perhaps she picked that
up there," I heard a woman say. "No one else in her crowd is
wearing one." Perhaps she had. In any case we wanted to see her
as both avant-garde and in all the magazines, and perhaps she
wanted us to, and him to also, for as long as she could make it.
What she was wearing was to be a curiously ideological fashion
that would get into our Sears Roebuck catalogues long before it
ever reached *Vogue,* and I already yearned after her pink-and-
green version of it, as all women alternately do yearn for wide
skirts. If she and I had been friends, I thought, as my mother
and I walked to the car, I would have had Miss DeVore make
one, tactfully of another color, but just like.

My mother did not speak of what we had seen. We sat on in
the car. We had to mention my father somehow. Often I was
the one to manage it. "Perhaps it was the Milwaukee client."
Who had delayed him, I meant. A man who usually flew into
New York late, required all-night conversation, and had once had
a coronary in my father's car, Mr. Sattick was difficult company
to phone from. Too late I remembered we no longer had a second car to meet clients with.

My mother took me by the shoulders and shook me. She was
shaking me out of my long compliance in our mutely held secret.
Then she kissed me. "No. The woman's died."

So it was, and for some months my father did not return.

In the weeks immediately following, my mother did a piteous but dazzling thing. You may think her hard as well. I prefer to think that it took hardness of a sort all women in her condition have in store. Remember too how much of a load she had of which she could not speak—a double one. Her solution was brilliant. Whether or not she got it from brooding on Towle I can't say or even doubt; I never imagined their conversations. Or their lovemaking. I never bother to dream of sensation in that secondary way. What I wanted were the facts and their meaning—and there my trade school of the intellect, as my father had called the junior college, did me better than grudged. For it seemed, according to my course in elementary drama, that whether in Shakespeare's times or now, a drama must do what the theater calls "externalize."

What my mother did was to join the community. First, she took a job—in our present circumstances quite natural. If she chose the library, where else would a literate woman who had never worked be employable? And in addition she did have the incomplete library degree that in Greensboro had been considered just the right tone of enthusiasm. If Craig Towle spent some of his time there, so did many others. Once employed, of course, she really had to go along with the other staff, to Luray's Tuesdays. On Saturday mornings, now that we had no man in the house, she might even have to appear at the hardware store, gravitating there along the accepted route of butcher, vegetable store, and baker, formerly ordered from by telephone, and so, after a cup in the tea shop, to the bookstore which supplied her with novels for the weekend, where she could appear in person for orders once delivered. On Saturday afternoons, once shunned as the busiest, she continued her circuit, even switching garages —at last taking umbrage, now that she was a lone woman, at Rudie the garage man's broad remarks, though the only other garage was at the farther end of town, where Craig Towle kept his car.

One place she never went near, and that was Cobble Row. Also, the time Craig Towle spoke at a college lecture series, she did not turn up, though since I was on the speaker's committee she had attended every other one. We did not ever mention this. Meeting him head on was not what she was after. Meanwhile, we began having guests, not always on the weekend, smart couples garnered from a long-gone past I had only heard about— their arrivals and departures always clocked to some inner timetable she had, whereby she could meet them at the station as smartly attired as they, and bubble off with them. It had always been her habit—as my father said, "never to leave the house without preparing to meet the King of France"—and she did not neglect this now. If the guests had driven down, she might take them to tour the little sights of town, where in their midst, nestled in their cars among their furs, she might be perceived to have her own crowd. "If you had only made the effort sooner," they said happily, as yet unaware she would never make the effort to visit them in return.

So it was my mother joined the community, with every good reason for it.

Even to a man as skilled in evasion as Craig Towle, it must have seemed that she was to be encountered everywhere, flitting his surface life, a proud hat at the restaurant table—though she never now wore the slouch one—a perfume and a low voice leaving the library's front desk just as he entered, her elegant legs still in short skirts; a woman with her past swinging idly behind her and her lips still ripe, her children well behind her, as his were, a woman grown and with a finish to her, in the perfection of middle age. But he would be clever enough to see what she was doing, and this I think was the final attraction, that her remoteness, and perhaps a touch of its skill, were like his own. It was the one thing, perhaps, that youth could not oppose.

As for "the young crowd"—which the town still called them, as if we had none of our own—they had departed. We saw them as seasonal. Last year they had been summer people. This year they would be at winter sports—which we could not provide. But thanks to their absence perhaps, the newest housekeeper at Towle's reportedly had so far stayed. Craig Towle himself was spending two days a week lecturing on the theater at Harvard, where, spotted in a pub frequented by medical students, he made the newspapers on a rumor he was writing a play about leukemia, which he denied. Since then the newsmen had neglected him, and us.

So the winter of Craig Towle's second year with us passed, and my father came home. Officially away on several scores, all true, he had first suffered a kind of breakdown not hospital serious, during which the therapists had advised no family contact. He had then snapped back by means of an athletic tour of some South American clients he had never met in person. Their wealth, until now never really credited, had turned out to be able to pay him all his costs, even to support for my grandmother, as well as what were to be many expensive family conversations on the international telephone—. his first remark to my mother when he came home, after exclaiming how well she had kept, being to express his gratitude that she had never given in to shouting intercontinentally.

To my brother he had written steadily. In hindsight often with real audacity, for what ordinary father would so have trusted a fifteen-year-old boy—or been able to? Though when read to my mother and me in parts, and for the factual report only, the letters had seemed only in the self-consciously manful style a traveling father might adopt for a boy rather small for his age.

He himself was tanned even deeper, and looked international too; by now I could see that he always had. He told us a lot about Rio, with due respect for its foreignness, but also as if it were, like New York, only the city next door. As he talked I began to see that while my mother was sophisticated, she had had to do it in dots and dashes, as a woman could; he was the genuine article. The conventions of being a lawyer had tended to obscure this. In our biennial visits to his office in Maiden Lane, where his long-time secretary bowed to my mother and called me "Miss" and my brother "Master," anyone could see that conventionality was in part what he loved the law for. I scared the secretary, I now think. I so much resembled him.

Once he came back to live with us, we were struck by how lopsided we had been without him. He was no mere breath of fresh air; all the old, ingrained habits a family gets were immediately upon us. He was the breath that made ours complete. Yet we were not to keep him. It came about in this way.

"My mother—" he said to us, when he had returned from seeing her home, after dining us all at a big but disappointing restaurant farther down in Jersey. He always referred to grandmother this way, as if in spite of his four siblings she belonged solely to him. Admittedly the others—three flaccid sisters scattered over the Sundays and a ne'er-do-anything brother, did not count with her. "My mother wants her grandson to come live with her."

He stared at my brother—who was not the only grandson. "I said if she would stop calling you her poppet, you had my permission to." He turned to my mother. He had a black and white stare, not formidable but opaque. "That Watanabe has too much influence." This was the Japanese student he had got cheap for his mother as houseman before he left, serving her grandiosity— "my Jap butler"—exactly as he knew she would accept, since he had his own share of pomp. At that steak restaurant, though he scorned it, he himself had sent the chef cigars, with his compliments. The dumfounded waitress hadn't known what to do with them, nor possibly the chef either.

My mother immediately ordered my brother upstairs. Ever wrong with him, she always did this the minute his needs were to be discussed, although no more able to talk with him than my father was with me. But I had her warm company; my brother had only the letters. Yet, always polite, he got up to obey. He knew that only her conventions opposed his going; the two of them were never mutually fond. When he was halfway up the stairs, though, my father said: "Wait. Do you want to go?"

My brother looked much as he does now, small of size by his own will, and precise from judging us. Though even then one was never sure whether that judgment was sardonic or flawed. It was he who had chosen the restaurant. "It's a glamorous house." He saw my father's nostrils flicker at that adjective—as we were meant to see. "Besides," my brother said, "there's nobody ever around here."

I wondered which of those statements my father, in his law-yerish, partitioning way, would choose to answer.

He smiled. "Ah well, you were always her favorite son."

My brother grinned at him. "She can keep calling Watanabe 'Knobby.'"

When he had gone up the stairs, my father leaned forward. "My mother doesn't get any less dotty. She's now wanting me to —sue people."

"Sue?" my mother said faintly. "Who?"

That never got answered, or not then. From the top of the stairs my brother yelled: "No dottier than us."

Next morning, though, before they left, out on the front steps where we had always exchanged our information about ourselves, my brother told me. "Grandmother wants him to sue Craig Towle. Oh, not for what you think."

It had been absurd of me—and of my mother, to pretend, as we often did, that my brother was only tagging along. "Not for money?" No one in the know ever gave my grandmother invest-ment advice. "What then?"

"She claims he sucked her life blood."

"She is crazy, then?"

"No," he said. "He sort of did."

The long old car came for them then, Watanabe—Knobby, at the wheel. Coming for both him and my father, and their goods.

Yet that evening before, I think my father hadn't yet decided on his new life. Or on which of his former ones he would re-sume. Of course, there were matters we didn't know of yet—to do with money—that he knew would shortly fall on us, and obliquely on him. As well as some matters he hoped we would never know? I'm not sure of that. I think that in the end we hope our children will know everything about us. It helps the burden, on both sides. I look at my own and think—yes, everything.

Once we were sure my brother had packed off to his room, my father turned to me; he always divided us so. "You've grown very handsome." His eyes traveled my length. "Rio would be astounded."

"Oh no you don't," my mother said. "One of us out there is enough."

"No," he said, "I won't. Do that. That market is off anyway, maybe. And my taste for it."

We knew all about this, our bread and butter depending on it. He was a good lawyer but could never settle on one branch of the law, as the sensibly ambitious did. Something at the core of him kept confusing his markets with his tastes. After all, he was only finally home, after so long away, because a lady had died.

We had had early supper, the town custom, and fine for those who had bridge games or civic meetings to keep, but here we three now were, in silence, and fed, the high pre-spring evening descending. We were not a family whom the gloaming brought together; dusk expelled us to our own haunts. But I now had no girlfriend; no boyfriend either. At this hour, Bill Wetmore, who in my memory continued to spoil all successors, was very possibly in bed, in a hayloft if Dartmouth had them, expounding on his Beaux Arts relative to some other girl. For seventeeners, the resources of a town like ours sometimes viciously contract. If I had still been a bobby-soxer—in the true meaning of the word, not my father's contemptuous use of it—I might have been packed off upstairs too, but that was long ago, more than a year. Now they did not want me to leave them. In the last deep blue light invading our dining room, which had a deep bay, I could glimpse the still frozen garden between us and the Evamses', every leaf craw and leftover stalk straining to become part of the wind. I had never felt so close to my parents as a couple. It was the "exquisite hour." I had learned that French phrase for it in one of my mother's books—yet none of it was for us.

Something had to be said, but not just anything. Any light

remark would be seized and torn. My mother said, "Is that a light on over at Evamses'?"

Now—we knew our next door neighbors' routine as we did the seasons, or our own worn decks of cards. One bulb on the porch, on a time set, night after night. The same in the basement and attic, when they were away. Lamps downstairs twice a week for the classes, with intervals when they practiced their pupils in the dark. I was a day scholar, and it was often dim there—thin gray shadow in winter and lustered shade in summer, but I never told them so.

Shouldn't there be?" my father said. "I forget. Though in Rio —all that noise, all that light—I sometimes thought of them. Their calm."

The two Evamses, who had met at a school for the blind and had been married from it, were the most equable people we knew. Mr. Evams had once been sighted, she never. Because of known genes, they had refrained from having children. Mr. Evams was in real estate, and went over a property so relentlessly before selling it that people were eager to buy from him. She worked in his office. But their real business was being blind.

"Not upstairs, there shouldn't be," my mother said. "They never have a light there. But at this hour, maybe it's only a reflection. I hate to interrupt."

"They would know what they look like," my father said. "I suppose?" As well as we do, I thought. Their dark as well as their light.

Their eyes were well formed, if a little sunken, hers under a formidable ridge of bone that a fringe of brown hair made doll-like. Their profiles, both delicately blunted, resembled. Moving as a couple, they had less of that angelic intentness which so often signifies the lone sightless person. Though they loved the theater—the smell and rustle of a top theater crowd was like a good wine, he said—they did not otherwise particularly hunt organized sound, nowadays seldom playing their records. The radio kept them clocked and informed, but was not constant. They enjoyed ordinary noise, they said, and the varying silences in between, which they now and then absentmindedly named to one another as one might classify cloth.

"The downstairs should be dark too except for the porch," I said. "They have no classes tonight."

After the teaching, mostly to young persons who would themselves teach, their great preoccupation was reading, for which they had a huge library, in a house otherwise too large for them. They hated the talking-books provided people like them. Their four hands passing over the braille were like a duet, and they kept the little rulers for reading it always in a pocket. The nicest thing you could do for them, an act of friendship, was to let their fingers interpret your face, and discreetly your body, for which they divided the sexes, exchanging chirps like tailors. "Our vice," Mr. Evams would say, "is touch."

"Maybe Brenda's been. And left the light on up there," my mother said.

Brenda was their daily, though the Evamses could have afforded a live-in maid.

"They always check, entering and leaving a room," I said. "At least when people are there." For they often gave parties, and at Christmas had a tree like other people, and even house guests. Other times, they lived in their comfortable dark. Mrs. Evams even claimed she could feel the presence of electric light on her skin.

"They said they would be grateful if warned."

We knew what my mother was thinking of: old porch conversations. The town had intruders now, like everywhere else.

"We better go check." My father included us. We followed him.

Our staircase landing, a high-windowed bay broad enough to hold a table, two easy chairs and the seven-foot draecena my mother never forgot to water, was our pride. A glass-helmeted light hung on a chain from the second-floor ceiling, hideous with red and yellow bezels but shining on a space always neat and poised. Quarrels paused on the landing; ideas began.

Darkness had fallen. The bedroom across the garden was brilliantly lit. Brenda must have been cleaning its windows when called away; a rag and a bottle of Windex lay on the sill of a bay the complement of ours, the curtains drawn back. The room, seen by me once or twice, was big enough for both a bed and a fine large chaise I had envied. The Evamses were on it, naked and entwined in a swoon of touch. There was no intruder but the light. Her skin, if it recorded, ignored. I saw how their noses matched, blunted one against the other, and their lips, and all the long line of their clasp, breast to breast, penis to mound, knee to knee.

I was tall enough to fingertip our lamp. In an act of friendship I tapped it to set it swinging and saw its prism glide over them. It was no sin to watch. I was interpreting them.

"Come away!" my father said.

"No, look," my mother said. "It can't hurt them. And one could almost wish to be blind."

I heard that gentle, baffled click of impatience she so often got from him. He turned and drew our own curtains, heavy draperies, thick with dust. That act couldn't hurt the Evamses. But I saw how our window, kept bare on our side, had taken advantage of them.

Our bay huddled now, its view gone.

"Craig Towle's wife's seven months along," I heard my father say. "They say she came back last fall to have it born where its father was. But for the past four months, she won't go out of the house. You heard?"

I didn't want to look at my mother's face. It might be rose red again, not from any radiance of our lamps. But I had to listen.

"Nobody told me."

So my mother had got him back again. And the town knew it.

The heavy old portières at the window hung without a stir, as horsehair does. Once, years ago, when they were last laid in the sun to air, lying on the lawn like a carpeted path to the Belgium my grandmother said they came from, my brother and I, having wrapped our summer-bare selves in those baroque amber and green folds, spent all a wriggling night with their short-cut, invisible hair-sheddings fuzzing our flesh, not knowing what beset us.

I rubbed my hands on them.

"Nobody," she said.

Upstairs at my own bare window, the bedroom opposite was gone. Perhaps my father had phoned. Too late, for all our retinas. The chaise lay stunned and white, on mine. Telling me that bodies lay everywhere, to be interpreted. I couldn't go over there for a lesson tomorrow and would find excuses not to go again. Our own outside light was now on, and in the winter garden the stiff weeds were being knocked about, and each time came back to plumb. The net around the Evamses, around us and the Evamses, was larger than any gossip, was invisible. If I were to evade it, how far from our town would I have to go?

Next morning, as my grandmother's car drew up, Watanabe driving, my father joined my brother and me on the steps, carrying his alligator overnight bag. This was the way he always left, for near or far. Leaving me, he gave that same click in the throat —like a sop to his gods, which for me was his sound. I can still hear it at will, as one can summon the coughs of the dead, or of those far away; who are not.

Women were trying to him, I think—but in the way we are trying to ourselves. He deprecated our berserks and our self-betrayals, as we do the gassy moods of the menarche, and saw our frou-frou as we often do, as less than true to our depths. I do not know whether or not he gave men more quarter, or even for sure what tolerance he gave himself. Although our grandmother's house was only avenues away, I would learn no more of him within the family. For the real purposes of living, my brother and he never came back there. I found I minded the hurt, but not the mystery. He too preferred that. Perhaps that was in part why he went. I looked too much like him for his own comfort, my brother now says, still researching. That is true. There is a picture of the two of us, taken by the ever photographically eager Watanabe, on those steps. My mother did not appear.

Yet it was she who was to save my grandmother's house. For

the South American market had indeed proved to be off, to the point of default. Meanwhile, my father's former clients in New York had felt deserted. Financial scuttlebutt of that sort often came true, he said, the day he first came back to visit me. "Like any other." The town had long thought he wasn't doing well—and now he wasn't. Yet our own house, as his marveling glance took in, was looking superb.

What had happened, of course, was that the day after he went, my mother had once again left town, that is, had run on back down home. She never gave up that option, my brother now says—and it ruined the two of them. Father had had to find a down home, too, or someone to whom he was home. My brother is ever fuller of explanations as time goes on—and ever more needful of them.

She left almost immediately, wanting me to go with her, which I wouldn't, though tempted. Normally she took the train, liking to get there gradually, but this time she flew. Summer school would be easier to do from here, and if I plugged I too might have a chance at a real college's scholarship. Besides, though this I didn't say—when would she come back?

"You're too young," she said.

"For what?" She had never taken that line with me; I was to have been like her, intrepid.

"To handle—the divisions."

I knew what she meant. But did she mean only those in our family, or between all women and men?

Since she refused to leave me in the house alone, it was agreed that Watanabe would move into a room on our third floor, caring for the other house by day, and teaching me how to care for ours, which was why Grandmother had allowed him to come.

I brought chocolates to my mother at the train, but it was only ritual. I told myself I was no longer that involved.

"Well, it's taught you housekeeping," my father said, that first visit. "You'd never have learned it down there. And Knobby says you help him with his letters."

Watanabe, corresponding with a top marriage bureau in Tokyo, craved a true Japanese wife but also an English-speaking
one. We understood one another. In a way we were both com-
peting for scholarships—and the marriage-bureau mail was
teaching me a lot. I couldn't stand the fishy food he singed and
chopped for himself, much preferring my own glop, which gave
him similar shudders. Meanwhile, as one does with the best service, I had almost the sensation of being alone, and yet was
comforted. He wrote poetry to his marriage prospects, in which
he outlined the measurements of the house he would build for
them. I thought this an odd combination, but he said firmly not
—and indeed, he had many acceptances, none so far to his taste.
In turn I thought he might teach me foreign perspective, once
inquiring whether he found white families mad. In Greensboro
the servants were a Trojan chorus, much quoted.

"You mean your family?" The walnut half he was rubbing a
table with halted. Whenever my grandmother saw him at this,
taking off what scratches he could, or tincturing the backs of old
mirrors, or boiling up agar-agar pastes to do she knew not what
to our reviving Hepplewhite, she said she would forgive him
anything, even her irritation that she could find nothing to forgive.

He discarded the walnut half and started with the linseed oil.
"With two houses rike these, why not you use them."

By then the town might be thinking the same.

"Oh, we get on fine," I told my father. "Only his radio. Woo,
woo, half the night."

My father dealt with this at once, going out to buy Watanabe
earphones, with that air men assume so easily, of supplying the
no-nonsense part of a house. I doubt it's a gene-connected talent,
though, or else it's in mine; left alone with the children a good
part of the time, I would one day do that supplying.

"Heard from your mother?" he said, coming down from the
third floor to report Watanabe already using the phones and
writing a letter to the tune of them.

"We talk."

"Who makes the call?"

"She does." I knew she never called the two of them.

My father shook his head. "Your brother won't talk to her. As for going South to see your grandfather, who would naturally like to see his only grandson—Tim won't hear of it, though I would gladly send him. He says he hates the South. How could he? He hasn't been since he was four."

Of course he hated it. It always took her away. And with me. I felt a twinge for my ailing grandfather, absent from the dinner table and with his naughty tongue quieted. "I'll go down there. End of summer." I would be my brother's substitute, as I often had been, as far as down home would allow. I wouldn't hunt and shoot with my grandfather—he would never have let me, even if he were well enough, but I could ride. Granddaughters were not the same to him, but I would do what I could.

I gathered up the box the earphones had been in. "What's that other long box?"

"That? Oh, that's for your brother. Army-Navy Store stocks them too. A pulley exerciser. He asked for one."

My brother was always trying to stretch his height. People used to say to me, "Why don't you give him some?" But now that we were grown they'd stopped that out of consideration— for him.

"What's that you're wearing?" my father said suddenly.

I had been having one of my mother's sessions in front of the mirror, like when the dresses came up north from Miss DeVore. Only, I had been trying myself on. Nowadays I reminded myself quite pleasantly of the six-foot Trilby in the old illustrated Du Maurier, which had come along with the furniture from the other house. Though I couldn't sing, I did have her noble foot, the one all the artists in that eighteen-ninetyish Paris atelier raved about—a Greekish drawing of which was in the book. I was thinking that if I swept my hair into a Psyche knot and brow curls, I could be a model too; Bill Wetmore had told me the 1890 goddesses were coming back. I had the foot anyway, and the neck. The onyx-and-green bracelet had seemed to go with them.

"That's Cartier, if ever I saw it," my father said in a tone strange to me. "I know something about those gewgaws. Nineteen twenty, I should say. Where did *you* ever—?" He closed his mouth, which my brother's does resemble. Well cut, if scissory.

"I swapped it. Not for keeps. Down home." As I looked at my wrist, the gewgaw, as he called it, did seem to have come from there.

I don't know where else the lies come from unless from a long way back, and harbored early. And I don't say he believed me. He knew where the lie came from as well as me.

"Quite a friend, he must be." He didn't ask what I'd swapped for it.

"Not a he. A she." My voice was as strange as his. "She looks something like—Bill Wetmore."

I think he and I were as smiling-close then as we would ever get. Most of all, he would know when the lies were only fantasies. I would trust him to the end for that.

He shouldered the box with the pulley in it. Holding stuff that way jaunties a man. "I'm going to take your brother away for a bit. Rio."

"But haven't they—?" Defaulted? I didn't like to think of him as a bad businessman. I didn't mind that much about my brother.

"No—that's why we'll go. The money's there all right. They were just being—Latin. I'll make him work it out."

"Him? How?" Hurt for my brother after all, I wailed it. Though I couldn't see him as ever close to me, we had been through serious times.

"Oh, not your brother," my father said, laughing. "Though he'll work out well enough." No—the man who owes me. He'll take care of us." His face changed. I thought he had never looked more—sophisticated.

And so the man did, ultimately sending my brother to college with an allowance fit for an heir—which my brother spent on

books, and whatever else would equip him to realize his dream—
a history post at Harvard. Where Tim is now, and ever will be,
unless he gets in trouble with a boy. Though nowadays perhaps
only Tim himself would think that scandalous.

"You wouldn't want to move over to your grandmother's? No,
I don't suppose."

"Oh, I don't mind her as I used. I kind of even like her—"
Spirit? Style? "Nastiness."

He laughed out loud at that. His mouth could lose its thin
line.

"I could hold my own," I said.

"I bet you could."

"But she doesn't—you know? *See* me."

Her eyes passed over me always, in a way that when I was a
child had frightened me. As if I couldn't be there. As if she
wouldn't have it.

I saw he knew this was true. His own eyes traveled over me.
"Well—you're no poppet." The eyes drooped guardedly. Finally
he put out both his hands to me. "She doesn't understand, you
see. That you're just a modern girl."

He did. That's what he gave me. I have it yet.

"Your mother'll be home in a week." Again his face changed.
Not darkened. Just—changed. "She doesn't know it yet. But she
will be." He slid the pulley exerciser box under his armpit. Held
it there. Clicked his tongue at it—his sound. Looked up at me
again. "You'll be all right then?"

I saw he meant for more than just now. I didn't know what
dangers he wanted reassurance I'd be safe from. But I knew I
would be. "I'll be all right."

We clasped hands on it. As he turned to go he gave himself a
shake, squaring his shoulders, the white forelock cresting. He was
a father anyone would be proud to take round a campus, and
over the years of my scholarship I would hunger for that.

We never met again in our own house.

My mother gave no sign of coming home. In our phone calls I
did not mention his prediction, and I did not brood on it. Probably it belonged to that general apprehension all the grown
seemed to share: once I had a future not tied to theirs, I might
escape it.

Yet during this interval I might have been too much of a loner
even for me if I hadn't found another interest, in the sitter
agency our school ran as seriously as a church sodality, and so
successfully that the neighboring towns could be excused for
taking it for granted that this was mainly what a junior college
was for. Boys and girls both were solicited, on the theory that we
were being trained for parenthood—as it turned out we were to
be, though not solely because of the children under our flashily
intermittent care. Since the boys did join up, we were given the
impression we were all advanced social thinkers, though in practice the boys were also under order to escort us girls to each
household, so that we might jointly inspect it and its owner for
lack of infectious diseases, honest intent with no risk of rape
from fathers or grown brothers, free soda pop and a working
television. If a girl didn't like what she saw, she could be driven
home, the bargain with that household forever dropped. The
idea was to make it clear to putative stranglers and other molest-
ers—and to the sitters themselves—that we traveled in twos.
Boy sitters were sometimes refused by the parents of girl children, but otherwise flourished. Since family cars were used in
rotation, we never could be sure who would drive who, but some
pairing-off for cuddling on the way home could usually be
counted on, so the sitter service was a kind of dating group, too.
One forgets, as the college's social affairs office maybe intentionally did, that in those years everything points to the sexual. For
some of us, of course, it will be that way for life.

At home it was lonely, but in a way that I loved. Knobby had
turned up the woman, not from Tokyo but from Kyoto, who
after due correspondence would arrive to marry him. Meanwhile,
in awe of the holy place she came from, he now drove all the way
to Rutgers University to have a Japanese professor there audit his

return letters, which was to work beautifully for both poetic exchange and the marriage, for although the fiancée who arrived would not be according to the picture sent—of the convent-bred daughter of the owner of a geisha house—but would turn out to be the mother herself, she was far more suitable for a man of fifty-five. Knobby, too, at the time was deceiving us, or else our own ethnic innocence had. He was a student, but not a young one.

My grandmother meanwhile depended on him for news of me, but never came near, or asked me by. That suited me but horrified Knobby, as did the disconnected state of our family. She had been told of my babysitting Saturday nights, he not being sure it was proper. Though her answer had been, "Well, I'm not going to be sitter to *her*," he still was loath. I finally explained to him that I ought to be allowed because I was studying households, which I was. I reminded him that he himself had remarked to me that in the States one could excuse almost any activity if one said one was studying it.

"What is it ours lack most?" I said one Saturday evening as we were cooking our separate solaces. I knew how sadly lacking he found the two households he commuted between.

I could see us pass now before that opaque glance of his. Ancient tyrant, but no protectress. Tender schoolgirl, even one so towering.

"Obligation."

He was wrong, but in the newly scoured kitchen this sounded like a sternness we perhaps needed.

I accepted some frail bits from his evening platter, always tactfully arranged as if it were to be shared. "I shall study that."

To approach some house with the coppery glow of life shining from it and ready to be dispensed, to enter another one gaunt with a tension readying itself to ride the evening out—or to learn after a couple of Saturdays in each that I had misjudged and must even switch these views, taught me more than the language of appearances. Unlike some of the sitters, I never opened dresser drawers; it would have been like using the dictionary for a crossword puzzle. That fine moment would be sacrificed—when the pattern leapt to its own logic as if from the recesses of one's own brain. A strange household, when properly observed, was layered like a street. I was learning my vocation, even before I knew its name. However I was to perform it—if not in paint or words, then perhaps by sacrificing bits of my own flesh, almost in the way Knobby pincered for me a quail's egg or a minute ear of corn, this observing was the adventure I was fitted for.

One night, a boy and girl picked me up. They were known to be a couple. He would deliver me, then her, then go to his own assignment, later calling for each of us around midnight and dropping us back at our homes, all in an order that would give those two some periods of time alone. I didn't mind. The sitter boys seemed to me either louts or prisses, the girls altogether too refined, in what I now knew was the provincial way. Similarly, I put them off, the boys and girls both, by clearly not being ready for what they were so ready for. All of them were itching to construct a household themselves.

So it happened that the skinny, nervously doting boy who was driving us, all the time bending his fancy mop of curls to the girl next to him, I being the third in the front seat, dropped me off first, and with a fast U-turn made off again, before I had quite seen where I was.

I was due at a house in a street called "the Arterial," where the small girl I was to mind, whose mother had phoned me, must never have anything made with wheat. I had wondered whether she thought I carried wheat around in my pockets. But they all had some special stipulation which meant that particular child to them. I could wonder what my mother's might have been for me, if I wanted to. I didn't.

Standing on the crooked path, I saw where I was, on that other girl's assignment, and sure as well that until midnight that pair, embarked on their routine of time stolen, weren't about to double back for me. I was in Cobble Row.

I knew the house. Once again I mourned Phoebe, only five

doors down from here. She would have been the only one with whom I could have shared this: how I was now walking up the path my mother must often have trod, slipping on the round stones in those dainty heels of hers, never vulgarly stiletto but curved in. How I knocked now at the witching door, thinking that I had never sat with a newborn baby before, which was about all this one could be. How Craig Towle, the dark man of all this town's sonnets, opened it.

I had to bend my head to get in under the door. Once inside, I could straighten up, though barely. The house was identical with the Wetmores', but I had been shorter then. Over there it had been dirtily sallow, a house handed down and not risen above, beyond a sunporch added on from the grandmother's earnings as the town's head nurse. Here, with the short, thick beams exposed, sprigged wallpaper and floors stripped from linoleum back to pine, it was trying to shrink my brain to Revolutionary era size and to ignore the rest of me.

Craig Towle wasn't. He was giving me the look older men did on the street. Sometimes a man muttered at me, often a short one, Big enough for you if you want, baby. When a girl my size wasn't a round-shouldered washout, that's what she got. Quickly I told him who I was. In case he didn't recall.

He did stare and stare. "Good Lord. Of course." His face didn't change, now that it knew I was my mother's daughter. It even came forward, the nose jutting like a guardrail. "How's that old beldame, your grandmother?"

How did he already know I wouldn't mind him saying that?

"Is that Penny?" came a voice.

In the room to the left, where the Wetmores had installed a Heatilator, the Craig Towles had had the old inglenook exposed, black iron pots hanging in its niches. Seated at its table, over a jigsaw puzzle, the bobby-soxer got up slowly. Though her name was Nancy, I never learned to think of her by it. "Oh—you're not Penny. Oh—hello."

"This is—" he began.

"I know who she is," she cut in. Once she must have been

quicker-mannered than him, in the casual ways we young ones were. Now and again this would show. Through the sloth. "I asked the bookshop lady who you were."

The silver-blond hair was dog-eared and gone greenish, as that kind of hair does when left to dull. Under the once-charming pink wrapper which she must be too much in the habit of, I saw where the baby was—still inside. Then why was I here?

He was watching. "Our live-in goes for the weekend. I don't like to leave her alone."

In those days, when there was only one thing to say, I often said it. "Then why do you?"

He cocked his head. I would one day use that same ploy. Listening for the motive, one ignores the speech.

"He has to work." When she stood that straight the baby stuck out. I saw she wouldn't have herself pitied. She even smiled.

"Penny and I got ourselves switched. Maybe you would rather she—?"

"Oh no. Not at all. Tell the truth, she was kind of a trial. I know the names of all the boys on your route. And their characteristics."

She had a delicate accent. I wondered how many languages she knew, not having had to wait until college for it. There was nothing wrong-in-the-head about her, I thought. She had fallen into the habits women sometimes did when left too much to themselves. Like me, she was learning the several thicknesses of silence in a house. What would a wife's silence be, when the man is with someone else? Such a young new wife.

"I'll have to have a phone number to call," I said. "That's the rule."

"Sorry, I don't have a phone there. That's why I go." He was still staring. "It's a hayloft. Or once was. Five doors down."

"Wetmores'!" I said. "Phoebe. How is she?"

"Off to college, I hear. I've never really talked to her."

"I wonder where."

"Somewhere around Boston I gather. From my landlady."

"I have—" the bobby-soxer said. "Talked to her."

I saw Phoebe, all scrawn and no great shakes as a scholar, but already in Boston. "Nurse Stevens always wanted her to go. But there was never enough money around for two. I wonder how they managed it." Under their eyes I heard how I was talking. Like the town.

"Well, I pay them top rent," he said. "Canny old bird. Brings me coffee now and then. But I don't get to use her phone. If you need to, you come running, eh. You look as if you could." He dropped a kiss on the top of her head, looking up at me. He'd kiss mine, I'd felt, if he could reach it. "See why your grandmother's kept so quiet about you," he said.

Then he was off. We could hear him scrunching down the path.

When he was gone she said softly and slowly, "I know who you are." Then at her direction we sat in the inglenook and had soda pop.

I went there four times. As we felt each other out, we switched to beer, were girlish with each other but never quite became friends. Even aside from what we never discussed, how could we? She hadn't finished college, and didn't give a hang for it. She had already been halfway round the world, if only in play, and expected the other half would soon be coming up. What I wanted to sacrifice for I didn't yet know, only that I wanted to. I could tell her that, and she wouldn't laugh, but that would be her best effort. I grew to love her instead, for what she was. The girls in the blue and yellow sweaters—I would never get over admiring them, even for their limitations. Though she would never again be one of them.

Sometimes, as she went chipping along in the voice of all her summer crowd, I wondered if that had yet got to her. She seemed at times to forget she had a baby in her. I know now that this can happen to anyone so fixed, at any age, and not only with the first. You are maybe sitting alongside the fire, even pleased with what you've got and are. Or in a room of cocktail slims, just before your time comes. Suddenly that birth date to come is a bull lowering at you with its upside-down eye. You could have escaped, had you been another kind of matador. For a minute you do escape, purling along in last summer's voice.

Other times though, the minute I came in I saw she had been thinking of nothing else but where she was, and why. Like the night she took me to see the wing they had had built onto the back of the house. Four bedrooms and baths for the guests— "Oh, we knew we'd always have them." Going down the hall which led straight from the old back door into this bright honeycomb, she was almost matronly; it happens with the first furnishings.

At the hall's end we came to a large room, bare and unused, built to the breadth of the house. A studio for him, built as a surprise. He hadn't wanted it.

"Great for the baby," I said. She did not reply. She hadn't chosen the nursery yet, or a layette either. He had bought her another house gown, though, since I came, exactly like the old one, as she had asked. The bedroom she led me back to had the same pale green. "My friend Julie chose it. This room was to be hers." Softly she named them all, each at a door. She herself had wanted six guest rooms but the plot here wasn't big enough, even with the extra back alley they'd bought. "He said maybe I would have to choose four. Friends. Choice was a fact, he said." No sweat, she said, her face alight. "With our crowd, the way we were, we simply doubled up."

So—he had married all of them. It must have been like marrying an anagram you only kind of remember from your own freedom time, I thought almost jealously. Our age—he married it.

"Why don't you ask them all back?" I saw how she needed them.

We were now closing each door, to save on dust. "No, no. They're too many for him. Too many young." I heard how she quoted him. "One of us is just right, he says." She closed the last door. He never lied to her, she said. But I wondered how much she asked.

I had to give her something of mine. I told her about Bill Wetmore. That he had existed. That he still hung around in my head. "Very destructively," I said, applying second-quarter psychology, letting first-quarter logic go.

"I knew there had to be someone, for someone like you. Is he tall?" Sharp-eyed from solitude, she'd alleged that I was growing between visits, and measurement had proven her right. Hadn't I better see someone? Good looks were no guarantee. Six foot and some over was enough. As her own cousin Venetia, kept too long from what could be done for you, had found out.

"He's a sculptor." And yes, tall, I said, amused. Though that didn't count with me.

She dismissed that. "Oh good. Then he can model you."

I remembered now, how that had been my own hope. *Sacred nudity*, he'd said to mine, *and such a stretch of it.*

I sat up suddenly. "Venetia?" And taller than Craig Towle?

She was sharp. "No, his wife was named Venice. I'd never met her. They were already splitting. He'd met the whole crowd of us. On Brown's Beach." The crowd had grown up together on that Boston enclave, from the age of tin dippers and pails. "He and his children—theirs—were staying with friends there." And little Tarquin had come along the beach, crying and lost. "We brought him back. Little Tarquin." She wrinkled her nose. "Her idea. Of what went with Towle."

"Did you ever? Get to meet her?"

"Once," she said. "She called me up." She seemed about to say more, then clammed up.

"She was a woman of ideas." I half-parroted it, intent on that group, cool as native plants on that strip of sand. We here had heard of it.

"A—?" She couldn't sit up further, the weight of the baby's water already grounding her like a sandbag, but her hair swung, silkier now that I had washed it. "How do you know?"

I felt my flush, my only legacy from my mother. Or the only

one that could be seen. Avoiding her in one way, we had come round to her in another.

The girl herself saved us. "He'll never talk now about his wife. Not a word. Only his older girl will—she hates it here. If we have eggs—'My mother never boils them . . . My mother wears only white in summer . . . Believes we should do this . . . Does not allow us to do that.' " She broke off, then said under her breath, " 'And hopes your baby has two heads.' Craig's banished her for that. I spoke up for her. No, he said. I never saw him so—so absolutely chill about anything." She lifted her head in pride. " 'No—' he said. 'She's reporting on us.' "

His other children now and then came and took over the new wing, and left their evidences.

"And Tarquin?" I said, curious.

"He never says anything at all. But he comes."

Perhaps she and Towle could take the baby into the old house, small as their room was, I said. "In there it would be more unique." She ignored me.

"So they come here," she was saying. "Dozens of them."

"Dozens!"

"Three. I like them, actually. Even that girl. Or could. But the minute they get here, they feel to me like dozens. Or their mother sees to it . . . How *do* you know? About her."

I had my alibi now. The old one, the permanent, it slips out easiest of all, from porches eternal. "You don't know this town."

"Don't I—" she said. And struggling up, she lumbered to the front door where my hat and jacket hung, and jammed on her head my hand-me-down slouch hat.

Why do women signal with clothes like that? Bracelets. Even candy boxes—that whole silly repertoire. If we knew why, we would tell you; it might be sad. The signal is always for oneself; I know that much. The hat kept my mother with me. I had brought her along.

The hat sat grotesquely, vying with the bobby-soxer's belly. Neither seemed hers.

After a while I said, "Keep it on if you want to. But let's get out of here. We're out of beer." Her Volkswagen convertible, new when she married, shone through the window. "Put on a coat and we'll go to a bar. I know one near."

She didn't move.

"How long is it—since you left the house?" I said. "I know it's hard. You get stir-crazy, yet you can't." I got that way myself sometimes, down in Greensboro, I told her. When you are in an inharmonious environment, I said.

Or sometimes when the old one comes up in your throat. I didn't tell her that. It hadn't happened yet.

But finally I wormed an answer out of her.

"Since the night everybody saw me. At the station. And—and saw you."

Us. She couldn't say it.

"Does he know why?"

She wasn't sure. She'd never said. Nor had he asked. "But he usually knows everything."

I thought of him in the hayloft, working away at Bill Wetmore's great-grand-uncle's rolltop desk, which was too big for the house. Working on us, the town.

While Phoebe'd got away, all the time quicker than me. With less to go on. Nor did I have to think hard on how the girl here had learned what she had, when there was Phoebe to talk to, with her lip rolled back.

After a while I said: "If you're thinking of wearing that thing until he comes, he never saw it, that day. Or us."

"He sees what he wants." But she took the hat off.

Now it was I who was staring at it.

After a while she said: "You must look like your father. I never —got to see *him*."

"He goes away. He always goes away . . . Yes, I do look like him, they say. In Greensboro especially."

She didn't ask what Greensboro intended by that. She was deep in.

So was I. I had come at seven, to stay until twelve. Soon their cuckoo clock would strike. Nine. Her crowd had sent it to her, from the Tyrol. Far places.

"He'll not come back, I think. My father." I stole a look at her. We were both so hemmed in.

The clock did strike.

"Please, could we go out?" I said. "I've never driven in a Volks before."

So we made it, the both of us. I got her dressed, pointing to a sweater and skirt out of the many that hung in her closet, when she stood mute. She really hadn't gained that much weight. Getting into the car, we even marveled at that. She drove.

Nobody was in the little bar near my mother's garage. The factory hours were long over. We sat at a table. Two men came in, salesmen by their talk, from the nearby motel. Soon they sent us drinks by the barman, who set the whiskies down with a flourish. We had ordered beer, as the men could see.

"What'll we do?" I whispered to her.

"Accept it." She smiled. "And if they get porky, I can just stand up."

I looked over at the two men, who were well-dressed but dumpy. "And so can I."

When they started over to our table—after all, we had drunk their whisky—we did just that, exiting without a look behind us, she with her stomach grandly before her, I rearing my neck. I was now taller than her by far. I drove the car back. I had left the hat in the bar.

Entering that house again was a downer for both of us, but I could afford it; I'd decided I wasn't coming back. Almost having a friend gets to you. Maybe she thought so, too. It's different from having a crowd.

"I'll walk back on my own." I still had on my jacket. We were in the tiny vestibule.

She nodded, slipping off her coat. Absentmindedly, she began to pull off the yellow sweater, too.

"Oh no you don't," I said. "Please."

"Okay—" she said, after a minute. "Thanks." The fire in the

inglenook was out. She poked it, leaning over with her skirt
hiked up. If you don't exercise, the pregnant behind sometimes
gets as big as the front. But she was still strong, only nineteen.
She reached over, tipping the heavy table toward the fire, and
swept the whole jigsaw in. "And you—you know what? You can
have him if you want him. I'll help."

"Have who?"

"Don't pretend, you noodle. Your Wetmore. I'll write Julie at
Dartmouth—she'll find him." She put her face to the fire. "I'll
get the whole crowd back. Flopsy and Mopsy too. My sheep-
dogs. And get in some cats. Cats *don't* suck babies' breath.
Though that's not why they're not wanted here. They're incessant movement—that's true. But babies love that, don't they?
And they *like* noise." She picked up a last piece of the puzzle
and tossed it in. "Anyway, we'll have a weekend party that'll—
and invite your Bill." The poker fell. Turning to the room, she
tossed her head so angrily that the tears whipped from it. "You
can get him if you want him," she said through a stream of
them. "Just be totally—." She hunched in, saying it. "Like me."

I put my arms around her. I'd just remembered something. I
likely would not be coming back here anyway. My mother was
returning. On extraordinary business, she'd said this morning. I
could hear the whole of Greensboro listening. I had better keep
it from her that I had ever been here at all. "Okay. But promise
me something."

"What?"

"Just—promise me."

"I do."

I couldn't say what it was. My own tears were streaming, and
not only for her. "Please—" I said. "Please."

"Say it."

"Please—keep yourself up."

She put her arms around me. I could feel her belly, but it
seemed to me that even my mother was in the circle, also my

father, and all our joint households—except Craig Towle. Together we breathed in the sorrows of the unrecorded world.

Down at the bottom, I saw our two sets of saddle shoes.

I was almost at our doorstep when I saw the light on upstairs
in the master bedroom, a term my father made fun of. For a
minute I let myself dream that the figure up there was his, but I
knew better. My mother and her extraordinary circumstance had
come home. Knobby's room under the eaves was dark.

Then I heard the car creeping to a stop behind me. Neither
we nor the Evamses had one. At this dead-end hour it would be
the men from the bar. I stiffened my long neck, which as the
armature of my height is my defense and my weapon, though
men are inclined to say No, it is the eyes. But when I turned I
saw the car was only the Volks. Had she come after me then to
spend the night, as unmarried girls do?

It was Craig Towle. They always paid me my five dollars tactfully, in a white envelope. I could see it in his hand. He beck-
oned me. I went.

"She says you're a breath of outside air. Thanks. I was afraid
she wasn't going to be able to hang on. But now she will." He
still held the envelope. "She's a lovely girl, you know."

I might be some man he was saying this to. I had no way to
respond.

"Who's that up there?" he said.

The shadow behind the thin draperies, in what would be its
tattered old dressing gown from Paris, was walking up the length
of the room, and returning.

"That? Oh—." She was going to miss the hat; she tabulated
her life by clothes no longer worn. I was glad I wasn't wearing it.
"That's—our Japanese butler. He sometimes irons up there."

"Ah. Didn't know they ironed. Never had one." He stared at
me as he first had at their door, absently toying now with the
envelope. "Remarkable. How you do resemble her."

"Who?" He couldn't be saying this to me.

He shook himself. "Your—grandmother. Who else?"

No one had ever said that.

He saw I hated the idea. "Disregard that. Perhaps it isn't true." He was still staring at me. "There's a group picture she once showed me. Of the family when she and your grandfather first moved to town. She was going to give me a copy. Now I expect she won't." He handed me the envelope.

"I don't want it. Buy the baby something with it."

He glanced up at the house. Had my voice been too loud? No, the figure was still pacing. It couldn't see us.

"Our hedges prevent," I said. "Seeing out."

"You are—remarkable," he said. "I might even explain. You see—I'm *not* a lovely girl. I merely acquired one. While—hanging on to something else. It's true she won't buy for the baby. I wish I didn't know why."

"Maybe because it's low class to trip through the stores for layettes and stuff." My grandmother's voice sure enough, though I was mimicking. "You're supposed to have it all in the attic. My brother was practically born in my father's bassinette."

I wanted to wound him. That's the first hint.

I'm sure he saw. "And what about you?" he murmured. Not really asking.

We both held very still. I could smell the work-sweat and the pearlike starch of his shirt. The cap of his hair, dark and silky, was some barber's triumph over bristle born on Cobble Row. Where they had no attics, but many a beaked nose like his, Englishy or Pole. Invisible wings of other revelries and knowledge stretched like a fay's from his shoulders. And had brought him back here.

Would it have been the same to someone from Brown's Beach?

So this is the womanizer, I thought. The word suggests a cockatoo, moving its head forward, and in. But this eye—I fixed on one in the starlight—is remoter than that. Any girl with him will move questward, in the arms of that remoteness. Or drop by the wayside.

"Look up there," he said. "At that bedroom. You have to."
He hadn't touched me.

Up there perhaps the figure was only putting its clothes away,
but it went back and forth still.

"People mostly don't marry for *who* the other person is, but
for *what* that person is. With rare exception. She up there—did
it about as badly as anyone could. Other than me." He stepped
back, into the shadow of the hedge. "I expect I'll soon be moving on."

"Then—you've finished your play?"

He froze. "No. I've scarcely begun."

"But that's what it's about, eh? About what you just said."

"I don't do domestic plays. Marriage ones." His face was a
scowl of distaste. "Nor leukemia ones." I remembered the newspapers the waitresses at Gilbert's had pulled out of the wastepa-
per basket after he left.

"Sorry—" he said. "I take advantage of you. Of your youth.
And I just may do it again." He moved to the car. "Maybe I'll
write about you."

"Not if—you're leaving."

"Hmm, that may be just when."

"Ah, you wouldn't—" I threw out in scorn. "Be writing about
me. Not if you can say so."

"No. But how can you tell." His glance strayed. He had had
exchanges like this before. "So that's Gilbert's house, over there.
Two lots extra to itself. On either side. Yet he wants mine."

"He won't get it," I said confidently.

"This town. This town. My God, how it knows itself. No, he
won't. But maybe you and I should collaborate."

"It's unfair. For someone like you to talk that way to me. Why
can't you stop?"

Knobby's room lit up.

"She's called to him," I said. "About where I can possibly be."

"Out being a breath of fresh air," he said. "Yes—why can't I
stop?"

He means his plays, too, I thought. And yet—he'll move

nearer. The comprehension was so heavy that I thought I would cry. Instead I broke out into a sweat and stood tall, hoarding my armpits. When he did come close it was like our doctor did, his breath cool and reserved.

"Sorry—" he said, "but if I asked, you wouldn't let me. Just a bit of research." His forefinger traveled down my right cheek, steady, not a caress. Then he slipped the envelope into the breast pocket of my blouse, his hand lingering for a second, and quickly stepped back. "Apologies." He said it twice. Then he was in the Volks, leaning out. "But if you ever want to talk—about the town—let me know. I promise—to pay nothing." The car started. Back of us, the porch light went on. "Ah, the butler," he said under his breath, and drove off.

So he and I finally met on our own. I had not known I wanted to. All the imaging and hearsay I had witnessed was true, yet now he was both more than that and less. I could think of half a dozen names to call him, words to describe him with, but no one of them alone would do. That was why the town called him Craig Towle.

The landing light went on now too, but I didn't need to look up. I had been doing that all my life.

My mother was an heiress. Legal notification—that all the property, excluding personal jewelry, of one Leslie Warden of New York City, had been left to her—had arrived the week my father had said it would; a New York bank's statement and confirming instructions had only now followed. In token of that, Greensboro, which during the interim had stood at hand to help her cope with any doubt about acceptance, had sent her off with a corsage now in an etched glass on her dressing table, rosebuds and stephanotis, in a frill stuck with a pearl pin.

"I hated myself for carting it along but I couldn't help myself." Except for weddings, funerals, and proms, our street, which grew its flowers for free, thereby achieving two kinds of grace, was stingy about bought flowers, and so always kept them overlong. My mother had never before done that. I mark it the first sign of her decline as a heroine of the sort I and some others would still take her to be. A woman of style—but style merely—has to rise continually, even to a bad end. Otherwise, there is so little place to go.

"So are you—" she said. "An heiress. Three quarters of the money is in trust, for you and your brother, as each of you attains twenty-five, or at the discretion of the trustees. And it's a lot."

"Not through Grandpa, then? The money?"

"No, poor dear. Though he sends you his love." My other grandparents did well enough on their pretensions, which included some fancy relatives, but the pension that allowed this would die with him. "No. No connection of his."

"Then who left it?" Who was this Leslie Warden?

She was plumper. I had just noticed it.

"Your father's—friend."

Who all these years, apparently—though who could be sure—had parlayed my father's support, and maybe his gifts, into the divers stocks and bonds which had been bequeathed. Or so my mother had been told—whether by the lawyers only or by my father as well, she did not say. It may be that she was told nothing, except that the money had been left.

There was no need to say why. "What a horrible act," I said. "You're not going to take it?"

She was not as quick to agree as I had expected.

"At least if it had been left to him—" I said. Returned, one might say then. Even if threefold.

"The jewelry's been left to him. There's quite a lot."

That was the second time I had heard that phrase.

"What tact!" I said. The morning sun was streaming in, showing us his empty dressing room at the bedroom's far end, shining with his special furniture, given him as his mother's wedding present, which Knobby had made lustrous once more. I had never before spoken to her that way. Last evening had left me with a feeling of success I couldn't localize. "Well, at least he never even wears a signet ring." On her silence, I turned. "Mother. You're not going to. Wear the stuff."

"For God's sake no," she said. "What do you take me for? He'll sell."

Then she came forward, in her furry morning gown. Last night when I came up the stairs, we had just embraced, under her "In the morning, my darling," and had fallen toward our beds. Bounding up early, with a zest I ascribed to her homecoming, I had gone for a walk, dressed in the jodhpurs and other rig bought for the promised horse we had had to flub buying last year after all, and had then brought her up a tray, knowing it took her days to divest herself of the South. Sun always made her blink; she was for later hours. "Feel as if I've—never seen you before . . . I haven't. Darling, you've gone and grown again." She'd never minded; she was old-fashioned only by whim. "How much is it now?"

"Six foot three."

She mused. She was thinking of my brother. When you don't love enough, your own disaffection still leaves an emptiness. I myself might one day know that for a husband, though never for a child.

She now surveyed me, her manner a cross between the grooms at Tipton's Livery down home, where we could ride for almost nothing, and Miss DeVore. "Handsome indeed, you are. In the new mode. But now it had better stop." She lifted a hand to the top of my head and rapped it smartly with the flat of her palm. "Stop, do you hear?" She listened, head cocked, the way we had crouched in the grass and listened for leprechauns when I was four. "Stop."

Then we laughed and kissed.

And do you know, I did stop. I believe you can talk to the genes to a degree, about their apportionment. Or they lie in wait, for what comes.

At the moment, I snitched a piece of her toast. "Well, I'm not planning to accept that money."

In her almost amused glance at my nibbling, I saw how I had always been provided for. Still, my flesh crept at any change in her stance, until then gallant to me. Like the autumn hills which surrounded all our meannesses. "You won't then? Refuse."

"I doubt if it's to be done that way."

Whether it would signify anything much, she would have meant, though I wouldn't have seen that, then.

I said I doubted I would want to live on that lady. "Even if the money did come out of us."

The phrase made my mother giggle. She had brought back

with her even more of the South than I thought. Or I was now more critical of her.

She saw. Whether or not she later went along with my notions of honor because of her own, or because of the delay her own windfall would prove to undergo, I do not know. She stared up at me almost flirtatiously from our now so different heights. "My God, how we're going to be able to dress you, my darling. And not from Miss DeVore."

When she sold our house to Gilbert, the town was not surprised, only analytical. In a place where all were so defined by their houses, any new turn of ownership shook those foundations first, and gossip might dwell on the buyer as much as on the seller—as happened here. Significantly, no one assumed my father and mother might be getting a divorce. As had long been clear, my mother and father were not the sort to ratify private changes of heart publicly. In the same way, though our family did not attend church, no minister had ever dared solicit us.

"She never did care much for your house, did she?" women neighbors murmured to me, in case I should need consoling. Meanwhile, as rumor of some inheritance reached them, they were more forward with me about Greensboro than they would ever have dared with her, probing me for description of our "plantation" there. When I said we had none, and that my grandfather had been a cotton factor, now retired, they smiled knowingly; we were also the sort whose prospects of wealth would have been kept from the children. "Is Warden on your father's side or your mother's?" one did ask, with the impudence of a person inside our house only because of the tag sale. My mother, gliding by just then, smiled, speaking one more word on the subject than she had to our real neighbors. "Both."

"Well, they're sure not selling any of the good stuff," the woman said to her friend, after. "And that's one in the eye for Gilbert Walsh."

Gilbert himself, with his wider horizons, may well have suspected my mother's inheritance had some dark non-family root to it, since, besides reading the New York papers cover to cover, as well as real estate journals and maybe even notices of wills at probate, he did know some of the details of the dissolution of my father's firm. Whatever else he did know he kept to himself, just as, even though he had not got my grandmother's house, he no longer spoke of wanting the house in Cobble Row. By buying ours he had moved up a step, and in our town one did not do that lightly, especially not a restaurateur, who had to be liked, and wasn't quite. As Gilbert himself said, "I have to go along with everything."

The last night she and I were in the old place, he and Luray and we were once again on the porch. Mrs. Evams was there, too. Mr. Evams had sent his regrets; he was involved in deciphering and authenticating an old manuscript in braille for a university library and didn't wish to leave it alone in the house. The usual things were said about intruders, though no one here had as yet experienced any, except for now and then a late-night trash-vandalizing at Walsh's Inn, as it was now called, and even that might have been the work of dogs.

On the porch, I no longer sat back behind the others; there were now not enough of us. Besides, I no longer cared to. My father and Mr. Evams, though never close friends, had between them kept up an unspoken balance beyond which gossip did not go. I realized now that I had enjoyed watching this, the way one watches a vanished handcraft. Instead, tonight I was the one being raked over.

"So the money for the house is all going to you," Luray said brashly. "No wonder your ma insisted all cash. Looks like you already begun to spend it."

They joshed their own child that way, but my mother bristled, though only I could see it. No one had ever called her a "ma" before, either. "Lord & Taylor. They had a late spring sale on cashmeres." She wouldn't say to them as she had to me: They have the only tall girl's shop where you should ever buy. She had put my name on her charge account, and the sum for the house in a trust Mr. Evams would be managing, with an allowance for me.

"It's for college." I held out my arm for Mrs. Evams to feel, adding softly, "Yellow. And the skirt is kind of a teal." Though she had never known color, she liked being in on the names of it.

"Well, you can sure afford a good one." Luray had wanted Gilbert to press my mother harder on the price, reportedly saying that there was no reason to treat grass widows as if they were real ones, but Gilbert had known better. "Which one you going to?"

"I've applied for three in the Boston area. But I'll go to whichever gives a scholarship."

"Scholarship? With thirty-seven thousand dollars in the till?"

"Can it, Luray," her husband said. "Girl has a brain, no reason she has to be poor to get paid for having it."

Mrs. Evams hovered a hand over the tea and coffee pots. "Which one of these is tea?" She knew perfectly well. She was only trying to change the subject, which she did, if not for the best; the blind can't know everything. Or perhaps, with all the loopholes in our family life, there was no best.

"Well-l, you can summer in Rio, then," Luray said—"in't our summer their winter? Sure be educational. A plantation." The town had determined we must have one.

"Dad and his associates don't grow coffee. They only deal in it." All my mother and I really knew was that my father and brother shared a flat with a Mr. Peralho, a longtime friend and one of the associates.

Luray served herself. "Well, I sure do relish a good cup of it."

Gilbert had his own irritations. He held out his cup to my mother. "You could have knocked me over with a feather, though. When I heard you were going to live with the old girl."

Since my father's installments of money seemed to be at his associates' whim, my mother, receiving her own new money in the nick of time, had applied some of it to my grandmother's costs, offering to go on doing so. She now bent forward with fine effect, pouring from the pot but also looking into Gilbert's face.

"My mother-in-law and I have an arrangement. I'll support her in the house for her lifetime. That way, she can be sure of leaving it to her grandson." She was telling him that he would never get his hands on it. But it was Luray who made a little telltale moaning sound.

I saw that Gilbert already knew. Sometimes I wished I owned a restaurant, for all you could learn there. Or that I could work at Gilbert's. But this my parents would never allow. Even in summer, none of the waitresses were college.

"I hear she'll make an upstairs apartment," he said, his face red. "That's desecration, the old Tartar."

"Why no, there already is one," my mother said. "They had it built when they came here. A sort of dower-house for the future. Families did that, then."

I saw that the Walshes, as recent arrivals, hadn't known.

I put my oar in, as my father would say. Inside our house, where his presence had been so infrequent, I forgot him, but outside here on the porch, in the shadow, all his savor, remote and careful, came back to me. "I wouldn't mind living up there. It's the prettiest part of the house."

I had chosen the wrong word. The rooms up there, as handsome as the downstairs though without any of its Victorian uglinesses, had that extra fillip, or strange rightness, which enclosure sometimes gives. I had only seen them once, and then on the sly.

"Oh, our Rosalie's already spoken for your attic," Luray said. "And her own phone. We would almost do it for that alone, I'll say. But then you can make an attic so cute."

Our own house attic was nothing. But I smiled to myself, seeing their tubby Rosalie trundling around among that other third floor's high armoires and gray-green leathers, and with her teenager phone propped on that altar-high desk.

Mrs. Evams said: "Those three servant's rooms off the kitchen here, that's what our Brenda envies. A real little flat."

"She could have a room over here," Luray said carelessly. Brenda was a treasure. "Scads of room, even after we redo. Then she could run back and forth to you."

"Thank you." Mrs. Evams never used contractions, and finished off all her syllables. These were what she had to spare. "We prefer our solitude." Her pale eyes and doll-fringe were pointed uncannily straight at Luray. I wondered what that domed forehead of hers would be like to touch. "In fact, no one over here has ever seen us as their responsibility."

"You bet," Gilbert said. He raised his hands in a shrug to my mother and me, ignorant of how, in our tight fivesome around the old wicker table, the airflow would tell Mrs. Evams that. "Anyway, these girls have everything worked out, don't they." He put one hand on my mother's knee, one on mine, and leaned heavily. "Boston. Seat of education . . . and medicine. By the way, Craig Towle's wife's gone back there to have her baby after all. Hit a snag. You heard?"

I'd never believed that party would take place anyway—the one she'd promised me. I saw my mother hadn't heard anything of this news either—though you would never know.

I stood up. I was just learning the power of my height. Gilbert, still leaning forward on us, was in one of our old wicker rockers. He went over backward.

I turned to Mrs. Evams. "May I go say hello-goodbye to Mr. Evams? I may go to Columbia Summer School." I had just then thought of it.

"We've missed you," Mrs. Evams said, her face lifted tranquilly to all these rushes of air.

As I went down our steps, Luray was helping Gilbert up. My mother was looking deep into the matching handkerchief Miss DeVore made for all her dresses. We made fun of them but never discarded them. When Gilbert had settled she said: "I know you hoped for us to let you have a lien on my mother-in-law's house. She'll burn it down first. But she'll do anything for our boy. And a girl going to college needs a background to come home to."

"She'll need a big one, your daughter," Luray said. "Don't lean back, Gilbert. I was going to offer for this porch set, but now I don't know."

"Don't bother," I called up to her. "Nothing of ours will fit."
I knew it was childish of me. Time I was leaving though, before I knew everything—which at that period I thought possible. Even that it wasn't me my mother wanted a background for, but herself. Why else would she ask me to stay, even for only summers and holidays, in the same house with a grandmother who avoided looking at me, though no small woman herself. Just because I wasn't my brother. Or he wasn't me.

Why would my mother put herself there? Some women might get a mean pleasure from bailing out such a mother-in-law, but my mother would never waste her life enjoying a grudge. I wanted not to think of what she might be wasting her life at. From my father I knew only too well what a man looked like, talked like, when he was separating himself from more than a woman. From a life. Craig Towle had talked to me like that. If he was leaving town for good, then what was it in my grandmother's house that would draw him back to it? Where my mother would once more be waiting, for him to pass by.

No person had yet made me focus as she had on him. But now that I had seen it happen, I could be afraid that I might do the same.

At the Evamses' the porch light was on. In the glass transom over the front door I could see my face. Though I could scarcely find the face or the rest of me as amazing as others often seemed to, when a girl is tall enough to stare into transoms, then it is good that she can take some pleasure in staring. I rang the gong. Then I took the key from its hiding place, as the students did here, and pushed the door in. From then on, it was a game we all knew.

I took one step forward, and waited. Then another, and again a pause. Finally, a third step, which—unless a foot or a shoe had somehow lost its characteristic, was the telltale one. I waited, forlorn. Change was my devil, these days. Then I heard the familiar cough—and held my breath.

"We missed you," Mr. Evams said.

The grace of it washed over me. I was admitted to the comfort of being blind.

Here, even before we were taught alphabet we were taught something of that comfort. I took off my right shoe. The prehensile foot has more than a knowledge of floors. I kept the left foot shod, so that it might feel how much it missed. It was now the sighted one. Just so, we had been obliged to wear gloves of kid, then of surgical rubber, until at last we were allowed to touch the braille-blistered pages with the true power of skin. Watching the reading Evamses play that endlessly mute piano, I would swear their fingers did not touch the page.

Eyes closed, I moved forward and sat down, inserting myself between table and chair without bumping the table's curve. My body had remembered the space in a kind of measurement. My thighs contracted now to the wooden mold of these chair seats. I knew where I was, in a way that with the light on and my eyes wide I never would. I could smell his shaving soap. For sure, he would smell the curdled sweat in which I had left our porch.

"What's wrong?"

He had a good teacher's voice—like a key turning.

"Oh—it's all right," I said, realizing that now it was. "But I am leaving. Or I will soon."

He nodded. I could feel it.

We were silent together. With the eyes mutually closed, or as good as, silence is a live thing.

"Why do I only know what I'm going to do, or what I feel—when I say it?"

He chuckled. "You have quite a voice box, you know. Perhaps it's that?"

We considered.

"Too good?"

"No. Some are. But that's elocution. Or opera."

We both laughed. Opera was too much for her and him.

"A good speaking voice listens," he said. "Yours does."

"Maybe that's all my vocation is? Listening?" They knew I wanted one.

He laughed. "Oh no. You'll certainly speak."

"I'm sure not a painter."

"Aren't you," he said indifferently. That could scarcely be settled here.

I opened my eyes.

"Yes, do," he said. "It must be harder to keep them closed."

Oh, they could be marvelously arrogant here. It was wonderful though, to be hedged in with them temporarily. People who got what they wanted daily because they had to.

"Watching the town," I said. "I can't stand to any longer. College is my only way of leaving it. Is that all right?"

"We'll have some tea," he said. "Turn on the light."

It was manners for them to let us do that. And it taught us what we were being given back.

Once, when in the dark at the end of a lesson he had instructed someone to turn on the light, a sighted student had said, smirking, "It is on." You can hear a smirk. He had never been allowed back.

Mr. Evams always made the tea, in the way the man of a couple will make the drinks. He handed me one of their Nippon cups, ugly in pattern but thin and light. The sofa was nondescript but quality-soft. The whole room was like that, an antidote for the show-off poisons, a narrow wisdom—pooled. I trusted it.

"What can't you stand about it?" he said. "The town."

"What they're hooked on."

"And what is that?"

I knew he would ask. The blind have to. I wanted him to, though I couldn't think what to say. Then—I said it.

"Their ways of keeping up."

He didn't answer; he often didn't. We rested so, while what I had said sank into me and out again, draining the sore.

"Would you like to see what I'm working on?"

The book was on his table, an old brown calf-bound volume, the kind that doesn't give in.

"Read a page," he said.

I washed my hands at the only tap I have ever seen in a

library, dried them on the roller-towel, and sat down, waving them dry. It's best to sit, for braille. The paper can be so thick that turning the pages can make a current. One gets to think of that air as like thought bubbling up, released.

These pages were so thin my fingertips felt coarse, and the marks were warped, like print under water. "I've forgotten it. Everything."

"No, it's French. Old French. Ronsard. The first ever printed for us."

"Why—we had him, second term. I learned one poem by heart. Or almost. *Quand tu seras*—"

"*Page trente-six,*" he said.

I read it out as we did in French class, translating line by line —only with my eyes closed. "*Quand tu seras bien vieille, assise auprès de feu*—When you are quite old and seated by the fire" . . . I could hear him listening, tranquilly breath-clocking the rhythm. My voice expanded, toward the finish almost baritone; oh, if this could be a vocation I would know what to do. "*Ronsard m'a célébré, au temps que j'étais belle* . . . Ronsard did celebrate me, in the time when I was—" I hesitated; "beautiful" was too many syllables. There was no English word that fitted.

"—'Young,'" Mrs. Evams said, arriving soundlessly behind me. We all laughed.

She accepted a cup from him. "Our new neighbors don't approve of our dark. They say it is an invitation. To bad characters. And downgrades the block." The cup rattled in her hand, her anger sifting up. "They were watching over here. They approved of you two. They want us to light normally. Like now." She turned to me. She always wore all gray clothes in winter, all white in summer; that way there were no awkward mistakes. Though once, when I had knitted her a navy-blue sweater, telling her how it would go with either, and how becoming it was, she had worn it incessantly. "You'll tell us the truth. Are we? An invitation?"

How could I warn them? How could I not? Hadn't I kept away from them, knowing I must? I thought of the white cameo of their bodies, ovaled against the pale furniture, Mr. Evams's mother's, which did entirely match both itself and them. I thought of Gilbert's hand on my knee and on my mother's, of his pudgy, inquisitive eye. Yet if I told them, I myself would break the spell forever. For them.

Opposite and up a flight, I could see our landing window, honorably shrouded ever since that night. Over this weekend the drapes would come down, not to be replaced. The Walshes liked a view, they said, and liked giving one. A good business habit, my mother had said, which must come from running that kind of restaurant.

I stood up. In this cued house I was afraid to open my mouth. Movement was only a deferral; no pretense was safe here. How they listened. How could I answer?

It comes through the body first, gesturing for the mind. All my life long I had watched that attitudinizing. *Externalize.*

I walked over to the nearest lightswitch and turned it off. They could hear the click. The voice coming in after had better be true. "Your dark—invited me."

You begin with truth. After that you can lie.

You *can* lie, even to the blind. The warm currents tell you, streaming from their taut audience, supporting the magic they crave as much as you.

"Of course, there's Brenda." I made my voice rich with mirth. "When you're gone, she tends to leave all the lights on downstairs. But once or twice when you were not. And once the curtains were left open, too. Only in the dining room. But probably you'll want to keep tabs now." Lying breeds saliva. I swallowed. "I loved seeing you."

So I found my vocation, in the theater of their dark.

Mrs. Evams put down her cup. "Luray said we depressed her. 'Like a vacant lot,' she said. 'On a first-class street.' " Her laugh tinkled. Then she kissed me, my sweat and all. I was pouring with it.

I wasn't sure I had gone over that great with him. He was an experienced theatergoer.

"I'm going away—" I said to him. "Would you two like to feel my face?" They hadn't done so in a long time.

Mrs. Evams went first, scarcely brushing my head with her astral shaping, then feathery over my whole outline. "My dear—dear. You're a goddess." Like always, she turned to him, as to the once sighted one. "Is she the beauty I think she is?"

His fingers planed my cheekbones for their wide angle, smoothed my eyeballs to a statue's stone orbs. He did the nose in one dash, then lingered on the lip points, and the lower lip's center infold. He curved his hand to cup my chin, tapping its cleft. "Your brows are dark, aren't they." He traced their flung frame. "Darker than the hair." At the ears, he grunted. "A flaw, thank goodness. Ears slightly jug. But the braids mask them." He breathed in one of them. "Ah, noble Hera. Yes, you're a noble girl," he whispered. No, I hadn't fooled him. Then he kissed me on both cheeks and gave me back to myself, his hands leaving me. I can still feel their sad, precise geometry.

But then, Bill Wetmore came back. He was just getting home from school on the incoming morning train, while I was only taking the outgoing one in order to register for summer school—but though the railroad had revved up its schedule as new city arrivals pushed into our hills, nothing much could be done about the two narrow yellow-brick platforms, from the scarred opposing sides of which two people who seemed to themselves inordinately young and hopeful for these parts could frantically semaphore—and later call it fate. "If you hadn't decided to go in that same morning—and if I hadn't missed the last train out the night before," we said to each other over and over, would say forever. He had spent the previous night in the Dixie Hotel near Forty-second Street, high-mindedly sketching from memory a couple of prostitutes who had accosted him, and the two men running a shell game scam just outside the bus terminal door. Both sketches we later framed and hung, just as that vivid night would later hang in our small talk, almost as if I had shared it, too. That night I had been washing my hair, as I did before all adventure, and had fallen asleep choosing which sweater outfit to float to Columbia in. It had been my last night in the old house, and I had taken the early train to avoid the moving men.

Would we ever have met again otherwise? He was slated for a summer session also, but down at Washington Square, a world away from Columbia Heights, and with plans to hunt for a Village pad to share. Truly we might not have encountered each other in the town either, each of us slopping about the house, lazy and alien, in the way students tend to do before they are reslotted. Though I would have heard he was home I would never have put myself in his way, instead, avoiding him because I still thought of him. And maybe proud because I was not as my mother was. While he, though he hadn't forgotten me, had never meant to start up again.

"Then I saw you."

Then he saw me. It became a canon in our tender conversation for him to describe that, and to credit his own presence of mind in yelling "Call you! Call you!" across the track, just before my incoming train blotted us out. Even the stray witnesses on the platforms, townspeople until then not known to us, were from then on enshrined, later to be puzzled at our shyly cordial nods. We were on that brink—remember it?—when everything is to happen in the appointed way, and will appear unique.

New buds often fuse out of an excess of their own honey and wax. Marriages can be made of this, or still later aborted because of it. You never tell the children anything of this. They, and the sketches, are what survive.

When I found out Bill Wetmore was illegitimate, did that add the final touch? They say that at times all young people wish to be that, or even imagine they are. Not me. I never dreamed of disowning either my family or the town, whether or not I left them. I meant instead to grasp them for all they were—if I could find that out.

At home, it was to be a hard summer for both him and me. His grandmother wasn't failing in the decent, elderly style which still blessed so many inhabitants tottering along the town's streets, but in the intense hospital agony with which more modern people ended their lives, a mode of dying to which as a nurse she had special access. As the head nurse at the local hospital, she was the focus of every possible medical angle and already had been fractured on many. In their own small house, to which she now and then remanded herself, her bedroom, filling with vials of sucrose or darker medicament, respirators, catheters, and other anonymous metal and rubber, became a paragon of what could be done at home. Solicitously never left alone in either place, in the Cobble Row house she queened it, waking to her own torture, to give her attendants gasped advice for more of the same.

He came home weekends. Phoebe had a summer job as an *au pair* girl with a family on Cape Cod. "She'll never come home again to stay," he said—and indeed she never did, becoming a zealot Bostonian, a dean somewhere, and not marrying. "She's the legitimate one. I suppose she has to prove it." His long, quirky face was all expressiveness. Later troughs would make it equine, lovable the way horses are. In his crop-headed, glinting youth he looked to me like the Arrow Collar ad of the 1930s, which he thought his father had maybe looked like, and in the sketches of small-town America, which Bill was doing for a drawing class—and later would become known for—I could see that both the fathers and sons looked like that too.

His father had been a Harvard boy who worked two summers at Pruyn's—the factory responsible for the workers' houses in Cobble Row. "He was related to some Pruyns, though not very closely." Which was why Bill Wetmore himself had a small trust fund. The rest of his father's identity had been lost in a sea of divorce. "I don't go to see them anymore." A couple of uncles and aunts, who lived between Philadelphia and Wilmington. "They showed me pictures of him in his baby clothes. Which seemed to be all they knew of him." And had sent the big desk in the Wetmores' loft. "He and some other kids were killed in a crash on the Saw Mill Parkway, on the way back to school." The word "kid" hit us like a pellet scuffed up from that roadway. It wasn't even the best way to Boston anymore. Bill's mother, the sugar-faced townie, already pregnant, hadn't known he was dead for three months. "I suppose he was weak. But how can one tell? Moral: drive back to school very carefully."

Bill himself hadn't gone to Dartmouth after all, but to the Rhode Island School of Design, where he was studying to be an illustrator. I saw that the idea of sculpture had dropped from him, as too heavy a stone. He was surprised that I remembered it, or that I asked about his mother. She had married the older worker from Pruyn's who had later fathered Phoebe, moving on to Detroit with him, where he died, from which city she had sent Phoebe back here at the age of three, to join Bill, already here. For a while she herself used to come back. "A thin woman I called Francie." He sketched her for me, a factory worker herself by then, with something of the town's Polish in her. "Then she didn't anymore." Now she was middle-aged and dead, with all her interim life invisible to him, though he didn't seem to care.

"Was *she* weak?" I asked, cupping his head up from the scruffy pillow on the floor of his Village friend's pad. That so well-shaped back of the head, still his best feature, and so cupped with promise—how my palm remembers it.

"I never thought about it."

"Because she was a woman?"

"No, I don't think so. Any more than you're only asking as one."

We lay back in the perfect equality of bodies just after joining.

Honey and wax, we had to meet at least once a day, traveling our dreamy train and subway miles between town and city, uptown and down, to touch or to know we were going to; otherwise we felt halved, the summer suddenly bottomless, its glow gone on to others. Unaware of how little this had to do with us personally, between us we balanced the world, each of us paying out to the other the history behind us.

"Grandmother managed it all," he said, letting her shadow cross us because she was dying—and was managing it. We had forgotten his mother. But what I see now is all four of us, she and his father, he and I, he and his father nineteen, she and I a little younger, all of us lying there, ready to be chosen by their issue to come. He had chosen most to resemble his father, and to doubt him. Whatever the genes plot, I believe we choose the family we can bear to have.

"Oh—grandmothers," I said. That kept him and me in hand-fast too. Mine now dowagered us from that third-floor realm I had once glimpsed—which only Watanabe was allowed to enter. My mother and I—"you two heiresses," as she now called us, had the rest of the house below—two august floors, a ground floor, and a second, in which only our own bedrooms seemed human. Watanabe was in the servants' quarters off the kitchen, which, too, we never saw.

Our own furniture, once it had been insinuated, had been lost to further reckoning. A sense of my father remained in the two guest rooms, the larger of which he had had as a young man, the smaller as a boy. My brother had lived in the latter while here—but from boyhood on he has never left much of himself behind. He and my father were always supposed to be coming home soon, but hadn't yet. Gradually, we were becoming correspondents only, my brother and grandmother in long letters on his part from which she read only the factual bits to us, my father in letters to me, cleverly short on description, sternly determined on love. I could sense there were lines to be read between, but couldn't decide which they were.

Once a week, Watanabe served the three of us a formal tea in the downstairs sitting room, for whatever exchanges were needed. My grandmother was more polite, as if she had schooled herself to this, now that we were in the house. She went out rarely, though she still looked too powerful for the sitting room's heart-backed chairs. When Watanabe came downstairs from her rooms with his pastes and his mops, he would exclaim "Ah—ee that fruitwood, and the desk, inlaid, she says, with zebrawood and white holly!"—but reflectively said nothing when he came down with her trays, after what I suspected were the times she talked to him. "What does she say to you?" I said, cornering him in the pantry. He flicked her napkin out of its silver-and-ivory ring. "Nothing she expect me to understand." But what did she do up there, beyond telephoning her lawyer and financial advisor, or a few town ancients she called her charity-friends—and once every two weeks, my father.

"She has a companion," he said. "When she wants." He tapped the side of his head. "Who? How can I say who? Ninety years to choose from, she can afford to change him. But I think it is only one."

In the upstairs hall my mother called the gallery, my grandfather's state photograph, silvery clear in the old style, showed a clean-shaven, shrewd-featured man with a mouth pursed like my brother's—nobody much to inhabit my grandmother's majestic head. Their wedding picture, when he was over sixty and she on the way to thirty, showed him as shorter and narrower than she. In the nearby picture of him in his office he looked more regal, his staff of men receding behind him in wooden-railed enclosures, each man decreasing in size, like a lesson in perspective.

A bachelor railroader who had gone into land sales and allied brokerages, he had lodged with her family before their marriage, and had continued on so as her husband, in her family homestead. The family had been New Jersey potato farmers, land-rich or land-poor as the times might be, of the breed who had Revolutionary teaspoons in their plain pine coffers and the new white refrigerator pridefully in the front room. Trenton had been their metropolis.

This was what my father had ultimately gone to Yale from, and not on a scholarship. One yard-long picture, taken well before he was to be born, showed the entire family of my great-grandparents' day ranged in a line on the porch of their almost octagonal hump-windowed farmhouse, always he said painted the yellow with fudge trim then considered a step up from Colonial white. My grandmother's parents center the line, staples also of their time, the huge farmer and his miniature wife, she soon to go down the birth-drain with a late last-child-to-be. Two spindly boys, my grand-uncles, flank her, one to fall in a war, the other to be the black sheep. Four daughters of the house flank him, all handsome and almost father-size. Two moved West and are lost to history. My grandmother, the middle sister in the picture, by age as well, is standing with her arm around the last-born and already looks to be the head sister. But that might be because I knew her now.

In that picture, my grandfather does not appear. Perhaps he had been still gathering his powers for the marriage, and for the long years ahead as consort in that house—not yet knowing of their eventual move away, to here. That happening had changed my father's college life, for it had given him a new background. "It was a bankrupt's house, got cheap with all its goods. For years I couldn't get over the notion that bankrupt meant beautiful."

Yet, though he could readily be made to talk about the old farmhouse sold when they moved, and my brother and I could walk its patterns in our sleep, he never talked in detail of his parents' life there, or why they had all of a sudden come here, to what my grandmother, always interestingly grotesque in her summaries, called her "honeymoon" house.

Verging on eighty by then, my grandfather had died in it that year—at a house party for undergraduates.

I went upstairs to the gallery, to check his photograph. No, he simply did not look as if he could have acquired all that force for her since.

Watanabe came up behind me. "A husband."

I had to laugh. Knobby had a passion for the ballet, fed by tickets from a niece, a costume girl for a celebrated troupe, who however scorned his wife-getting, and had informed him that "husband" was ballerina slang for a male dancer who was a trust-worthy partner but would never be a star.

"What's it like up there, now?" For weeks my grandmother had been clearing out things from the third floor, not relegating them to the attic above her, but sending forth a stream of pack-ages and cartons as neatly bound as if for holiday mail, which Knobby was however required to deposit at the town dump.

He looked down at the tray he was carrying. She ate well. Under some handmade domed pottery dishes, which had been brought out when she moved up there, the lamb-chop bones would be picked clean, the butter plate blank. A rough sweet-sour came from her wineglass. In a tentative, stealthy unity not otherwise acknowledged between us, we three females were getting at my father's wines, which had always remained in the cellar over here. A case had even been sent to the Evamses, and I myself intended one day, perhaps at summer's end, to take a bottle or two to the city. My grandmother still lorded it over these bequests, but in an odd way, as she became more remote in her eyrie, she had become more generous.

"Knobby. You haven't answered."

"You can see the hills, from the—what you call it? Cap-i-tain's walk."

"You always could." I loathed that enclosure, reached by a last twist of steps from the third floor. It had murky amber panes and a floor like painted hide, where your steps could only circle and never stretch. I had no desire to see our hills from up there.

"It is like a leaf viewing," he said. "Only the leaves are gone."

I followed him downstairs into the pantry. "You know what I mean. The apartment."

"It has not changed, your grandmother says. It is the same."

"Then what's all this stuff from?"

The packages for this week's dump day were already ranged down along the backstairs which led from up there. That disposal, oddly contested by my mother, would come up on tea day, which coincided. My question was a silly one, what with all the closets and drawers in this old stockpile of a house, and in similar houses here. People on our porches censured themselves every springcleaning for their accumulations, leaning back into these with Cheshire-cat smiles. I had even heard it suggested that people got senile quicker in cities, with less storage space to remember from.

Some of the drawers up there, I thought I recalled, had a tooled-gold line around the keyhole. I couldn't recall any knickknacks; maybe there had been none, or none to engage a child. "The same? Like what? What's it like?"

Knobby had never looked me up and down before. I hadn't realized a person like him could do that as well as any of us, even if bowing to the privilege. He was going to say something special. He often did—but as I check back now, never with such ceremony. Now he turned to the packages, bowing to them, and then again to me. Somehow it was inserted into my mind that it was an honor for each of us to know the other.

Sunlight from over the sink warmed my hair and fell on his clasped hands. "Very Samurai."

On tea days my grandmother comported herself like company, often wearing a hat for the drive to follow, for which Knobby, too, put on a chauffeur's cap. If being without income had made her almost benign, her autocratic public manner remained the same. As she shrank in size, though she was doing it hardily, she seemed to have come into the more spiritual promise of those great-flowered dresses, which now whispered around her with a tuberose perfume so heavy it affected the tea sandwiches. She seemed to be able to look at me now, though still not casually. Often I caught her contemplating me. I always stared back. Though I can despise people in small ways, I cannot hate them. They interest me too much. My stare never downed her. She seemed instead to sink into it almost fearfully.

My mother couldn't rise to what she called "your grandmother's act."

"I don't think it is an act." We were waiting for her in the sitting room. Two of the charity friends, very old people also, had just left the house—and this, too, had been going on for weeks. Always they left with a bundle or two. Surely my mother had noticed this, though she never said.

"Ah well, you're the acting expert," she said.

My cheeks mantled with red, as the old expression went. At the well-known acting academy to whose summer classes I had transferred, hoping to qualify in the competition for full en-

trance in the fall, we were collecting these expressions and practicing them. The teacher was pleased with those of us who could
blush; I couldn't do it on command, but some students never
had blushed at all. As to the academy—my mother had cheered
me on, crying out the minute I broached going there—"Of
course, of course—how is it we never thought of it for you?" She
had put her hand on my wrist then, just as now. Saying, "But it's
—it's the person herself who has to think of it first—isn't it? Or
it won't work." But yes, she had said, oh yes.

Each yes and but of hers had mounted to true recognition and
delight. That's what I was, an actress. Without knowing it,
that's what they had been fitting me for. All the planes of our
family, our street, our town—had contributed. As a newspaper
would one day note. But she granted it first.

The hand on my arm was very thin.

"I wasn't making fun," she said.

"I know." I wished she would; she worried me. My mother
and the city had collided, though with her usual tact she never
went in at the same times I did, and never asked to meet me
there. Clothes arrived, from stores with bleak French names.
Stark outfits, with sudden spurts of frill. Too much black, even
for the suburbs we now were. Swooping hats. She would dress in
them and after hours of rapt preparation be unable to leave the
house, sinking back to regard herself for hours, wineglass in
hand. Dressed like that, there was after all no place to go. Once I
heard her say this to her mirror, nodding from her divan, "All
dressed up and no place to go." When in the city myself, I once
or twice peered into hotel lobbies where I saw she could belong
—but on what errand? The worst of it was that she knew beforehand the dressing up might come to nothing, yet didn't stop.

Today she was in all too perfect gray, silkily pouched on the
vanished hips. She saw me looking at her new stiletto heels.
"Don't worry. I dress for the drive. But I never get out of the
car."

A mirror was opposite. The house had many, and she tended
to place herself in front of them, not for pleasure. "I used to look

like a provincial just a little ahead of the crowd, didn't I? Or too
good for it." She smoothed the ravages under her eyes and at her
mouth. "I always did dress for what might happen. Down home,
we do that. But now I look like a widow with hopes."

Her accuracy made me flinch.

"Yes, it started down home," she said, giving it home's inflec-
tion. "We attitudinize. That's so you don't get too close to our
hearts."

I must have brooded.

She was handing me a glass of wine. "For better or worse, I've
taught you the same."

"For better. I'm sure of it." I was flushed with all the first
rose-pinks of the theater, and they had told us we must prepare
to be hard.

I was wrong. Attitudes may get you into drama school. But in
the end the heart must be exposed. It wouldn't be Bill Wetmore
who taught me that.

Another old person was coming down the stairs, one of the
fading ones from our own street. He nodded in at us, holding up
his cane. "Just look at the one she gave me. I'll leave my old one
in your bin." The cane was an elegant briar, with an ivory grasp.
He accepted a glass of wine, but with a gander over his shoulder,
as if allegiances must not be confused, and went quickly out.

She laughed, then knit the plucked brows that gave her face
an undeserved shallowness. I think she found that useful, or had
once. Mine are what hers might have been—heavy and straight.
A woman's face can have too much character for quick luck. But
I prefer to leave it so.

"I wish all the stuff went out to those poor dears," she said.
"There's another load in the front hall."

"Why do you bother, then?"

"Why indeed. You think I want the stuff, whatever it is?"

"Old clothes, old underwear, Knobby says. Old papers she
can't bear to burn, but scissors up. She goes through everything.
Maybe it's a kind of rite."

"Maybe."

"Then why do you care?"

"I promised your father. To keep him posted." She took a second glass of wine. "Don't look so amazed."

I wouldn't nowadays. The lines of communication can be down but not cut, only sagged from a slow, weaning wind equal to any storm. Yet one still communicates. The one who long ago first wheedled for it, does so once again; in duet, the one who in response long ago promised whatever, again promises—and at times the roles may even be reversed. Where that kind of power is exerted, distance doesn't count. As every grave-digger knows.

"He said she might well do something strange, if we came to live in the house."

"Did he say why?"

"He thought her memories may recently have been disturbed by something. She wouldn't say what."

"But what has that to do with us?"

She got up and walked about, carefully picking up her sharp heels from the mahogany floor, which gave her the gait of the larger birds who walk so. I would one day use that gait in a part I played, scarcely believing that I would ape her so, would do such a thing—but I did. "I saw you in the gallery, looking at your grandfather."

"No one ever mentions him. What was he like?"

I thought it was the wine that made her slow to reply.

"A good man—they said later. The way they say it when they mean—dull. He and I only spoke for ten minutes. It was at your father's college graduation party." She peered into the front hall, toward the long double parlor. "They cleared all the downstairs for it. Sprinkled rosin on the floor, for dancing. Banked the place with flowers. And after all that—had record-player music. Your grandmother had never heard of hiring a band. A Victrola— from the farm. But we loved it. We thought she meant it to be that way. None of us girls rightly knew your father, you see. In those days it was still mostly girls who gave the parties, and he didn't know many girls. My school was only what they used to call a finishing school, more for marriage than for college, but we were near enough New Haven to know a lot of Yalies, our senior year. And one of them got a group of us to come. I was on my way back down home anyway." She looked up almost shyly. "And I had my own new graduation dress." She and I exchanged smiles. "Linen, it was. Starched to a fare-thee-well. So when the old gentleman gave a funny spurt of a sound, I thought it was my dress crackling, and almost giggled. Old men hold you tight." She arched a pointed toe along the mirror-brown floor. "Your grandfather died while I was dancing with him."

Someone was coming down the front stairs. A little old lady appeared, scuffing a package from step to step down the long flight, her fluffy white head bobbing above it. Taller than she, it was apparently light. Like a triangular sail, it bore her out the front door.

"Packages can be strange," I said, in a deep weirdo voice.

We laughed until we were weak.

I felt better then about leaving her here alone, as I did day after day—even about leaving her for good, as I knew I was going to when I could. She could go down home, where laughter was easier; perhaps she should. Why do people ever leave what suits them so well?

"Why did grandmother and grandfather ever come here?"

Bringing everything with them except the farm machinery. And we'd have brought that—I had heard my father say—if there'd been a way to move it. Even so, the best things here came from the bankrupt. The house we left was the best thing we had.

I answered for her. "I know. They wanted to give father a good background."

"So you heard," she said. "Ah, you were born listening. Anyway, that's how you came to be born. I don't think your father would have married, except for that day."

"Married you, you mean?"

"He and a friend were to have gone to be law partners, right in New Haven. That man never spoke to him again."

She clasped her hands behind her head, swinging from side to side, defiantly. I had never seen her in that posture. "You see, I was sort of—made interesting by the event. They thought I handled things so well. It was just manners."

I knew those manners—Greensboro's. Sometimes you didn't know why you had them, but you went on with it.

"It was thought proper for your father to escort me home. By train of course. They weren't the flying kind. A long ride. And it was school breakup time for both of us. June. And after that— there was down home. We lived in the factor's big house, then."

And the furniture was theirs. And my father liked manners.

"And I'd brought him there."

She'd dressed for something to happen, and it had. I don't suppose men ever know that feeling. She was still pushing her toe along Watanabe's shining floor. Of a sudden I felt mired in what women do, and choking to get out, even if a stage might make it worse.

"There were flowers here, everywhere," she said. "The aunt who lived with them had an eye for it. Little pots of those pocket flowers, like pansies with the mumps, all down the side of the dance floor. When his father and I fell, people thought we'd stumbled over them."

My grandmother could be heard now, coming down the two flights. She still had her decisive step. Whatever had upset her memory, it wasn't mere age. Like many hardy, immovable elderly persons, she seemed less vulnerable to death than the middle-aged—and never spoke of the chance.

"You never told me, Mother. Why not?"

"Women are always exchanging their mistakes with each other. Men never do. You'll notice that, one day. You do the same as them, hear?"

It was true she had no women friends. "Even with you?"

She put her arms up and around me. "You're no mistake to me."

Over her head I saw the packages in the front hall. "Hey-y."

Crossing a finger over my lips, I ran to them and pawed them over. Some felt like framed glass. I chose at random, a small one of those and a soft one, one of several about laundry-package size, and was able to hide them in the boots-and-rubbers closet under the stairs and stand at attention, before my grandmother hove into view. I moved well, the school said.

My grandmother passed me without comment. Behind her, Watanabe carried her car rug, a fine affair of taupe plush. He loved these ceremonials, and often was asked by her to choose their route. In everything but money she was head of the house still.

Knobby brought tea. I always had a lot of it, with milk. That seemed to fascinate her. Her own people, both the huge Yorkshire farmers and the little nimble Irish like her own mother, had been great tea drinkers, with lashings of milk. Tea had brought the two sides together. I heard the story again, sleepily; would it never stop, that family essence ever steeping in one of our two brown luster pots, ever diluted by the hot water in the other?

"You've brought her along well," she said to my mother, approving my skirt. I was not allowed to wear jeans or slacks to go out with her. "Though in my day we wore sleeves. And—underwear." I supposed she couldn't bring herself to say "bra." If she knew the word. They must have had other names for them. "I hear she's even—seeing a boy. Is she?"

My mother smiled at me, lounging in her chair. "Are you?"

I smiled back, seeing Bill Wetmore standing before me, redorganed, his eyes intent on that bushy part of me which wasn't me as specifically. Men always look more specific, to us. "I suppose I am."

My grandmother's hands were trembling. Age was nibbling even her. "We didn't know how to do that. How to bring a girl along."

"Or a boy," my mother murmured after her, watching her exit to the car, Knobby toting behind her the first load of castoffs to stow in the trunk.

My mother, putting her hat on, made a fright-face at herself in the mirror. "Nor did I."

I missed my brother sometimes. Tim wrote every week that he
and my father would soon visit. He seemed to believe this.

"I'd go visit them," I said. "If they'd send me the money."
Tim was working these days, subbing as a teenage jockey at a
track. But he would come back for college eventually. My father
was the one who had put the family out of focus for me—
leaving, yet not leaving. I couldn't get past him until he became
forgettable. I already had an idea that maybe my mother was, or
one day would be. Maybe all of them. Tim said we all made him
feel flanked in, like a horse in a crowded starting position—but
that may have been due to his size. Though I rode well enough,
of course I could never be a jockey. Yet big as I was, I felt flanked
in by the horse who wasn't there.

"I could advance you some of your money ahead." The hat
she had chosen drooped gently to her shoulders, framing her in
its glossy dark bell.

"Not for that." No, he would have to send me the money.
Against all his pattern I knew so well, I had dreams of that.

"Aha. You're weakening. What would you use it for?"

I shrugged, shaking my head. Bill Wetmore would use it, he
said, if he were I. He claimed artists were excused from both the
consequences of money and its sources.

Knobby came in again for his last load. He took his cap from
the hall tree and sat it on his head at an angle. Until lately he
had worn it straight, but as the time neared for his prospective
wife to come, he was becoming more offhand American; even
his food had changed. He was preparing to enlighten her.

Picking up the load, he nodded at my mother—"Somebody's
still at it. I checked." And went out again.

Somebody's still at what, I wondered. She would soon eluci-
date, as they said down home, and of course she did, toying at a
last brown parcel with a gossipy foot. "Some nosy's been picking
over our dumped trash. Wraps and ties it up again. Does it on
the dumpster's day off. Leaves a donation for the dumpster.
With a note nothing's been taken."

She and I exchanged what I now think of as the peccadillo

smile. That familiar one which recognizes the accepted flaws of society, or of some member of it. I know now such smiles occur at every level, from the White House say, to the close-ups in the subtler movies, but in those days I thought them indigenous only to where I grew up, and even in the act of performing one, I felt mired again in all the rhythms taught me—for it was the smile of all our little social-lying selves.

The dumpster, for instance, so-called because to run the dump in all its phases was his official job, was also guardian and tender of the cemetery, each chore excusing his absence from another. We all knew that where he could be found soonest was at the pool hall, cueing for tips, but since his was that fringe life which makes other lives seem real, the town was proudest of him for his absences. We too always left a donation at the shack he kept his mock office in.

On the way there I usually sat up front with Knobby. That day, my mother sat there. Broad though the old Lincoln was—it too had been the bankrupt's, it could not accommodate both my grandmother's hat and my mother's with the separation each wearer required. I sat with my grandmother, in the back seat. Not so long ago that might have frightened me, but today I could sit pleasurably ensconced in a jelly of my own feelings, a broad band of which, paling from dark rose to nude as it left me, seemed to outline and protect me, as a violin case does a violin. Only with Bill Wetmore was I ever bare of this strip of—what was it, mapped receptivity?—belonging only to me. Even then— he would say—he had to wear me down; getting to me was like walking through a bead curtain, until at last we were together, in the foreplay of sex. He himself had never felt a feeling-band, although at adolescence he had been all quills. He drew a picture of us so—"you in your aura of snatch, me in my porcupine karate belt"—which he clearly wanted me to save, as women do, but I did not. What I felt wasn't all snatch.

In the end, gesture, not sex, would be what would release me. The studying of it, the learning of it, the watching for it, helped me break out of my pupa case, if that it was, by means of those body starts and facial moves which were now seeming to me to underlie all human drive—as in class we were taught how the phalanx underlay so much of Greek art. Meanwhile, such practice became a focus apart from him. This I didn't tell him, and scarcely acknowledged to myself. It would be a long time before I had gestures of my own.

I could tell my grandmother was nervous, fiddling in her lap with the collection of calling cards she always used as we went along, to locate and list where old houses and acquaintances had been, or still were, though she never stopped to visit. Before our family arrived the town had never heard of such usages as cards, nor had she. According to my father, she took certain customs from old novels and etiquette manuals found on the shelves of her new residence, not noticing their dates. "And bang, instant aristocracy," he said, though the town had balked at fingerbowls. "It's the women who have charge of daily life," he wrote me once. "I had to hunt my way out of that." I wondered who had charge of his dailiness now.

I studied her hands, noting how the corrugated veins of an old person were rather greener than the accepted blue. How the earlobes also became prominent. How in fact her good Knox hat of tan felt, that staple for those of her years and social standing, made her look like some old soldier from an as yet unidentified garrison.

I had forgotten that she too was staring.

When we got there, the dumpster as usual was away. The dump itself always reminded me of some harsh engraving; it was mercilessly clear to the smallest details of its accretion, while its greater outline rose in those pure, swarthy dunes that in religious tracts depicted either heaven or hell. At the bottom, an ashy substance had formed out of the once natural clay mixed with all detritus, strewn with shell and shards of crockery whose blues or flower bits one might even recognize. Next rose the enormous inventory of appliances, baby carriages to cookstoves, mattresses yawing their cottons, enamel bedpans and three-legged chairs upended, all under a constant fluttering of newspapers, flopping rolls of vinyl, and the hushed whirr of whatever other substance took the wind. At intervals during the year a caterpillar tractor ground all this down. At the very top, the cone rose to be bald earth again, and finally, weed. Going down the other side, one would pass these layers in reverse. No one was supposed to climb here except the dumpster himself, in his hipboots. Far to the right, where the main pile sloped out, his cart reared tongue upward, like a plow. Overall there was the smell of burning, in itself a heavy river to cross.

We parked the big black car to the left of the shack. There was a side road which led to an area marked for current disposal but we never drove up there; instead, Knobby would unload from the car trunk and trundle off for the first of many trips, stepping delicately. He never wore boots. A white kerchief tied around his face made him look like a victim rather than a bandit; I had given up puzzling why. The sun, always lurid through haze here, had a special stasis, because we never seemed to hit rain. Take it or leave it, a dump was always some sort of parable. There could be no other reason why I could be so bored in this cul-de-sac and yet hear behind it the blind plashing of a greater life.

While we sat waiting for Knobby to return, my grandmother took out her scent bottle, offering it to my mother, who took out her own, then to me, which I refused, though I hadn't bathed since yesterday. On weekends, when Bill Wetmore was in Cobble Row with the old nurse, I never saw him. It was a comfortable charm to keep his spermy odor between my thighs.

The door of the shack now and then swung. One could see the table where we left the tips, flanked by the dumpster's chair and woodstove, and on out through to the back, which was open and doorless. A car stood there, too decent to be the dumpster's; now and then he made private deals with those who had more to leave here than could wait for the pickups he did for the town. Often there was even money on the table, a tithe that we kids never more than dared each other to take. The devil's mark would have appeared on us if we had stolen it.

I had gone to grade school with a girl bearing such a mark, center of one cheek, who was supposed to have done that. Actually, her strawberry mark must have been with her since birth, yet at one time or another she would have been dared, as we all were, and the story must have got confused, as often happens to children who are marked. When I had been dared I had just laughed; perhaps she couldn't afford to.

It was peaceful here, like maybe at the end of the world when the smoke would be clearing, or on one of those metallic, overcast Sundays when there was nothing else going. Far away, Watanabe appeared, making his way to us slowly, empty-handed at last.

"So it's gone," my grandmother said. "The last clutter in my house."

In the town it was not unusual for a woman to straighten every drawer and cupboard in her house before she went for an operation, so that all might see her fine habits if anything went wrong. But my grandmother never went to doctors.

"You won't die for years yet," my mother said from the front seat without turning her head. "You have to wait for your debentures to come due."

"That's what they're there for. To get me to a hundred—what else? Pays to have something to wait for." A chuckle came from under the Knox hat. Money made her cheerful. "Whereas you're not so lucky. Your ship has come in."

"Not all of it," my mother said.

Watanabe was slow in returning. As he neared, we could see he was taking the little sips of oriental meditation he sometimes did, to make us remember his nationality. Yet this impulse, to cock his head to a birdcall, or pause to pull a grass blade, was no less real and lyrical.

Externalize. All the beginning world of it was in my lap and at my eyes, pure and hard in its physical manifestation, only waiting to be sorted and skeined by me, and given back again. What I would be doing with my body and my voice would be a recognition of the world. The stage-to-be for me, even if it was not to be that Chinese box of a thousand linings, the theater, would surely arrive.

"God, isn't it wonderful!" I cried out to it. "To be waiting."

Dumps make an echo. No one else said anything. Watanabe came up to us, taking off the white handkerchief. Now he was Knobby again, offering my grandmother his arm. She hung her big cretonne knitting bag on it, and walking under his ardently hovering attention but not leaning on him, made for the shack.

She was going to pay, which for her was like taking communion and absolution both. Before leaving her check—never paying cash even here—she would have made private assessment of what merit she meant to acquire by such an act, and of how much that merit was worth to her. Here at the shack, according to Knobby, she always left something adequate. If money was the kind of emotion she could best transact, then in this particular exchange she was being very scrupulous.

I think now that an obligation which had been at the core of her life had finally brimmed into all the crevices of her being, as can happen in age, when one tries to tidy up these ragged tides which will roll on without us. Who can say whether she did this too belatedly? One judges an action by its effect—and there I was.

I got out of the car to stretch my legs. When I could afford a car of my own I would buy some old Thunderbird or other model which would accommodate them. A wind had come up. At the shack door the dumpster's two geranium plants strove like dancers to meet it, but had to stay where they were. I could stretch freely, and in rivalry with those two poor tethered skimps I did so, from waist to shoulder to neck to arms, yawning at the sky. When my head came down again with happy expelled breath, I dropped to a squat, stomping from foot to foot, and shook myself like a wet puppy.

I still use this old muscle relaxer, taught us by the school's dance expert. If it works, I hear only her seamy, Russian-doll voice. If it does not, I see into my mother's face, straining against the windshield Knobby had polished almost to air, her

big hat tremoring like a bell. The face is never shallow to me
now.

Following its stare then, I saw what must be the crown of a
man's head bob up once, twice, along the bald rim of the big
dune, and sink down again—the unknown trash-picker maybe,
unaware he had company. Then the whole man stood up, complete.

It was Craig Towle, dark-vested against the sky, chin up like
the world's figurehead. That's the way he looks when alone. You
may begin to ask how I know.

In the same moment that he bent his head and saw our car,
my mother stepped out of it, closing its door slowly by leaning
backward against it. She stayed that way for a minute, pressed
there like a second figurehead. Then she walked forward, in that
rocking way women take on when they confront, and stood
there, one hand on the car's hood. My grandmother emerged
from the shack.

With any luck, my grandmother might have been spared the
sight of him. The dumpster's tin doorsill was stuck high in the
sand, and Watanabe, who will never reveal what or how much he
sees or saw, was suddenly disentangling her skirt from one of the
geraniums, and shielding her close. My mother and I would have
been her natural points of reference. Who bothers to scrutinize a
dump, especially when done with it?

But just then, Craig Towle moved. Or some small, crinkling
avalanche occurred in the dune itself; its sides were blanched
with them. My grandmother raised her head.

I try to see us as he must have seen us, three women angled up
at him in an acute triangle, my mother at the apex. One old
woman known, one woman better known, one unknown. Did he
move on purpose? If so, to which?

I know his hands were locked behind him—and do not unlock
without reason. I know my grandmother tried to scream, because
I learned right then that great age or sadness may not have the
breath to—and have since heard a renowned stage presence give
that same rasping whisper, which the last row of the audience

could however hear. I know that the package he must have been holding behind him fell and skittered from him, to slip down and disappear between a pile of old roofing and a mangle, and that the package resembled the flat, laundry-size bundles seen an hour ago.

My grandmother cried out—"Are live ones not enough for you? Must you have my dead girl too?" But even while it was happening I was unsure of the sequence of it. For, all that time my mother was standing burning-still.

Knobby, holding my grandmother like a relative, whispered in her ear. He would be asking if he should retrieve the package. She shook her head. "Leave it to the law. Leave him. Look at him up there. On an ash heap. Where he belongs."

Craig Towle opened his mouth. But she turned her back on him and got into the car, summoning Knobby after her.

Then my mother moved, without a word. But all the gestures came to her. First a signal to Craig Towle to return to the car behind the shack, which I saw now was the same Volks in which the bobby-soxer and I had gone to that bar. Then the signal that we were not to wait for her. She knew the right gestures, or they came to her. From where all the gestures come from.

As we backed up in order to wheel around, Watanabe, who handled that car as one stroked a cat, let the motor die. From my seat in the rear I saw him stare straight ahead, his narrow eyelids almost closed, his cheek wet.

Outside, my mother was walking up the dune, her high heels sinking in the ash and glut, so that she seemed to make no progress but continued toiling on between two streams of rubble, one on either side. Above, Craig Towle was looking down like a diver, at the stratum of found objects and destroyed ones which separated them. I saw him make the dip a man makes entering the jungle, to push the matted stuff aside. I saw him draw back, and try again. In my mind, she and he never meet.

In the car, now moving, I took my grandmother's wrists in my hands. If she shivered, she let them be. This was an enormous advance for both of us, for as far as I knew we had never touched. I couldn't have done this a year ago. Being with Bill Wetmore again hadn't made me any tenderer than I would ever be—a level which is not mine to judge. But it had taught me the non-exclusiveness of flesh. Or of human flesh. We are too unique in the world not to touch when we can.

My grandmother's pulse was steady. Below my ear I heard her respiration, faster than the rest of us, from that incredible engine her heart, carried so long. Her card case lay on the floor. As I picked it up, she disengaged her wrists. "I don't get strokes." But I was beginning to understand her.

When we came out of the road from the dump and onto the highway and paused there, she rapped the back of the driver's seat. Knobby had on his cap again and sat like a chauffeur.

"We've had our visits. Drive home."

It took time to get across that highway, which had replaced so much farmland. The cars kept streaming by.

"Grandmother—" I cried "—why don't we go to the farm!"

She turned her whole upper body. That is unusual for those so old. They tend to be immovable, except in the appendages. The whites of her eyes had dulled, but the brown pupils in their almost purplish rim had not. "Because we came from it."

Her voice sounded surprised that I had had to be told.

We crossed the highway.

"I'll phone your father this evening. That man must be stopped."

We passed through Cobble Row, those chunky, deep-rooted houses. They had not been stopped. He would not be.

We passed along our own street of fantailed windows and gables gawked high enough to satisfy the tallest. I wasn't that sure of us.

Her garage had once been the carriage shed, openable back and front by wide crescent doors. Knobby parked inside and went out the back. She always required a cup of tea "to rest me from the drive," which was served her in the car, and we were not asked to share. We bore her no resentment. A taste for luxury of that order must be admired, my mother had said.

We always left my grandmother to it, often not seeing her again until our next drive.

This time, I stayed. Quiet wood was stacked against the walls here, in pew shapes I had never seen disturbed. Yard-long lengths of narrow moldings were bunched together and upended in their corner, maybe since the beginning of the house. Opposite these, in its own metal-walled corner, the sturdy kiln my brother and I had once vainly asked to reactivate was surrounded by rows of the red clay pots that were its product, and were still hosed down whenever Knobby washed the car. Yes, it was restful here. It had never been bogeyland. Curious how in that high-varnished house, ugly but energetically functioning, no place ever came to be that, even then.

She wasn't staring at me now. I wanted her to. "Grandmother —who lived upstairs before you did?"

In the moment I asked, of course I knew, as you already may. But watch us work it out in our own way.

"It can't be cleared away," I cried. "It can never. Why should it be?"

I was wrong. Or half wrong. A life can be cleared away in a whip's crack. But those opaque old eyes finally saw me. What's more, the green-knotted hands laid hold of me, took charge of me, in what was going to be a connection. I might not want it, but it would be one.

"Hush—" she said. "Shut your mouth. Your mother says a person learning an art is very sensitive. So you should know when to." She pointed to the kiln as to a grave. The painted china she now ate on had come from it too. My brother and I had always been told that both china and kiln had been the bankrupt's. We had always suspected they were not. "Hush, girl. Girl—tell me about your boy."

When *you* tell *me*. I didn't have to say it—only to put my hand on the kiln from which all that china had come, my foot against all the red clay pots there was never a plant in the house for now—and stand tall, arching my neck.

I didn't speak. She couldn't. In her face I saw why. I was her bogey.

It can't be cleared away—that I ran.

That night, when I went down to Watanabe's quarters, he was somber. Quirky as he could be over our national differences, caustic on how all here in his adopted country had an unnatural friendliness but no deeper code, our own family ups and downs always affected him, making him unsurer of where he was. I was sad too, at the sight of how in our serene egoism we had made a servant of him in spite of himself, no matter how he balked.

As provisional dowry for the new wife, my grandmother had offered to give him a few of the goods he had cared for—some beds, chairs, and tables, but only to lend a fine desk and sideboard he himself had repaired. Instead, he himself had made all his and Etsuko's furniture-to-be, whose yellow-gray wood and simple lines my mother said were like a rebuke to ours. One oak prie-dieu he had accepted—"Since you worship otherwise"—hanging some scrolls above it and placing some mats before it, to make a kind of shrine. All Japanese houses had them, he said, even the most modern.

But did these also have a setup for a game called Pachinko, in his youth very popular in Tokyo? If his wife-to-be turned out to prefer Ping-Pong, he said, they could substitute, in much the same space. As the time drew near, he had begun to realize how much of daily life he and she had failed to discuss, in favor of certain dreams and pretensions. Now it would be too dangerous. In consequence, the old cottage piano he sometimes played had been pushed over to our side of the basement and covered with tarpaulins; he wanted his wife to see him not as the music student he had been, but as he now was. All his hi-fi equipment was prominently displayed.

When I dared to ask the reason for this afternoon's tears, he was proud. "Respect," he said. "To the moment that makes you see."

When I asked, was that like a leaf viewing, he did not respond.

"Can I have some of your tea?" I liked the plummy stuff, but he was more in need of it. Whatever vision he had had of us that afternoon, our prospects had made him panicky about his own.

Yes, he said over the tea—walking back toward us he had come upon Craig Towle behind the biggest dune, in process of rewrapping a package Towle had then carried back to the top almost absently, replacing it where it had been dumped. They had been too far apart to speak and Knobby had thought himself unseen. Returning, he had said nothing, only wondering how to tell my mother who the trash sifter was. Nor had he seen what the package contained.

I only wanted to know one thing. Did he think Craig Towle had dropped the bundle toward us on purpose? It had been the kind of gesture which put me in mind of the *Aeneid,* a mist to me in high school, which thanks to Mr. Evams I had begun to understand in braille—the sixth book particularly, with its "Here be lilies" and other hails and farewells.

"It was the wind," Watanabe said dolefully, looking round the careful rooms he had prepared for so many months. "It is always the wind."

PART TWO

PART TWO

"So this is the farm," Mr. Peralho said, standing between my father and my brother, in the cow parsley and ragged robin of what had once been a potato field. A merry brown keg of a man with brindled hair and a black moustache, he was at home here as he was everywhere else, in his palely woven deerstalker suits from the last supplier in Scotland, and boots so engine-turned they must be able to walk by themselves. During the weeks since the three had flown from Rio he had become everyone's favorite, by from the first partly acting like one, spending hours in my mother's darkened bedroom, adjacent to the two rooms, formerly my father's, which the three men now shared indiscriminately, or hobnobbing in the kitchen, saucepan in hand for a steaming café-au-lait, or brewing maté, for which he had brought along the proper silver-crested gourd and long sipspoon. Though he had yet to be asked to our third floor, my grandmother, bringing out her best downstairs tureens, made every evening meal a state dinner, and Watanabe seemed cheered rather than not by the extra forces which had brought on all this butlering. Perhaps he and our guest had even had after-hours sessions over his own destiny, for Mr. Peralho, who tossed out words like that with an impressively accented calm that he well knew resonated, was also confessedly a midnight man.

Only Bill Wetmore, always at my side since his grandmother had died, could not bear him, even on this bright excursion day holding back, chewing satirically on a stem of wild garlic. A few feet on from us the field ended abruptly, at the edge of acre after rolling acre now given over to lawn. My father had wanted us to approach this way first. "Following the potatoes—" he'd said, with an eye-crinkle at me. "Then dip right, at the pigs."

"And left at the cow barn," I breathed, giving the old responses. "Where the cats will get their supper, except for the old tom that ate green peas with his paw."

"—Then in at the truck garden, past the scarecrow—" my brother shouted, so that we all looked at him. Newly a dandy in tailor-mades, he smiled back at me crookedly.

In the distance the farmhouse, sleeked and unporched, rode too high on its new and profitless green. Of all the random buildings so well-known to us by description, only the barn remained, staunchly bigger than the house, as had once been practicable.

"Lost its ballast," my father said.

"House was never Revolutionary," my brother said. "It's not even 1850." In the way of those who wear special ties in order to be seen, he had also begun to be ponderous. At the time, the manner was unduly heavy for his whittled bone structure, making him seem like a bird carrying too big a worm. Always sisterly, I had told him as much, when the manner had been tried on me. "Ah, but in academia," he'd said, "they'll only see the worm."

His aim was to research in the Beinecke Library, though Mr. Peralho was agreeable to either Harvard or Yale.

My father glowed, proud of both of us. Ballast was what he had gained. His health was clearly now in tune with his looks. Browner than ever, his skin was almost what Mr. Peralho's was by nature, and in ease, too, he now resembled him. As I told Bill Wetmore, he had unshouldered some responsibility—probably us at home. Something missing in him haunted me though, until seeing him with my mother I identified it: he no longer had his

censorious click. If he had opted for the sensual life, I said to
Bill, I no longer blamed him.

"Don't daughters usually?"

Not this daughter, not anymore, I'd said meaningfully, but
Bill Wetmore had not been amused, even when I added that at
least from Brazil we didn't have under our noses week to week
whatever my father's life down there included. As, after all, he
and the others now had the two of us. "Brazil—" he said "—
does that excuse them everything? In spite of his Beaux Arts
relative, he still disapproved of other countries, in the Cobble
Row way that going away to school had done little for, and
though he meant to go to Europe some day, as we all did, he
tended to think of the rest of the world as backward. I recalled
too that he no longer had ambitions to be a sculptor. Without
knowing quite why I saw these things, or that he saw the change
in me, I was beginning to estimate him.

"Gentleman's farm—" he said now, shifting his chaw.

He and his had never been farmers enough to criticize. He
saw I was thinking that.

"Gentlemen—" Mr. Peralho said serenely. "Two."

His acquaintance with the farm's most recent owners was why
we were here. I thought of how many of our taken-for-granted
family barriers had melted in his presence in the short time he
had been with us. My father had never volunteered to take us
here, might not have refused us—but then my brother and I had
never asked it. There were always mysteries at the bottom of all
families, as our street had long since taught me. I do not think
even now that we had more than our share. But whatever the
initial premise on which my parents had built their lives, this had
been compounded by their habit of not speaking of it, most
importantly not to themselves. Manners had excused this and
indeed united them; they both had the remoteness of the polite.

My grandmother would have been moved by more anciently
lurid conventions. But she or we weren't unique there either,
except in the details. All families are bound to a primal contract
so visible we come late to thinking of it—that legend-making

which begins the minute we are born. How delightedly one watches children, ours or not, compounding this in its earliest stages, innocently aloud. But it's not we professionals who keep the legends going. The rest of the world merely conceals its performances.

On the path to the house, Mr. Peralho seemed to skip, but when you looked at him square he was ambling like the rest of us, though we were the entourage. It was the same in our kitchen, never before a place for men, to which my father and brother now gravitated, following after him. I would have too, except for Bill Wetmore.

"What nationality _are_ you, Mr. Peralho?" my grandmother had said with just that emphasis, after a day with him. We already knew that his name, like his native language, was Portuguese, his fortune from the Cauca Valley of Colombia, and his birthplace Brazil.

Smiling, he gave her a kindly poke. "Latin greaser."

Eating soup next to me, my brother spluttered, muttering He'll have her in his pocket now; isn't he marvelous?

On my other side Bill Wetmore said low, He'll tell anything, won't he.

My brother said, not so low: I heard that.

Hush up both of you, I'd said, busy watching how sparsely Mr. Peralho spoke. It was answers, mostly.

Up ahead on the path, my father was momentarily alone. I ran and attached myself to him. For days I had wanted to. The happy change in him had made me hope it might be easier. But he was always with the other two. Now I remembered how good walking with him was. We had the same stride.

A lot can be said silently between two who share that. I could tell—stride—that he would prefer me not to talk—stride, stride —that he could not himself find anything casual to say—stride, stride, and stride—and that both of us knew—saunter, saunter— that I was going to speak. "Is it Mr. Peralho's money that makes him so cheery?"

Stride—bump. We were out of step.

"Who told you that?"

I was caught. Shift to get in step again. "Bill Wetmore said it."

"Shouldn't wonder." Quickstep, quickstep. "No. It's not the money."

"What is it then?" Hard to keep up. Like when I was small. Full stop.

"Acceptance."

I stopped too, still small.

My father looked back to where Bill Wetmore lagged self-consciously. "Whatever Bill Wetmore says—is what he *is*. I suggest—you consider that. I beg you to."

He made me walk on. "I've always banked on you to speak for yourself. You always have, best of any of us . . . And why do you keep calling that boy by his full name? We know who he is."

I hadn't been aware. I guessed at once, though. Craig Towle —always fully named also. I had them both in my head.

Up forward on the path, the pair turned briefly, then Mr. Peralho urged my brother on, taking him amicably by the arm. Their steps did not match. My brother slipped his arm in Mr. Peralho's.

"He can't see anybody else for beans," I said. "You're his father. Don't you mind?"

I was wearing a belt with silly dangles. My father touched them.

"I accept it," my father said. Then he took my hand, the way he used to when we crossed a street. The calm I felt is with me yet.

All four of us met at the farmhouse door. My brother spotted my father and me at once. "Oo, lovey-dovey."

My father looked at the oak door, shook his head at the brass knocker.

"Not our door!" my brother and I said. We were both free-handed now.

Bill Wetmore came up from behind. He had switched to a

long stem of last year's straw that waggled all the way to his cheekbone.

"I'll bow out—" he said. "Thanks very much for—everything. Been eating with you day and night." He lifted his chin at me. "Call you."

"Thank you, Bill," my father said. "I've been meaning to. For what you did for my wife. In case we don't see you again." He gave him a long look. "Otherwise—come on in with us."

"Yes, do," my brother said. A giggle spurted from his mouth. Lack of control is his agony, but he's always kidding himself he has mastered it. "As an artist you really owe it to yourself."

"Thanks—no," Bill Wetmore said. "It's not—my farm."

Mr. Peralho said, "Na, na, na." Each sounded placating in a different language. I saw his eyes didn't match. One was a genial brown, the other had a hazel flaw in it, like the tip of a gold knife. He reached out winningly to take the straw from Bill's mouth. "Give him a cigar."

The door opened shyly on two gentlemen, both in jeans, both with hair cut boyishly close to the pate. They and Mr. Peralho greeted with fond ceremony, cheek by cheek. With pleased cries of "Rio!" my brother was drawn in. My father shook hands with them.

"And who's that good-looking young man going off?" the one holding back a big dog said. "A new friend?"

"No," my father said. "Hey! He has no transportation. How's he to get back?" He ran down the path after Bill.

"Uh-uh—" my brother said. "Not a friend."

The dog was sniffing my new boots. I get on with dogs. I dropped on my heels to him.

"Pity about Leslie Warden," the dog's master said. "We met him more than once. A fine man."

My father came walking back. "Wetmore says he'll hitch a ride."

"And who's this beauty?" the other gentleman said. He

smiled from my father's face to mine, then at his partner. "We think we know."

"This is—our daughter," Mr. Peralho said.

I called Bill for hours before I got him, at about eleven that night.

He'd had a hard time getting home. "But I enjoyed it."

"Can I come see *you?*" I never had. "I'll take the hearse." His name for my grandmother's car, which weeks back he had driven a lot for a brief time, helping me take mother where she had to go. She would not enter his old Volks. No one had used the hearse since Mr. Peralho, who had friends everywhere, had borrowed a silver Citroën from a friend in Doylestown who ran an agency there. Watanabe was in California, waiting to meet his wife.

"I'm not asking because of you." He would hate me to apologize for not having left with him. "Because of me—" I said.

"Did you stay for dinner?"

"*Al fresco.*"

"What's that mean?"

"In the garden." I had just learned this. The meal had been wonderful, simple but everything of the best, with one or two items I had never heard of either. I wolfed it all down as if it were knowledge. The farmhouse's interior had been mannishly suave, fixedly looking back at the people in it, in the way of places always set for company, and of course it now had nothing to do with us, though the word "Farm" had been retained in its new name—the other names given it by previous owners being bantered—all the way back to us, who had never called it anything.

For drinks we were offered everything from kumiss, drunk by the artist elder gentleman ever since his years in Morocco, to Pernod, of which only my brother partook. The second gentleman had spent his fateful years with the first one. What else distinguished him was not disclosed. They admired my new riding boots, and my father for having had them made to my spe-

cial last by Mr. Peralho's little Spaniard in the Calle So-and-so.
"Not that other leather butcher," they said with laughter. It was
revealed that Mr. Peralho owned an apartment in New York to
which they had been, and which it seemed he now hoped I
would use during my drama-study years, since it was hardly ever
occupied. My brother's Harvard future was also brought forward,
Mr. Peralho's genial right eye presiding over both these statements.

I saw our hosts weigh the balance between my brother's physique and my own, and tuck some mutual judgment back in.
"Isn't she something!" they said to the air, to my father, ready to
warm their connoisseurship into affection, if he and I would
allow it. "Oh, she must come visit, when you're away." I saw
what their friend Peralho had meant by "our daughter." Friendship was their family, and I could become a property of the
unique sort they could not otherwise acquire. In quite another
way, my brother had already been absorbed. Meanwhile the two
of them moved with quiet dignity through all they had been able
to acquire on their own—their books, art, opera loves, barn studio, and the elder one's ringing professional life, the two of them
meanwhile inclining their boy's pates in the most experienced
conversation I had ever heard.

On the surface theirs was a seamless life. I hadn't lived long
enough to know that in the end everybody tries to make one—
that even the adventurer, maybe breaking with every rule except
the bedouin, still gathers some sameness to himself at night. But
as I sat, childishly mum, at that cool marine table, while the one
hipless boy they had in the kitchen kept replenishing our water
glasses and his twin outside pruned a sandy, yellow-green shrub
whose leaves, the second gentleman laughingly said, resembled
banknotes, I sensed what any child would, that whatever is this
seamless keeps something at bay.

The water glasses were extraordinary, each goblet footed with
the cloudy-crystal body of a woman. As the willful-mouthed
houseboy piled my plate and the two hosts cozened me shyly and
sweetly, I felt that while I was here I too was a kind of amulet,

and that the Dollies and Ginnies and Millies who peppered their
affectionate chitchat might be something of the same. Even
though this world I was temporarily in might be like any house
presenting itself for company while covering up any subfamilial
rages—I glanced up at the serving boy—there was also a fealty
here, as delicate and accomplished as the napery on the table.

I could see why my father, who never preened himself in our
house, could stretch so at ease; even if his fine brown hand from
time to time closed anxiously on its napkin ring at some sally
from my brother, whose cockalorum manners were the only false
note. Once or twice I caught my brother himself casting sheep's
eyes at me, pleading for my understanding. He had it. During
dessert, a sense of enclosure momentarily beset me. I listened to
my own femaleness, thundering small in my fingertips. Yet I
could perceive the quiet attraction, or even the fiercer one, of a
world from which women's agony, even women's inner entity,
were barred. I myself was feeling how that could be. Under the
table the dog's huge russet head made eyes at me, as benign a
dog as I had ever seen.

Before we left, they showed us where the pheasant run had
been in my grandparents' time. They planned to revive it.

"But not the refrigerator in the parlor," I said, and everybody
howled, the dog barking at us. My father could not take his eyes
off me.

Out on the steps, my brother hung back. The elders were
already at the car. Steps make Tim confessive. Or he has to
educate. "Sis—."

I said to him what I said to my mother when she attempted to
tell me the facts of life. "You don't have to explain."

When we all left, I too was kissed.

On the phone to Bill, I burst out crying. "They were so nice.
So terribly nice."

Emotion can do very well on the phone—especially if you
wish to be saved from it. He was spared my real tears.

Meanwhile, I could hear his answer clearer than if he stood before me. "You're not going to be crazy loyal?"

In turn, a phone voice can't lie, even to itself.

Though it may pause.

"To whom?"

We were to meet at the hayloft, giving him a couples of hours' time. His grandmother's house, emptied of all but the bundles for the welfare and the leftover medical appliances, still stank of bones gone bad. She had left neat directives for the disposal of all her effects except those. The house was to be sold to satisfy the liens on it which had paid for his and Phoebe's education, as well as to fulfill a memorial bequest to the hospital, although he had been informed that he and his sister could have first-purchase rights for a short period agreeable to the bank and other lenders, unless a hot purchaser came along. My father had advised him that this arrangement, though it had little basis in law, was likely to be honored by small-town decency. But Phoebe didn't want the house, even if she could have paid for it, and Bill had barely enough money from part-time jobs to live in the city —on hope.

Our house had become his oasis. The day my mother came home from the dump, walking, he had been in the empty house on Cobble Row, ready to go back to the city. His grandmother's funeral had been two days before. Because of that, he and I, parting in the city and agreeing to meet there on the following school Monday, had not even communicated while in the town. Young live-at-home people, conducting their divided lives, have a fierce sense of those partitions. In my own house I was another person, a totality of my history with the family. For hours I might not think of him. Whenever I did, my lower limbs might swim with our secret unity, but I kept him and the tiny apartment where we met, just as I kept the school and the city's daring streets—at the other end of our first train ride together.

In the house on Cobble Row that day, he had just flung the old casement wide. The wind we had felt at the dump was still up, a dun, hurricane stealth that bypassed us late every summer, on its way to the coast. Behind him, welfare bundles lay on the floor and the rented wheelchair, oxygen tent, and intravenous feeder waited to be picked up. The Wetmores' economy had never much needed the dump. He had just about decided to take what food he could to the city with him, and hole up there until Monday, drawing. He never got much done when I was there. He wasn't thinking of me, except perhaps in that reverse way.

He was about to shut the casement when my mother floated by. Her hat must have been pinned, for she wasn't holding it against the wind, and her shoes dug from step to step, as if by themselves. The body in between might have been all silk, blow-able. He took all this in with the quickness that was to make him so good graphically, so poor at paint. Her arms were what floated, like scarves. The face, as it bobbed near, had the dedication that madness brings. "She's beautiful, isn't she?" he said, telling me. "I never saw that before."

He jumped out of the low casement into the flowerbed and called her by name. She had a hard time stopping, as if on a vehicle that wanted to roll ahead. He thought she recognized him, and that she perhaps was not crazed after all. When she swayed, about to fall, he grasped her. She held onto him. He said her hold on a man was something that man would never forget. "The bobby-soxer's dead—" she said. "Everybody knew it except me."

Craig Towle must have tried to drive her home from the dump, and she must have refused him. Several porch-sitters on the road back to town reported seeing a car like his following her anyway. The section nearest the dump was made up of old wood-frame cottages, the early seedbed of the industrial part of town. Mostly pensioners lived in these, or the bachelor tag ends of old occupations. Watanabe, out looking for her on his own, talked to one of them, a retired signalman for the vanished freight rail-road. "Sure, they paraded right by here, him in second gear; looked like he was pacing a greyhound."

Nearer town, the trail disappeared. What had happened was

that she had gone into Walsh's Inn, where Craig Towle had not followed her. Gilbert and Luray weren't there, but the barman was, and a few regulars. She told one of them, a veteran Legionnaire whose picture made the *Sentinel* every year for selling the most poppies on Decoration Day, that she had never been in a bar alone before or at that hour of the day, but that she recognized him. I recognize a lady when I see one, he said. She paid for her own drinks, he said, out of a little silver change purse.

My mother never went out of the house without carrying a handbag. Inside it would have been that chain-silver purse in which she had carried her mad money since she was a girl. All girls of her era, she had long ago told me, had toted such insurance against having to climb out of a car. "On a double date mostly, when couples tended to egg each other on." Or a blind one, when you hadn't picked the man yourself. No girl of her acquaintance had ever admitted to having had to use her money. When I'd wondered at that statistic, she had answered in that sudden, ambery drawl which brought Greensboro right back to me: "Reckon they stayed on—in the rumble seat."

She had had two drinks at the inn, about all that her five-dollar bill and some change would have paid for. Nobody there had dared offer her one. She would have sat on the barstool, sipping like a poster girl, a slim pointed leg hooked on the brass footrail. "I been nipping—" she told them. "That's what we call it down home."

Down there, one rarely saw anybody you could say was out-and-out drunk, but Southern company never went without a glass of something, and its lawns and days were crisscrossed with errands and droppings-in, business or household, which on the instant qualified a person to be company. Nipping could become exaggerated, like at the "old-crowd teas" which also served as our birthday parties from the time of our christenings—crepe-paper hats on our blond heads as we grew, and the darkies snickering, not always at us. And old ladies walloping their cars home afterward. You could draw back from nipping "on doctor's advice," or lean into it gentlier and gentlier, especially if you were a woman.

a were like our Miss DeVore, no one ever saw you
tiny bit blank, and you could always cut cloth.
Miss DeVore in the morning," was all down home
with the men, of course, hard drinking did not have
to hide.

I think people drink in order to be able to tell the truth to
themselves. Up to then, my mother had abstained as she could.
What she would do, once Bill brought her home, was to hide
herself. Where she had been brought up there was one more
alternative, if you found yourself sliding too far. You could go
away, but not to an institution. Many of the houses down home
were just right for that. My grandmother's, with its two-step
drops here and there into separate suites of rooms, much resembled those. As my mother's separation wore on, I sometimes
fancied that even as a girl, come there that party night in her
graduation dress, an inner something unknown to her at the
time might have seen ahead to the possibilities of that house.

I don't know whether my mother ever fully realized that the
house had already had what one might call a harboring experience. To her there would have been no connection between her
plight and that other once-upon-a-time life upstairs, which I
would come to know as not hidden, but staged. At any rate, she
was never to mention it. From her own wedding day on, perhaps
she had been in too deep for other considerations. To me, as I
myself grew stagier or was trained to be, plight became the exact
word for her situation, so troubledly between the archaic and the
real. She had come to that dark room of hers too unfairly, and
not through maidenly shallowness.

Taken into Bill Wetmore's house, once he had persuaded her
there, she sat in the only chair left, staring at the old beams and
at the Heatilator in the inglenook, sipping at the water brought
her as if it were contraband. All the Cobble Row houses are from
the same early builder, who knew only one way to set up that
stone. Seeing the piled floor and the gear ready-packed, she said:
"Ah—clearing for a guest wing, are you?" We would get to know
that murmur, made with such effort. Then she saw she was in a

wheelchair, Bill said, and sprang up in fright. All those who se]
hide are afraid of forced incarceration. She would not enter his
beat-up old Volks. "No, I can't go home in that."

Nor would she ever enter it in the following weeks, when he
and I drove her to various doctors, first at our behest, then at
hers, on what we thought were her fool's errands, until we realized she was stocking her room with vitamins, paperbacks, every
requirement for a long indoor siege except the food she knew
would always be brought to her. We always had to take the
hearse, which Bill drove, and she still dressed for the ride, even
on the day she asked to be taken to the police station. "To lodge
a complaint?" I said, fearful. I could scarcely hear her answer.
"Oh my dear love, against who?"

What she did want, nobody could have dreamed. "I've come
for a breath test," she said to the old captain at the desk, so low
he had to ask her to repeat, and so imperiously lorn that he did
what she wanted. We two helped her unwrap the endless head-
scarf in which she had encased herself from head to neck and
down to her shoulders. It was exquisitely done, Bill said after; did
you notice? Like that old Elizabeth Arden ad that went on for
years, he said, in which the model had looked to be ready either
for surgery or for immortal mummyhood.

While my mother was breathing into the tube the officer
whispered: *"Has* she been driving?" We shook our heads, no.
The results were positive, he told her, though the percentage of
alcohol wasn't high. "Ah, I've been nipping again, have I?" she
said. "I wasn't sure." She wrapped herself up again abstractedly,
as one put away an article long possessed and known to be break-
able, if no longer so cherished as of yore.

On the way out, she extracted from her purse her packet of
breath pills, a small box of the lavender-flavored pastilles which
used to be sold at the cigarette-and-candy stalls of good New
York office buildings. Nowadays I procured them for her as my
father had. I had thought of this habit as one of the little city
encrustations with which women like her, not quite of the provinces, would flavor their life. In the car she offered us each the

purple box; we each took one of the tinted squares. They are seldom found anymore, but I can still build their essence on my tongue. To Bill they were like eating perfume, but he accepted one, for which I still honor him. She flashed a sane look at him. "Tact. You two will live on it."

Officially we waited for those saner looks; actually we feared them. The orphic insights of the disturbed are the hardest to tolerate. Or to congratulate them on. Yet once inside the house, we always tried to delay her leaving us. "You no longer wear your big hat," Bill dared.

"Oh, Bill—" I warned. The day he had brought her home from his house he had had to order a cab, paying for it out of the money he had earmarked for his train fare. He was always broke before Mondays. On the way she had asked twice whether someone was not following them. No one was. It was raining hard by then. As he helped her out, the cabby noticed she had left her hat on the seat, and handed it to her. She had ignored him. Bill had accepted it for her. Standing with her head full up to the driving rain, wet to the skin, she had said: "The weather must not be allowed to sympathize." Running out to meet them, I had seen the cabby shake his head.

That too had stayed with me—and when I had seen her eyes. The soft armor which from that day on coiffed her only made more evident their gaunt stare. Now that other saner look again flashed in them, first at him, then at me. "She no longer calls you Bill Wetmore." I felt the twinge of surprise one does when a parent gives warning of what one's inner self has scarcely yet noticed. Then with the side-wave of the hand with which a passenger on a receding boat indicates the elements to those on shore, she went to her room. Picking up the purple box she had left behind her, I thought of the years of her chocolates, and of how long her fastidious habits had obscured her from us.

So that was how Bill Wetmore had become an intimate of the house. Having spent his fare to bring her home, he could not go to the city, though he had not said so. He would borrow from me anyway that next Monday morning. Meanwhile, there he was on our rubber-matted, brass-edged top front step—a flesh and blood figure, bred to me on dirty bedpads and river-park corners never shoddy to me, which I thought I knew as well as my own. We stood there half aghast, spun toward each other from funerals, bad errands, and weekend dearth. I myself invited him in to my other life. To his credit he was reluctant, out of certain doubts. But he entered it.

My father hadn't come home at once. Though my grandmother had called him in Rio, her story of the dump must merely have borne out what he had expected of her. Or, in my mother's case, what he did not care to confront. Yet, as could be seen after my luncheon at the farm, when he did come it was in the spirit of having us all confront everything. Bill Wetmore must have done so at once.

Watanabe watched us all with that servant devotion which is the most sophisticated of any. I would have caught on to a lot much faster if I had been willing to watch him in reference to more than Bill. On him, Watanabe and I vied on silently. Though by now our family fluctuations must have exhausted him, and he had been still busy as well with his efforts in anticipation of his wife, he disapproved of Bill's driving the hearse. He disapproved of Bill and me doing jointly what should have been my private filial duty. He looked sardonically on Bill's constant presence at meals, and on our table manners when together. After the first meal he brought out fingerbowls, his face smooth with gratification when Bill tried to fit his whole hand in one. After the second, he added cigars from my father's old humidor, later tut-tutting over Bill's sadly chewed butt.

When he one day came upon me giving Bill money, he turned a curious shade of tiger.

"Knobby disapproves like a father," Bill said. Under Bill's influence, which I, untutored, saw merely as healthy and masculine, for surely a young man so slim and well-featured would not be coarse, I began to think Watanabe outrageously funny, and worse, to show it, sometimes in cahoots with Bill. I do not now think that a servant's devotion should ever be ridiculed. Though from well before Sancho Panza, people have not agreed.

My father caught onto Watanabe's sly sabotage at once. "Fingerbowls?" he said, looking down the table at Knobby. "Ah, cigars—" he said, looking down the table at Bill. My brother, sniggering to me, said: "I never much liked either of them."

My brother reported that my mother hadn't been that eager to see him. For that reunion he had gone to her bedroom ahead of my father. "And when our father followed me in, she went mum. One would think," my brother tittered, "that she was off men altogether." He was always to be as monumentally wrong about her as she was about him. But the hurt was eternal. "I see the favorite is doing fine," my brother then said to me, and went up the stairs to the third floor to see my grandmother, as he would be allowed to do every day of their stay.

When my father came out of my mother's darkness that first time, to Mr. Peralho and me waiting in the corridor, he came first to me, and gripped me by the upper arms. "I had no idea. No idea." When he had last touched me we had clasped hands only. I now felt that he had not acted unwisely. What a daughter admires in a father stretches so far beyond the sexual. That fussy Viennese uncle, Freud, on whom the world has so long depended for the key to its sexual shackles, had had his rabbinates confused. What I felt in my father was the holy ark of authority, brought into the domestic cave for all our protection. There my mother was our innerness, but one stretching far beyond the decorative arts, or even those of the psyche. Where he phrased life for us even when reticent, or was meant to, her life worked beneath phrases, even when she spoke. Who they slept with had less power to hurt me, or to inspire me, than what they withheld of those other powers—or gave. And surely he would give me his confidence.

But my father turned next to Mr. Peralho. "He's bad for her. So am I. Juan—what's to be done?"

As your parents grow old, you become the authority. But I was not allowed that time-lag. I saw my father, still in his prime, cast aside his own authority like a jackstraw. And not to me. The corners of our upstairs hall, filling with bloodlight, crept forward standing there autonymous. Jealousy is yellow to me. I sink into it like into plush, in my ears its shifty tambourine shake.

Just then Knobby came up the stairs with my grandmother's afternoon tray. Once upon a time there had been buzzers all over the house, connected to a church-shaped wallbox in the kitchen, inside which the little flags had gone up on signal, each slotted to a room. Knobby had reactivated the ones to and from the third floor. He and Mr. Peralho nodded. They might already have had a midnight session. My grandmother had first dined with us the night before.

Mr. Peralho twirled a hand toward my mother's shrouded door. For her?—his eyebrows inquired. Watanabe pointed toward the third floor.

"Ah na na na," Mr. Peralho said. Reaching, he took over the tray. Holding it, he bent to my mother's door. She had hung from its top a voluminous drapery I vaguely remembered as once worn by her. Of darkest navy, too curved for a door, it hung disconsolately, good neither against sound nor dust. Mr. Peralho wagged his brows again. "Cashmere."

"She's always liked *luxe*," my father said.

"And you do not?"

Knobby had vanished down the stairs again. There would be plenty enough of that handmade china my grandmother fancied, for him to furnish up another tray. Unlike the inherited hand-painted stuff in half the better cupboards in town, which had been done on Bavarian blanks shipped for that purpose, this set had been made from scratch, in heavy brown and blacks I liked.

The two men had forgotten me. I hid in thoughts of china, like a child.

My father had not answered. He still had his noble looks, though two newly pouted lines framed his mouth under the tan.

Mr. Peralho saw that too. "Those with her trouble, they need liquid by the liter. *Other* liquids. And my dear, dear man"—the two dears spat out like shot—"they need to have the *first* tray."

Then, holding the tray waiter-style in one hand, he rat-tatted on the door and sallied in with his deerstalker's stride.

We waited, but there was no sound.

"Is he a doctor?"

"A—medicine man. Without portfolio."

"Is that where you went? To him? When you were ill?"

"So you know about that," my father said. "No. I knew him from before."

The questions were backing up in me, pouring out with the mud like the pebbles do when the dams of childhood break. "Like—Leslie Warden? From the time when you knew him?"

I meant that to come out like shot.

Why didn't he crumble? In those days I thought all you had to do was to ask the questions, for the arks to slide. Like Babel in the Bible.

"So you know about him too. Yes, from when I knew him."

He looked at the door. Still no sound.

"Let's go down," my father said. "I find I want my tea, too."

Neither of us moved.

"Who made all that china? Like in that kiln, in the garage?"

"One of the aunts."

In family parlance, that meant one of my grandmother's sisters, all dead. His own sisters we called by name.

"The one—who lived upstairs once?"

"When she did, yes." His eyes brimmed, not with tears but with story, though he did not go on. Perhaps he thought I had had enough. Or he waited.

Do houses breed habits? Or do the habits of a family breed the houses? Had we as a family always gone upstairs and shut the door?

I had one more question. Why had they left the farm? I was about to ask it.

"You should take Leslie's money," my father said. "He meant it kindly."

"No," I said. "I wanted yours."

Haylofts are fine for a beginning. Soft and prickly, jocular, with a cushiony golden light even when there is no longer any hay. Innocence seeping out onto the floorboards. But that can't be repeated. That nothing can be quite, is the first lesson. We tried.

The loft was different. Lying on the floor afterward, I already knew why. At my side, Bill Wetmore seemed not to. One glance at the desk where Craig Towle had worked, his chair, his daybed, was all it took. We had an audience.

"You're so thin, all of a sudden."

"Too thin?"

I have small breasts that lie flattened against the chest like lappets. Many girls have them, but it is a shape ignored. Beneath them my body is narrow, with hardly any indentation at the spoon-shaped hips, so that the long, long legs seem scarcely separate. I am soon to find that shorter and chunkier men go mad over such a body, and also, that since clothes hang almost in their own folds on such a structure, such a body is not surprisingly the ideal of the fashion trade, where so many men like that are the moneybags. Gossip blames the gentlemen designers for wanting women androgynous, but one ought to remember that the sexual sanction of those other men enters in.

I still thought I could never bear to copulate with a shorter man. I knew nothing as yet of the attraction whose very violence comes out of inbred standards departed from.

Bill Wetmore was the standard choice for me, as our schoolmates and even our elders were prone to emphasize. Tall men do as they please sexually. I was to be the grateful one, and I was. He covered me well, the head and toes extending beyond me, the cave of the eye little more pronounced than mine, the feet only slightly less arched—but the square-bladed shoulders satisfyingly alien.

"Too thin? For art?" We had already had this tease. But now I cast a look at that desk, so sequestered with its chair.

"Uh-uh." He liked to be applied to as an artist. "But it changes the drawing."

"You saw me only last week."

"I know."

We held each other. Nakedness was the only real seeing, back then.

"When you called me, you were crying."

"I know."

"Why?"

"Don't ask me. Now I'm not." My tongue licked his breast-bone. How safe I was. "I hated waiting. Why did you make me?"

"I was—thinking . . . and believe me, that house is no fun to be in."

"No other reason? Why you never ask me there?"

"Why should there be?"

So there was, then. But his reason wasn't what I silently im-puted to him—the thought of my mother tripping those cobbles once, a few houses down. Or of Phoebe, once my friend. No, his house wasn't good enough for me, now that he had seen ours. But that sort of shame has to be lived with, before it shows.

We all but fell asleep, in that lulling amity which would never come again.

I was the first to sit up. "I have to leave."

Other women will tell you that more often the men, married or single, lovers or not, are the ones who do the leaving. And of how they, the women, loathe being left behind. But it would be a long time before I came to that.

I stretched, yawning, deeming myself in full command. Per-haps, in a way I was. Certainly he saw me as so. "Wish I had a horse. All the way over here, I was wishing it."

"Instead of a Lincoln. Of course." He leaned back on the pillows we'd taken from the narrow daybed, his mouth wry. To him, I and mine were the impracticals who always landed money-high.

"No. Instead of anything."

Horses are health to me, and a way of being in woodland. So they were to my father, too, who had taught me to ride. To him too horses were for riding, not for ownership. To me as an adolescent, also perhaps a chance at being in command. I'd never minded our having to rent or borrow them. But to Bill, even to wish for one was a matter of class.

He was still leaning back. Youth integrates some faces only briefly. I can't swear that I even then saw, in what he called his Philadelphia face (as if to him all Philadelphia had only one) those flint-shaped peasant eyes. Yet I saw something, or heard it. "Well—you have the boots," he said.

I got up, still nude, and went over to them. They were lying on the floor near the desk, where I had discarded them like the properties we tossed around the stage before a tryout or rehearsal at school, or else carefully arranged. I had shed them before I rightfully knew where I was, in the dark of a space once so much my own stage.

They lay in what my brother had high-voicedly pointed out as "all their amaranthine beauty." Gifts excited his stinginess, as porn must do the impotent. The spurred ankle of one boot lay across the other's calf. The bootmaker, he said, had thought from the size ordered that they must be a man's.

I turned on the desk lamp, a plain brass gooseneck. A pocket of manila envelopes, a clutch of yellow pencils in a rubberband, a stapler, and a box of typing paper lay on the desk top. The center drawer, opened, had one typewriter ribbon in it, used; the file drawer was bare. The chair was metal, and pillowless. The daybed cover you could buy at any dimestore, and looked unused. How could this small array have put so much intent into a room? Putting the room itself into another history entirely, which even in the evening's new air smelt of its own mulch.

"Has he gone for good?"

"Don't know. He took the typewriter. He said to get rid of any stuff, if he didn't come back."

I sat down on the splintery floorboards. Soft, camel-colored socks had come with the boots. I slid them on, conscious that Bill was staring between my legs, at what he had told me was undrawable. Once he had had me shave down there, in order to try. This had been just after the Chicago Institute, posted one of Bill's drawing books by an instructor of his, hadn't bought it but had held onto it for a respectable time. Illustration had then still been a dirty word to him. I had sat for hours with my legs akimbo. No, I can't, he'd finally said. It still looked like a Hasidic's mouth to him. Impossibly vulnerable. Impossibly arrogant. Put it away. Oh he could be fun, when he had still been Bill Wetmore.

I sat on the chair to draw on the boots. What purpose had sat here for so long in our town, where now my own buttocks rested? I was remembering Craig Towle's sweat and the jut of his nose. And his cool throwaway promise. To pay me nothing. For what nothing could pay. He must be much more than solvent. But he would understand my father, down to these boots.

"So he took the typewriter." I thought of the man who could gather up his intent and take it away with him, maybe all over the world. Through all towns, all wives, all deaths. Not a fair man, probably.

I stood up. Yes, I still had the boots, gift of my father. "I'm not crazy. But I am loyal. And I'm going to go on being."

Bill would have to count that in, I meant. If he kept on hanging around us.

He got that. But he asked anyway: "Loyal to whom?"

"To—everyone. To Knobby, even."

He reddened at that. "What an aristocrat. But then—you know who you are."

"No, I don't. Not—all of it." I found I didn't want to tell him more about us, about what until today I had thought of as the mystery of the farm. Now that I had seen the farm modern version, was the mystery once there even more alive, having migrated past our third floor? Past my father and brother even. The family mystery, migrating on, even to me.

I stared at him, aghast. There waited for me matters I didn't want to tell this person to whom, it seemed only a minute ago, I had wanted to tell everything. It was a bad loss. The bottom had dropped out of that safe place in his arms.

"You know who you are—as much as I." I wanted him to stand by his own folks: the woman Francie, his mother, and that vague outline, the old workman, his stepfather, to whom he was unrelated, yet through him linked to all his own working forebears here on Cobble Row. And the old nurse, that witch of the winding sheet, of whose death, in its common stench, he seemed ashamed.

He would even sell this house, if he could rid himself of it handily, and be glad of the price.

America is full of people like Bill—the man to whom I would one day try to explain Bill Wetmore and my quarrels with him— would say to me in this same loft. Elective orphans—the West Coast crawls with them; no history on their backs except what's new. Or there are the *selective* orphans, this man would say, with his hooked smile. Those who keep a few picked ancestors around, for show. That's the other Coast. Ours. Like your Bill. William Wetmore Storey—would he have been your Bill's sculptor great-uncle? Or perhaps a cousin?

Cousin—I would say. Yes, he turned out to be only a cousin, several steps removed. You see too much.

For, as that man would tease me, I was an aristocrat—but only in the common way. I romanticized other people's trials, along with my own. To that, he said, the stage would add its own exaggerations. In the end, if I and the audience were lucky, we might both get hold of the truth.

But right then, what I said to Bill was childishly direct. Schoolgirl-style repartee—I'm not sure there isn't a place for it.

"You'd sell this place, wouldn't you. Just to hang on to your father's baby clothes." I flung out my arms. "This place."

Under the riding moon the hayloft lay around us in rumpled shadow.

"You buy it," he said. "You have the money for it." He got up from his lounging, always his ultimate gesture even in the pad in town, and turned on the loft's solitary bulb, flicking off the gooseneck lamp. Maybe he'd sensed that audience after all.

"Only one way I can pay you back. I'll draw it for you. What you're hanging onto."

There was paper on the desk, pencils handy. Materials for that brand of explication always are. I leaned over his shoulder as I often did, fascinated by the streaming leadpoint or pen nub which bred people in lightning outline, never seeming to lift from the page until the last dot. Then the instrument would uncover its brood, hatched in a style half fairy tale, half carica-ture. As their maker would one day tell a newspaper diffidently: one made them just askew enough to be recognizable.

He had already drawn three heads when he dropped the pen-cil and picked up another, then another, scowling at the num-bers on them. "Eversharps. Too soft, really. Or too hard. But they'll have to do."

In the end he used both hard and soft. I had already identified the heads: Mr. Peralho, my father, and my brother. At first he populated page after page with their three figures, in what I took to be at random. Then seizing on the stapler—oh, he was always quick to make use of what was at hand—he fastened all the pages together in what I saw was a progression even before he slipped the whole length of cartoon on a line of wooden wall pegs next to the window, in whose center the moon had risen, after all almost full. He had numbered each page of the cartoon.

On page one my father appeared, downstage front, neat as a pin, the way he had been in his commuting days, and about to drop to our platform from the train. A few heads were behind him, all women. In number two he was alone, walking stage right. Mr. Peralho, slightly rubbed in outline, appeared on num-ber three, behind him a map of Brazil. Number four, they met, feet planted on that map. Then came a succession of sketches—coffee plantations, the harbor of Rio, bars, and evening parties, the figures of the two men gradually nearing, then linked, often hand in hand. Then, as my brother appeared, my father, though never disappearing, faded backward, until, in a similar progres-sion, Mr. Peralho and my brother were linked. Except for the clasped hands, neither couple was seen any nearer to each other

than lolling side by side on sofas—these however enormously
stuffed or torturesomely elegant, and in a mise-en-scène of increasing vulgarity. There was only one page one could call ob-
scene—on which the three heads, drawn with the fuzziest thick-
leaded pencil, shared features indiscriminately, seemingly to be
one person, one sex.

"Do I have to title it for you?"

I couldn't speak. One goes mute. Or I do, once a thing long
borne, even admitted, is phrased. In the same way, when one
finally leaves a man one has lived with, one may do it silently.
Everything will have been said.

He was talking in my ear now, in the earnest way people do
when they prate of what they think the general world disapproves. Special friends, he said. That was the fancy French
phrase for it. I would have thought better of him if he had
produced an unfancy one. Our house stank of it, he said. Probably that was why my mother was as she was, he said. Possibly
that was why my grandmother, even. Things went backward,
and forward too. I must get out of there. For good.

I found my tongue. "Houses that stink. You seem to specialize
in getting out of them."

A ring of moths was circling the bulb hanging at eye level
between us. They kept passing, freckle-colored, between his face
and mine. Light beaded his blond evening beard. Two nights
without shaving made him a vagabond. Behind him the sashless
window had its casements wide, framing the dead factory two
streets beyond, across alleyways rarely frequented. Anyone looking up could have seen us, framed in its low-silled triangle.

"They've weaned you," he said. "In a few weeks."

No, *he* had. Bill Wetmore, become Bill. He's whatever he
says. You begin to remember it. As you look at him.

"Haven't they. From our whole time together."

A miller moth flew in, bumped the line of stapled pages, and
clung. My shirt and pants were on the peg farthest from me,
unreachable. The sweat ran down my bare legs. I reached.

"No you don't." His long arm, gaunt with drawing muscles, barred the cartoon.

"I wouldn't. Tear it up, if that's what you mean."

"Sure?"

The moths hypnotized me, not one of them yet burned. I had come here to be safe? Here? I flipped the miller moth from the page it was pressing against, fluttering vainly. It ricocheted the room, thumping the walls, then joined the circle. The cartoon jiggled at us. None of my father's letters to me were indicated in it. Or my brother's hurt. Or Mr. Peralho's generosity. And we three generations of women—in this account of our house, where were we?

In his own way, this soul mate of my summer streets was farther from me than those he had drawn, no matter what their sins were, either against me or all the squared-off households of the world. His were sins of omission only. But those are the ones their owners never can shake.

While those three—they were the sensitives. They knew who they hurt. My father knew. As for my brother, he knew that no one would ever love him enough to be hurt by him. Even my grandmother, whose hurts were now all in the past after one last try, would never sue *him*. That's all right. Out of all this my brother would make a personality of the kind universities harbor —and in the end perhaps love.

Mr. Peralho and my father would meanwhile make amends if I would let them. They would help me with my professional life. When nobody's to blame, that's the best way. But that takes a seeing I was too young for. The yellow bloodlight remains.

I tore the cartoon down the middle because I knew I was going to be doing something wrong with my life.

Bill was there to hit me for it. Under the blow we went down together, clutching. The moon watched him plow me. I felt his apology pour in. Sex would no longer be the same with him. Now that I saw I could manage him. Or we had both been managed. That's the animal after-sadness they talk about.

Downstairs, somebody pounded on the door. Craig Towle,

come to rescue me? I don't have a phone there—I heard him say again. That's why I go.

"Somebody saw us," Bill said.

I stretched up a leg, clenching my toes on the light bulb's dangling string. Two tries. Then I pulled us into dark. In the dark I drew Bill's shirt over me. I would pay Craig Towle nothing at first. Not even my nakedness.

The two who burst up the rickety stairs each had a flashlight. One was the old police captain who had been so decent to my mother, the other was our former sheriff, Pat Denby's father, dismissed for drinking but on some nights still employable. Since cops have to travel in twos, the town thought it might as well be him, in order to help out his kids, all of whom now worked. Most nights were dull here anyway, except for the odd smashup. Or somebody going to the theater at a windowsill. When a widow phoned, the two officers had cynically waited. When the factory watchman down the alleyway reported us, they came out.

"What kind of kickshaw you making up here?" The captain was irritable. He had been asleep at his desk.

Mr. Denby was the kind of drunk who turns a nasty weak white on his day to be sober, and a bully by that same nightfall. He didn't like me and mine either, for giving his son big ideas, like getting away to school as my brother had—or for having a quality view of his garage door. "Why'nt we pull these two in. Less maybe they've got a bottle on 'em." His son Pat Junior's nice smile sat on him like a bow tie on a donkey.

The two flashlights were dueling with the moon.

The captain was one of those fine leftovers still bred on small streets, a man with a seagoing profile even if only at the prow of a town, and with a good family doctor's responsive slouch. What other kind would have taken on Denby for deputy?

"Haul *you* in, I should," he said to him. "Man's on his own inherited property. At least for tonight. But don't nobody turn on that light."

Then he spoke to the "man" as to a boy. "You two have any more peepshows in mind, take that train of yours to the city for it. Somebody thought murder was being done. With two houses on the Row dark from death, people get nervy." The beam of his flashlight searched out my foot only, though I was covered with the shirt. "Known all the women in your family. Do what they want to, every time." In the white candlepower my foot did look like Trilby's. Maybe that's why I didn't feel shamed. Or because I am what I look to be. And the captain did not intend to shame me for it.

The beam switched from me to Bill. If Bill, according to my father, wasn't what he looked to be but what he said—then, he said nothing. I would never see his face clearer.

The beam switched back to me. "Just be sure you want to," the captain said.

They went down the stairs. The moon had won out. But the miller moth lay dead on the floor.

Who were we to think ourselves a pair who had evaded the light? Or the layers on these streets? I found I didn't mind that for any convention's sake. But those who lived by their secrets had a second power, a separate if parallel time sense. One could acquire a taste for living like that.

Then there were those who were allowed only one circling of the lamp.

Two houses dark here on Cobble Row. She had been dead for weeks, the girl I had baby-sat with, and I had never since given her a thought. Dead of her own baby too long aborted inside her, it was said, and not a peep from her until too late. Perhaps she too had been trying for secrets.

It takes a long time to become a friend. She wasn't granted enough time to become mine, but I would become hers.

I poked the moth, which lay without color or injury, a perfect specimen.

"If you're not feeling too singed—" Bill Wetmore said, "I'll take you home." Yes, sometimes he still inhabits his full name. A droll remark will do it, lodged in one cheek like a quid of tobacco. Those long-flanked cheeks, now his face's prime feature, seem to me like the supple calves of a smaller person who shadowily inhabits him.

We are all of us one creature, Mr. Evams said—a creature unevenly distributed among us. Listening to a person, he said, he could sometimes hear the separate ones in each of us. Though with Mrs. Evams, love prevented him.

No, I didn't want to go home, where all the unacknowledged parts of us were gathering. "I'll stay here with you. You're a man of property."

That was always where I would hurt him. "So am I—" I said, softer. "A woman of. And neither of us has got it."

And soon it was going to be morning, in whose tonic reality all the properties of this world rise up. The city never seems property to me. It's where both he and I would have to go to find all the gestures of the world. It's for that I want the layered street. Onstage—they say—one can always spot those who do.

I picked up the cartoon and threw it into a corner, not wanting to see across whose face and figure it had torn, or at what moral point. It flopped to the floor like a poorly made paper dart. Later Bill burnt it in the kitchen grate. No use of course. The three figures shot up straight as flames, my father the tallest.

"Leslie Warden's going to buy this house," I said. "Would you consider marrying it?"

Our daughter, as Mr. Peralho had called me, was to be married from her own background as once arranged by her mother, in her grandmother's house, her father and brother attending, accompanied by their friend. The two gentlemen from the farm hoped to be back just in time from their autumn tour of the elder's artistic connections, renewed yearly continent by continent. Phoebe would arrive, with her precocious student-deanship-to-be already securely in ego. Mr. Evams, hearing us cast about for a minister, had revealed at one stroke that he had once been ordained, as well as how well the blind hide what they choose. When I remarked this, he replied that all the handicapped were adept there, except perhaps his wife, who was such a tidy package of goodness she had no room to spare. I thought him lucky that the one thing he couldn't see in his all-but-sighted divinations was how her domed forehead, always facing him with love, sometimes willy-nilly went past him to another, my father. As for Watanabe, who when he and his wife returned home to news of my coming marriage, had made a feint at quitting us—he had been restrained by his wife Etsuko's advice, to which he now applied as to an oracle—and by his furniture, so much of it built in. However, at a suggestion from my mother, always more sensitive with servitors than we Northerners who

gave them freedom only, we were not to call him Knobby any
more.

She came out of her room two weeks before the wedding date,
unwrapped from all her cerements. The face underneath, almost
wantonly restored by those months under the coif, was pink with
misplaced youth. Her tongue too now and then slipped into
observations that might have grown like herbs in the dark of her
room. An outsider wouldn't now have noticed her dress one way
or the other—her final refinement, conscious or not. For me this
was the great loss; I still wanted her to be as conscious of everything as she had been for me once.

Etsuko, a wholesomely compact woman with a nose a mite
coarse for the ambassadorial front she had acquired by assisting
at state banquets, took with passion to my mother's absentee
elegance. We were to understand that this was the air the great
geishas cultivated in their decline. Meanwhile, she had wormed
her way into my mother's wardrobe, admiring and repairing for
the next phase to come, and heartening us all by assuming that
there would be one.

"Father thinks Mother now resembles Wallis Windsor more
than ever," my brother said. "I agree."

I could see what they meant—that semi-morganatic duchess's
abstractly embittered, extravagantly cared for later style, and the
Japanesy eyelids of certain small, middle-aged Southern women,
and men too, whom one saw down home being deferred to at
country-club tables.

"She would have to be a ghost of something for him. Or else
—" Or else how could he stand to be in the same house with
her? I didn't finish. Mr. Peralho was behind us.

"Some women are never fully appreciated except by other
women," he said. "Or else by certain men." He put his hand on
my brother's shoulder. "Your sister is not one of them."

I never knew for sure which eye he was speaking from. Yet I
knew he would not lie. I saw, too, that my brother had begun to
trouble him, less by his oversilvery blurts than by the lack of
decorum with which he let his meanness show through.

"Watanabe says Etsuko would like to do you a wedding dress," Peralho said.

"Only she's afraid her arms won't stretch that far," my brother said. This was a reference to how Etsuko had managed to get rid of the Pachinko setup.

No, Peralho would not be sorry to see Harvard loom.

I was wearing granny dresses now. In the Village they all were, often with bare feet on the hot macadam, which mode I too had tried, gratefully cured by having had to wear hipboots for my part as Portia in the school's exam play for scholarship candidates. The theater would let you try—and help you cure—almost everything. "Oh, grandmother wants me to see if her wedding dress can be altered. I haven't seen it yet." Just to stand up in, she said. And she would order a repast. Under her softer glance I felt new, the approved child of my former self.

Down home my grandfather was now truly admitted to be dying, and my other grandmother not well, which might mean anything. Miss DeVore, the natural inheritor of all weddings, had actually died. We had had no wish to assault them with my mother's state, or to have them up here to see, as they surely would have, that bride and groom were already living together. Other peculiarities of our house—in its family extension to friends, cousins, or what could be taken to be, were more like theirs than any other in town, and would not have had to be explained.

I was having to explain to myself the new warmth there. A house filled as its spaces deserve, even with such an assorted company as our three women, four men, and two servitors, has a rhythmic undercurrent that the happiest prototype foursome of man, woman, and two children cannot achieve. One seems to be living more, and with more variation. Peralho, still having his midnight confabs. Etsuko burrowing in my mother's closet, emerging with cries of discovery. My father, trying to teach his prospective son-in-law, without seeming to, how to handle a cigar. Watanabe spiraling meals out of a genie larder these days incandescent with greens and fish, and tawny meats. Even the

trays, going up the stairs for all their sad or abstruse reasons, but
sustaining life. Even the sexual undertones—from my mother
and grandmother in their severed cul-de-sacs, to the three men
in obscure command of twin beds, a studio couch, and a paterfa-
milias bedstead—to the Japanese couple, busy at a correspondence love confronted—and found good. For Etsuko had been a
surprise, but not a bad one.

As for Bill and me, we never made love in that house. At the
pad we were almost at a standstill there, too. What with my
school rehearsals for the *Merchant,* a cast picture of which had
appeared in a city summer supplement, my father-guided efforts
to get the trust money to buy the house, and Bill's job hunting,
there was scarcely time. Our part of the house's rhythm was a
lazy, never ominous sense that we were leaving it.

We were not going to live in Cobble Row. Would we ever?
Enough for me that I had acquired the place, or what I saw
when I thought of it—a moon and a window and a bit of torn
drawing, like a painting with only moral to it, and a lamp now
relinquished, on a hunched desk. To own the house before coming of age I had had to spend afternoons with the law and the
bank, learning that the weather in all offices is the same—watery
with judgment. My father helped me, apparently without con-
sulting Peralho, but if that was so, it came too late. "Do you
know why you want this?" he said. "Yes"—I answered truthfully
—"and no." He made one more try. "Even at the last minute,
you don't have to, you know. Do all of it." He saw I didn't
understand. "You can have one without the other, you know.
The house. Or the boy. Or you might even consider having
neither. It's the most important time of your life." If he and my
mother had felt so when they married, that was no recommenda-
tion. So I did not reply.

To me, this time of my life felt like an interim. At school, in a
melodrama we had performed, there had been a line, from of
course the heroine, a role which I did not play: "Shall I barter
my brideship for all the bad faith to come afterward?" Note all
the *b*'s, the visiting director from London said, lecturing us on

alliteration. We would find it in the worst rhetoric—and in Shakespeare. Our job was to make it fit to speak, either way.

I felt no brideship. Few at the school would have, except perhaps two girls who had been disqualified as students and had gone back to being girls. As for the barter, we were learning from both melodrama and sacred William that one could only be wary, watch for what one's innards were up to—and maybe have a care meanwhile for the w's. My house would be cleaned up and marginally painted for a tenancy, the income to go back to the trust. Once it was bought, I got the bills for that, Phoebe got her half of the purchase price—which the bank had raised rather than be accused of preferentially lowering it, and the hospital had got its memorial—all so quick. Each transaction had had a different weather. The learning piled, and now that I had been accepted at the best professional drama school in the country I made what use of it I could.

What did I feel about this period of my life? That I was involved in one of those lengthy bits of stage business during which you pass the time, while the real intensities build. Any regular in the audience out there could have told me that on any stage you do not merely pass the time.

As for daily living, we were going to be one of those summer couples from the hinterland who perennially transplant into the winter pad. Bill's student friend slipped us the lease over a jug of Gallo and awarded us his mattress, which we had earned anyway. If we ever turned out to be anybody here, he said, he would come East to visit us, on his first sabbatical. Being somebody was not a concept I had ever given much thought to, not considering that it could ever take precedence over being yourself, but I found that Bill understood thoroughly. It was the way he was going to pay us all back for what we were. Even Knobby—who had privately and sweetly said he would miss my calling him that —was to get paid back for those meals with fingerbowls.

At the big house, I never practiced gesture. If able, I would have made the place off bounds even for observing them. For school, however, I had to learn lines overnight, and these I did in my bedroom there, so neutral a territory that my old bed and dresser set surprised me freshly each evening. A room of my own was not what I wanted. This is a fact that many people of my profession, who when flush tend to buy ballrooms and ocean terraces, are forever having to relearn. Better to buy the moon when young.

Meanwhile, Bill was practicing his pencil on all of us.

"A leaping jackanapes—" my father said. While I strove to keep my own persona plain, as young actresses did then, and as is comfortable to me, my father was becoming more rhetorical. "And I could wish he'd go back to chewing weeds," he added, surveying the inroads on his Havanas. Bill was becoming good at them.

"No, he's better than that," Mr. Peralho said. "He has something. You'll see." Still, he hadn't again offered us both his flat, which Bill had rather hoped for.

"I already see," my brother said. Bill always drew him accurately enough, but always alongside the highest armoire. "Wish he were a photographer. So I could smash his lens," he said louder, Bill just then entering with his notebook. Bill never answered his jibes, except with another lightning sketch.

"What he draws best are the women," my father said, when Bill had gone outside again to catch Watanabe in the old car, a sketch he thought he could sell. "Maybe it's the Beaux Arts influence. What I mean is—those *are* drawings." Which Bill distributed with largesse, always to the unexpected person, a tender drawing of my mother to Mr. Peralho; one of the queenly Etsuko playing Pachinko after all—to my father; and a cabinet-photo style study of my grandmother to me: "You can start a gallery in the new house." He always now called it the new house.

"He never draws you," Mr. Peralho said, focusing those unmatched eyes on me.

"He's already done me."

I was surprised when all three men burst into laughter, and half pleased at their joining, as another instance of that elusive warmth. Where a sex has difficulty from the world, it swarms in congress. The swarm can repel, but it also attracts.

It is awesome, to confront all the divisions at once. Yet who can regret knowledge?

Etsuko, quietly clearing the luncheon table, watched the men go. They were off to the farm, where these days they spent many afternoons and some evenings. The leisure there, my brother said, was like lying on velvet: "Once it was called repose." I was saddened for him, seeing how he always chose the once of anything. "You're invited," he had told me. Bill was not. "There's still a chance for you, they think."

"For what?"

"To get off your seesaw."

I knew that, yet I was impelled to go on as I was. There are swarms made up of only a single person.

Etsuko came around the table now to point out a huge dress box that stood in a corner, then folded her hands with her usual economy. We both knew what the box held—my grandmother's wedding dress, sent down from upstairs. On whatever grounds, I planned not to wear it.

"Stay," I said. "While I open it." She missed her daughter, I knew, and their former communal life. I had grown to like that merrily splayed nose of hers quite as much as I admired the suave ebony of her head, meanwhile watching both sides of this lady deal with the husband whom she had got by a trick she had trusted herself to work out. She and he were more complicated than I would ever decipher. Where their nation left off and their own personalities began was a division I might never know. But while he meditated, and she acted for herself, between them they furnished me the kind of audience that gives one strength.

Boxes. Women so love them, acquiring all kinds; discarding is harder. But cleansing. They are what bind us to the house instead of the road. This one, of taped, stout cardboard from long ago, streaked where the gathered dust had been wiped, was marked in black crayon in a strong round hand with *s*'s like our turrets: WEDDING DRESS. NESSA'S. A nailbreaker of a box to open.

Inside, tissue paper as fresh as day. See that, and drop into the abyss where time goes when it is worn out. How dare it leave this behind?

The dress was that hard blue-green people used to call Prussian blue, with a bodice like a cuirass to match, on a skirt that could have stood by itself, all of it of a heavy stuff with a shine to it, not wool yet not silk, quality in every inch the way the provinces do it or once did, the name of that kind of yardage, of its mercer and its maker, all lost. The dress? Solidly here.

Etsuko held it up, or tried. Nessa was my grandmother, to be sure, and still a tall woman. But even the shrinkage of age would scarcely account for the height of this thick daytime costume with its long-waisted top, or for a skirt length that would surround her ankles in folds. It was handsomely sewn, but perhaps they had lacked a Miss DeVore.

I dropped my sweater right there on the dining-room carpet— who was here to watch now except the two dreaming women upstairs?—and slid the dress on, Etsuko's hands gliding from hip to sleeves to neckline, to help me. Her arms were long enough for this performance no matter what size the model, her face serenely intent. This was her profession—to attend the adornable. I have never felt closer to my sex as a sex. The thousand-and-one hidden professionalisms of women—there should be an Armory Show of them.

Still, no art of Etsuko's could account for how snugly this bride-to-be fitted into that other, as the mirror over the sideboard clearly showed. Otherwise, the dress was not becoming. What an oddity its owner must have been, in this stiff collar, high as a parson's, that hid the neck, this bodice so tight over the breasts that its wearer must have had even less there than me, and these long, ungainly sleeves with a dribble of lace at the cuffs, as at the costume's hem. Dust-ruffle, that used to be called —why did I of the short-skirted generation still know this?—and that such a ruffle was more often attached to a petticoat? Instead, the dress had long inner pantaloons of the same sturdy white as its lining, and the lace border had been sewn straight on them. There was no dust on it. Maybe the church aisle had been well swept. Or red-carpeted.

By my wish, we were to have our ceremony at the Evamses'. Both they and Bill were extremely pleased. Mrs. Evams was in a froth as to whether their library curtains should be open or closed, in order best to chastise the not-to-be-invited Walshes, who had continued to complain of the eeriness next door to them. "Their life is an open book, they say." Mrs. Evams's forehead had a special glow. "Then let them see what five thousand books must look like, when *en fete*. All of them in braille."

Mr. Evams, hearing Bill's glee, was more thoughtful. "We shouldn't wish to take advantage of other people's—vengeance. Are you sure, Bill, that your father-in-law-to-be won't see it as a slap—having the marriage here?"

Oh no—I'd interposed for him; we were all to come to my grandmother's house after, for a wedding dinner the Watanabes would cook. "If I'd still been living in our own house—but I'm not. I have a lot of backgrounds, you see. And your library—." I hadn't said it out. They knew I loved it, but not wholly why. It belonged to a house where the people in it had felt my face.

I would never wear this harsh dress over there. But the costume room at school could well use it, and in several roles to come, I hoped, so might I. A good period costume protects the actor inside from the mannerisms of his own era, yet is strong enough for any passion. I found the pantaloons allowed for free stride, the collar and cuffs nicely neutral. The best of such costumery denies the real extravagantly enough so that everybody out front can take comfort in that illusion, one that they are indeed there for. Yet surely this tight shell I was wearing was meant for workaday, not for a wedding? I could sense the person in it going over the accounts, monitoring a kitchen or a garden, working with the hands at the domestic preoccupations of those times in this house, maybe even wearing the pince-nez that would more or less fix the period for the viewer. A character role inhabited this costume, not a star.

Watanabe now appeared in the doorway, bearing the big tray.

So it was tea day; my grandmother would come down; no wonder the men had decamped. She could be beakily amusing on life in the old market towns of Jersey, informative on how linsey-woolsey was not the same as the woven coverlets that now were so wanted, or—like a parrot taught the swear words of another era—engagingly direct with the people she was with now, in her angered way always making us feel that this is all we were to her. But dinner with her was long enough to have to watch her comport herself as the star she had become. What had changed her from this subsidiary being I was wearing? The rage, even at ninety enlivening her? Over what?

These are the questions—Miss Pevsner, head coach at the school, told us—that actors must ask about every character. I felt as proud of her guidance as some do of the psychiatrist. Even now, waiting in the wings to go on, I will find some adage of hers lurking too.

So, I didn't mind if Knobby made a face at the dress. Actually, he had no facial expression. Disapproval was merely a kind of stillness on its usual state of non-change. "That is for the wedding?" He himself had of course brought the box downstairs.

"Don't worry. I'll ask mother to countermand it. Is she coming down?"

"I had no signal."

When she was coming down or had a request, she pressed her own bell, now also reconnected, whose wire raised yet another of the small metal flags in his signal box. It takes so little to enchant a house forever in memory. That little does it for me.

So—would she sleep away the afternoon then, maybe to arrive downstairs at dinner, once she knew from Etsuko that my grandmother, sated by her own matinee indulgence of tea and ride, would not appear? Then my mother would be the center of everything, not that she ever wanted that alone. I think she wanted only one thing always, but that desperately. One man. At one time. One man at a time? Not quite the same thing are they, Miss Pevsner says. And—which man?

Knobby still stood there. He wanted me to ask him something.

"Yes, Knobby?"

"That gentleman is coming to tea."

"Oh—the old man with the cane. That's nice." Austrian born, he was full of tales of his service with the Lippizaner horses of Vienna, before he and his wife had emigrated. Sometimes she came too, clearly for the tea. Even the crotch of his trousers was elegantly sharp for such an old man, Bill said. And he always carried the gift-cane, as token of his thanks.

"No. The man from the dump."

"The dumpster? Whatever for? She paid him."

It was known that the dumpster pawed over things at his own pace afterward, and sometimes censured people later for their own castoffs; he liked objects and appliances to keep on going. That baby carriage—good as new if you fix the springs, sure you don't want it? No? Then, mind if I give it that sister-in-law the new postman, her name's . . . Always identifying the receiver, even if the "Donor"—as his insisted upon receipts were always marked, didn't have a prayer or a care who. And often the receiver didn't want the thing either.

"No. The other man."

Etsuko squealed. I had stepped backward on her foot. But she nodded understandingly; clearly she knew all that story. She said something in rapid Japanese, at which Knobby frowned: he did not like her to take advantage that way. "My wife say even a ninety-year-old lady have a man-story in her life. And that now the young wife is dead."

We all looked at one another.

"He telephone," Knobby said. "Want to take her like old times to restaurant. She say no, that time is over, she don't eat out again. He to come to the house."

Knobby did not eavesdrop. Up there, he was required to listen, so that my grandmother might discuss it with him afterward. I could see her at that, casting him her thoughts and

conclusions like some major-general to the aide-de-camp bringing him the campaign lunch.

"My mother—" I said. Closing my eyes for a minute, I felt
myself be her, lying sleeping, unaware. Mr. Peralho had torn
down the material hung over her door to no avail; sleep was now
her drapery. Then I opened my eyes, shamed; an actor's inhabi-
tance of others can go too far. Or she was too close for it. "He
won't have known she's here, will he." Not seen on the street for
months, she was rumored to be with her dying father. Next
week, if she was well enough, my father actually planned to take
her down there, along with my brother, who had at last agreed to
go. To get Tim there, she would make that effort.

What effort would she make here? Or should I?

He could come and go, that long-dreamed-of guest, without
her ever knowing. If she slept. And if I let it be. It's not fair what
circumstance does—or is it? Even Miss Pevsner could not say.
But if by chance my mother woke, then surely she should not be
allowed to come down to that tea table unwarned. Yet *allow* was
a word I did not enjoy.

"I go up to her," Etsuko said. "Maybe I say nothing. She want
to come down, I push Watanabe's bell." She went off, up the
back stairs, Watanabe following. Only when they were gone did
I see that they had left it to me to decide. Was I to hustle him
out? The word was an indignity to her. Perhaps she would sleep
through all. But should I let her? That's her lookout, I hear you
say. But what was mine?

Too late I heard my grandmother begin her descent. I came
halfway out of the dining room to the edge of the front hall. She
had a callous step, I told myself, exactly like her conversation.
Yet somewhere behind both must be the woman who twenty
years after her marriage to that state portrait upstairs could still
speak of her honeymoon house—even if all her love of it had
now gone into the furniture. I didn't much credit her for her
recent charity to the elderly; any town like ours has powerful old
women who dispense. If even they and she were vulnerable in-

side their print dresses and behind their tyrannical dinners—
then all the world must be. Yes, Miss Pevsner, I see.

The door chime rang. I heard my grandmother call from halfway down the curved front stair: "I'll go, Watanabe." She never
did that. Yet what did I know of her nevers?

Just in time, I retreated to the niche under the stairs, in whose
closet I had once stashed two of the packages meant for the
dump. Forgotten during my mother's worst time, then remembered and opened, the flat, laundry-shaped one had revealed half
a dozen knitted silk-and-lisle men's shorts and the same number
of vests, all from Hanro in Switzerland, and all unworn. My
grandfather's? Bill, shown them, said they were too fine for himself. "Try the 'Three'—" he'd said, his name for my father and
brother and Peralho, but I hadn't thought of applying to them,
and under his glance never would. Etsuko had taken the underwear gleefully, exclaiming over the workmanship, but Knobby
too had refused them. A wasteful country, she sighed, bowing to
make it seem a compliment, and that got my dander up. She
never wasted emotion, or not our kind—did she have it to waste?
"Use them for dishcloths," I said. The other package had been a
framed snapshot of two bikes. No owners, just the bikes.

A last clump of a shoe. My grandmother was in the front hall,
then in the entry. I heard her open the front door.

"Nessa—" a man's voice said. No more masculine than many.
But with an edge. Of what? I had never heard my grandmother
addressed by her first name before. No one would have thought
themselves old enough. Except this man.

I heard them seat themselves in the sitting room across the
hall, where the tray had already been laid. Back of it were the
two parlors where there had been a graduation dance once—
perhaps why we were not encouraged to use them. These led
around the rear to the dining room and a small anteroom
through whose arch I had come into this side of the hall. The
archway was fretted with niches for the tall plants which were no
longer kept.

The murmur of their two voices came like an itch. The sit-

ting-room door was open but I was too far back under the stairs.
If I crossed the hall again, back to the archway, I could hear. I
tiptoed into the archway.

For a while I heard nothing but the clink of tea things.

"All true stories are private," that voice said then. "Comes a
time when they're no longer that."

I couldn't hear my grandmother's reply. Perhaps she made
none.

"Besides, I have the story now. I think—all of it. That's what
I came to tell you. To let you be the first. I shouldn't like you to
hear of it from others. And I'd like us to be friends, you silly. I
hear you wanted to sue."

This time there was a reply I couldn't get. He must be the one
nearest the door.

"Ah yes, the dump," he said then. *Mea culpa.* But I'd do it
again. For my purpose."

Again, a reply I couldn't hear.

"Higher than God's? No. No. Just—for my god. The work.
Nessa, hear me out. I'm not the man I am in my work, or seem
to be. Just—a man. Doing his best for it."

This time I did hear her guttural "And never mind the people
in the way?"

He was silent for a while. "I can't always keep it separate.
Keep them. Yes, that's true. Though they have been known to
cooperate."

I could hear his smile. And hate him for it.

My grandmother would have seen it. I heard her clearly this
time. "And my daughter-in-law? Did you work her in, just for
your purpose?"

I was amazed, never having heard my grandmother speak to
any outsider except socially. Or to any of us in this way. Adult to
adult. And who had I heard speak in that same dead-on voice?
My father, to whom she never in my hearing had spoken so.
Who himself spoke in it—I now believe, trust in, and sorrow for
—only to me.

"No," the nearer side of the tea table said, "Though I was to blame there. If any of us are to be. For these sudden—irruptions. I had gone to her to get to you, you see. For that connection. And a little, yes, for my first wife. To hear of their joint youth. One never knows what perspective one will find. Which might explain. And even heal . . . Your daughter-in-law was my wife's generation, you see. My first wife's. Who'd left me. And returned again—and left. Because of the work she'd thought she'd married me for. Her rival. It was to have been only the jewel in *her* crown. When it's nobody's—not even mine."

That's what makes the edge in his voice, I thought. That.

"Your daughter-in-law would never have done that," he said. "She wants—only to be a man's jewel. In an affair that goes on and on . . . But she knows nothing of what I wanted from you. You knew that. Nor would I have asked."

There may have been an answer. I never heard it.

"That's why I could go on with her," he said. "She had nothing to do with the town. There's always one person or more like that in a town. Lovely as she was, she was something of that for me. And I took it from what she said once, that she was used to affairs. Perhaps I shouldn't tell you that. But there was already one affair in her life, she said. One that had gone on and on."

My father's? O my mother. The only affair she knew of to go by, went on and on. That's the way she saw any affair—as going on and on.

I was breathing so hard that the dress tore. Surely they could hear it, that split at the breast?

They were too occupied, but one day, on a stage, I would repeat this, and even the balcony would hear. A trick, they said. Which could never happen in real life. To trick the truth into being, is that despicable? But it works. And who taught me that?

"And then—" my grandmother said. "I am ninety years old. And then you wanted to bring me your new juvenile."

"I can't talk about that yet," he said. "But she wasn't—new. We were together even before I came here. That's why I came away."

But she followed him. I wouldn't have had to know her, to

know that. Some follow, some are followed. And gender alone will not explain it.

He was talking with a rush now, maybe trying to. "Anyway, I haven't damaged you, Nessa, not at all. I've brought you out. And about time. You'd have died without letting on, wouldn't you? But you're the better for it. Come on. Come on." And then I heard him push back his chair. He must be going round the table to her. "Ah, Nessa. That's the girl."

She was crying. Maybe in his arms. A ninety-year-old woman, and a hard one. Hearing the grace of being called the girl one still is.

He must have sat her down again. "And I'll do your story justice. You may even be proud."

"It's not my story," my grandmother said. "That's why I thought I must sue."

Again a silence. But somehow lovely, after an old woman speaking refreshed and silvery.

"And what about your secrets?" she said, lulled. Or was she? "You must have some. What about them?"

He didn't answer quickly. "Ah, that's for my middle age. Which has finally arrived. I'm not good enough at it yet. At getting at myself. But one day I'll get my secrets outside myself. For all to view."

So he too needs help on this, I thought. Even he.

"What's that?" she said sharp and sudden. "Who's that?"

It wasn't I. No one could mistake who it was, walking rat-tat, rat-tat along the upper hall. No one who had ever lived with my mother's heeled step.

"It's your middle age." My grandmother had got her cackle back.

"People said she was in Rio. Or down South. Or I would never have—. I must go." A side door led from the sitting room, to the sunporch. I heard him turn the heavy handle.

"No, you'll stay. And let her do you justice." My grandmother gave another cackle. "Who would think I could talk like that."

"The one who taught you," he said. But he stayed.

Up there on the staircase, my mother paused. Etsuko had awakened her after all, and had told her who the guest was. In spite of Etsuko's mixed *l*'s and *r*'s, and even in the dregs of sleep, my mother had risen to that name, straight-backed from the pillow, Etsuko said later. "Like a ghost." Where we here have the loose feelings we term personal, the Japanese move by obligation. I had the obligation to let her show herself, Etsuko said. To let him see the ghost he had made.

She had tossed over my mother's head one of the soft, colorless shifts she had sewn for my mother in the more staid style of her own country, then had whipped my mother's hair into points on her cheeks and had brought her the high-heeled shoes.

But it must have been my mother herself who put the bracelet on. A woman knows her own paraphernalia, and must keep with it.

As she came farther down the staircase and passed me, I leaned back behind the arch, but those sleepwalking eyes would not have seen me. Then she went in.

At first, I couldn't hear her or them—as if she had brought her own soft muffle with her. Or maybe nothing was being said.

Then I heard him say how well she looked.

"I slept," she said.

Then he said that after their last meeting he had thought he better not get in touch with her.

"I am still sleeping," she said.

To brush a man aside yet hang on. Perhaps the women who do that are ghosts from the beginning.

"You wouldn't have minded her. My young wife. Nobody would have. That was her trouble. So I had to."

No answer.

"The young can be like a drug," he said. "I married her crowd. Then I had to keep that from her. I hope I did."

Yes, he was just a man. May I remember it.

But also the man who would one day write *The Troupe*—that movie. Saying to me in the dark of the preview—"Yes, here they are. And I'm rid of them. They were never right for a play."

"Ah—" he said now, "you're wearing the bracelet. I hunted a long time for that."

"He hunts well," my grandmother said. But from their silence I surmised they were ignoring her. The quiet went on so long that I thought he might have taken my mother in his arms.

I craned forward, out from under the archway.

They were on opposite sides of the table. She stood there, cloudily. He was leaning toward her.

"Perhaps—." Leaning farther, he took hold of the circlet on her wrist.

My grandmother, sitting between them, stared straight ahead.

"Perhaps we—" he said to my mother.

My mother drew back her arm, leaving the big empty circlet on his upturned palm. "I shall go on sleeping."

His face. I have to begin seeing it now at my own distance. Inclining toward her, and even at that moment, as it would one day incline toward me, a face with one ear better for a certain kind of listening, saying to me: It's beautiful and terrible, that moment when the sanity and the madness join.

Then my grandmother cried out, pointing at me in the arch there, where I stood tall as that other figure once had, tending the plants in its armor, the blue-green dress.

Pointing at youth, the double—as Craig Towle will soon tell me, will keep telling me.

The double, rising always the same, yet never quite.

So now we enter the opposing dream. We cross the bar, to the
person opposite.   Craig Towle.

PART THREE

PART THREE

"I hope to do *all* of you justice," he said as we left my grand-mother's house. Back in the sitting room, my mother had re-treated as she had warned, falling like a cloud on Etsuko's willing breast. My grandmother, fulfilling her own prediction—that she did not have strokes—had listened to his explanation: "Those two dress boxes must have been marked wrong—one for the other—at the time they were stored. The one you sent to the dump had a cream-colored dress in it, much smaller than the green one. I presume—*your* wedding dress." Then, making no comment on his maraudings, she had gone up the stairs alone, only leaning heavier on the banister. To me he'd said only, "Change out of that. Into your own clothes. And come. Out of this house."

As we leave, it seems to me that all the women of our upstairs float eagerly along with us, hovering around his head to be veri-fied. Along with all those before us. "No—" he will laugh, the day I say that—"the woman under present scrutiny will always hold back. She is nemesis. In the same way that one's latest work effort always is. Until it issues," he says, his eyes locked inward. "Then it is done for." And smiles lightheartedly. By then I will not tremble at this issuance of women from his pen, or even from his bed, but I will know better. Men who write about women wear them like laurel leaves in the hair.

But that was late in our exchanges. Or lessons. This is the first of them. He has hurried me to a destination I still cannot believe, though we are chair to chair.

"Yes, that was melodrama," he says. "And it depended on dress. Women let themselves be humiliated by that, I know. That their lives should so depend. And what melodrama—a switched box! An honorable ruse, but only if set by the gods. I had nothing to do with it. I wouldn't dare."

But the owner of that dress I had worn might have. I could still feel its peculiar quality. Those who instruct us, as he was instructing me, tend to forget that the young are not learning solely from them.

"What did it say on the box that did go to the dumpster's?" I said. "The one with my grandmother's dress in it?"

He doesn't answer at once. He is never quick to. "Of course. Of course. I thought what was marked on that box was simply your grandmother being her lordly self." He leans toward me. "When, all the while, it could have been—what I was looking for?"

What he starts at once is the collaboration. With anyone. It's his way of looking at the world. Though flawed in him, as in any of us, I still see it as a great one.

See us there, then. The man who holds a person face to face, and if interested will work you over with his pen afterward. Yet to whom—if you have to have your story, you would go as to an internist.

But I had the safe feeling that the story he was after was not mine, or ever to be mine. For the past weeks, spent so much in the company of "The Three," I had worn riding togs and those boots, half being, if tongue in cheek, what they may have thought of me. But leaving that house, shedding that dress as he commanded me, I had grabbed up the work jeans and T-shirt with the school's insignia on it that a lot of us first-year students wore. The second year, we were told, is when you achieve your own style, or shed it; wait for that. I had no such needs, and from then on wore that uniform or a plain jumper straight through school. Such clothes keep one from thoughts of costume. The costume is the last part of a role, we were being told. Lack of it may even be a boon to any girl who is thinking herself out.

I thought of the dress I had discarded, lying on the bed back there, breastless but uncrushable. Like a shell waiting to be filled with meaning. Like me. And both of us could wait.

While I look at the floor here, which has been newly swept. The dead moth gone. Then at the desk, no longer hunched in solitude but covered with typescript. Then at the moonless window, vague now with afternoon.

"I finished the first draft of the play last night. I wanted to do that here. In the town."

That last phrase has delicacy; the craggy face has a dainty tongue. And an economical one, when moved to tell you more than what it is saying. Acknowledging the town as an entity. Joining the two of us over it. And telling me the play is about the town?

While I am both gazing at him—oh, I shall get his every gesture—and enumerating this place.

"Yes, nice, isn't it? They've sold the place to somebody, I understand. But nobody's living here yet. I still have my key. Maybe we can go on working here."

. . . If I were to jut my chin and neck now, as I did back then? No, after youth one can't get away with it. But it's not the limberness that goes; it's the unselfconsciousness . . .

"You know." He makes the two words equal. Brushing away non-intimacy is natural to him. Can he help it if each recipient takes it personally? As he leaned toward me, his shirt still had that fine-pored scent of a good laundry, the collar not like any I knew. Neither elegant like Mr. Peralho's, nor button-down broker like my father's, yet better than what Bill would buy even if

he had money. Nor like Tim's, whose lapels hung like field let-
tuce. "I can't tell how much you know," he said. "But you
couldn't live where you do and not know some of it. Nor be as
you are.

A noncommittal collar. And too close. I sit back in my chair.
Then he says the unforgettable.

"And besides—I *saw* you."

Anybody in the theater knows what that means. I held my
breath. How was I?—we students all said, crowding to each
other after the performance—in which we had all been the
same.

His arm reaches for the desk; his hand smooths its edge. One
never knows which of his gestures come from intent. Behind
them is that longest harbored intent of all, a medium he lives in,
moving him to its dictates as water sways a fish. Yet he can move
like any other man as well.

"You're not Portia yet. How could you be? You're a beginning
animal."

—I see myself back there, my face lifted, becalmed, in the
way of those who want to cry but hold still. No one had ever said
it so well.

"But you have what I want," he says—and I approve the
harshness. We are matched, I think. He too sees everything.

"There was a family picture Nessa showed me once. And
wouldn't show me again, once she saw it wasn't her I was looking
at. What you know—is there. And it's in the dress you had on,
that went into the wrong box. Or was put so. And in the letters
she has burnt or got rid of this past year. No letters came to the
dump."

He could admit that. Then I could speak.

"When you stood up, there. At the top of the pile." Like a
statue a town has erected to itself without knowing so—and the
man himself oblivious. "And my mother was at the bottom." In
her big hat. "And the ash and cinders began draining from beneath your feet." And she, climbing, climbing toward you in the
same seeping rhythm, remained always in the same spot. The

dual question hung in front of me, fixed as that gray landscape and flaring sun. "You did start it, didn't you. That anthill moving." A slow seepage that could go on for days, which was why we children had always been chased from there. "And were you —moving toward her?"

Or back into his own life?

He smiled. When it comes to the world's dump piles, that smile said—in that ashen landscape you are still a child. But I won't chase you from it. "I moved toward what I saw. Toward Nessa and you. Once I saw you together. With the whole town behind you. I've been doing that ever since. That was the afternoon I came back here, and began."

I got up and went to the hayloft's window, away from the thrall he might put me in, safely back in my own. There are certain lonely paintings I love. Never any people in them, but haunted by the absence of people—in the angle of a footpath maybe, or under eaves brooding as low as guardian wings. Here the bottom of the town composed itself in a straggle of cobbles and warehouses chinked with light, at the base of one of those streets which incline up to the dots of personal houses, and a marketplace. I almost forgot him, there behind me, hunting his play. Or testing it. And hunting me?

I might be young, but I had an idea that the two should never be hunted together.

"Shall I tell you? What the play's about?"

"I already know."

"Who, then?"

"Somebody young."

He laughed. "Don't look so sullen about it." But his voice was dashed. "Yes, young. In 1927. Come. Turn around. I'll tell it—as I found it. In props. Prop by prop."

I knew what he meant. In improvisation class, we were dealt situations to dialogue over—and sometimes a hasty assemblage of objects, perhaps a still life on a table, of ordinary objects, a handbag and a notebook, plus some oddity—a flute, a doll's shoe, a knife. But he hadn't found his properties merely, or been dealt

them. He had burrowed. This was why our class improvisations
were so weak, though no one at school could quite tell us why,
not even our haughty mentor muttering of Aristotle's unities,
and of her own one *succès fou*—in Strindberg, at an age little
more than we were now.

What was missing in our arranged prop fancies was the real
dramatist's lack of shame. And the real actor's. Down in the
mud, for the glory of the theater. Not to roll in it simply, but
because it is there. And is not always mud. And what is mud, my
dears? Stare at it long.

"First prop—" the voice behind me says.

He holds that yard-long farmhouse photograph from my
grandmother's upstairs hall. These stiff old shots are often that
shape because of the length of the porches, and the size of the
families disposed along them. Browntone, on backgrounds aged
to yellow, they harbor a stillness one doesn't see in the modern
technique. "I just now snitched it, from your grandmother's.
While you went upstairs to change."

I had run up the backstairs, Etsuko vanishing out to her and
Watanabe's ell. He would have gone up the front stairs. To take
the photograph, which had hung in the hall to the left, he would
have had to pass my mother's door.

"Was my mother already asleep?"

He will not answer me. Not because his former lover happened to be my mother. As I will learn, he will not ever talk
about his lovers. His silence then would be his only acknowledg-
ment that she had been one of them. To him, his lovers are
inviolate, not for their own sake, but because they are his.

"Just face the camera." He's smiling broadly now. One of his
forefingers reaches around the photograph's frame, pointing to a
head.

She is facing the camera too, my great-aunt Mary Leona, in
her family called Leo for short, the last born. As often with
those, she appears the handsomest, and to me, the most modernly near. When I was born she was still alive.

My grandmother, in the photograph still a young woman, has

her left arm raised so that it may rest around her much taller youngest sister's neck. Nessa—as I will grow used to hearing my grandmother named—*is* still alive. But in the photo Leo next to her seems as vigorous. A photograph can be made to do this, the person in it toning forward to whoever will agree to revive her or him. We are maintaining Leo. First Nessa, in the long, long run that travels away from a grave. Then Craig Towle, arrived like a bolt out of the blue. And now me?

Does he know that in grandmother's eyes I have long been what silly old women, leaning over my cradle or bemusedly gripping my soft, untutored hand at graduation have sometimes exclaimed: "The living image!"? When did she start not being able to look at me square?

Or does he think he has discovered me all himself? He sets the photograph flat on the desk, and reaching into a drawer, places a magnifying glass on its surface. "If the photo itself weren't under glass this would do better. But see there."

"No."

"You don't agree?"

"I mean—I don't have to look."

Actors dislike authors with reason. When the material is good enough we begin to forget it is theirs. They begin to stand between us and what we must make our own. They themselves shadow it—sometimes even against what they want of it. And we, outside both it and them, are the ones who have to make it be.

And in this case—I was the material. At the same time enraged—as a target might be—and proud. "I've been in that dress."

In how many greenrooms, in how many theaters, he must have heard the cast chattering of their positions in the play, confirming or inveighing against those as people in real life discuss their destinies. And had been grateful to overhear, or desperate?

"You're an actress all right," he says. "But how much do you know? I mean—of this?" He tapped the picture. "Of—Leo."

I thought of the pottery in the garage. Of the apartment my grandmother now inhabited, scattering her flowered dresses— why did female ancients so often wear jungle prints?—on all that severe wood and manly green leather, one sight of which had stayed in my mind like part of an archive not yet gathered. One dating all the way back to Phoebe Wetmore and me fiddling in bathrooms like small girls do, she the leader, giggling to me what her grandmother, once a layer-out of dead bodies, had reported. Or to my mother's account of my grandfather's dance with her: "little pots of those flowers like pansies with the mumps, set out all around the dance floor." Flowers—the aunt who had lived there then had had a way with them. Flowers also then always kept in the empty niche where I had hidden this afternoon. Once, my father, coming down the stairs white-faced after a bout with my grandmother, had stopped dead in front of it to say: "Leo always kept that niche full of flowers." Who was Leo? "My Aunt Leona," he had replied, but had never again spoken of her. Why had I not forgotten any of it?

"I remember everything about her," I said.

He smiled. It's his business to know where all the lies come from. And though it may seem strange in an actress, I have never properly learned to lie. That's from having been with the blind, he'll tell me later. But I am not sure.

"I haven't told you what was on the box that did go to the dump," he says. "In that old-fashioned writing they used to call 'Palmer script.' In black crayon. Ha. On yours too, eh. But first —what did *your* box say?"

"Not mine." Any more than that other box, all those boxes, wrong, or belated, opened or bound up again—were his.

But he could wait; he knew what he wanted. I didn't have that advantage. And that's when we give in, move with the tide, even marry. Hoping we'll learn from the tide itself what we want of it.

So I tell him.

"Ha. Just 'WEDDING-DRESS. NESSA'S'—eh? How the womenfolk used to mark things, in the old days. Even the stuff in their own

dresser drawers. As if they knew all the epitaphs beforehand."
He bends toward me and takes my cold hands in his. My extremities are colder than normal. Tim, my brother, used to tease that the blood had to go so far—until I found out that his hands are as cold. My profession warms mine. His is no good at that.

But no matter. Craig Towle is talking to me. And will not stop. "Those boxes, those bundles at the dump. They are yours. And they are mine. Don't forget, I come from this town." He let go my hands then and said low, like a creed: "We inherit them."

The hayloft window frames him. What do we inherit, what did we acquire? This window—how divide it? If the moon comes up I'll leave now, I think—I'll take myself out of his grasp. But the moon did not rise.

"The boxes would have been marked and mixed up at the same time," he says. "Maybe at some crisis."

At once I knew what day that had been. Glinting down all our lives, even mine. Why don't we go see the farm, girl? Because we came from it.

"What?" he says sharp. "What?"

"The day they left the farm. For here." And then I give up. "Okay, tell me what it said. On Leo's box."

"It said, 'Not a Wedding Dress. Mine.' "

I am looking at him from a long, long distance. I am leaving the farm, with them. Am I crying over that box? For her?

"Yes, yes, yes—" he said. "Come sit down. And let me tell you a story."

For the first time I think of him as a man with children, the ones we in town never seemed to see. My father, when a very young one, used to say that very phrase to me at bedtime. Although his stories were always about the little girl who was me, I never accused him of want of imagination, indeed helping him fill in. And now tell me about being a little boy, I said once, startling him. About when you were one. He never did. Perhaps that was kept for Tim—who would never say.

"Any story," I say, hardening. "As long as it's not mine."

When this man is about to make a killer remark, he telegraphs it with the slightest lift of chin. Fencers do that, almost as if they want to. Craving the rhythm, not the kill. "Planning to avoid yours, hmm. By marrying?"

So he pulled out like a thorn what had been drugging my days, puzzling my nights. "How do you know?"

"That you're marrying young Wetmore? Heard it at Walsh's. Everything's on the menu there."

"I mean—why I am."

"You just now told me. You're avoiding—something else."

"Did I?"

"But you yourself—hadn't caught onto it?"

"Not really."

"It's a common enough cause. For marrying."

I toed the floor. The workmen had cleaned well. "Yours too?"

Few beard this man on his own motives, I would find—he being the professional grandee of motives; I saw him hesitate because of that. And speak the truth because of it. "No, I did it to find out. That's what I do."

So *I* find out from him early. How the animal hides in the professional.

"Well—" he says, "aren't you ever going to sit down?"

I leave the window slowly. I hear the breath drawn between his teeth. "The same fairy-tale gawk, it would be. The way you move. I can see it. I got in as deep as anybody can after thirty years—but maybe I'm not done yet." He watches me sit. "I knew it when I saw you. I could write a line for each one of your bones."

"But I am not—like that person."

"I guess not." Did I hear though that he had had a wild hope? "But—with what you are—and with what I could do—perhaps you could be."

It takes me a minute to understand he might be offering me the part. That sometimes did happen, even to beginners, in some agent's grubby office, or in the producer's dreamboat motel. Otherwise—it would be tryouts for tryouts, showcase theater for the lucky ones willing to work for free, and the gossipy grapevine at the unemployment office. At school we were all coached on the odds.

"Oh"—I say—"*Pygmalion.*"

"Christ Jesus," he says. "Education."

"No. Movies."

He laughs. "You're a worthy—"

"Opponent?"

Only a phrase, tapped out in the rhetoric class at school, along with "mortal enemy" and "fast friend." But it told him, he said later, that I too watched language.

"Collector."

He watches me examining his desk, no longer bare, as I first saw it, stacked now with typescript at one end, a typewriter at the other, and in the middle, retreated to a last stand, a long yellow pad scrawled in a black as heavy as subway graffiti, and a felt pen.

"I play Russian roulette with those pens. I seem to be able to buy only one at a time."

But has squandered two years, he tells me, tracing Leo everywhere. Town records. Town newspaper. One photograph—at a flower show. "Of the winning plant only." A music society that by rumor once sang for a year or two here but had no history. Two ancient shopkeepers, now retired, who remembered the best customer of their apprentice days; the grocer who recalled most a telephone voice; and the past owner of the bookshop, who supplied a list.

"How do you describe a recluse the whole town knew?"

Who baked cookies with rosewater, but once ordered a whole sheepshead in order to taste the eyes—cooking it according to a Turkish recipe—and read Milton's *Areopagitica.*

And wore men's underwear ordered from Switzerland.

Who gave handouts anonymously, the source being known to all, but must never be thanked—which induced a shyness almost hysterical. Who once traveled, it had been thought, but thereafter never would hear news of the world—only of the town. "Yet who did not faint at the sight of blood"—once rushing from the

house to pick up a child seen to fall from a neighbor's window—
and once taming a young bear that had wandered in from the
Poconos and was scavenging the garbage cans. "Who—according to the minister of the Dutch Reformed Church, whom I
tracked to his nursing home in Reading, was the happiest person
they all knew, and not at all strange?"

He reached behind the desk. "Then at last I lucked in. Those
old biddies and geezers Nessa began bundling the effects to—
they're not Nessa's friends. Poor old war-horse, she may have
none but me. They were the music society." He brings up a
couple of framed pictures, cabinet-size, and holds out one. "The
old Austrian says Nessa gave it to him. More likely he sneaked it.
Nessa had them all up there this year, he said, one by one.
They've never seen the place. Asked me not to tell his wife about
the picture, which is why I have it. He had been in love most
with Leo's voice. But his wife would never forgive. Ah God,
know them? They must be in their eighties."

"They come to grandmother's for tea. She's younger. And eats
without speaking. Nothing in common with each other—and it
has gone on so long. But they still act out their domesticity.
Scary."

I see I have thralled him. He's slow to hand me the picture.
"Yes—scary." Then comes that shift—a professional screen
dropped—which even his children when grown will never learn
to anticipate. Tarquin, who often comes to stay with me these
days, especially.

"Well, my dear, here you are," says Craig Towle. "In 1923."

Yes, the dead hold very still for interpretation. The heavy
cardboard that even then maybe only provincial photographers
still used makes it easier. Am I looking at myself three years ago,
but long-skirted instead of short, calico instead of my tartan, in
the background a barnyard instead of a riding stable, hair
cropped close instead of my new bob? They say the twin always
looks different to the other twin. If I could see the hands I would
know how far likeness can go—surely no two people have the

same hands, but these are thrust in the pockets, ungirlishly. I
used to do the same. Farmyard boots.

"The hair was cropped because of scarlet fever. Then, Nessa
let drop once—for a while Leo wouldn't let it grow out. The old
guy had never seen it like that."

"No?" But I might have done the same. You are fifteen, and
you don't know what you are, much less who. At the same time
you are full of life. The only people you know to have a crush on
are other girls. Every day your features vary, seeming to grow on
different days, the nose your mother's, a small woman's, the chin
—your father's, as a youth. Let's cut your hair mannish, says
Phoebe, who has been taking a mail-order course in beautician
stuff. Then let's go in the bathroom, and fiddle. The nurse isn't
home to catch us, but later, when she sees my hair, she crosses
herself, then comes to twitch my cheek. "Any spots? No. Crea-
tures like you don't get spots, even at the age they should." And
I'd thought she meant diet—the lamb chops and beef juice they
didn't get on Cobble Row. Granny says not to hang around girls
like you, Phoebe says next day, fiddling, her face hot.

And all the time, the person you are in love with is yourself.

"See anything?" he is saying.

"So what if I do?" I have to swallow, though. "Leo looks like a
modern girl."

Maybe it's my expression makes him hand over the second
photo so silently. The music society, taken in the downstairs
hallway of my grandmother's house. The young women are all in
dark surplices; the men wear flowing ties. The Austrian has high
color and light wavy hair.

"They all got a copy of this one," Towle says. "He had his
tinted."

Leo is in the center, leaning against a niche from which palm
fronds spill. It is a pose in which divas of that era used to let
themselves be "caught," as if staring at a basilisk from which
they cannot look away. The gaze is deep, the lengthened eyes
lucent enough to compete with their jewels, and in the best of
them the brow is broad, the cheekbones well planed and easy to

highlight, the mouth mobile. Leo has no jewels, only the structure of a face I know too well. Though mine was not destined to
attain what Leo's already had—gone past a girl's curve or a boy's
narrowness to that questionable human marble which unites.
Leo's hair, superabundant even in the pulled-back 1930s coif,
keeps the question alive.

Nowadays my own face is my dear machine. Make-up bat-
tered, speech-inflected to the smallest muscle under the skin—I
watch it daily, but only for age. It is mine; I have earned in it.
But in those days it was only what had been given me. Down
home had been the first to approve of it, though dismayed at my
other growth. Behooves you to keep yo-seff mo-ah a lady than
most, heah?—the dear sweet ladies said. The Evamses had approved of my face almost as if for good conduct—and it had
helped me get into drama school. Seeing Leo's face did not scare
me. I felt myself safe from that kind of beauty. Or if safe is not
the modern word, say then that my body had already declared
what its intentions were. What I felt, looking at Leo, was awe.
My face, too, would someday be mine alone.

I turned the framed photo over. On the manila-papered back
all the names had been inscribed above the date—May, 1932,
and in a young hand the name of the taker too.

"Do you sing?" the voice at my side asks. I shall resist letting
the man who owns the voice become more than that.

"I have no ear." Such a good strong instrument, our school
impresario said, holding his head. And listen to her shift key
twice in ten bars. "But I can imitate—even opera singers, for a
bar or two. It's not really singing."

"Which singers?"

"You'll laugh."

"Try me."

Oh I would, again and again. What I wanted was for Craig
Towle never to come near enough to drop out of the myth that
the town, and I too, had made of him. Never to become an
ordinary man, in a room with me. Or even an extraordinary one,
unimaginably near. And I was afraid that I wanted him nearer.

"Chaliapin."

He didn't laugh. "Where from? *Boris Godunov?*"

"No. I don't know that. 'The Volga Boatman,' just the 'Yo-o-oh' part. And Kirsten Flagstad. Not the Valkyrie cry; it's too sustained. But the first bars of the Love Death—*Mild und leise,* and a few words on—I can do that. And John McCormack's 'Jeanie with the li-ight brown hair'—not always, but sometimes. That's the hardest." The Evamses, though they couldn't take opera in performance, had a wall of old records I was free to play, and had listened to me with glee.

"Tenor—" he said. "You have quite a range."

"It's not singing. It's like—talking. But from the diaphragm. And with what they call *timbre.*"

"Do one."

"Uh-*uh* . . ." I give it that down-home lilt. You can snow people with Southernism, if you're good enough. From me, it surprised him. But he caught me looking in my lap anyway, and looked over my shoulder.

"Why—your father took that picture. That long ago."

"Wasn't *that* long ago. Or not for him."

Then he does laugh and laugh. "That you—should have to tell me." He sobers. "Maybe I've been thinking too much that way. Of a period. I don't want a play to be that; I never do. Yet even my own early life here seems to me out of a family album. It's the town—and the reason I left it. Still forty years behind."

"No!" I say. "It's not."

We sit as if over a chessboard. At the window is the town I could never paint as it should be. "It's not like that," I say, in a deeper voice than I have ever before let myself find. And deeper yet: "Not at all."

What an old trick, dropping the voice with each repetition—but I didn't yet know this. All the tricks were passion once.

"I'm the one who bought this place," I say, with the same alto joy. Now that I see why I have bought it. To own what you love —and can't get away from. As people do, never sure of which comes first. "That's why there's nobody living here."

Has he heard me? His head is cocked—he might be one of those students the Evamses crave most, who at the height of practice appear to be listening to decibels beyond the ken of the sighted. He isn't yet sure of what brand of creature I am.

A flush creeps from my neck to my temples. Old-style actors in the sticks used to hold their breath to turn themselves red, we were told—and were applauded as they reddened. But this crept of itself. If he wasn't sure what I was—I would never tell him.

"Leo wore gloves half the time, claiming an allergy. Know any reason why?" His tone is strange.

I hate him for it. "Kid in my sixth grade, white kid, her arms were all liver and pink; said her mother was frightened by a stoat in her sixth month. But that's just the town, eighty years behind."

"Your round," he says—and seizes my hands.

They are comely, and small for my size. "I have my mother's hands," I say. And I'm a bitch. Let him know that.

He puts my hands back in my lap, slowly. "The part's yours—Portia. Now—let me walk you through it, though. That a deal?"

How will I feel when I inform them at school, I wonder—proud or shamed? Answer: I will know what bribery is.

"And then—*you'll* walk *me* through it, my girl. With every thing you know about it. Or feel."

Why do I tremble, like a prisoner offered a cigarette? Answer: because you are savagely learning more about the business of life than you have it in you to confess.

"So—you're my landlord."

It was my window, even if I couldn't make the moon rise in it —the same limits under which the rest of the town owned its property. The Row will buzz no more than it always has about me and mine. He leans toward me, a shorter man than he seems. The crown of his head hasn't lost a hair. He doesn't gossip; he takes one into the ways of the world. The back of his head is not as well-shaped as Bill's.

I face him squarely. Again I hear that intake of breath, and this time I know what I have done. I have assumed that pose.

There are divas who must go to school to become one. There are
those who come out of the town.

He tosses a key in my lap. I let it lie. Then toss it in the air
and catch it. Then toss it back. I will hear his story to the end.
As he gives it, I will add to it, until at times it will seem that I
am playing all the parts in this family. In many voices. The voice
of young Nessa, grandmother-to-be, and the harsh crank of her
when old. The twanged Boston of old medical records never
resolved—and how should they be, when nature itself has refused to?

"Some facts I'll imagine," he says. "Some I know."

And will it also be the other way round? Some I will imagine,
and he will confirm?

Through the air the packages will come flying toward us, under the glare of an ashheap sun.

As he begins, both our faces are incredulous. He has given me
the part. I have inherited it.

The day we leave the farm, the men who come to move the tractors, all men from the district, say the cows already know. All machinery is being cleared off as a condition of sale. This is not a dairy farm; the herd is a small one, personal. It too will be led away at four o'clock, by which time we will be gone. The furniture, when auctioned off, may have been shamed by the low price set on its dignity, but most neighbors have much the same stuff, and no call for new. Only the grand white icebox remains in the parlor to greet the purchaser like one of those huge, retarded hired girls who around here are sometimes included in such deals. The buyer, our leading banker, is coming to take possession, denying that he is acquiring us for the sake of our fields. "That barn is chestnut," he said. So perhaps there's hope. A lot of the household stuff is made of that wood too—no point in saying it. The newspaper has congratulated him for saving the finest farm in the township. The township is Cranberry, New Jersey, but that kind of bog tilling—half nature's and half raucous bands of pickers and babies made in the bushes—is not what we have ever done. That morning, the slightly acid smell of potato fields stretches as far as the low-level brown horizon, as if it always will.

It is on record—as told by an old woman dining in a restau-

rant with a man who, though a native of the same state, doesn't
know beans about its farms—that Leo, the sole reason for the
move, was the last to leave. Though it's not yet time to go.
"Look at that crew," my grandfather says, then shouts to the
men shifting the John Deere. "Put her in neutral, you lunk-
heads," but they know he's only yelling to explain away his red
face. The machines whine on and down the driveway, which in
those days was dirt, though fine-packed. "Where's Leo?" Nessa
says, as she has said how many times since Leo, fresh from the
dead body of their mother, was placed in her arms, she then
younger than Leo is this day—"where's that child?" Though the
child is now seventeen.

Leo was born when their mother, the tiny, cramped farmwife
in the porch picture, was fifty years old. Six had already come
from that worn uterus, and when it was made to expel its one
sure beauty, the mother's heart had already failed. Nine pounds
nine, the record says, though in those days the doctors, all family
doctors proud at the christening, used to weigh their own hand
as well, for emphasis. The mother had brought one treasure of
her own to the gaunt house and its giant farmer—a set of
pointed coin-silver spoons, and when the baby was placed in
Nessa's arms to raise, she wondered whether she would get the
spoons too. Didn't. They were lost—which is what a family has
to say when there are eight women going over the bureau drawers. But she got everything else. And her doll-child, too, heavy as
it was.

Now, sir, let's not put on the farmhouse stuff too thick. Or the
old days either. There is that inside part of us which passes from
one to the other even in a city, or towns like this one. Cranberry
was the same. Then there are the outer things, which if you're
trying to live till your debentures come in, can change into the
new world they didn't warn you about. Good for the arteries, if
not for the soul; take it in stride. But to find where Leo is—at
the moment saying goodbye to the cats in the barn, though
that's not finding—you'll have to feel the changes between then
and now. Not just by reading the old newspapers, but as if you

were us then. What you'll have to know is how we named the nameless things. No doubt you think we mostly didn't, when it's just that what you and we won't name are different. In Leo's case, what you have to hold clear in your mind is the state of our household nakedness.

Like when Nessa married. In part because she was over twenty-five and that was nearing thirty. In part because her own father, that huge bulwark, had had to go into the nursing home for good. Leaving her and the lodger alone on the farm. A man of sixty, and of such substance that his lodger status had been all but forgotten. Now it would be revived. If he had been one of those poor neutrals that can dangle their lives out on a farm without notice—but he was a bachelor with as good a jowl and gold tie pin as any married man, only wedded to his business, which involved a lot of traveling. There the men would assume he took care of himself as regards women, even if he didn't talk of it—while their women would not think of it. Bachelors could be bachelors in those days, dividing off into the shy or the selfish, the rake or the mother-bound or the duty-held, plus a large class, wistfully envied by even the happy husbands—those single men who were consummately taking their time. The name for these was "latecomers." Grandfather, though tardier than most, had always been classed that way, and so it turned out. Perhaps he'd had Nessa in mind all along, only hadn't gotten around to her. And if the affair was a bit like uncle and niece by now, that had been heard of. There was no kinship involved, the porches said. And meanwhile, all that substance, most of it in paid-for land.

As for Nessa, so long tied to a father who demanded, and to the doll-baby, a big girl now, on whom she doted, and out on a farm, fine as it was, that isolated by its very acreage, who else could she have been waiting for? It was World War I, with the young men gone or going. On market days in town, she never let the child out of her sight; on the rare church Sundays when the father could be torn from his fields, no one else being allowed to drive the Buick, she dressed the child fit to kill, in bought clothes from Trenton. Some who knew no better even believed the child to be her own by-blow. Farm families, used to animals, often do that kind of taking in. But even in those rigorous times, when doting was less taken for granted than abuse, nobody wondered that Nessa spoiled Leo. Some persons, when spoiled, respond only by bringing light into dark corners. Even in Cranberry, where the state of being good, the onus of it and the rules for it, were thrashed out all the week and winnowed on Sunday, it was standard to remark that Leo, with whom old and young were so easy, must have been somebody's love child.

Only the animals gave Leo trouble. There are some people whose essence bothers them. Nothing so serious as souring the milk, but still a restlessness sweeping the barn when Leo's chore was to scrub the milking machines, a lack of empathy on the part of dogs. This is hard on a farm-born person, and even harder if you have to shift farms and go into service, as the sisters would have to do, if and when—since the only good brother was a dead hero—the farm was sold. But then, as is on record, the lodger bought it. And the marriage did. Though such things are not written, they can be found out.

On the night before the marriage, the sisters are sitting in the grand main bathroom—once their father's—that Leo will now no longer share. Share is not quite the word. When the two are here together the door is always open. While for the two, just to begin to use this bathroom once their father was dead had been an act of daring. Farmers, even rich ones, are not thought to have much latitude in these matters; however there are three toilets in this house, of ascending status and eras, plus three privies outside, all used in pecking order, up from farmhands, hired girls, and children, to family women and men. Children used the attic, with chores of chamberpots, until high school, when girls and boys paired off into rooms with washstands, the boys meanwhile using the toilet off the pantry downstairs, or one of the privies, girls going to the "other" bathroom upstairs, the women's—pleasant enough, with fake tiles added above its old wainscoting, but nothing like this marvel of oak and zinc. When their father became a widower it became his exclusively, as befitted a father with two girls left in the house. The boys never got a chance at its splendors, perhaps part of why they enlisted early.

But this is not the only protocol. There are no levels of undress in this house. Their mother was never seen without the housedress into which she was reborn from behind closed doors, at break of day. Going "down the hall" in bathrobes and slippers, one crept, carrying the bellyache or the secrets of puberty and the soap and towel for them. On lesser farms, foolish men in the fields sometimes had bare torsos, but not here, where even in a broiling August no man was seen in his undershirt—then called, with a dainty hiss as the women slapped the washboards, his "singlet." Home laundry was enormous, an everbearing crop that prospered along with the farm, as if, as they grew richer, their bodies must sink further out of sight.

At around seven years of age, children assumed care of themselves in such matters, as well as the guilt for any lapses. Boys were freer; they could bathe together even indoors, to save hot water. One was not frugal with one's girls, each of whom, bathing alone, might therefore come to think her body uniquely hers, until some accidental revelation. These of course occurred, and some by intent as well. But where by age ten a girl's own impulse was to slip her nightgown over her head before she let drop the bathtowel, it wasn't strange never to have seen a sister's nudity, and even dirty to do it. Everybody was communally shy, and approvedly so. And so it was in all of Cranberry, except maybe in summer, in the bogs.

No wonder that a baby given one to tend—to wipe its milky burps, support its frail neck with middle and forefinger, nip together its fat ankles while diapering and sprinkling talc on its pink curves, might turn one delirious with flesh—and responsibility. By age eight, late in-the-day but the sister is such a young mother, the child, by then lengthened into the gawky, is sent out to maintain itself among these privacies. From then on it will stretch itself into the adult like those lily bulbs one is told to keep in the dark until a certain day—by some plant nurseries guaranteed to be Easter.

No wonder—Leo. Whose Easter will not be early but late.

On Nessa's marriage eve, Leo is eleven going on twelve, and sitting on the edge of the oak housing that conceals the bathtub, dangling legs still black-stockinged though tall for that, the face longish too, and faithful as a pup's. Watching Nessa, who after a flushed, tearful hunt for her father's razor—vowing she wouldn't marry if she couldn't find it—is tremblingly shaving an armpit's virgin hair. The atmosphere is hushed, charged. The door is for once closed. Even though there is no one else in the house.

Are all the young now born without this delicacy for the body? Or in some do these shynesses still burn? Is there still innocence? Or was there, in your own time?

If so, then remember: the crude sob that innocence can give when it is broached.

"Was that somebody, Leo?"

No one. Since the engagement was announced two months ago the groom has quite properly not been resident. Leaving behind what had been his own quarters, a room at the farthest end of the front ell of the house, and a bathroom he himself had installed years back. These now will be for Leo, who tonight will move in. Leo was eager to do that last night, but Nessa said no. She wants all the formalities. A bride marrying an older man often does. The ritual holds one steady.

And note how Leo, the gawk, was the forward-looking one, even the adventurer. Always eager to drive to town, to try a new game, or order anything from astrology charts to ant houses to be sent through the post.

Hard to believe that it was Nessa who was shy.

She has finished one armpit when Leo says, "Can I do the other one?"

It is allowed. Nessa arches her neck and arm, as one does for the dressmaker. She is wearing a new camisole, one that will not go into the trousseau because in the making it has been botched. Under it her breasts are flattened by a cambric band.

The virgin fluffs of hair fall lightly on the camisole. The sisters, though they still hug like mother and child, have for years not been this intimate. The air in the room seems to them harshly ritual. It is erotic, but neither of them would know.

Finished, Leo sets the razor carefully on the washstand. Then —what is the child doing? Blowing in the armpit, at the last nicks of hair. Nessa, still raised her arm, holds still for it. It is like a soft nursing. Their eyes meet. They are saying goodbye.

Then Leo says: "Now, will you show me? The place where he will put in his gun?"

And is slapped, even before Nessa cries, "What are you talking about?"

And is answered, as Leo's tears sprout.

Now this was still wartime, remember? January 1918. Was it the Germans or us who had that cannon we called "Big Bertha"? Hard to remember, easy to tell you why. For a while, that was a joke name for the male organ. In school, notes were passed with crude drawings, in pencil only. Ink was too aboveboard. One such note had been slipped into a library book Leo had brought to the librarian's desk for stamp-out—and Leo, who hadn't a prayer as to what the note meant, was shamed by the librarian— who snatched up the note, rough-tongued the whole waiting line, and sent Leo away. Not saying why.

On a farm, animals tell you everything—except about humans. But farmhands josh among themselves when out of hearing. Ears can be sharpened for it, and chores sought. So Leo, who was not too welcome in the barn, came anyway, to set out the pans for the cats and learn what they could not tell.

"His Big Bertha," Leo said, standing tall, not to be humiliated again. "And will you put yours in him?"

There was actually laughter. Yes, Nessa did that—who wouldn't have? But there was no shaming. As for explanation, Nessa said hastily, "I'll show you in a book. It's time. But not tonight."

Understand, please. It was her wedding eve. She was book-enlightened. But neither had she herself ever seen a man's parts. The uncle lover and she had to date only kissed and pressed a bit. It was not to be brooded upon.

That faint roaring which begins all over the untutored body and has no part to cling to per se, or not yet—if she had at least hinted. Not explored—one can't expect that. To check up on a child's fantasy—unnatural. And perhaps all with Leo was still as it should have been? Or nearly?

We shall never know. If up in Boston ten years later they couldn't put a time or even a sure name to such a thing, who are we to?

That's easier. We are those who let it be. Which includes Leo.

The book is procured, sometime later. Not a very good one, no pictures, which by that time Nessa may have thought unnecessary, for Leo, spurred by injustice, will not go back to the old library but manages to get a card for the high school one—and why else would the child go all that way?

As time goes on, Nessa thinks that the heat of the married bedroom, and the arrival of the four children who so quickly come from it, must surely have informed. Meanwhile, Leo, who might have been jealous of them but is not, is like a second mother to the eldest boy, her favorite. Everybody's . . . Your father, girl.

Nor as Leo sails through high school, winning an honor or two, and even smarter than those signify, is there ever a shade of anything—offshade. Girls then are protected even from themselves, all down the line.

Once or twice Nessa senses—what does she sense? But she and Leo are no longer so close. And life is busy. Out where they are is too far for a child to have much company of its own, but an active farm in that part of Jersey is never dull; market days and fairs are now regularly attended and Leo is outgoing, liked by all who come and go. Wanted a heifer once, for the 4H competition, but was persuaded to the garden side instead—as was more seemly for girls in those days—and to a Home Ec course in making clothes. Running in to Nessa once to say: I want never again to have a boughten dress.

So—Leo, who at thirteen asked to be called Leona again, later plumping for Lee, then much in style, but finally falling back in with family habit, to Leo—was left to mature. "You have, haven't you?" Nessa said once, clutching her forehead as if she had forgotten a pie in the oven—"I gave you a belt for that. And you know where the napkins are." And Leo, almost fourteen, replied: "Not yet—" but shortly reported otherwise, in the proper muffled voice.

But the night before the wedding all Nessa said finally was "Come. Haven't shown you all my trousseau. Only the bed linens." So Leo was shown the slips with drawn work, the gown of pink satin bands alternating with see-through lace, and the pantaloons with open crotch. And was after all allowed to sleep that night in the new room. And the laundry labors went on.

So we left it. People are not animals.

So—some years down the line. Nessa's eldest, and only boy, is now past ten, already interested in the law and training himself in debate. Leo acts as his foil. A tall handsome pair with a family resemblance, they go everywhere together on their bikes, even once to Rutgers, to hear real debating teams, which the two never yet have—and to put their dreams for him in working order. After that, whenever they come back from hearing the real pros—college men—the dinner table crackles with argument snapped back and forth like rubber bands, and all according to rule. They were never to fight except once, when he wanted Leo to follow him at some sport into which a woman couldn't go. The time they heard the Cambridge-Oxford teams on the radio, they stayed up all night to hash it over afterward. If they could have, they'd have biked over there.

Then—Leo pedaled ahead of him. Into beauty. The Boston doctors took pictures later, front, back, and sideways, but medical photography, not for the other. Can't be described. Big eyes —but big feet and hands, too, not the ideal. Didn't matter, except to Leo, who said later that Garbo had made it all right for big feet but had done nothing for hands. A modest chest, for some tastes. But the expression was what did it, the whole carriage. And the neck. Some Greek statues have that front-swelling; Boston said nothing about that. You could look for hours at it and at Leo and not decide—and not know what you were not deciding—only happy with what you saw. Like when you hold a solid healthy baby to you, not too young to squeeze. And full of the power of the milk. As if you have the world all in one place. Or there is somewhere you can get it.

Well, that was a lot to put on a face or a person, and funny— Leo got mad if you did. Then along comes a man—blond piano-tuner's curls poking down his forehead, though he is a church organist—and Leo begins not to mind. Too weak-chested for the war, he'd been, but still with a look of being left over from it. And a name to match the curls. But the worst is—he comes from somewhere else.

One day Grandfather takes this man to his office in town, the land office, and swings his watch seal at him: "Why does a thirty-five-year-old man suddenly want to marry a teenage girl?" Nervy of him; nobody ever asked him beforehand about his intentions toward his own wife-to-be—but maybe that's why he would ask.

Because of the way Leo and I sing together—this man said. Tenor and second alto—pure gold.

Have to do more than sing, the old man said, and when he got home told Nessa that he didn't like the lay of the land. At twenty-one, Leo would have acres of it.

Now—land brokers have connections all over. Next Sunday dinner, when the couple asked to be engaged, or the man did, our grandfather says, in full sight of the table to which all family have been invited, even Nessa's black-sheep brother, "Do people have land in Illinois, Mr. Swazey?" Then the men, eyeing each other, go into the den to drink what isn't communion wine but from that bottle like a big yellow gem, pulled from under the rolltop desk. "Sorry this desk isn't a musical instrument," our grandfather says. "Or Mr. Swazey could play for us." They are all sipping. Then the black-sheep uncle, once one of those two spindly boys in the porch picture, undertakes the function he has been invited back home for. "Ever tune a woman, Swazey?"

Who knows what he himself thought he was? It's no sin to be skinny from music. Or to be skipped by a war. Or not to be from the town where you are new. And no, he never had. Been with a woman. But what that poor goaded man did was to try.

Leo never said where they went. But where else would it have been but the choir loft, after practice? It's a rich church, and a stingy one. No full-time sexton. Does it for a garden, plus other payment in kind, and holiday cash. The field land rolls almost to the back door. Men and tractors go home early, out a side road that doubles back. These two, Swazey and Leo, wouldn't have been the first. Close-fisted as the church was, it was always open for Christ.

And for Christ it was—the only one stern enough to watch real innocence, and in sight of His own organ pipes. Leo had on the green dress.

Always wore it when with me, saying it was her best—Swazey told them. But I couldn't get to her in it. And maybe neither of them quite wanted him to. But the dress was like a maze to which he had to find the key. In the dark. And by then they were both eager. Or so he swore. For Leo had made him strip.

See them, in all that their nakedness meant to them. Leo's hair, dressed in what then were called "book curls," came loose from its clasp, mingling with his, Leo's chest pressed to his narrower one, the hips spread like a swan under him, the long sinewy legs twining with his own. And moving on his face, the big hands, not unwomanly, now ungloved. They were not that hairy, nor was the rest.

If Swazey hadn't been such a ninny, we would know more. Had there been more than love play? He swore there had been a love act, and what he took for a normal one, for there was blood all right—when his hand, straying down Leo, encountered more than he had bargained for, and he sprang up with an awful cry. Strained my throat, he said. There was only the one light to turn on, above the bench in front of the organ panel. Leo lay staring up at him. "There's too much blood, I think." There was; Swazey's whole hand was smeared with it. But that was not what had affrighted him. Under the blood, to one side of what a woman should be—his phrase—there was more.

In his high school they had all known a boy whose testicles hadn't properly descended—and whose later marriage had been annulled. That was the closest he could come to what Leo was. Adding to it what his own blood still felt and would never forget: where he had been, if shallowly—its seam still seeping. "You're not normal," he said, hunting for his handkerchief. The shawl he'd given Leo as an engagement present did better, the paisley blending with the blood—which after all wasn't that much, to have had to ruin such a shawl for. But he never could stand the sight of blood.

Leo, so wrapped, looked up at him—he was still naked, you see. "Are you?" Leo said. "What's normal?"

Hear their voices in that choir—pure gold.

Could it have been that, if they had been left to themselves? Who knows what matches can be made—have ever been made —between those found to be too various?

But hush—all voices except from back then.

That night, those two got Leo safely home and in without notice, thanks to the green dress. Nessa, who always waited up but only called down the stairs, heard the other bathroom going for hours afterward but thought she knew why that might be and kept quiet, maybe with the inner wrench of mothers who think they know what has happened, only worrying the worst, or what to Nessa would be when it went on and on; had Leo had a miss? That bathroom had a woman-sound to it, Nessa said all those years later: you can always tell. Then, after a while, all that running water stopped.

But the next night, the young man came and asked to be "annulled." Asked for a "conference," mind you, with Nessa and the grandfather both, Leo being "requested" not to be present.

Oh, it was all quotes from whatever fancy etiquette books he got them from—anyway, a far cry from Sunday after-dinner whisky interrogations. These Jersey burghers, with their Frigidaire in the front room where a Hardman & Peck keyboard ought to have been—he had them right where he wanted them. It was quite an aria, what with his venom at his low reception in Cranberry, plus the insulting style that inferior-feeling persons take on when in the saddle—yet over it all, as he wrung his wrists and tossed his head almost awry, the caw of a bird rejected by the flock.

What he told them was that Leo was a man.

Now: the grandfather. Who dealt in land, yes—but those are often brokers in all trades, as opportunity calls. Regret the passing of the type, those bluff bachelor veterans of the all-night hotel and the poker antes as full of blue jokes as chips, who stroll into marriage with a background of pretty nearly everything. And die dancing. But still the kind to step out of his portrait at the right time.

"Now that's a fair question, Mr. Swazey," he said. "What is a man? What do they say to that in a town called Tophet, back in your native state of Illinois?"

Gone long since. Swallowed up in steel mills. Maybe never too sure itself of any other music. But as grandfather stepped forward, the young man stepped back.

Subsequently, it was announced that Mr. Ruskin Swazey, Fellow of the American Guild of Organists, had left our church to take on another not disclosed, the engagement to Leo being terminated by mutual consent. It may occur to some that he was paid to go quietly. Hard now to think of Nessa as not aware enough to ask, but she only grew money-wise after they moved.

The black-sheep brother did ask. "Pay off that pretty-boy?" He would have smelled more than a love-spat, and payoff was the way he lived, though restricting it to within the family. Hard to credit that he would imagine the real case. But he was good at suggesting what dirt he'd collected, without specifying. So in the end they had to pay *him*. They were used to it.

For many weeks Leo was not seen outside the house. Then

one day, some weeks after, Nessa and Leo left for the clinic in Boston, to be away some months. Long enough so that in later years the legend grew, as harmless ones will about spinsters who so love children, that Leo, whether or not undergoing psychological treatment, as was let out, had also had a bastard while there. Nobody really came to believe that, since anyone who knew Aunt Leona later knew she would never have left a child behind. Even a dead one—for that too was hinted—would have had its memory openly kept.

As for the clinic, it didn't do that much, old Nessa said. "They wrote Leo up." But Leo fell in love with Cambridge and all the learned societies with meetings free even to ladies, and a campus where even country people could walk. Meanwhile, the grandfather had been busy again at his brokerages, and it soon would be announced that Nessa had at last found—and had got him to buy her—the honeymoon house so long owed a younger wife. For this would be the story that would harden around that snob Nessa among all the farmwives she had abandoned for town elegance, and would outrage all the friends of such a fine but foolish gentleman. So Nessa assumed that burden too. If the iron did then enter her soul—as she admitted to her interlocutor in one of the ruby-glow, chalk-green restaurants where he was wooing her old age—"that's how old women like me are made."

But who had made the decision to go to Boston when Philadelphia was handier, or indeed to go anywhere medical; who had thought of it?

Leo had. "It was the only way to get the child downstairs," old Nessa said, the word "child" issuing like a bell from her wrinkled mouth. "After seven weeks."

For when they went upstairs the morning after the young man had had his conference, they found the bedroom locked and a note slipped from behind the door. Leo wished to be left alone for a while. Would they kindly leave supplies—food, and books to be asked for, in the bathroom adjoining, which had doors common to bedroom and hall, each lockable. "I do beg both your pardons," the note said. "But do not try the door. I ask you this with sincere love. If you do try, I must kill myself."

They did as asked. Ever after grateful that they had. For in those weeks Leo was allowed to forge the character such a creature might best have. It was like with the rain on the fields which they had kept but no longer farmed by the work of their own backs. One must have its double season, gloomy in rooms pent with damp, but outside fresh in the nostril.

And the character would be noble. Leo did not leave them to despair. Little notes came, assuring them of health, grateful for supplies, mentioning their quality. Trays, if not eaten bare, were never sent back without something gone. Far as they could tell the closed room remained as clean and sweet as the bathroom did. A note came—"if you hear pacing, it's just exercise." No pleas for something special or extra, as from the invalid or the wounded, ever came. Instead, they began to feel that they were helping, and this was a vindication of Nessa, who had set the tone—never to press. My grandfather's tact came more naturally. Such is ripeness.

About the third week, a note issued asking Leo's nephew to obtain a list of books. He ran all over for them, even to the state library. Where had Leo got the titles from? Some from the learned societies—Montesquieu, Pascal, and a man named Gide who might still be alive. Books telling you straight out what to think—or diarists deciding. He was instructed to ask the librarians as well, for other books on conduct. After this came a raft of those pocket-size Little Blue Books, which boiled it all down— and after that the dry-as-dust medical ones, heavy in his bike basket, for which permission had to be specially given. Young as he was, how had he got it?—for he had. And somewhere in all this, maybe reading behind Leo like a courier who dares to open the letter maybe containing his own destiny—did he discover what was wrong? One knows only his own later choices.

Once—he did tell Nessa—in an old copy of stories by a Gerard de Nerval, he came on a piece of paper tucked inside, with one word slashed across it: *No*, and he read the whole book to find out what Leo had said no to. Suicide.

And once, when he came in with an armful of books, Nessa said desperately to the ceiling, "Leo. Leo. Leo. What is it all for?" and stood there, wrung out.

"Leo's debating," he said.

"What?" his mother said. "Debating what?"

But he had already gone up the stairs.

I was more of a mother to Leo than to any of mine, old Nessa said.

And still later, once the grandfather was dead, had the awkwardness between him and Nessa come about because he was the only accomplice left?

He was only a boy, old Nessa said. Why did I harden against him? Because—I was hardening.

Then came Boston. For which trip Leo, thinner and with long hair ever after kept so, came down wearing such tweeds from the self-made trousseau as were suitable. At the bottom of the stairs they all kissed. As after a wedding. Leo would never offer to do so again, not even to kiss a child. But would gather other warmths—in the way that young persons do gather their talents.

When they came back from Boston the grandfather met them with the car and drove them home. The ice was thick on the front steps and the sky the color farmhouse sky gets that time of year, as if snow is its sole industry. The house, newly painted in chocolate and gamboge, sat there like a plucked chicken, with only its rhododendron bushes to hide it. Know how that plant's leaves hang down in points in winter? Leo touched one of them. "Don't despair." The grandfather, stomping in his arctics, found his key, and the ladies lifted their skirts and went in.

Inside, he blew his nose. Those big handkerchiefs of those days, they hid a lot of tender men. "Nessa, make us some tea. Leo, come into my den." Leo was easier with him than with me, old Nessa said. Leo was never as uneasy with men as women were trained to be. Nor as hard on them. And what was said in the den? "I've traveled," Leo said. That was all. But it was when

Leo went upstairs again—though they heard the door shut softly and not lock—that he said they must move. If only from under the increasing pile of books alone, for these were all over the upstairs hall now, some in neat piles to be returned, and some bought—though he didn't mind that. And he didn't expect this to stop.

But it was as if the books were hunting us up, finding us out, my grandfather said—and of course that's what Boston eventually did. "That's handled better in a town," he said. "A new town." And from there, the son must go away to school. "Where he can settle his own debate," the grandfather said to Nessa, with the sole fierceness she ever saw on him. "Listen up there" —he said then. "I believe Leo is opening the door."

And when Nessa went upstairs: behold—the door to Leo's room was open. That's how she thought of it: behold.

Since Leo's tenure, the lodger's room had gone through all the teenage stages. Then had come those storms of dressmaking which can crowd a young person with all the patchy fogs of ego —witness that girl who Nessa's son would one day marry. Now Leo's room had become the lodger's again—decent but anonymous. Only one book remained, one from their own Five Foot Shelf of the classics; Nessa couldn't see which one. Leo sat bent over it.

Nessa was about to tiptoe away when Leo's wonderful voice came out to her. If a trillium could speak, that would be it. The dark red ones.

"All clear."

Back there in the hayloft, the afternoon is fading.

Sheets of foolscap-size paper lie scattered around us. He gets it from a kind of homespun cooperative in Cornwall, he tells me. The oat-colored pages mean work to him wherever he is. My own long thoughts seem already to lie among them.

I'll make tea," he says. "Toilet's in the corner there. Ah, of course you know. And I have some stuff to eat, if you like. Or I could take you to dinner."

"Walsh's?"

We laugh. And I think, yes, we both come from the town. "No, we can't leave the farm," I say, standing at the door of the little latrine I know so well. "I mean—we haven't yet."

"You're an angel." He sees my scowl. "Sorry. I know you're not a child. I meant—thanks."

"I know I sometimes am. A child. What I can't stand are—"

"What?"

"Ordinary responses. I mean, token ones."

"It was just a phrase. I pick up language."

But we are both silenced.

You're an angel . . . *Be* an angel . . . Do we both hear the bobby-soxer's crowd?

"You may be too much of a sibyl," he says after a while. "To be a good actress."

He sees me droop. Arrogance deserts me fast. "It's just that in this case, I am your material. We are. My family."

Candor will always reach him.

"Go to the bathroom, for Chrissake," he says, and then— "Sorry."

We laugh. He and I are going to do some laughing, I think. But it will be only about us.

He must scrub the toilet himself. I like these small clean ones where one communes with the ammoniac human smell, with one's own. My house.

I am becoming part of the town. He thinks he's wooing me to do what he needs. But it's the town, all the people back there, back there in the secret life, among the old postcards and tatty lace. One doesn't expect to find a power there, sitting in that antique dark.

He and I share his cold cuts and beer. It's not hard to go back. It's not easy to go back.

Leo is in the deserted barn, with the cats. They've never minded her presence; cats don't care. They are circling for the milk that will never again be here. The herd has left, lowing its uneasiness, the farmhands too, touching their hats. "Bye, miss." The sun slants in everyone's eyes. "Bye."

An empty barn has no more revelations. But for the sake of those one has had here, one might come to say goodbye to it. After the dresses are packed. "Where is that child?" Nessa cries. "Ah, there you are."

Outside on the front lawn, the banker has come to say goodbye, and to see that the sellers take nothing that now belongs to him. Some people steal their own plants. The last of the machinery hobbles away. The first van of goods has gone on ahead. The sun clings like snuff to the women's dresses. Leo's is tobacco plaid. The odors are April lazy. People stand still.

Then my father comes out of the house in his new schoolblazer and cap, calling: "Leo's rocker is still upstairs. They left it."

"Told them to," Leo says. "I've rocked enough." The voice is rich and amused. Even in the later decline of Leo's beauty—the nose too noble, the neck cords tensed with song—people will remark on that voice's positive joy. And now that swelling throatline—was it Greek?—takes the sun like the plaid.

"If I'd thought—" says the banker, who is recently widowed, gazing at Leo and taking new note of Nessa and the grandfather —the gap in their ages. "Still—you all aren't going that *far*," he says. "And Miss Leo—" he says, turning "—you are to take any you want of your plants."

But Leo has fled.

"Far?" my grandfather says. "Far enough."

So they leave. Oh, spare me, my old grandmother will say at ninety, but in the end she will describe. How Leo gathered and gathered the plants until it was well past dusk, with each armful asking reassurance. Like a nun going into the convent, only here in reverse, Leo kept asking whether the world outside the farm would have the proper furnishment. Was there really an upstairs in the new house—above the upstairs? "It's a bankrupt's house—" my grandfather said "—it has everything."

"Does it," Leo says, suddenly calm, and absently adding on

another plant. "Then I must burn some things I still have in the cupboard up there. I was going to put them with the plants."

But on a farm one does not leave a fire burning. So my father brought down a portfolio, and a hamper. "Clothes I bought in Boston, Nessa—that you didn't know about. Except for the shoes, a monster mistake. But I'll take it all with me. As a lesson in extravagance." As this was said, Leo's voice failed. Theirs was not a world in which anything could be kept private, maybe all the more because of their lack of nakedness, and Nessa, who must have known about the clothes in the hamper—all male ones, began to bawl.

At that point—at that exact point, old Nessa said: Leo became my elder. Both of us accepting that. When you're the elder, it's easier to be brave, Leo said. But I would put it another way. Leo thought it was my turn to be young.

The portfolio? Letters, old Nessa said. In a house in town they can be burnt, even fifty years later. And were. The hamper? Here old Nessa's voice failed her, then found itself. Those, sir— articles of underwear and other garments—were in the bundles that went to the dump. The shoes, pairs and pairs of a high-buttoned style with the brand name Sorosis, Leo would wear for life.

And the life, loaded too into the van?

What a tale, the man in the restaurant says in spite of himself. Like a folktale.

We were not folksy, the old woman in the Stetson hat says. We were folk.

Sorry.

Accepted. One day—I may tell the girl, my son's daughter, about that life, the old woman says. But just now, we are leaving the farm.

My son—that girl's father—is leaning on the porch-rail, picking at his blazer buttons, which he hates. He has been hating a lot lately. "Our bikes—" he says. "Leo's and mine. There's no real room for them. Why don't we ride behind and follow you?"

Two British Raleighs, the pride of his existence, formerly. "And the plants will bruise them."

Everybody laughs, even Leo, who quickly adds, "It's miles and miles, yes, but he and I have done more: let us try."

So we're ready, but no one moves, even the grandfather. Those cows knew, Nessa said. Potato futures are down, though, her husband says, rubbing the grizzle at the back of his neck. Potatoes—the boy says; at school, that's what I miss the most. No one laughs, all their four necks hunched out, shoulder to shoulder. You could paint them, hankering face against hankering face, locked toward that buff-colored crop-lined horizon, sealing now with night.

"Your window's open, Leo," the grandfather says. "Somebody go close it."

"Let Mason close it," Nessa says. That was the banker. "Let him try."

The wind whips the curtain out. Nothing funny about that; there's often a night wind.

"Nessa—we're all trying," the grandfather says. A man without temper. A rock to lean on. Yet one needs more.

"Somebody's still there," the boy says. "Looks like somebody's still there."

"Does so," his father says, and climbs in the second van.

Driving down the road to the highway, they have to pass the entire front of their house, the van with the two in its cabin crawling heavily, the two bikes wheeling behind.

Out on the highway, the house fronts them again, following as it can. It understands why they are leaving, and is flying a white flag for surrender, nobody will say whose. Somebody's image is still in possession there. As the four faces recede: land broker husband, wife and sister, boy nephew, Leo—or grandfather, grandmother, my father-to-be, and Leo—Aunt Leona, each face sees who has been left there, each in its own way.

Upstairs, in the lodger's room, the androgyne rocks, debating what to be.

"*He* was a great actor—Leo." Craig Towle got up to turn on the desk lamp. The prosaic flooded in and retreated. It would not dare the two of us, I remember thinking—a young judgment.

"I assume you know the life—Leo's outer life," he said. "The eccentricities a whole town was made to accept. The kindness that flowed."

I *pre*-sume, was what was said down home. Taking for granted that a life, outer or inner, was not that easy to get to. *We* were the actors; couldn't he see that? The kindness was what was real.

"Ever see his tombstone?" Towle said. "Worth a trip."

I hadn't. But when I went, I would go alone. And I would be taking the part for Leo's sake as well as for myself. How black the window was now, how dark the town. The moon would rise over Towle's final word on us, but not without me.

"*She*—" I said, rearing my long neck at him, and scuffing the place on the floor where a moth had been. "She."

"I want this room to shine for you," Mrs. Evams said. "Yet I want it to blaze." She didn't have to tell me why. We were in their library, with all the windows that faced our old house—now the Walshes'—opened wide. I wondered though, what vision of light was behind that high, polished forehead, what concept possible only to the blind.

To attain it she had gone to the local rabbi and asked to borrow every branched candlestick he knew of in his community, then had ordered dozens of natural beeswax candles from an up-country apiary. The five thousand books had been cleaned by a corps of their students, who had been able to find scarcely a speck of the dust she had said she smelled. Two of them, two young men in their best jackets, now stood by, holding candle-snuffers for any emergency, and flanked by bins for resupply. She had wanted no girls, because one could never be sure what girls would wear. The two boys had been chosen in part for their jackets, which she had made them describe. One in a woolly brown that blended him with the leather bindings, one in sharp white, they did look like acolytes. One of them was sighted, for safety's sake. Both were smiling.

I had given up counting the candles, all honeycomb patterned and twisted to a point that burned true even at eleven in the morning. Luckily the day was as soft as taffy waiting to be pulled. Brides' weather, Etsuko had said, coming in to wake me, who had never had to be waked before—and adding hastily that this was a good omen too. She always had a polite one handy, often drawing out a wrinkled slip of rice paper to confirm it, from somewhere in her invisibly seamed garments. But this omen I felt had been improvised.

I was already wearing the biscuit-colored dress she had made to my design from yardage bought years back by my mother to take down to Miss DeVore but never used, and now cast into a plain shift banded low at the waist, and with an irregular drift of skirt, of a kind I still wear. The wedding was not to be until four, but I had dressed early—for the candles.

"Does it shine?" Mrs. Evams said, facing the windows, her arm at my waist, weightless but unprecedently there. "Does it—do that?"

Across the street at the Walshes' a smart gray van from Trenton, there when I arrived, was now being emptied by a uniformed crew of two who were delivering unidentifiable gear inside. Now and then there were nervous shadows at the Walshes' windows. Perhaps they were planning a rival party. No one was to come here except family.

Mr. Evams, suddenly behind us with the quiet footfall practiced in this house, had heard her question. I could feel that he knew of the activity across the way, but glancing sidelong at his face—at the aquiline nostrils expanding, and the wise eyes, blank with infinities always changing, I saw that I was not to signal to her of whatever, high up on her own alp of vision, she hadn't sensed.

I would miss the cues gathered for me in this place, more than I knew how to say.

"The room blazes," I said. "And it shines."

At four, Mr. Evams, wearing a surplice, grouped us around the oak table at which students always stood in a body for the more difficult or unique instruction. On it lay the ordinary braille Bible always there. Today, another book lay beside it. I should have recognized it, but trembling, I was noting the order in which he had placed us, for no one ever left this table without turning to fingertip the face on one's left, the face on one's right. And I hadn't yet told anyone what I was going to do.

Mr. Evams had made a masterly dinner party of us. Placing himself at the head of the table between bride and groom, so as to conduct the service, which was to be as agreed, a civil one, he had put my father on my right, in effect to give me away, though the service would not press him to do so. Next after where Bill would be on my left, came my mother, after her Mr. Peralho, surely now family, and as the staff she often leaned on when awake. At his left was Tim, at once placated by this, then my grandmother, who would want him next to her, then Watanabe, whom she would want also. Etsuko, as his spouse, came next, though on his left. Her delicate scent and graces would soothe Mrs. Evams, by etiquette on my father's right.

And so we come round again to the bride, the minister—and the groom, entered last, as grooms when flustered sometimes do. He was wearing his best, a jacket I could see my father thought surprisingly decent, not knowing it had been left behind by the former owner of the New York pad, to whose pleas to send it out to him Bill had responded, "Should *you* turn out to be somebody, I will." The style of that had pleased me; he might still be Bill Wetmore. But was that why I was marrying?

As we settled in, my mother reached for her purse and a slight pressure went round the table. To watch her sip from the flask now always with her—given her by Mr. Peralho, who swore it held only fruit juices—was still not comfortable to watch, for by this time we knew she slept even when seemingly awake and with us. Now and then a remark would escape her, she always staring at the ground as it did so, and on occasion lifting the sole of a shoe to look there, as if she walked on needles, always self-directed, one of which had pierced its way up.

Mr. Peralho had formed the habit of reaching for the hand in the purse and kissing it to quiet it, but today he kept still, his mismatched eyes almost crossing, in evident prayer that wedding manners would sustain her. The hand came out with one of her lavender lozenges.

Next to Peralho, Tim fluttered up at him, seductive, anguished and smart-alecky, all at once. I knew how much it was costing him to blurt nothing. Across from me, was even my grandmother—having noted my dress—stretching her lips in approbation? Etsuko, in bliss over the dress, Watanabe holding the printed cotton foldover bag carried by men in his home city, from which he intended to scatter a ritual something, my two dear blind guides—and even my father, who this morning had given me a check, muttering: "Something blue—put it in your stocking," and adding that it came from the sale of his lawbooks, as if nothing less would do—how did I know what all of them were thinking? Was this the common lot of brides?

Across from me, Mr. Peralho was checking our circle with his keen, flawed glance. I liked him more and more. Last night he had come to me to volunteer not to be present, as not being family. The two gentlemen at the farm weren't coming either, he said; I guessed he had so persuaded them. "No," I had answered, "you must come." This is our daughter, he had said to those two at the farm that day, with his one off-color eye hopefully marking it, though he knew I was not that and never would be. The other eye, unflawed, must know as much about acceptance as a man could. Today he reminded me of the poll-watchers at election time. Nothing partisan, for or against a particular candidate, can be said within so many feet of an election booth —or of this oak table. But never glancing at any of us too long, was he letting me know he was counting the vote?

Mr. Evams was about to begin. Though he was to marry us in his capacity as a justice of the peace rather than as a minister, he had indicated he would not do so without homily: "A few tags."

Yearning not to hear that man straddle what he could not approve, or pretend to be as blind as the sighted—and do all this for me, I turned to my brother, whose verdict I knew already, its blue glare fixed on Bill. Once he had come upon Bill and me scuffling in the back hall where my grandmother's house divided, a prosy arena where snowboots could walk in and slickers hung. Hatracks make me horny, Bill had been growling, clasping me wetly. Now I've got you where I want you. "No you haven't," Tim had said from behind us in his bow-tie voice. "You've just got yourself where you want to be." And flinging up his hat, which had lodged like a goal-shot on the hatrack's top hook, he had passed us by.

"Well——!" my grandmother said now, in the voice that knows itself to be a yea-sayer. I dared not trust that voice, even though I knew how it had come to be.

I could trust Knobby, but he would not speak. Though if that bag of his could have held something even better than a finger-bowl to show up the groom with, it would have.

Etsuko, mother of geishas—for by now we knew there were two—would always cancel out his vote.

And why anyway had I left the counting until now?

Bill, studying the grain of the table, had his drawing hand in his trouser pocket, where it would be abortively moving . . . "Have to be careful in buses, I do. Take me for a pervert. Never sit next to a girl, I don't. Only next to you." The groom. Who will stand there totting up his own charms and other scores the way smart people do crossword puzzles—in order to keep other conundrums at bay?

My father is the only one looking straight at me, clearly thralled in a hot attendance he sees he should have given me sooner. But that is all he will give me. Plus something blue. He is like me—but in what way?

And Mr. Evams has not begun. When the blind won't look at you, you have done something bad. Or you have not done what you should.

"The faucet!" Mrs. Evams cried in sudden agony. Releasing us.

One of the candle boys ran over to the tap where we students washed our hands before braille, and shut it tight—and Mr. Evams began.

Though he goes on inexorably with his pre-marriage sermon, I do not hear it, nor will I ever be able to recall more than the edge of what he said. Perhaps he counted on that. For down the arc of the table my mother, the forgettable, has raised her head, intent on the big double door to the corridor, which creaks lightly, as if someone waits there.

It is only Terence, the Evamses' Sheltie. Not trained to be a Seeing Eye dog, but sired by and brought up with the one Mrs. Evams had used early on, he has learned his fierce obligations anyway, waiting to be admitted at every room where she is engaged with people, always entering any classroom a half-second before she is done. He will know when instruction is over.

My mother stands up. Etsuko has dressed her cannily, not too elegant, one dull jewel. Except for the turban she always wears, which keeps her out of all eras and frames the two fever-spots of the cheekbones, she looks like the mother of the bride. Perhaps that has cued her sufficient strength to come down the table to me on her own. Mr. Evams's skein of words falls silent. She puts her arms around me. They were always long enough. "He's come for *you* this time, hasn't he. When I saw you go off with him I knew he would." I whispered back that it was only Terence, that I could see his muzzle through the crack of the door. But she knew better. "No, you know too much. Do what you must. But be careful." We might have been mother and girl on the train again, putting the flats of Jersey behind us—and for a minute we were. She gave me a squeeze. "You never did like chocolate." Then, still holding me, she raised her head to the rest of the table, spellbound there. "I see it all from my window. It's just that I cannot always wake."

Still in her arms, I felt the shiver she said that with, pushing me to look out these windows, across the street to our old house —and I saw what the Walshes had done. They had given in. Heavy drapes, sculptured like marble, now blocked ground floor and landing; upstairs, every break in the façade had been packed with lace. They had curtained the whole house. It's only what a town does, of course, even if the Walshes had had it done tighter than the street had ever seen. "Yes, tell them—" she said. "For me too. Tell it all to stop."

The candles helped persuade me, pulsing their gold. There should be candles upstairs here at the Evamses too, around that cameo bed—attesting to what ought to be. Behind us all, the tap rill-rilled. Across the way, my mother came to a college party in a dress that crackled compliantly with death, and won a strange groom, who as a boy had kept snapping a picture with nothing in it except two bikes. On the third floor of a house much like this one and the one across the way, my grandmother keeps a companion. In a gentleman's farmhouse, kitchen boy now quarrels with garden boy over who loves who—but in the grain of a past that maybe resides there yet—maybe in the old horsehair plaster of the walls, maybe in the night creaks an old barn gives forth like coarse conversation—a rocking chair rocks, debating. I have obligations to all of them.

"I can't marry anyone right now. Bill—if you can wait, one day I will."

Etsuko, never too stunned for ritual, makes a wavering Japanese sound.

I face my father first, because of those two bikes that pedaled steadfast all the way here. "I've been given the role of Leo, in Craig Towle's play."

And Bill? Wild for an adversary, he peeled off his filched jacket and flung it behind him. Then he fled.

My brother's jeering *"He'll* wait" followed him.

"That was unkind," Mr. Peralho said. "But perhaps too cowardly slow to be heard. I better go after him. Perhaps to order a picture. Perhaps—one of you. Come along." Tim followed him.

"Tim has the sweetest tooth of all—" my mother's whisper came. "But I couldn't foster it." Then she looked down at her shoe, and Etsuko and Watanabe, who knew the signs, led her away.

My grandmother came toward me. "When you want to come to the third floor, you are welcome."

My eyes filled. So did hers. She turned to my father. "Take me to dinner. In my own house."

He put his arms around me. I was a little taller than him now. The time for looking at each other eye to eye had passed without our ever knowing. I put my head on his shoulder. What he said came to me in vibration. "I am glad that you were born."

Terence, the Sheltie, came through the door for his charge. Mrs. Evams, making a sign to the candle boys, went out with him.

"They're all leaving me," I said. "Why does it feel so good?"

"They're wedding each other," Mr. Evams said. "You've made that possible."

The acolytes were putting out the candles one by one. They had a system good to watch too, the blind one first, following the heat of his hand in order to quench a candle, the one who could see following him to the next. When all were quenched, they left.

"Are we in shadow?" Mr. Evams asked.

I nodded.

He smiled. "Thank you. I would marry you myself, if your ears were not so jug. But I have a present for you." He led me to the table. "For not having made me complete that service."

He was giving me the Ronsard, and I knew why.

I was the beginning animal.

That was the beginning of how I have come to live in my house. I had never lived in one that did not have strong reasons for me and mine being there. People like me will always find reasons for why they must domicile themselves in a place, or even doom themselves to it.

In a town like ours, the merely expedient—to work in the hayloft, with Towle a few easy doors down the Row from me, was also the most troublesome. I wanted that too. I wanted the town as audience to what it would immediately conceive to be corrupt, and I knew to be pure—or professional. Perhaps I needed their help to keep it that way. But of this I was still ignorant. Can you remember that bracing joy—of being ignorant?

So for three months Towle and I would spend every afternoon that I wasn't at school in the loft there, in slavishly sexual concentration—and with never a touch. For me it was all for Leo, for him the play—on which he talked business with a vigor that shocked me. To me "business" was the theater's compelling slang word for the business of life as transacted on stage. I was surprised to find that even a man like him would have to hunt backers. "Oh, they'll listen." No worry about that—and their agents would ploy. But getting up the ante for a play like this one wouldn't be easy; some money would be repelled. And he wasn't having a star. It might have been hard to find one. "Though I didn't choose you because of that." Nor for the brief news value in an untried actress, nor worse—for my family connection with the play. Or worst, even in my possible bodily connection with the part. Though many would slyly think so. Until they *saw*—he said—and again that beam of light went through me. To be seen *being*—the thrill that cauterized any wounds I had.

Often we went into the city together on the morning train. I think now of the poker players behind us, in those first weeks their ears growing through their hats, and not a card heard to drop—as he and I discussed the Boston clinic's report on Leo. An anciently evasive essay, as much mumbled as written, its language reminded him of the gothic romances of its day. "More monkish horror than medicine." The doctors had vacillated over what to record, and while satisfying themselves of the situation had decided that in the case of a living person, "non-concealment" would cast "contumely" on the patient—and even disbelief on them.

Our own argument was always the same. "She urinated as a woman," I said, "I feel sure of it." Behind us, a chip was at last tossed into the pot; perhaps they were getting used to us. But when he answered: "Remember when they were in the church— he must have erected as a man," the players got up and moved from their own consecrated spot. After that, we sat at the car's end in the seat where the conductor kept his supplies. In that seat, we settled it that part of Leo's organs must have been vestigial; we would never know which.

Later still, and not on the train, I told him what I would and would not ask my grandmother. "She would never have seen Leo in the nude since Leo's puberty." But at the hotel where they stayed in Boston?

I searched among the small authorities that with practice seemed to be coming to me the way the fingers acquire thimblework. I don't believe in spirits. But spirit transmits. "They wouldn't have shared a room together. But I'll ask." And I would also ask her—because I thought I already knew the answer—to describe that lovely babe at birth. I would ask anything that gave my grandmother pleasure, or relief—no more. I thought of her now as an old tree transplanted, its dreams and comportment still on the farm into which I had projected myself by inheritance—where he could only research. He and I were changing seats even with respect to the two of us. But he knew that sooner than I.

"I won't press you to ask—"

"My father? No. Don't." But in my researches, at night before I went to sleep, I did ask him, and slowly he was telling me.

When we actually met it would be at Mr. Peralho's apartment in town, where he spent much of his time. Peralho had gone back to Rio, Tim being at Harvard at last—on probation. My father was staying on to help, in what we all knew was a matter of Tim's conduct. My mother was not now a consideration, or rather to us a permanent one, not subject to change.

Meanwhile, in the loft, where the town surely imagined me in all the carnal positions a girl and her mother's lover would try, I was walking back and forth as Leo would, limbs hung so, arms held thus, and trying never to posture. I no longer thought of it as a role in a play, his play. Our practice *was* Leo, coming alive between Towle and me.

The school was partially taken into our confidence. The voice coach, accepting the challenge in his own high decibel, was acquainting me with recitative, in a range from falsetto through countertenor to second alto, to light baritone; and one day, among a pile of old discs—Peter Pears, Bidú Sayão, Kathleen Ferrier, I found the voice in which I could sing—for four words only—but perhaps could learn to sing-speak in: the dark alto vehicle of Rose Bampton, long before she made herself suffer upscale into soprano—singing *O, rest in the Lord*. The next phrase—*rest patiently in Him*—I could muster, though not as well.

Miss Pevsner, the drama coach, not confided in, was highly allusive in the Strindberg style. After her class, which Towle sometimes came to watch as he did the voice class, he and I could laugh, our sole time to, and even that helped, for I began to wonder at Leo's own reliefs—what had been broad enough, or grotesque enough to make a Leo laugh?

"Found that out yet?" he said one day in the loft, at the end of a long afternoon. Each day I reported to him on my outside labors, if not on all my thoughts. My grandmother was away at her one indulgence, a summer stint at Chautauqua, taking the Austrian couple along "because the lectures will help them with their English." After forty years in this country!—but both she and they had to have an excuse for her charity. I was glad of the delay. Over the weekend I had been to see Knobby and Etsuko. She had shown me a picture-book, lent by the ballet niece, on the Japanese male actors who played women. She had charmingly refused to let herself understand why Leo's case might not be covered by such a switch, I told Towle, and miming, I began to play Etsuko in Kabuki gesture, until warned by his glance. I had better play no one but Leo. For the time being, I must be no one else.

At the moment I was having tea with gloves on, in an effort to find out why Leo might have worn them so often. I took them off. Absurd. But Leo would not have been a fool. Then why? In the pictures the hands were well formed, free of rash and not really large enough to be hidden either for vanity's sake, or for maidenliness. Neither of which, I decided, Leo had suffered from. But those hands would have had their own gestures—perhaps unique? Gloves of thin kid, like these found in a thrift shop, would restrain them. I flexed my fingers. "At times maybe one would simply want relief—from being reminded. Of what one was." Whatever that had been.

He was always as attentive to these revelations as if he were at a seance. Or as a lover might watch one disrobe. Or might listen —the day beforehand—to one's dreams? Though I knew he stared at me, I had never caught him at it.

"What Leo laughed at." I made it a statement, not a question —as if like all these matters, it was there to be found, a jewel mislaid but somewhere safe. "Maybe. I didn't find it though. Knobby did."

"Oh, you talked to Watanabe—good girl. No telling what Nessa might have let fall—or he's picked up."

He spoke so idly. I understand artists' casualness with their own work. The way a sculptor, showing the studio, will cuff a statue the way a father cuffs a child. Roughing up what no one else must. But Towle, when offhand, unnerved me, unable as I was to tell where "the work" left off and he began.

"I speak to no one about Leo but you," I said fiercely. "No one else." Then I caught his stare. I had become easy with his smell, heady but now not dizzying. The eyes, brown-pupiled but no longer liquid with youth, were like a fence, scarcely divided by the nose. Out of his presence one thought of the nose as a hook; returning, one saw that it sloped. Of course one doesn't see a body's whole import in its eyes. But one may see the flicker behind the fence, or the undisturbed brown. I thought to myself: in him the idea of only one other besides oneself, of that exclusivity between two people—one for one—which my small world and many books had taught me to long for—is not there, is simply not there.

"We'd been making cookies," I said shakily, and certainly in my own voice. I had wanted to do even that in the persona of Leo. Knobby and I were alone, he watching quietly; I had told him nothing. Just as I needed the sieve, he reached not into the drawer but in a cabinet above, on the side where the set of brown-black pottery dishes was kept, and brought down an odd-shaped one from a corner that held strainers, tongs, and other kitchenware, all, as I now saw, with the pewtery shine of old implements. "The best," he said. "Make the flour like silk." He knows, I thought; Knobby understands what I am doing. This stretching back to be another person, in order to honor them. That natural tribute to one's ancestors, which one performs time after time in daily life.

"Then, all of a sudden, we had this big plate of cookies. And nobody to come for them. And Knobby said: 'Children should be coming for them. Our family house Kamikura, they come like clockwork.' " He said "crockwork," but I had long since stopped grinning at his accent or his specially trotted out phrases. "Knobby wanted children, you know. But Etsuko's turned out to be too old. And then he said, 'Children are monsters. Dal-uh-ring monsters. With them one can laugh.' "

We two were quiet. As at each of these discoveries when they rang true. It's a solemn thing to reconstruct a life. This was why in spite of all, I could approve of him and maybe even why—as the town became aware of what we were up to—it let us alone. I would not know Mr. Evams's role there for a long time.

"I'll visit the day nurseries," I said. "As Leo did. Everybody thinks they know what it is to be a child. Especially someone my age. But I'll go."

I finished the tea, bare-armed. Arms in long gloves move differently at the elbow, protected as they are from excessive gesture—was that it? But which such gestures, of which sex, would a Leo have been seeking protection from? Even to the oddity of wearing gloves inside the house. And when one wore them, in or out, did one or did one not touch the face? "Makeup," I said. "Are we back to that?"

Would the Leo I was feeling my way toward have worn it? I felt not, but Towle maintained this might be because I didn't wear it myself, except when acting. "For you it means the stage," he had said. "Not what women feel they have to do." The play, as so far shown me, had had a scene in which Leo, as Aunt Leona, returns to the church after years of avoidance, wearing too much rouge. Painful—but too beautifully written, he said, and had discarded it.

It still amazed me, that in his mind the scenes changed from day to day, and might do so up to dress rehearsal and even after. I had thought that somebody as eminent as he wouldn't do that, or have to.

"May I never be—that eminent."

I wasn't too stupid to see that my use of the word amused him. But I was still to learn that he was leading me through a part, more than I would ever lead him toward his play.

Only yesterday I had challenged him—did he really know what he wanted his play to be? "Of course," he said, quick, "I want it to have—a haunting provincialism." I saw that he both grudged and loved saying that. Then he lowered his head, to slap me down for it. At these times the nose has a definite hook. "Exactly like you."

"Look, Towle, don't stare," I said now. "It puts me off."

"Good voice, that—" he said at once. "Make note of it."

I did, and of how it had come without thinking.

"Does it scare you?" he said. "To be becoming someone else?"

I nodded. "But not enough."

I rubbed my face with my hands—it hadn't changed. Leo would have had no beard, we had agreed, but I was becoming ashamed of our practice, so mincingly literal. I stared at my palms. The children. Eyes like magnifying glasses spying at the pores of adult flesh. Luray Walsh's mouth corners, for instance—how repellent their thick pink, wet with beads of saliva, had been to me when I was eight, the year the Walshes came to town. Younger children see even closer, with the same gaze—open to first principles—that they give to the Silly Putty in its staple primary colors and to the building blocks.

"The children—" I cried, "could Leo have worn the gloves for them? Maybe not to touch them." Not to repel. The conscious monster, protecting what it loved. "Oh that would be—" I couldn't find a word. "Oh, how can I know, at my age, how Leo felt about them?" The loft echoed. "How anyone does," I said, in my own voice. That was the key. In what I said—and in how I said it, both. But I wasn't ready to know that yet.

He knelt to pick up a piece of paper, one of his everlasting notes to himself. "What we're doing—it's for real but also *not* for real—can't you learn that?" In his cool distaste, I heard that I had become too partisan. Was he mulling whether he would have me in his play after all? Deciding that what we had done here was about all the use I would ever be to him?

He stood up and went to his desk, fingering the big pile of script, of which he had fed me only a scene here and there. "Yes, the children. That will be it." He didn't mean how it had been for Leo, but how it would be for him. He handed me one of the scripts. The pile, always changing, had never been so high. "So you too have come to that conclusion. Good girl."

He dropped to his haunches, in front of me—later I would note how he always did that when explaining a part. "Here. Time you read it, began learning your lines. As well as learning how I may change them." He stood up over me. "Going out to get us some dinner. Might have a few drinks on the way. Are you too hungry? No? Good." Climbing down the ladder which led up here, he still faced me. "Read between the lines, remember? Not just bung on."

"That's unworthy of you," I called after him. "But teaching corrupts."

The play in that version began in Boston, with Nessa and Leo walking on the Common. The hospital and the hated doctors one never saw, except as a background chorale, in half-dark. Though the two walkers never left the stage, there were flashbacks. One to Nessa's wedding eve, not confined to that bathroom but including it. One to the time when she first held the babe in her arms. The order of these scenes was not yet certain. There was also a flash of the farmhands in the barn—though Nessa was there too. The two main characters, Nessa and Leo, were sometimes there in the flesh, sometimes only in the spirit, and all variations of this were played on. This he called spirit-shading, and I supposed it to be his method—he replying when I said this, that yes, he supposed so, since the method had been around since the millennium.

He didn't like the analytics our school so fostered. Even with only those two walking, his stage was often densely packed, but the shadings were never intentionally cloudy. "I write to make things clear," he said, "and don't you forget it."

The second act was all Leo's affair with a man, one not so silly as Ruskin Swazey. "I think he was not silly," Towle said. But the scene in the church was there. It was to hang in the mind, the directions to the stage designer said, "like a postcard painted by Raphael."

There were no suggestions as yet to the actors.

I hadn't got to the last act, when he was back.

He fended off what I was full of and about to say. "Pizza? Or quiche?" He always brought both, as well as other delicatessen, laying out the food and beer like a picnic.

"I never thought Nessa would actually be in it," I said. "Does she know?"

"Eat."

I was hungry, with an anger against him that added zest. All through our association he would play on that anger.

"She does and she doesn't know," he said then. "It won't matter." He put out a restraining hand. "Come come. It would matter to your grandmother as you know her, maybe. But not to Nessa. Or not that much. And they both want the same thing." He reached for his beer. Not a stage pause. In his own life he never acted; he was one of the few people I could trust not to be theatrical. My father was another.

"She wants Leo to live," he said. "For as long as *she* does."

I was near tears. Such violations were new to me.

"Eat."

I did; my appetite these days was huge. I thought again of prisoners. As I was to always to do, when I must act at someone else's behest counter to my own. "The lines. They're—kind of primitive. Some—are they to be read double? As if the character wouldn't know all it's saying?" It was a relief to call Leo the character. I began doing so that night.

"Read those plain," he said harshly. "Leo would know everything."

And there we utterly agreed.

When we'd finished, he said: "See you haven't read the last part. Go ahead. I'll nap." He stretched out on the couch. He often did that. I no longer stole secret looks at him, as one does at a male sleeping. He was no longer that to me, I thought.

I bent to the playscript. Up to now it had been all continuity —a flow. But in this final section, not an act in the usual sense, more a charade, the actors spoke in stylized cries, as if in echoes of an old theater craft that everybody might have forgotten. The stage was filled with them—with the town. And children were everywhere—urged away from hot pokers and sneaking cold biscuit, kneeled to and scooped up, and fed warm cake. And all, all were imaginary. Not only to Leo. Spoken to, their answers could not be heard, except at the end, when Leo did hear one of them, who emerged into the real. A boy of fourteen, speaking in low peroration.

I saw how heartrending that could be—or could be played— the two, he and Leo across the stage from one another, separated by that dumb throng of the imaginary.

But all of the scene was spoiled for me, spoiled, spoiled—by the presence of the town girl—she the silly essence of all those small-town girls whom banking money or land money would send into the world to boarding schools, only to come back—and in physique like those bow-mouthed, frill-necked cloth dolls that the divas and housewives of Leo's era had had in their bedrooms. A girl Leo now loved. And more imaginary—I thought scornfully—than any of the throng.

Towle was smiling. When I said nothing, he yawned. "We could have production money now. And dates. And two winners willing and eager to sign for the girl. One from Hollywood—who can act up a storm, by the way. The other, from Broadway via Park Avenue, doesn't have to. She could lisp that part in her sleep."

"But what's she doing there!" A girl—such as my mother might have been—at the time.

"I knew how you would feel."

"I hate it. It's not true."

"For Leo? Why not true for him?"

"Her!"

We were both standing now. Even if he had been as tall as me, we would never see eye to eye. Why must I always seek that, with men especially? Whereas with women—Etsuko, my mother, even my grandmother, I had a warm tolerance for their variation, and with my girl classmates could argue amicably half the night? Because we already had a common ground?

And the play's end—that boy, leaning against the two bikes. How did Towle dare?

"I'm going to see my father."

His eyelids flickered. "So I'd hoped."

Mr. Peralho's flat was in one of those large apartment buildings on Cannon Place, where my father said old money on the run came up against new.

"Slightly on the run," he added, looking out with me on the East River below. "Nothing serious."

The river, with so little now of the gear and traffic of a live waterway, must be only a print of its former self, and on the run too. To a gelatinous shoreline not far enough across, and holding almost still, mere window bric-a-brac for buildings such as the one in which we were. Massed together over the East River Drive, all on one side, these apartment houses gave off a gray money-light. Flowers dotted them, at closed casements. Terraces did not flaunt but hid. The windowsills here were lined with plants inside the panes. Across the water a sign said PEARLWICK HAMPERS, a vista from a factory fairy tale. "These places seem to me like hampers for *people*," I said.

I had mostly been asking my father mild questions since I got there, to get him used to them. When talking of money, older people, men particularly, are always glad to instruct.

"Well, the florists' bills on this side are certainly large," he said. He had already told me that the West Side, where our school was located, was the side of the city where people thought about money even if they had it; the East Side was where it was kept. As I would see if I came to live here during the play.

"Is Mr. Peralho's money old or new?"

"Old. And not on the run."

"He's kind."

"I'm glad you see that."

"I like him a lot. Or else I couldn't stay here."

"Neither could I," my father said.

The flat was sleek but shallow, scattered with photographs artistically arranged, even packed with them, in the same style as the sitting rooms of the two gentlemen at the farm, who had so keenly enjoyed naming the originals. My father had made no move to, here.

I went to a good-size study of a man, hung on one wall. "I seem to know that face."

"T. S. Eliot? Yes, the resemblance was remarkable. Leslie himself often said, 'I look like that poet with the large but weak nose.'" My father's mouth folded inward, as happens when people quote the dead.

"Was *he* a poet?"

"He played bridge for a living. On ocean liners, when he was young. Later—here. Those he won from helped him invest. It was nothing to them." My father inched closer to the portrait. On our porch that had been the way he used to defend me. But the bloodlight once in my head had faded. A great leveler I hadn't yet named was pushing it out.

"That why we're talking so much about money?" my father said. "You still minding—how you got yours?"

The curls I had grown to play Leo swung in front of my face, startling me. "In the end, people don't mind, do they?" I said.

In my new voice. "And as for me—if a person knows what the other person is. And accepts that." I dared not look up. "It's like a view. One gets used to it. Is that bad?"

"Think I'll buy myself a drink," my father said.

He brought me a small wineglass filled with red.

"What is it?"

"Punt è Mes. It won't hurt you."

I thought: They talk flip here. These people without real streets to refer to. Or closets of a depth to hold their lives. But serious things could be said that way, too. It's just another style. Take it in. "I just thought—maybe I ought never to begin?"

He stared into his own glass of drink. Was he thinking I blamed him for my mother? They give us their own burdens, I thought, but we are never to present them.

"You take all of your heritage so hard," he said. "So hard."

Is that bad? I can't ask that again, I thought—and then I saw what was tipped against the swinging door that led from the dining ell to the kitchen. They had no back door here, no real dining room either. Though I supposed a view could inhibit just as much as a Taj Mahal lamp. "Why there's the old Raleigh. Your old bike." He used to ride it home from the station, in the early days.

"Not mine. That one's long gone. There was another like it, at your grandmother's. I've had it revamped. They're too heavy for the city. If I were going to stay here I'd get an Italian one. But I hope not."

He was always one to say what he felt—only never saying much.

"Why would you stay?" Of course I was busy now, too busy for him.

"It's Tim who shouldn't drink."

With so much else Tim shouldn't be doing now, that too? "I'm sorry."

"Not really. No one is. That's the trouble."

"Not even you?" The horrified question shot from me.

My father gazed at the plants. "I give what I can."

They were a mixed lot, those African violets and worn bego-
nias, assembled without concern for their separate sun needs.
But not too clumsy if tended for honor's sake. If I stayed here, I
would water them.

After a while I said: "Those pocket plants we used to have at
home—it's not the season for them?"

"No."

Down below, a barge urged itself grudgingly north. It was
carrying piles of real coal that glinted in the water mist. But with
every foot farther along this sector of river, didn't it risk becoming a mere paper cutout for these residents above? My father was
watching it also.

"Ask me the questions you came for," he said. And I was not
surprised.

"Pocket plants were Leo's favorite, weren't they."

He nodded, still tracking the barge. Not asking how I knew.
"But Leo had pockets everywhere. One never spent a day in that
—*presence*, without receiving some gift."

"Cookies."

"Not always tangible, those gifts. But you could always sense
them."

We seemed to be breathing in unison.

"You're like that sometimes," he said. "When you come from
the Evamses' especially. And maybe you'll be like that on stage."

How could a barge grudge being looked at, or having to go
north? Onstage though, we imputed to a property what we
wanted it to be. And backgrounds were tailored to us. Yet wasn't
there a chance that the inanimate was as suspended in emotion
as we? And that this too, was heritage?

"Other times—you're like me."

What are *you* like, Father; what are you really like? I knew
better than to ask it straight.

"What—*are* we like?"

His answer came quick. "We give what we can."

How kind he was, to take the blame for whatever we were.
Who had shown him how?

Could *you* give *me*—Leo? I was about to ask. But it happened that I moved—to see the last of the barge.

Or scow? I know nothing about the sea, although the idea of a sea somehow moves me toward the generous, as it does most people. As that vessel turned, I saw a woman sitting against the south wall of its small cabin, a child at her feet. The camp chair on which she sat was distinct in the sun. Did her shoulder also have the storyteller's outline—how could I have seen that from so far? Far enough to see my mother telling me her story bit by bit, on trains in flight, on striped porch chairs in the evening, or in the silence drawn under big hats—often with her shoulder so curved. The legends told by women drop into the same sea as the legends told by men, but even a woman born of a woman has to learn to fish for them.

"Did Leo ever study for the law?"

"Yes. By correspondence only—and reading. And passed the bar exams. But never practiced. That was why I went in for it, later. My idea was—we would practice together."

"But when you graduated—Mother once said something about your—planning to go in with somebody from Hartford—a friend you graduated with."

"Did she?" He turned from the window and took my hands in his. "Your mother's a sibyl. Who doesn't know she is."

"She refuses to," I said. "That's the trouble."

We held onto each other eye to eye, exchanging our blindness and our sight.

"So will you be, one day," he said. "And you won't refuse." He let go my hands. "During law school, yes, I had a friend. He and I were, as the saying went then—inseparable. Nothing more. Men could still do that then. Be close, without other thought. His father, who was a judge, agreed to help us open an office up there. Not Hartford, New London. And maybe in Boston, later on. And I spoke to them about Leo, my aunt, that privately educated lawyer. It was a time when women were coming into view in the labor field especially. There had been a woman Secretary of Labor in the Cabinet. And Mrs. Roosevelt. And my friend and I planned to go into labor law. So he and his father were open to it . . . What are you looking at?"

"A barge. A scow. And now it's gone."

"So—my friend came to the graduation party. Intending to meet Leo. Who was not a recluse, you understand—do you understand? Only retiring, in the way many spinsters then were. Helped with the family work, both the heavy and the pretty touches, and then went to their rooms. Appeared for meals, or didn't. Some were made into slaveys. If they were loved—they were made into characters. The town did a lot of both." My father peered after the barge. "It's all gone now—the spinster cousins and aunts and sisters who stayed at home. Sometimes they helped the family make them into characters. It gave them a status. And freed them of criticism maybe. For their one central lack . . . And in that respect, Leo was no different . . . What's wrong?"

I was awed, that's all. "Nothing. It's just that I never knew you thought that much. About the town."

"Oh?" He smiled at me. "Everybody in a town thinks that about the others. That's what a town is."

And the difference between men and women may lie elsewhere than where we think. A woman slopes over her hoard of the past. My father, leaning again into his, squared his shoulders as if taken aback.

"In those days Leo's quarters were slightly off limits, but nothing sacrosanct. Few outside of the family were received there, but partly only because there was so much room downstairs. The houses afforded that. So families might either receive together, or scarcely at all. Except for the town children, who ran in and out from house to house. Upstairs all of us could be pretty much private to ourselves. So bringing my friend upstairs was—a kind of occasion. Not much noticed—the house that day being in preparation for the party. It was the day before. My friend was at the moment the only guest. The girls hadn't yet arrived. That evening, they would."

The river was ready again for the next batch of whatever. I am

more used to the city now; I can love it for what it is. Apartment
buildings are all the same, rich or not. They are barracks, with
starers everywhere along the façades. A city is audience.

"So I took my friend upstairs to meet our possible partner,"
my father said. "My Aunt Mary Leona, called Leo. And Leo was
waiting for us. Dressed like a man."

On a river, the revelations rise and sink. Any stranger may fish
for them. But a house can be set for company, with all its signifi-
cances plain. Until now I had thought of our once sturdy farmhouse as desecrated, like a plowhorse made to wear pompoms
and strut. But now I saw that the two gentlemen had massed
their photographs of European tours, their bric-a-brac and even
their boys in the garden according to an instinct honest for
them. Maybe even the suave barrenness of the fields had been
intended. It was what they had had to do.

I strained toward Leo with whatever empathy I had been born
with, or learned. The aunt who had ridden from the farm with
my father, bike to bike, the hamper of male clothing bought in
Boston trundling ahead of them in the van. Who maybe saw my
father and his roommate come into the house still flushed and
innocent of what their linked future could be. Leo the debater,
watching all belowstairs from the captain's walks that both our
family houses had had—haylofts of a kind. Who later would
surely have seen the girls fluttering around their tall host, the son
of the house, as handsome as he was remote.

I strained toward him, the nephew. Taker of pictures at an
early age. Of Leo and a music society, when he himself was just
able to pen his name. My father the lawyer, who had never had a
business partner. But in whose New York office there had always
hung what when questioned he had said was "an art photo"—
which he said was what one called pictures with no people in
them. Yet that one was strangely inhabited. A picture of two
bikes leaning against a wall.

"Leo let you see on purpose."

How loudly I said that. But then—I was not at Evamses'.
Look at those huge speakers in the bookshelves—what mam-

moth music must issue from those. Quiet as the cardplaying here would have been, this had been a high-decibel house.

"That's what Leslie said."

How it must have mattered to them. For my father to tell me this.

"We discussed it endlessly. As to what the purpose had been."

The false Mr. Eliot looked down on us. Not a face that would have come to no conclusion.

"Perhaps you have an opinion?" my father said. "From what you and your—collaborator—know of Leo?"

I saw—or heard—that my father thought Towle was already my lover.

"If you yourself could say—" he said stiffly "—I would particularly value it."

And I hear how faithful my father is. How much it must matter to him still, that those he has loved since should know Leo, that Leo should live again in such a dialogue. First with Leslie. Now with me.

Only my mother would have been debarred.

While my father and Leslie Warden discussed "endlessly" whether or not my father had been in love with Leo, and Leo with him? And whether or not for Leo this had been as men love women, or as women love men? That face up there would have thought of it. And of how the two must never have loved as my father and mother once had, or as he and my father. I could only feel that they had not. But that face could have been told.

This apartment was a place where everything had been said. I was not going to. Nor would I ever ask for sure when and how my father had found out what Leo was. Leo would not want me to. What Leo would want me to know I must find out for myself, or it would be worth nothing. And if it was worth what I was beginning to think—then I must tell the world.

"I think—Leo did not do it from jealousy."

"Indeed not." From my father's tone, he has never bathed in that yellow light. Or else had been taught otherwise. "It was done from grace. The way Leo did everything. I feel you should know that. Before you begin."

"I feel—almost as if I do." True. But I won't be asking my father anything more. How odd to find one's father more innocent than oneself. It heals the jealousy, but leaves another kind of hole.

What I want from Leo is the bitterness as well. Even from that half person, or double person, the hidden part that hides in all of us, and anneals our lives. And perhaps because I want that annealing for my own life—I will find Leo's.

"When you and your friend confronted Leo? What then?"

We were talking as equals. To do that with a parent is heaven. But it is not done with both parents together. Perhaps that is the bitterness.

"My friend—as you call him—turned tail and fled. And I had to go after him." My father bent his head in anguish. "No, I didn't have to follow him. Leaving Leo. But I did. All the way to the station, to which he demanded to be taken at once; he kept waving his arms. *In flagrante delicto*—he kept saying. But that means 'taken in the act.' Maybe he wouldn't have done that well in the law. Anyway, I never again heard from him." My father raised his head. "That was the worst. That I turned tail, from Leo. And fled. And the next day—your grandfather died."

"And Leo?"

"Leo came down to help, as usual. Dressed as usual. My Aunt Mary Leona. Not quite as slim as when we rode our bikes."

"Did Leo and my mother ever truly meet?" *Truly* was my mother's adjective.

"No doubt, in a bevy of girls. Girls traveled more in bevies then."

"School is a bevy—" I said.

"But I remember Leo at the kitchen window after the funeral, ironing the dress your mother had worn to the party. And saying to me: 'The touching way that girl says *down home*. She should not be put to traveling all the way there alone. After such an experience as hers. We owe it to her to escort her there.' "

I opened the window and leaned out—toward that train my young father and mother took South together, the first of the many she would travel later with me, or alone. "And you and Leo never spoke of it. Of what had happened upstairs." I said this with authority. I don't remember in which voice.

"No. But that's how Leslie—happened. I found a person—the person, to whom I could speak of it."

And had been faithful, through death in hospital, to him.

Another barge was now passing upriver. The Pearlwick sign held fast, a document for a time. We in our town had its product in our bathrooms, wicker at bottom, pearly flip lid—and inside, beneath the week's soiled laundry, an ever-ready supply of rags lively with memory.

I leaned out the window.

"Careful," my father said behind me—and I would be. I was a vessel filling. It would be a sensation I'd learn to live for.

"How did Leo die?" I knew my father had been away in military service at the time.

"Heart. The mitral valve was said not to be as it should be. A mild defect in some women, not ordinarily life-threatening. But in Leo it was more."

I wasn't surprised. As Boston had said, Leo was more, not less. Adding in sermon that this was what a monster was.

So at the door, I asked my father after all what I had come to ask: "Do I play Leo—as a she? Or as a he?"

He stood stock still. One never asks without telling. I had revealed what I knew. "You don't mean—just dress?"

"No." Boxes, so interchangeable, teach better than that. And a town's dump.

"Dress means nothing. Nothing." I saw an Oxford-Cambridge debate one year. The year I was waiting to marry your mother. They wore black tie, those striplings. To debate with the gods and the dons. And presumably—with themselves. I also saw the oracle at Delphi. A hole in stone. Behind some artfully disposed boughs—and some German tourists." He laid a palm on the apple of my throat. "The oracle is here. I can't tell you more."

But downstairs, looking for a taxi to take me to my first rehearsal, he said: "I find I can give you two bits of advice. One possibly useful. Cannon Place is the pits for taxis."

We walked over toward First Avenue and picked up a rover.

"And the other?" Out here I was alight with the city, standing as straight as a rocket pointing up, the towers around me ready to be knocked every which way like in an Art Deco poster, by me in my path.

"Don't paint yourself into a corner, with Towle."

The cab door closed before I could answer. As he had intended. So I never told him that Towle had already done that, to me and Leo both—but only in the play, and that I would hang in there and paint us both out of that corner. For though I had been born to my mother down home while my father was still in the service, and Leo, dying before they at last came North with me, had never seen me, it was to Leo I owed my birth.

Leo gave my father my mother.

We give what we can. And are taken in our acts.

"Say another!" my grandmother would cry, each time I came. By instinct she had recognized what recitative was; she never said "Sing." So I gave her whatever the voice coach had newly come up with: two lines spoken from the diaphragm in Kabuki declamation, or five bars from one of Canteloube's *Songs of the Auvergne*—as sung by that voice like a sliding knife—Madeleine Grey. I always ended with John McCormack's "Jeanie," her favorite. My theatrical training fascinated her, as long as I kept it practical—what one literally did onstage, and at what salary. She had no interest in ambition or myth. Nor as I vainly hoped, did she ever blanch at a certain sound in my voice and hold up a dreaming finger—*Leo!* And I saw she wanted no tender questioning. She had had her recitative.

I could even acknowledge that my loving inquiries to her wouldn't have been as kindly intended as I had conceived them, and in any case would have been answered in that other language, the esperanto of two generations back, which might sound cognate but really wasn't. While to her mind, my generation spoke a patois out of that nowhere—the future—which always corrupts.

It even seemed to me that my grandmother had no subconscious—that such a concept had to be connived with by the carrier before it was wholly true. I and my kind, born into a world of accepted double meaning, lived there as in some amniotic fluid that would never quite drain. My grandmother, untouched, undivided, moved in that primal world of gesture which could never become obsolete. It was no wonder she would rather hear me *say*.

We never spoke of the third floor. I was on trial.

And what did I expect to find there? The greenwood heart of a house, beating on like in some old opera libretto held in the fist, while I waited to enter that forest of sound, poisonous and sweet?

Though it was I who would have to perform.

How that would happen my grandmother understood better than me.

At the time, I was living in three places and fully occupying none of them: Mr. Peralho's in the city, my own house, in which I had never slept but sometimes mused, and my old room in her house, where I memorized lessons quickest and slept when I had to. I saw myself the way the age I was wants to—as a smart nomad where others were foolishly settled, a true solitary, but engaged as deep as any devil in the passing scene.

My father, Mr. Peralho, and my mother—attended by Etsuko —had left for Rio on what was to be my mother's trial visit, their caravanserai making a sensation at our local depot, for at Etsuko's hint—that this would be a gentle way to get my mother there—all had been dressed in white. By then she and my mother were as fully in step as some nurses become with their long-term charges. To Etsuko, risen from a lower class to near lady by means of an elegant smirch of brotheldom, my mother plainly embodied some myth a Japanese woman would burn altar tokens to. In that shrine, my mother, swerving in tune with habits of tint and finickiness not far from her own, felt puppet-safe. My brother, arriving red-eyed either from a binge or from being dried out, but very entirely sober, said: "Southernism isn't that far from Buddhism, y'know," also pointing out that Orien-

tals mourned in white. And switching to tennis whites and head-
band, he had accompanied them.

So Knobby, Nessa, and I were alone. I was determined to call
her that, but had not yet attempted it.

Then one day, Knobby rang me at Peralho's, saying "Tea at
five, any day after school. Upstairs. And I am not to bake but to
buy. At Lundgren's." He despised the town bakery's confections
because my grandmother assumed these to be hospitality's
height. Much later on, I would be reminded of her by certain
born-to-the-purple patronesses of the drama who served Cheez-
Bits and meals cooked by Irish maids, with her same haughty
ignorance—or wholesomeness?

At five o'clock I climbed the stairs. I found her seated in front
of a huge platter of pastry.

Actually, Lundgren's cornets filled with buttercream had been
our splurge as kids. Out of disappointment at what the third
floor at first glance had come to—an old woman's lair, heavily
draped and scattered upon—to her satisfaction I ate three,
served me on the Haviland that was the town's acme of taste. I
was given no time to ask where the harshly burnt, squat pottery
she had been using had gone. I scarcely was given time to look
about me, though this abruptness was nothing new.

I had responded to the story of her own youth with one of
those bouts of sympathy the young give the old of such stories,
quite without understanding them. It's hard to estimate, or even
believe, the resentment of the undereducated, particularly in
one's own family, even though much of the populace in our
country of émigrés or lost provincials is often in the same fix. My
father and I had risen above her. Though this was an external
pride, inwardly she could never forgive us. Or wanted to cut us
down to size. Her early life had engrained in her bones that life's
version of the status quo. She was aware enough of that life's
other strengths. Yet she belonged to that class which wants to
quash its own legends in favor of the kind they can buy at the
stores.

For the former resident of this long room, hidden and fenestrated as any room in a fairy tale, this may have helped.

But all I saw now was my grandmother's impish, at times almost evil, urge to make us admit we were indeed—only folk. It did not occur to me that she had brought me there for a purpose of her own.

"You don't fatten," she said, when I had finished the third cornet. "We don't. Farm bones. And in our family—now and then a woman as tall as you. Never the men. Always had to marry short, those women—if they married. You maybe should keep a string on that boy."

"Oh, I will." I had. A student at school who knew him had reported Bill was joining the Coast Guard, but two drawings of his had shortly appeared in a Greenwich Village rag of some distinction, and when I phoned the pad—to congratulate, though in a funk I hung up instead—he had been there. And had known it was me?

"He may soon be living with a girl called Marilyn," I said. This had been a joke between us: that for the sake of drawing practice, he might one day have to replace me with what he'd called a "svelte dumpling," of that name.

"You could get him back just by wiggling your little finger. I saw."

I looked down at that finger. Yes, I could. That was the trouble—and that I might. "Men don't mind now. What size a girl is."

I saw she didn't believe me.

"*I* was minded," she said. "And I was nowhere near what you."

Towle had dared to question her, why shouldn't I? "But what about Grandfather?"

She wanted to be asked. One day, I will watch a great actress of eighty smear her nose with a finger and a Greek snuffle, hawk and spit and even fart her immortal lines, and then say to us other actors in the wings as she exits, in accents already like a

lost bell: "At that age, at *mine*, one wants to do and say everything."

"He was a prince. A prince. But he came too late."

"But you got your honeymoon house."

Her eyebrows, furry and mannish now, flexed, but I felt no
shame. We begin that inquiry early, some of us.

"Doesn't matter when," she said. "Does matter how. But now
—I'm away from it."

All this time, glancing about me as she would allow, I could
see nothing left of these quarters once secretly crept into and so
well remembered—though we must be in that very space.

"Upstairs—" I'd said beforehand, "you're sure she's inviting
me upstairs?" and Knobby had nodded without expression, although in *déjà vu* his noncommittal nods were often full of it—a
reversal I recommend for study to those who would understand
his nation.

Now, looking again, under the many shawls and the scarecrow
garments, and past a line of shoes of too much experience, lined
up like a bench of the unemployed, I saw that my grandmother
was living in a room Knobby must have made for her out of
those screens called *shoji*. Almost a one-room house this place
was now. Ordinarily this would have pleased me, in the way a
dollhouse or a box-within-a-box does tantalize. But this room,
though Knobby must tidy it, was inexcusably rumpled with an
old person's living. The old have random ways no riotous youth-
ful mess can reproduce. The stasis of memory is going. The
relationship between ordinary objects is no longer the common
one. A fine impermeable dust settles—nothing that can be
cleaned away. Age wrinkles the air.

So—once more had Leo escaped me?—and my grandmother
had helped. I had no conception then of how far we will go to
keep the mundane always with us. And to hold love separate. Or
that my grandmother's image of that separation might be as
fierce as mine.

In the next second, I see how tall the screens are. That other
room, of furnishings maybe not so high in scale as a child would

see them, must be shielded behind them, pushed, like most attic memories, with its back to the wall. From outdoors, if one glanced up, the fenestrations were still the same.

"Where's the master?" she says suddenly. The interrupter is her role, will be to the end.

I know who she means, of course. "Craig Towle? He's in Canada, drumming up money for the play. There's a whisky distiller up there has backed him before."

Though I'm not sanguine—Towle had said. That man never saw the play he backed. He was advised. Nowadays those ginks choose their own write-offs. I might lose out to Black Angus bulls. Or to a government arsenal up for grabs—.

The tinny lingo he fell into at those times, was it meant to warn me, in our too detached joint corner? —"Good for me to go"—he'd said. And I'd quipped: "Too many women around?" For we still had our differences on Leo.—"No, never that," he'd said, his lower lip suddenly indenting, the peaked eyelids widening, a man clearly remembering sex. I'd held onto my acerb pose but I too was recalling a past. The room thickened, or our bodies did, toward each other, with the swelling that comes like a seventh sense. —"No," he'd said.—"I just need to keep in mind how gothic you all are."

Then he'd looked me up and down in detail, the whole length of me. No doubt recalling all that fancy self-imagery he had extracted from me, which in the guise of our getting bodily closer to Leo I had been foolish enough to let him in on—all those allusions collected from other men. He looked me over head to toe, from noble Hera's braids to 1890 goddess neck, to the flat breast lappets some men were mad for, and lingering for an infamous flick of a glance, his first, at the crotch of my shorts —behind which lay what Bill had likened to a Hasidic's bearded smile. His survey traveled down my bare legs, now out of riding boots, to the Trilby feet. Oh, I had told him all, with what now struck me was my own lechery.

Then he'd gone down the hayloft stairs, tossing me a final blasphemy, which coming from him it was—a quote of my father's, on his lips. And hadn't I savored that too? "Oh, it's all right. You're still a modern girl."

Had he really gone to Canada? Where else might he go? And had he gone only for money or sex? Where would a man like him go, for advice?

For it had become worrisomely clear even to me that the play was still a shambles, its shiftings not lively and natural but hectic and slow—and with only one plus. The fake girl-character, Leo's "inamorata," as he had called her, had faded out, along with any mention of the two actresses who'd been so right or so eager for the part—and had not been replaced. Something else was needed, he'd kept saying. "Or someone. The narration—haven't hit it right yet," he'd said, not meeting my glance, then turning to stare full at me. "Once I do, it'll flow," he'd said.

Now I think to myself, perhaps he already had hit it. Or has another studio somewhere. Men tire of haylofts. Although he and I hadn't shared what one normally gets there, perhaps he has already got what he wanted.

"At least he's never asked me for money," my grandmother said. "He's honest there. But only because he doesn't care about it."

That was true. When he talked of backers you could tell.

"But never trust those who say they don't care about money, your grandfather would say. Only look harder for what it is they do care about." She was staring at me squarely enough now. "Have to hand it to Towle; he tells you. Keeps telling you. How he only has his eye on one thing." She leaned back, with the ratchety croak that had once been a laugh—"He thinks people care about *that*"—then fell to musing, cuffing and cuffing the knob of her chair in one of those repetitive movements that were accumulating on her like an equally silent repertoire. "Knew he was a sneak from the first. Happened I needed one. And am old enough to admit it. To talk your heart out to, there's nothing like a sneak."

I felt mine there. My heart in my mouth.

"Just so long as you know the bargain, girl. That one day the talk will be turned against you."

At nineteen, how consciousness hurts. "Sometimes *he* levels with *me*, about Mother. My own mother. I don't like that."

She pursed her mouth, shrugged.

"He said Mother ate chocolate the way other people drank wine. And that when she drank wine, it would be the way other people ate chocolate." I'd excused myself when he said that, and had gone down into the yard on the other side of the house and bawled. Then had hardened myself—in the interests of the theater and what one could honorably do there—to go back up the stairs and hear more. "He said that my mother was the bankrupt among us. Bankrupt from mirrors. Her life." I had listened to that without bawling.

"Clever," she said. "But only what everybody knows."

"But he didn't get to know it from everybody!"

She banged on the chair knob. "No—didn't I say!" Then looked at her hand in surprise. "But I've got this place out of it. After he and I talked—and I'd had enough of it, I told Watanabe what must be done. It's hard for me to be myself, these days. And maybe won't get easier. Watanabe knew exactly what to do. He always does. And so he did when I told him to bring you. 'Bring that girl,' I said, 'for me to listen to.'" She gave me a sharp look. " 'And to listen,' Watanabe said."

"That's what I've come for," I cried. "To listen." I hadn't thought of her listening. "I'll do both," I said more humbly. "But first—could I go behind the screens—to see what's there?"

"Do as you like," she said. "Too much light for me back in there. I'm done with it."

I get up slowly, and walk in. So there it is—childhood's greenwood, in shadows subtle as in a forest where animals almost move. The high chests are quite as tall as I remember them, the leather inlay of the open desk is as buttery an olive green as once. Light comes lucidly through each small pane of the two casements, yet since every other pane is leaded, the luster is as hoarded as it should be. Watanabe, coming here to clean, would surely stand in verdict: yes, very Samurai. There is even a rocker, too elegantly spindled to have come from the farm. But when I touch it, it rocks.

The drawers are everywhere slightly open. Knobby would do that to counter mice and mold. There's nothing in any of them. But books fill the breakfront, all behind glass, tight against one another. To reach for books under glass always tires me. Such books are so often the kind one doesn't believe. These look more like armor than like friends. But to one side, on a table, there is a small shelf of worn volumes, humped between a pair of bookends of the kind schoolboys once made during the hour called "Shop." We had had a pair like these at home, from my father's school days.

A confirmation Bible, from its freshness rarely used since, is next to one of the Little Blue Books—by the Robert Underwood who billed himself as an "Iconoclast." Next came a green-and-gold edition, lovely to thumb, of the *Cathedrals of Europe*, next to that a coverless cookbook, yellow-spotted and very early, printed in our own county. I would one day ask to have it and be given it. The recipe for sheepshead is there—and in the margins, the only examples of Leo's penmanship. Almost every recipe had been tried—marked with a large check, or a cross, or even a "Nix," and some of the old ingredients had had their current substitutes noted. For isinglass, a penciled "Cornstarch?" and below this—"No—agar-agar."

I keep that cookbook to remind me of the everchanging pharmacopaeia of women; maybe Leo did so also. Nothing on that shelf brought me nearer that creature's spirit. Certainly not the miniature copy, printed by one Thomas Mosher, of John Donne's *Biathanatos*, an apology for suicide. Alongside it, as if in answer, a healthily large Newman's *Apologia Pro Sua Vita* had been stacked. The last book on the shelf was much worn. Duns Scotus? I had never heard of him, as most have not.

A short preface stated that Scotus, a British or Irish scholastic commonly called "the Subtle Doctor," had died in 1308. Asserting that any knowledge of finite truth rested on that ultimate truth which is God, he had denied the individuality of matter.

This I could not understand—God helping or not. And am not sure even now of what a Leo would make of it. Would a Leo have wanted a denial—or an affirmation? But the huge engraving that hung frameless above the shelf—that I could appreciate. Its fine-print title said: *Château d'If, State Prison off the coast of Marseilles. Illus. Comte de Monte Cristo, Alexandre Dumas.*

I had never cared for Dumas. But the prison looked like what it was.

Lying on the table beside the shelf, there was a portfolio of red leather, stamped LETTERS. Empty. Towle had reported such an article, brought from the farm, and gradually filled. Letters to people we never heard of, Nessa had said. Letters to books, long-ago books. And the authors dead, most of them. Letters never sent. She had destroyed them all, unread.

Resting my hand on the red leather, looking up at the Château, I made a vow. "I'll write your letters, Leo," I said.

I found my grandmother asleep, or nodding. Was she half awake? With those who can destroy, one is never sure.

"Nessa?"

In extreme age, the pupils of the blue-eyed either go greenish, like cheap glass looked at from the side, or clearer in their own color, with the clean innerness of flint. But her pupils were that brown which rims with mauve, as if from an ever-perfected past.

"Go back," she said. "Go on back in, my ewe lamb. No, I'm not done with you. But that girl is here now. The one he's writing his play about."

I climbed the twist of steps to the captain's walk—as I had every day since. I needed an ugly place to be. The house below was empty. My grandmother, for months the target of the old Austrian's plea to let him and his wife show her their country, had given in, half out of amazement, when she discovered she was not expected to pay for them.

"Every Austrian has a nest egg," the old man said, and that

had sealed their kinship, for though my father had been conned into paying her expenses, all along so had she. Also, such a country seemed the right sort for a ninety-three-year-old's first trip abroad. "Travel's like housework, isn't it?" she wrote my father, who had never done housework in his life. "Why didn't you say? It clears the head. At my age that counts. By the way, I said something to upset your girl. Don't remember what."

He sent the letter on to me, saying he well understood what she meant about travel, though her version of it was a demi-pension outside Vienna, where their party would stay put for three months. As for him, Rio was now home—perhaps the reason why it hadn't yet helped my mother, although she had been slightly roused by her new Indian nurse. Etsuko, lingering on in the name of duty, had finally persuaded Watanabe to detach her by promising to meet her in Japan, to which until then he had refused to return. "As for your grandmother, take her with the usual grain of salt. Her age is certainly wandering; far as I know she is not yet ninety-one. Maybe those debentures are the draw." He concluded by saying that I was the only one of us who had not traveled, which he would someday help me toward, though of course I was busy—and how was the play getting on? "We will all return for your debut, of course."

It was his first real letter, and I treasured it.

By then, I had also had a note from Towle. He was at the family beach house with his children, saying that their presence was useful since he was keeping the children's scene in, though rewriting it.

> But Leo is no longer the main character. I was pretending that to myself. As well as to you. What I'm doing now works. Hope you'll understand, once I've got it all, and will agree to play your new role. No more—until I see you.
> Watch for the flag.

For rendezvous we had used the red flag on the mailbox of my empty house, which no longer received mail or sent it. Whatever the mailman thought—when he stopped for the pickup flag and found nothing—went into the granular underdust of the town. For it all goes somewhere, I believe now. If the flag was up when I came by of an afternoon, it meant that Towle was still in the loft and at work, in which case I continued past it to the back-yard of my house and sat on a torn, tan-striped garden chair whose seat sagged as the weeks went by until I was almost on the grass. I remember that humped waiting, excited but mindless except for the pattern between my knees—and their jump—when he called me to come up.

I rarely went inside my house. When I did, at first only Phoebe was there, if feebly. A mere arrangement of light and the sound of a name, in the way of persons not seen for a long time and once known too well. But then Bill joined us, and with that I couldn't yet deal.

But now I slept there every night, on the mattress the Salva-tion Army had refused, Towle's letter beside me on the hall floor where I had tossed it, where if I left it long enough it might tell me all. There was that virtue in owning an empty house. Or three houses to be alone in, in a kind of spirit-travel, in which I was going from one to the other, out in other company only at the school, which would shortly recess. Not before teaching me that very few egos, there or perhaps anywhere, would ever have as much time for me as my own. My getting the part had been a nine-days wonder. That a role—or a play—might evaporate, was not.

"That's the theater for you," the voice coach said, basso profundo on this anodyne which would perhaps serve us both best of all. "In the mornin' and the evenin'." He had just re-hearsed "Mighty Lak a Rose" with two boys slated for a televi-sion commercial—canceling my final lesson for theirs. They had a job. "Read in *Variety* that Canada weren't the only ones backed out. Hear Towle's gone away. To revise, it said."

"I know. I had a note."

"From Towle? Signed?" Mr. Margolies hummed a certain three bars—his own signature. "Save it, if I were you. Never know when one'll need a testimonial."

"Him? Or me?" I said, and left him shaking his head—in six/ eight time.

So here I was, in recess, when one is supposed to learn nothing. Or else, as they advised at school—to go back to life. But I seemed to carry my life with me wherever I went. Which practice, as Miss Pevsner had warned, could keep one unprofessional. A group of students was going to Spain, to wallow in the scenic and forget that they would soon graduate, but I told them that I had an obligation. "To Towle?" said a boy who fancied me in a light way and had declared I had better learn that style sooner than later. "Come on—shape up." No, not to him, I said. Other students had dropped me bids to parties in the city, but Mr. Peralho's was to be painted; I couldn't stay overnight there—and didn't want to, though I already knew that the city in dead of summer is operetta, is nice. Ambition is in its own dead swoon— or at the shore.

Towle's note had been sent from Dorchester.

As for me, I felt at the height of physical and mental power, ready again for the scenery of sex, or to board Shakespeare on strophe after strophe, or to strip to its core any blood-and-thunder script a casting agent would toss me—my own history waiting second by second to burst from my veins and deal with anything, if only there were something with which to deal. Meanwhile that half-obliterated postmark from Dorchester, whose oval I had turned this way and that to read for sure, lay in my mind's eye like a seashell for which I would not stoop.

In those days the train to our town took at least an hour and a half. I boarded a slow afternoon number known as the "Philadelphia freight," whose wheels seemed to be deploring their own slackness: *Tsk—ull, tsk tsk.* Only the morning trains had many men on them. I thought of the two in whose company I had traveled this route with such intent on my part, such significance, each man only half joined to me, each riding with one shoulder pressing forward beyond the two of us—and the division between men and women seemed to me the heaviest I would ever bear. Perhaps that was why Leo had never ridden the trains.

In the town as I hurried home on foot the evening sun made dark dunes of the narrow streets near the depot. Children, poor ones, were still out playing in all the networks children maintain. I knew none of these little webs anymore. But what if one had known these, stepping along in one's Sorosis shoes, steady, steady, between all the signposts of generosity and will along the path one had made for oneself? Had had to make.

In the kitchen I concocted my nightly meal of sandwiches with lurid fillings, meanwhile missing Knobby, presently walking the misty streets of Japan, maybe toting that same cotton bag he had brought to my wedding, which had held not rice but paper blessings never scattered. He had given me a private handful instead. Of all the people I would miss later—and I would become faithful to the point of neurosis there—he cast the least burden. Perhaps I could have asked him about Leo. His language was more cognate with our country's past than with its present. As is often the case with foreigners here—though only they seem to notice.

Sandwiches make me optimistic. I went up the stairs singing for real, passing the locked third floor, for which I now had no need. Up the pie-cut steps to the triangular landing, through the tower space with its purple and amber bordered panes and slanting floor, and I was out on the walk itself, a lacy three-sided railed balcony that surrounded the mean-sized tower and excused it. Here I could survey the town, and more and more it was Leo's town, for I felt sure that after the hidden errands of charity and other shy forays of Leo's day, those shoes, pair after pair, wearing like iron and yet wearing out, had mounted these steps.

What I was seeing, and daily more familiar to me, were the lanes that people's workpaths make. And that these have little to do with whether a town council has paved with macadam or tar. The path to the factory was trod early but by few, all older men lumbering along as if linked by one and the same arthritic twinge. At 6 P.M. twenty or more women of all ages flounced or sagged from the new department store, the cleaner's and the other service shops, their sharply coiffured heads of white or blond, russet, or brown dotting erratically between the houses, until each singly entered her own door. On Friday nights the two beauty parlors, one a Nook the other a Bower, took in the disheveled and sent out again these sedate blooms. The doctors' offices, most now in one medical building, seemed at some hours to disgorge more than they took in, and at others to do the opposite. The exception was one granddaddy house only a block away, a replica of ours even to the tower. In that house's similar carriage house the town's reigning doctor kept the special-built Packard that doubled for funerals as needed, in the mortuary run by his son-in-law. One went to this doctor as a last resort. Through both his door and his son-in-law's the patients entered at stately intervals in a thin, selective line, to exit in identical lines and with much the same mien as before, only somewhat nearer the grave.

I watched this theater of the ordinary with the eye of one who had never traveled, and with the aid of a pair of opera glasses found in a case with the music society's gold stamp on it, inside the glassed-in bookcase I had after all opened. Possibly the books there, all of them on law, contained much to do with what I was seeing: how people moved, divided, connected—and were mowed down. People were a crop.

Why did I feel it necessary to tell myself I was seeing the town as Leo saw it? Because I was seeing it with love?

I was doing "Oh, Rest in the Lord" when the front doorbell rang. Leaning over the railing I saw the police car at the curb, but couldn't see who was below. "Door's open," I called, leaning out farther.

"Don't *do* that," the police captain's voice said.

He climbed the flights at a stately pace, nothing like when he and Denby had stampeded the loft. Once on the landing, he leaned in, framing himself in the tower's doorway. "Nice lookout you've got here."

"Built for sea captains," I said. "Emphasis on *sea*."

"And only accommodates one?" he said. "That's a change. What the hell you up to now?" But he had already scanned the plate of food, the schoolbooks dumped on the floor, my decent shirt and braids, and neat ballerinas, and I could see he was relieved.

"Rehearsing, for a play."

"I heard. Who's the leading man? No, don't tell me. Heard that, too."

"You heard wrong."

He grinned. "With you, I always hear wrong. Don't you do anything—*downstairs?*"

I had to laugh. "Who phoned you this time?"

"Nobody. Keep my ear to the ground. Have to, the kind of crime this town mostly commits. Murders in haylofts. Voyeurs in braids." He pronounced it *voy*. His eyes went again to the opera glasses lying on a box of Kleenex for polishing them.

"I was studying the town. How it would've looked to the person who owned those."

"You don't say. Tell you something. This is a real town. Not some play-acting. People worry about you. Know you're alone." He bent over the Kleenex box to scrutinize the glasses, but didn't touch them. "So—who belongs to these? Our local genius —and lady-killer?"

"No. He—he studies on his own."

"Bet he does. So then—who?"

"It was a long time ago. Thirty years."

His eyes crinkled. "Try me."

"Mary Leona. My great-aunt."

What he did then—he stepped inside the door frame, over to where I was. There was room for two on the walk after all. Lowering that big head of his from left to right, he checked the view, then stood still for it, his hacked profile forward. If there had been a ship's wheel up there, his head could have manned the whole walk as if from a prow.

When he said: "So *that's* what he's onto—" he no more had

to say he meant Craig Towle than one of a pair steering some old packet boat always on the same course would have had to say to the other—*South, southwest.*

Then, still looking out and over the town, he said—"Leo . . ."

Not a question, not just a statement but in the way two inhabitants would refer to what a whole town knew, but didn't talk about.

So—I nodded back.

That rough-cut mouth didn't change, nor that big ear, which had to keep itself to the ground. I had to answer to them.

"Was." It came out a croak. My throat hurt. "Was onto. Now —I dunno."

"Uh-huh," he said. "Saw the evening paper. Too bad."

The local paper came at four o'clock. Its delivery box was down there at the edge of the lawn. But the paper had been stopped.

"The play—" My voice broke clear. "They've announced the cast of the play!"

He turned, shaking his head slowly at me, the way he must do when he came to a house to report a crash—and a death.

"Towle's young wife—the one who died? Parents in Boston are suing him. For neglect."

Then he patted my cheek, which was what he must have come to do—and to check on the view from here. After which he did pick up the opera glasses, handed them to me, and went back down the stairs.

There was someone staying in the Towle house—and I thought I knew who it was. Once or twice a day the Volks, not so new now, passed my grandmother's house, going slow. Towle usually drove with his left arm out the window, but the car was on the wrong side of the street for me to see the driver. I didn't think it would be he. At night, from in front of my own house, I couldn't quite see whether there were lights in that other house down the Row, but as one by one the houses in between went dark, the cobbled path in front of the fifth house down was still luminous. Whoever was there stayed up late.

Each morning, waking early and ravenous, I would walk over to my grandmother's. At that same hour those workmen who still lived on the Row were making their way to the old factory, the few young apprentices slamming by in their cars, the elder men still on foot, as befitted men who all their lives had made furniture by hand. On a pearly morning, one could see clear down the Row to the nineteenth century, to where the factory's low buildings, all of cobble too and improvidently made to last, clustered like a village, among trees dwarfed by age or else by a decision to stop growing. No apprentice with any get-up-and-go to him ever stayed there long.

One day, halfway down the Row, a new car glittered, its hood like a long upper lip clamped in disdain. A tow truck, from the garage at this end of town whose habit was to repair at night and deliver in time for those who drove to their jobs, was just drawing away. By the license plate, this car, not a big car, almost mutinously small, worked in Massachusetts, if at all. My brother, who had once been mad for foreign cars, had classified this kind as not like a Jag, for show, but if you wanted to hide your wealth like the Chinese—as he had recently reported some Bostonians still did—this was how you might go.

At dusk of that same day, just as I was leaving my grandmother's house to go to my own, this same Citroën drove by, at a crawl. People unfamiliar with the town tended to do that, often stopping dead to have a look at our impressive turrets and bays, though this car did not. I hadn't yet left when it returned from the other direction. This time I could see the driver's arm, a woman's, dangling. Maybe from long intimacy Towle and she both drove the same. Surely this time the car would stop. But again it drove on.

Why did I go to Towle's on my own? For a purely physical reason—to deal. And because I had never yet dealt physically with Towle himself? That too, though I wasn't conscious of it. I was doing what we call instinctual. I had spent my short life watching the patterns of others: I wanted my own to begin.

Our old hearse of a car had also once been elegant. I drove it there not for that but because I had seen what walking a set path in this town could do to you. The car stopped with a jolt in front of Towle's house.

She opened the door.

"I'm—"

"I know who you are." Looking up at me she said that while I was still on the doorstep. Her accent was a shock, but I had known beforehand that everything here would be. The bobby-soxer had said the same more softly, but as clear. It could be that every woman associated with Craig Towle had waited to say that to some other woman in good time.

"Aren't you going to come in?"

I bent so as to enter and came into the light. Women's eyes don't widen at me; they fix. One of her hands slipped into its pocket in the enviable white slacks. The arm, in its short white sleeve, was a little gaunt. Her gray-blond hair, streaked chastely only by time, but clipped and polished to a silvery shoulder-length casque, would swing only when she wanted it to. She was not beautiful, but the features were still crisp. She had that style which partakes of the expected and knows itself wanted—the style always just coming in or never quite gone out.

She would never be what I was, or with persistence could come to be, but she made me feel as if out in a world where as a beauty I would be the dragon and she would use every steel she had. She had been surprised, but I saw that I must give her no advantage. So I said nothing.

"I was going to come to you," she said. "But I waited. And here you are."

I saw that she was used to her own simplicity, or sparse way of doing things, which she might take to be sense, or even kindness, and no doubt was used to being admired for. I did—but the stage teaches the value of pause.

I had had a second shock. In the inglenook where the bobby-soxer had once had her puzzle, the table again had a gameboard on it. I suppose inglenooks breed the same habits. As I came farther into the house, a light-haired person, as slim as the bobby-soxer had once been, arose from the table. I saw at once that this was a young man, or a boy almost that—but still it was a shock.

"This is my son Tarquin," she said.

So this was the little boy found weeping on the beach, and picked up by that swarm of girls, bright in their dotted halters— those sweet sophists, lisping of youth, whom his father had married.

He hadn't been that little—as he has long since told me. He was eleven, but hadn't got his growth. And wasn't lost, but crying with rage. At the way his father was getting out from under as usual, knowing he could always depend on her to hang on.

"And those girls, all over me so cutesy; it wasn't for me but for him. I saw the whole thing."

He doesn't resemble his father; he has her features and height. Except for that he would for a while recall my brother to me, though I soon saw that his femininity wasn't physical but that of a Picasso clown-boy, who at the time had a fey interest in miniature objects, which he collected and cosseted. What I'd mistaken for a game were some of those. In youth many mother-reared boys have a certain femininity which they are hard put to express. If Tarquin has certain ambivalences they are not of sex. By now, like most of us, he has dealt with them, in that imbroglio of adolescence out of which the real sex-to-be rises bare-toothed.

"Come, sit down," she said. "I love inglenooks, don't you? Tarquin, clear that stuff off."

She was false and she was hard—was what I first heard.

"Thanks. I just saw your light. And knowing the house was empty—. On the Row, we kind of check."

"Civil defense?" She smiled; she was a veteran of all kinds. "But you don't live on the Row."

"Not yet."

I saw Tarquin stiffen. He loves that house.

They wouldn't have known about mine. As for her, I had merely confirmed what she already thought: this girl too wants to marry Towle.

"Indeed." She had a tendency to smile as if she knew everything. Sad, powerful women often do. "Know who I am?"

I glanced at Tarquin. "I do now."

"I want to talk to you. Tarquin—go chop wood."

He was staring at me. He would know everything she was sending him away not to hear. "You're the girl in his play, aren't you? I'm sorry for you." Then he went.

"Am I?" I sat down in the inglenook, opposite her. Oh, I thought I knew how to play Portia now. "I know he's been working at your house, in Dorchester."

But drawing-room comedy was more the way it came from my

mouth. When you are being schooled in many modes of playing, they tend to emerge all tumbled.

"How old are you?" she said, with that smile.

I put my hand on the checkerboard Tarquin had removed his collection from. I had better be cheeky at once. "We're advised professionally—not to say. And I haven't asked *you*."

She sat quite still. "Craig said it. But I didn't believe it."

I wouldn't ask what. She had waited. So could I.

"That you were—'a Venus of the mind.' "

Who could help flushing?

" '—Who—hasn't yet found her natural dress.' "

I sat back. He was right. Though that was nothing new.

"But then he always has a phrase of that sort about the women in his plays. He did about me."

"But you weren't an actress."

"No." Everybody would know who she was, her smile said. "Those he *writes* about." The casque of hair swung. "I was the first."

And proud of it. She would have liked me to be a Portia worthy of her, if I could.

"Yes, he did say once—that he might write about me."

I take advantage of you, he said that night in our yard, the night my mother, an heiress, came home—and I may just do it again.

"He doesn't do well on women, the critics say," she said. "Each time he's tried, it's come to nothing. But he always thinks he'll do better—once he's slept with them."

She didn't smoke. But onstage, any director would have told her to light one now. For the pause. "But you haven't," she said.

I had no manner left. "He told you?"

"He doesn't have to. I only have to open the door to him, to see the trouble he's in. Oh, come. Isn't that what you're here to ask me? Whether you should? A lot of them do."

"The young ones—" I said. Yes, I could see how they would. In this time where all women were becoming friends.

"They're all young."

Was that her triumph? That they were?

Lips can go stiff; I hadn't thought mine could. "The girl who was here. Did she come to you? To ask."

"Oh, poor girl. I knew her, you see. All those girls, one saw them about. None of them knowing for love or money what to do with themselves. Her new stepfather, a strict Frenchman, the kind that keeps its girls in convent till they marry, and the mother going along with it—we all knew that girl was having a time. The sort of godawful time one does, at that age. And so, in his way, was Craig."

Maybe wearing white helped one be honest. Or he had taught her his brand of it—of everything, even to the way she drove.

Her head did bow, though. "He and I were split, you know. Wasn't as if I had a stake in it. So—matter of fact—*I* went to see *her.*"

If I had a real rapier, I thought—not the dull foils they hand out in fencing class—I could make that bowed head roll.

She was studying her fingers. "It's the Frenchman who's making the mother sue. And not for money. Not even for costs. That makes it bad."

"Costs?" I said.

She misunderstood me. "It's a legal term."

"I know. My father's a lawyer. And—my great-aunt was—Leo?"

But the name meant nothing to her.

"Ah, then you know." A look of calculation pinched the long, inbred face. In some ways she was oblivious to what others felt. She had attitudes instead. Nowadays one often sees her kind among the women of new principles. "But perhaps your father won't like you to testify."

"Testify?"

She put her hands across the table. "I apologize. I misjudged you. I was bowled over. And I can sometimes be a hag. Whatever you choose to do about him—Craig—about that, I mean, you're on your own course. It can't change things now."

Can't it? For me?

She didn't hear. Or perhaps I didn't say.

"Yes—testify. It's what I came down here for. Craig doesn't know I'm here. To ask you to testify that you observed him and her closely. As you did, I know. That's how you and he met, he said. Testify that he even engaged you to sit with her. That he did *not* neglect."

The room was hot, airless. She and Tarquin hadn't opened the door to the new pastel wing. Those pretty rooms I had tripped through, and the soft voice saying that incessant movement was not wanted here—what was neglect? *I'm* not a lovely girl, he had said.—I merely acquired one.

To speak the truth and admit it even to one's own shame; what's it do to that hooded eye of his? Is it wrong for a face to be that much on its own?

"What did she die of? No one really told any of us here." My voice was husky. Maybe that angered her.

"Toxemia. But when a baby dies in the womb, the mother must surely know. That late in the day. But she let it go. She let it go on. Horrid. She was a depressed girl."

But one who could be cheered. When we marched out of that bar past the two salesmen who had sent us drinks, her belly well ahead of both of us, she had laughed hard enough. "He said she wouldn't buy a layette for the baby."

"See! You have only to say."

"And that he wished he didn't know why."

She slumped, rubbing her face. People who do that must feel they have two faces. Or want another? Under the rubbing hands the face so often doesn't change. "He knows too much about us all. For his own good. And he'll always testify against himself. Every time."

How had he taught her that? *Venice.* How that name unlocked her for me—all the way back to our front porch. Had she kept up her Italian? Was there still a sloop? I could see her opening the door to him, to their summerhouse with its ancient bulletin boards still crying their causes, and closing it, closing it and opening it.

And was he teaching me the same?

"Venice—"

She wasn't surprised that I knew her name. Everybody would. Or anybody connected with him.

"What was the phrase he had for you?"

No doubt a winner. Suitable for a lifetime of use.

"Oh—that. He used to call me—a woman of ideas."

"He still does," Tarquin said, reappearing at the kitchen door.

"Tarquin. Stay the hell out."

He was only getting at the order of things. Like me.

I stood up to go. It was awkward getting out from between that small bench and table, even if one had no belly. No, I didn't like inglenooks; I wasn't built for them. One tolerates them—as I wished I could again—for a friend.

"Then you will?" she said. "Craig need never know. You could come forward, of your own accord. That could be better still. Say you will. I'll have our lawyer call."

"It would be worse if I did testify. Far worse."

She scanned me—up, down. "You mean—the judge or jury might get other notions?" She drew a sly breath, already hopeful that we were conspirators.

Tarquin could be seen in the far corner of the kitchen, head averted, but not too far away for a normally keen-eared boy. It was no concern of mine. The order of things has to go on, will go on.

"No. It wouldn't be of any use. He had an affair with a woman in town." I had to swallow. "On and off." It hurt to say that, one of my mother's catch-all phrases. It was what she would have said. "An—older woman. There isn't anybody in town who doesn't know. And the bobby-soxer knew too."

"Who?"

That had slipped out. But I saw she knew whom I meant anyway.

"Nancy?" She whispered it.

If I was going to cry I would do it for both of Towle's women. For the lanterns swaying in a girl's face, at a depot, the entry to a

town. And for a jaunty slouch hat. "She knew from the moment
he brought her here."

She didn't ask anything more. In the scheme of her life,
maybe an older rival wouldn't do. Or it was enough that the
phrase he had dubbed me with—"a Venus of the mind"—even
echoed her own name. Though perhaps he had done it uncon-
sciously, in that grand slump of release where such slips are
made. Ruthless herself, she would be the one person his con-
science need not serve.

I would keep my mother from her as I could, safe in her own
poor web. But I myself could see how the younger ones would
seek out this woman, as moths do the death lamp. She had a face
not to be rubbed away, emerging as she sat there, the casque of
hair framing it. The face of a Joan who to avoid the stake has left
Rouen for Paris, for anywhere—and is still burning.

Later that night I lie thinking of what *I* will make happen.
This is a dream best dreamt in one's own house. Lying on the
Salvation Army mattress of one's choice. Eyes awake.

I have my own gestures now, or enough. His I shall steal from
his own testimony freely given, fed and coached me over a
prompter's book of afternoons. To be confirmed by the man
himself, when he arrives at my door. Who will be traveling—
according to the mailman's red flag on the box and the telegram
inside, by plane and train straight to me, his star witness for so
long. As men go first to the girl they have not yet attained. It is
very late for that. But I am dreaming well.

The curtain will rise on me seated naked, left of center of a
divided stage, with my back to the audience. So risen, it will fix
me in the mind of all, in a style simple if unnatural, for the rest
of my life in the theater. Or my theatrical life?

In our profession, one migrates constantly between, he says,
emerging from the wings—and at the same time entering a door,
my house door. Onstage that is simple also. The problem of
costume is easy too, Towle says—if you think it through.

Or perhaps he will say that later—later still.

At first, when he closes the door behind him—for at his knock or ring I will stop this dreaming and go to the door to let him in —all he will say is—Your hair has grown since I last saw you. And I would still be clothed. Though lying in wait for him.

This is a dress rehearsal, when one may do the same thing over and over. Again I am on my mattress, with my back to him. My shock of curls falls to a triangle mid-shoulderblade, not too short for a handsome woman, he says, not too long for a beautiful man. Note those adjectives, transposed too. Our unaffected days are over. Language too must twist as bidden. We have painted us into this corner, Craig Towle and I.

Except for the glowing mind of the dreamer, the house lights are dark. But she lies in wait. Somewhere along here there will be a dialogue. Once he is inside my door.

"So you'll play yourself," he will explain. "Yourself—in your town."

His tone is as holy as if he's asking to marry me. "For me the focus changed like lightning—once I saw I was trying to conclude—what one cannot conclude. I saw that the real focus wasn't Leo but is you. What *you* saw, and how *you* grew—in the town."

I do not quite hear my reply. Do I ask him whether *I* am what he thinks he can that easily conclude? But I hear his next lines.

"It's not a matter of ethics for me. But of obligation. To what I see."

"Nessa says you're a sneak."

"So I am. One of a long, long company. Now and then honorable."

"How do you know? When you're honorable?"

"When what I do—exceeds me. Then I know."

His face will darken then. *(Use the blue spotlight.)* "When my own life creeps in—then I don't."

Yes, those were his exact words, once. He would have been thinking of the bobby-soxer maybe. *(Anyway, whenever that happens, use the blue.)*

"And Leo"—I'll say—"couldn't you have exceeded there?"

He will assume that posture—more a stance than a gaze, though the eyes are steady, quizzical—which always made me feel the apprentice I was. This time it will not. "Maybe *you* could" he says. Even on your own, someday. I wouldn't be surprised if you could. But not me. Or not without you."

Is it then I will tell him about the third floor? He has been hunting the mystery of Leo so long—and I am honorable. Lying awake.

So why not take him there? Now as well as later. Montage is easy, where one plans ahead. And the lighting more professional. Would I really let them use that crude blue? Yet his words will remain his, when or wherever he has said them, on early trains, or on a whole hayloft of afternoons.

How will he look going up my grandmother's stair—grave? Gleeful? No, he will look as always. Say that for him—he is never two-faced. As for me close behind him, I am shivering. I should be smelling only the mystery of what we are after. But the long-gone dead are the one odor one cannot smell; that is what they are. Even Leo. And was there ever really a shirt starch that smelled of pear? What draws people to Towle is the odor of a meditation that both repels and attracts.

Now we are there. The screens that Knobby so tenderly arranged are behind us. We are in my childhood. We are in that room as it was in Leo's time.

Leo, if there, follows us like that shadowy black crew Knobby saw at the Osaka Bunraku, who moved the great ten-foot puppets, everywhere at once. The rocking chair is stilled, and will remain so throughout.

We—Towle and I—are the cleverest. Where I've brought him now, one has to be made entirely of artificial light. Where, as I have been taught, the true word is that much more true.

He is hunting the books. He finds them. I say nothing here. I found them so long ago. But if he asks me again, as he did once, whether it is my opinion that Leo when up here alone always dressed like a man, I will not now be too shy to answer that women do not find the trouser as comfortable—that it would depend upon the crotch. Or that women clench with the physical, whereas men in some non-somatic way exalt it.

Yet I must honor him. Somewhere in his absence he has come to the conclusion that outreaches either of us, rearing over us like a puppet come alive.

How is it we have got to the captain's walk? I did not intend ever to bring him there, even in dream, for he will ask me what I see when I look out there at the town, and will I want to say? Even if awake? On the ugly floor there are now no dead flies; perhaps it is not the season, or else someone has swept. No ghost, only Knobby—yet what shoes am I wearing? Pointed, high-laced, brown leather, marked Sorosis—Size 10? The size happens to be the same as mine, but I am not fit to wear those.

"What would Leo see," he keeps asking, "—when standing here?"

"Or, pacing," I say. Leo would pace.

He's waiting as he so often did in the loft, or as one used to see him in his earliest street exchanges on a town curbside, or in the hardware store. Listening, the way a deep-sunken well seems to, luring yet remote. I am not—am I?—going to cast myself in.

Wake!

I am awake. And will remain so to the end.

"I see the town lanes," I say. "And their crop."

It's then I see the inner light of a face like his when it opens—the light that makes him Craig Towle. He and I standing there are one day to be mere holographs of bodies remembered, but this was—ever will be—a light.

"So—we have no more quarrel," he says. "You've seen that too? The one creature we all are? In whatever shape. And a Leo —only that particular shape."

Then the face closes, and we are onstage again, that much farther inside my door.

"But if I'm to play myself—won't my own life creep in?"

"I'll see that it doesn't," he answers.

So that's all I'm to play, I think, standing there in the only clothes I keep by me here, my worn old yellow sweater and skirt of teal blue. Only the narrator—one of those roles that the students in the greenroom scorn. "Then—who's to play Leo?"

Either of those two actresses would be a draw, but neither will do as well as I can by now, as he must know. Then it comes to me: why did he never talk of it? He'll do as old Will did for actresses. He'll have a man play Leo. Opposite the narrator. Me.

Just as I'm about to speak he answers me.

"You. You'll play both yourself—and Leo."

Then he cries: "Don't move!" For I have finally understood him and I am creeping away from him and from Leo, away and out of that corner, back into my own life.

He comes downstage after me, with that wooing directorial whisper the school is teaching us to obey. "You'll play both. Sometimes you'll be a womanly Leo, sometimes a manly one. But always—the creature we all are." He looks me up and down. "With a capital C."

Nobody says that in a dream; it has that everyday ring. This is not a dream then.

"Not the monster," I say, quick to his cue. "With a capital M?" I have never really scanned his body before; the head and face are always so intent.

"Only the ordinary monster we all are."

How is it we are nearing this bed, with no curtain to halt or hide us—not even a scrim?

This is the nurse's mattress I'm using, I tell him; it has been scrubbed. But has he no bed of his own, five doors down?

He has come straight here. To warn me and all of us here of how our circumstances are now entangled with his. "The lawyers —they'll get at all of you. Or they would have." But he has outwitted them. We need say nothing.

"A whole town?" I say. "Need say nothing? How?"

"Except among yourselves. It has been done before." And he sets the briefcase with all of Leo in it on my bare floor. "It's my town too, though it may begrudge me that."

"And how will I—say nothing?"

He comes closer. The footlights shine harshly up, on all of

him. "I thought of you all the way down. How week after week you were there with her, with my young wife. How you must have seen—watched—what I do. Yes!—people are variation. I can't help that I see it. That it enchants me. And is all mine to use. I should never translate that into personal action. But I do."

How has he outfoxed the lawyers?

He has admitted to the charge.

He has admitted to the charge.

One must move on, he says. *He* is moving on.

"This old mattress—" he says. "That old nurse, my landlady. All my working nights over there in the loft, I think of it. How she wrapped Leo for the grave. And all she would answer—when I interrogated, pleaded, was: 'One wraps.' "

I sit naked on a divided stage. Would one use number eight, that deceiving rose red?—for he too is shedding his tired, experienced costume. Above us the old wooden beams hold up piously. He was born on the Row, under their like.

There is no size now to either of us.

"Think of it," he says. " 'One wraps.' And I even offered her money. Well—now you know what I do. All of it."

Then his forefinger traces down my right cheek. He is staring at both of us.

But in the dim aisles just beyond us, who are those two, sitting as audience? A woman not yet sleeping her life away? A live girl?

Master of the ash-heaps, how he bells all of us along.

"Craig Towle—" I say in the soft voice of all the women of our town "Craig Towle. We understand the apportionment. Without being blind."

I am to be his privacy—for one night.

Then at last I will rise against him, knee, crotch, breasts, neck, mouth—crying my one line, rehearsed since the day he met me, a small duenna stumbling down our stairs in her new plaid skirt —*"No. I am the bobby-soxer. I."*

His face is a well. I see a light at the bottom. I cast myself in.

The doorbell rings. He has already knocked. Once again, I open the door—as in years to come I will open it, over and over, now that the dream dreamt too well has become memory. God —isn't it wonderful, not to be waiting?

We both know that it is he who is dreaming now—and that anything I say will be a lie.

"Come in—" I say. "You will pay nothing."

Time to speak in the full, grown voice. Nothing less will deal with it, with Towle, with us all. Today, after so long, we are all of us together again, like players from the original cast of some sturdy old vehicle, now met again somewhere on the road. Except that all day we have been in the exact place where we began, with all the town foaming through the doors. Some of our group are still in the town and of it. Some who were once with us are absent, each in the way peculiar to them.

This is the day my grandmother's debentures come in. In fact, whatever she was holding at such high risk came safely due a year ago, but she kept mum. Our informant is Gilbert Walsh. "Actually what she bought were ten-year bonds with a Dun & Bradstreet rating lower than a baby's bottom, but at an interest rate higher than an angel's. And with about as much chance of maturing. Have to hand it to the old girl."

What has incensed him most, now that he is our mayor, is that the town has had a centenarian without knowing it. Almost missing its opportunity to celebrate the pure air and customs which have made her possible, plus a good crop of others in their late nineties, now crowding up.

The story sent to the metropolitan dailies will make no mention of Cranberry, her birthplace; Gilbert has property rights here, in every direction where real estate values might soar. Nor does it say precisely why she hid her age—this smart old bird who doesn't paint or quilt. "Plays the market right from here"—the mayor is quoted—"from a bedroom only one and three-quarter hours from Wall Street. At the age of one hundred and one."

It is rumored that when Edward Evams, head of the town board, was read this draft, he said: "Strike that 'only,'" even though he himself is in real estate.

However, the depot now has a fleet of cabs.

Today strangers have used them, getting off buses and trains with the simple urge to see another town, any other, for the day. Also that rookie reporter from Philadelphia's Main Line—sent out to see what town in our state could possibly be not Amish, not Pennsylvania Dutch, and still be quaint. Gilbert had sent out flyers only to banks, country clubs, suitable churches, and the like, but a Grandma Nessa's Day is hard to keep high class, even when discreetly engraved.

"Age isn't high class"—Bill Wetmore said. "Neither is it quaint." Nevertheless, he did the drawing for the flyer. Nessa looks quite nice. All his drawings do; people always look a trifle better in them than they could achieve on their own.

I have accepted that this will always be the case, as well as the reason why. His sour tongue comes from that underground Bill who will never be comfortable with what he is; any sweetness runs to his so successful pen, which endows people with what they too can never be born to, or buy. He never draws me. On my part, I no longer bother to make any distinction between a Bill and a Bill Wetmore.

I still feel the loss—of not bothering. Yet, so far, no one has superseded him. Not to our surprise, the full sweetness is in the children. We live like many, on the divided stage of parenthood. Though we do not have to do it all in one house. He lives in the city, with his drawings. I live with the theater, in and out of this town as it takes me. The children live with that other entity—us.

Today all of us, children with their parents, families with their town, even strangers, are running toward the world. Our own townspeople walk proudly on foot as able, from open house to open house, unleashed for the day to check for themselves on whatever may only have been gossiped, although the ladies organized by Gilbert into the welcoming and clean-up committee, have been, as he says, indefatigable. And always rewarded. For by the custom of such committees, its members have revolved all the livelong summery day, no lady under the onus of having to welcome in her own establishment. What a joy, even to the happy or the house proud: for the day, every man jack and jill freed from the melodrama of one house.

Except for us, the group standing in the hallways of the main house, its niches now filled with public flowers, the kind that will wilt as they should, once a ceremony is over, meanwhile remaining neutrally alive. A few of the ladies are carting off these bouquets, casting brave glances at our group—known throughout the day, as in funeral homes, as "the family," though we number more. When they catch our eye we nod back majestically; today everything here is theirs, including us.

Tim is down from Harvard. Bill's sister Phoebe, at his side until a moment ago, ever nervously humming over her Boston deanship, and most so with me, hasn't waited for her ride back with him but gone on, with a parting lip-curl to me: "I don't begrudge you owning our house; I couldn't wait to leave. And so convenient for Bill, isn't it? When he bothers to come."

I won't correct her—on who bothers, him or me.

Nor did I check her when she boasted to her students—as she did the time I accepted her invitation to perform for a night at their new theater, that a "famous" actress now lived in the house where she herself grew. To introduce me as "not obscure," which is how I feel, would not have interested her. Those characters who play the smaller parts in our lives never alter; it's we in the major roles who must show change.

Bill is here from the city as I am, though separately; if he wishes to stay over in my house here he may, and I will not necessarily leave. I understand better now how things might go —in a house in Dorchester.

My mother is here, and awake.Though temporarily not in the hallway, she will return. My father, here with her from Brazil, is standing with Mr. Evams. I can call him Edward now. Two men who have had losses, they seek each other's company now like those odd-men-out uncles one sees at all such celebrations.

My grandmother's day is over. She is upstairs, maybe even alone, though of course constantly attended, and more delicately than she has been in years. Etsuko and Watanabe are here from Japan.

We have all paid our personal devotions to her, but will not quit here until all strangers are gone.

Luray Walsh prowls over to me. "Those flowers those gals are picking off . . . Don't they know any you bring home, a dinner dance, a wedding, always die the next day? Even in the refrigerator. Florists don't send their best, these affairs. Gilbert has to watch all his official tributes."

He follows behind her. I appreciate him more now. Born in the Row, not ashamed either of that or of bettering himself, he has kept a kind of rude mental health, based on his inner contentions. That's not my estimate of him but Mr. Peralho's, who liked to dine at Walsh's occasionally and to talk with its host. He would be sorry to hear that Gilbert is thinking of giving up the restaurant.

"That was a lovely corsage you presented Nessa," I say to him. "In spite of what she said."

We all laugh, but it's Tim who snickers it aloud. " *'Plant it!'* " Nowadays, when Tim has trouble with his effusiveness he uses a handkerchief to quiet himself, pressing it on his mouth against another explosion. Which is a pity. My brother, whom some once thought a repellently pretty boy, is not a handsome man. But with curls set as close to his head as are his ears, and that fillip to nose and mouth which comes of routes exhausted and even conquered, he is often a beautiful one.

"My mother's arranging her death," my father says. "Just as she arranges everything."

"After what she said to that reporter?" Luray says. "No way." She means to console, not to contradict, but Luray always over-reacts, and especially with him. I used to think her vulgar. The young are so refined. Now I see a vigor refusing to give in.

Maybe my father does too. His once prematurely white hair is now in better tune with his age. "That poor rookie. He went green at the gills."

Ma'am—he'd said—*Ma'am, why'd you hide all that good money for a year?*—and she'd answered: *"Because I didn't want to die."*

A whole town, sitting in its community center, had risen to its feet to applaud. If they didn't know about her bet with herself, they could imagine it. And could chortle over her antics later. *But then she turned on that young fella*—I heard half a dozen tell later—*"and said:* 'WHY, BUSTER? THINK I WAS SAVING IT FOR YOU?' "

"And I hear tell that at her request Edward here is teaching her braille."

Gilbert, after all these years, is only now first-naming Mr. Evams, who takes it in good part. People adopt a certain famil-iarity with the bereaved, Edward Evams says. Or are only then able to. And if the bereaved are smart, he says, they will take balm from it.

As for grandmother, whose glasses are now as thick as the cataracts they replace—it was I who put her onto studying with him. Braille is almost like another sense, I said to her. It tells you things beyond the words. And she answered in the eerie way she sometimes does—though I can never pinpoint the remark that will elicit it: "Ah my ewe lamb—I always did what you said."

Mr. Evams now says, "Well, I have things I must do for my-self, I ought to go."

They all look respectful, not suspecting he may only be bored with them or with the occasion, in the normal way. He contends that people are often sense-confused about the blind. "Some talk as loudly to us," he said this morning, "as if we blind are also deaf. I shouldn't be surprised if some find it remarkable that we eat."

These days I've caught him wincing when he says "we." I have observed on my own that if he refers in the most ordinary way to the sexual life, men in particular find this strange. He usually never speaks of these matters to me. Nor is it easy to catch him wincing. Though his face is never blank, or not to me. Rather, it is a fine obscurity, well-guarded.

The last of the ladies' committee sidles past us, pausing regretfully over the large palm in the columned niche just inside the doorway, but after a whispered confab leaving it behind.

"Who sent that one?" Luray asks me. "I have that kind myself."

"Dad and I."

My father and I smile at each other. All the niches are now filled.

"Bet she gets a lot of flowers for free," she says to him. "All those plays, gee you must be proud." She turns away from him, to me. Her left profile, when arched, is boldly good. "That last one. Loved your outfits. But whyncha ever be in a musical?"

Tim has to use his handkerchief.

I say, "Nobody's picked me for one, so far."

The last stragglers are emerging, from corners we thought emptied, some via the back stairs. Among them are the two gentlemen from the farm, who have been upstairs to pay their personal respects.

"Hoping not to intrude!" they chorus.

They are assured that many do come nowadays—and Nessa loves it.

"Beautiful!" the younger of the two says. "Of course, we tried not to remind her we come from the farm. But at home we so often think of her . . . Why, Tim! Long time no see!"

My father and I won't let on that she as frequently refers to them—as *That pair of matched bays. Who let the farm go to grass.*

I haven't seen them in years. "You two look exactly the same."
They do, both their shaven pates only a little dustier.

"He's been ill," the elder says genially, "but our usual round
away has cured him."

The younger one says: "His usual. Sicily, Thessaly, Capri. Ca-
sablanca, on the side. Then New Delhi, Kashmir—and a new
one, Sidney! Then back to our Swiss spa, where I fell with a
thump. If he ever adds Russia I'm done for. But never say die.
You heard though, about poor Rasselas?"

The dog. They do look frailer without him. "And you, my
dear, they say to me, "We see everything you do. Bliss!"

One kisses his fingers to me, the other my hand. "Come see."
They nod at my father, who had been to see them two nights
ago. "Bring her." Then they sally for the exit, their eyes wiser
than anything they said.

"I will, I will," I call after them. "If he doesn't, I'll come on
my own."

There I can talk of Mr. Peralho, can pay him the memorial I
have not yet been able to, having no one to share it with. To my
father I had said, "I relished him." Ducking away, he had managed: "So did I."

Bill says from his periphery, "Those kind never die."

He has hung around longer than usual; perhaps he meant to
stay the night, if I hadn't just said what he disapproves. I usually
manage to.

"Just draw them, Bill," Tim says. "That's enough."

Even he now knows that Bill's silences are those of a man so
sunk in the visual that some things he cannot see.

My father is not so tolerant. I may always come to Rio, he has
said, but not ever with Bill. "Some do, Bill. Die. But yes, just
draw. Or have a cigar."

"Have one of mine. Of these." Bill offers them, each in its
separate tin case.

Gilbert says: "Those. Give my britches to have two of them."
He gets them.

Bill stops short at Mr. Evams, who is next to me in our circle.

In spite of being unable to treat him as an equal until lately, Bill
has always been afraid of chivvying him. "Smoke too now, do
you? Thought you didn't, once." His eyes flick toward me, in
sullen innuendo; of course this Mr. Evams can't see, though the
others do.

But he can hear. "Thanks, yes, I do nowadays. Occasionally.
But let Gilbert have mine."

"See you in the city," Bill says to me, and leaves. By prear-
rangement with me, he will pick up "the kids" if I am performing when they come down from summer camp in Maine, but out
here he rarely mentions them—as if he and I are involved in an
affair which they pre-date. In his choppy lingo—born of car-
toons, and the cafés that cater to "singles," where he is one of
those table adjuncts who adhere to that policy—he never formal-
izes them into "the children," and they in turn, at age nine and
seven, keep up a charming chatter with him, drawn from his
own paperbacks. He has his apartment, which is no longer the
pad. I have mine, which is no longer Mr. Peralho's. In either
place, we are entirely different with each other from the way we
are here. Curious, that he should be the city lover I once plotted
in my teens—the married one.

"Funny—" Tim says. "Minute Bill goes, I always feel we've
been too hard on him."

Luray is off to the kitchen, where she no doubt hopes to
encounter the Watanabes and perhaps lure them away to work
for her. Now she's gone I don't mind opening up to the others
here: "Funny, Tim. I feel the same."

My mother enters: she has been with the Watanabes in their
quarters and is in a glow over the treasures they have brought
from Japan. It was during Mr. Peralho's gasping invalidism that
she rose again, my father had told us. "Like Undine from the
waters." Though she didn't nurse Peralho, she had kept the
landscape of the sickroom full of charms against the evil day:
books and games and gossip, and all the odd toys that riches
could buy. She had even brought in a renowned juggler, who had

enchanted her—and Peralho—by proclaiming one of his routines as especially designed for men with eyes of two colors.

Greensboro took care of its invalids with lively cackle and chronic visiting—and this was what she had done. It had cured her.

In Rio, she and my father now live quietly. She has an admirer, not a lover, an elderly Brazilian colonel of German extraction, who remembers her birthday three times over, and takes her to military balls. In appearance she is now very South American in the old style, one of those tiny macaws seemingly in mourning for Paris, who are never out of silky black. It chills me to report her to myself by appearance only, but she would wish it. She admires me for barnstorming around the theaters of our hemisphere as I can, and has once seen a performance that came far enough south, but although my father comes north for the others, she as yet has not.

At home, their view over the harbor is a vast sweep of glitter, but they stay much inside. My father, going out to shop for grapes and imported cheese, overrules the cook's menus, sorties once a week to his card club, and pads the house in velvet slippers with coronets, fingering his small, faceted amusements the way he does the paperweights on his desk. There he writes letters to Tim on the general unfeasibility of the law, and billets-doux of praise to me.

"He'll break out yet," my brother says. "I open each letter like I would a time bomb. But—you know? It'll be in a good way."

Last night my brother informed me that he himself is marrying. For the past two years he has had a relationship with a visiting professor at the medical school, a British surgeon who had brought with him a wife. "A small dented blonde," Tim said. "Who stayed with the child. And in our presence, him and me, spoke like one." The husband, asked by Tim at the outset whether she knew of his extramarital tricks, had replied—"Poor dear, she hasn't a prayer."

That had festered, Tim said. "Couldn't get it out of my rumpty-tum head." Besides, half the men in his own crowd were dipping into bisexuality; it was the going thing. Though he has no intention of pursuing that. "I'm an historian. I know too much about the going thing."

In the end it was the sight of the woman's untrammeled gaiety with her little boy that had wooed him, plus seeing her staunchly doing her duty at those faculty functions from which the surgeon was often absent with a lover who, unlike Tim, did not have to comply.

She and Tim had discussed everything; she was bright. Questioning herself on why she had chosen two men of the same ilk, she had decided that at home it was often a matter of whom one met; she had been taken young. She thought the same might be true of Tim.

He finds himself deeply happy in a woman's bed. Always before he had been post-sexually depressed. *Post coitum*—Tim *est Tristram*—the surgeon had quipped. Tim and she have discussed my father, my mother; they have discussed me. I don't press him for their verdict, although these days I am beginning desperately to want someone's. He is too nervously intent on having mine.

As for children, they plan on having their own. "I'll grow a patriarchal beard—" he says, smiling easier than I have ever seen him do—"think it'll look well?"

The surgeon, he tells me, is coming out as gay, and going home to lecture about it. "He'll describe his, er, operations, in a flowery style tipped with blood," Tim says. "Poor dear. And go in for rough trade."

He waits for my verdict; I am astonished to hear how much he wants it to be Yea. "Not because I'm marrying. Marriage isn't the question, quite, is it? And if it were only for that, I wouldn't ask you, would I?"

"No." That reverberates in my own rumpty-tum head. Which thanks the British surgeon for what must be his word. "But I'm not a historian. I mean—I can't seem to see—the going thing. Or go in for it."

"You're straight. And how you hew to it."

"Sometimes I think—too straight?"

"No—hew on," he says. "We all must. We all do."

And I think: he has seen it too. He has seen the lanes people take.

"When I was in Rio—" I say. "Know what Mother said to me? Know how they sit at that window, she only by day, he only by night? She and I were watching the harbor. And she said to me in that sleep-walking way—the only time I saw her fall back on it—"Go with the weather. I never could.""

Tim and I don't touch; we never have. But for once, even with him having to stretch to pat my cheek, or me bending down to let him, it wouldn't be grotesque.

"Turn around," I say. "Round and round. Slowly. Slower. Like you're at your tailor's."

He laughs but obeys. His suits are still custom-made, but not so obviously. I see a small, stolid man, who in time will blend in, except for that head, whose beauty will pass. It will not forget the cockalorum path. Nor will it try to do so by disclaiming those still on the path. In the end Tim will be a distinguished man, but only for his history.

"Yes—" I say. "I'm sure of it. You're taller."

We both laugh until it stops hurting.

"You're not any shorter," he says, "but it's okay."

And I am glad of his verdict.

As we go into dinner, twelve strong, what with my parents and Mr. Evams, the addition of the Walshes with their Rosalie, the Watanabes, now seated at table and both watching closely the native girls who are serving us, the Austrian—predeceased by his much younger wife, and my grandmother's closest runner-up—and of course Nessa, out of her wheelchair and loving it—I say to Tim: "Now that we two are grown, and even the others as they get older—you think we're all becoming yea-sayers?"

He takes his place at Nessa's left before he answers me. "Dunno. But if so—Yea."

That was the eve. Now the day itself, Nessa's Day, is over. We have eaten the buffet supper Gilbert has had Walsh's Inn cater, charging it to the public domain. Nobody in town has objected to this double role, his habits there have even contributed to his election. He confuses all our interests so well.

"Fine meal, Gilbert," my father says.

"Best Italian cold cuts—mortadella not spared, lobster mousse, mocha meringue." Gilbert smacks lips, always red, that with the years have merged with his face. "Never give anybody what I wouldn't want myself."

The very last of the stragglers, an unknown, emerges from the downstairs bathroom with what must be a grandchild who has had an accident, ducks apologetically at us, and drags him off. Now even this stern house has that sleazy ease of the aftermath of a good party, the last sparkle draining down into the dirty glasses, the tinklers in the kitchen still at their task. Now surely the family is to be courteously left on its own, able to ease its corsets and shoelaces, to dabble again in the cold cuts, exchanging a "Think it went well, don't you?", and to say—"Phew!"

"Well, Gilbert," Mr. Evams says, "I'll take that ride home."

But Gilbert doesn't want to go. Everybody sees it. Mr. Evams has sensed it. Gilbert is mulling something, and hasn't the nerve to say.

My mother, who hovers so well, steps forward. Like many who have given up emotion, she has replaced it with the most delicate sense of the social order. "Shoot—" she says, that dainty Southern expletive which my father says can only derive from Shit!—"Shoot, why don't we all go out on the porch?"

All of us stare. My father says: "Is my mother safely upstairs?"

We all giggle. We know where she is. On the third floor, from which all except one of the screens have been removed at last to make room for today's rites, the Watanabes are showing her their slides. But the porch and its furniture are famous—a three-sided veranda's spread of matched wicker: sofas and love seats, end tables and footstools, two full sets of chairs, one lacy, one knobbed and spiked—and a contingent of heavily hatted seven-foot lamps. No vandal has ever dared this array. Nobody ever sits in it.

My mother leads the way. Half over the doorstep, she draws
back. Close behind her, we too stop short. Every seat out there is
occupied, in each a head bobbing, white or bald, or capped.
They gaze up at us like guests at one of those summer hotels
where there is always a competition for porch chairs. We must
make a pretty sight, clumped there in the doorway. They keep
their stare, timorous yet defiant; they know the status of this
veranda and they have conquered it.

These are the ninety-year-olds, waiting for their bus.

"Why don't you, Gilbert?" Edward Evams says. "Go on. Go
ahead."

Is he asking the mayor to disperse them?

No, never, but he has been called Ed, and in his mild, inexora-
ble way he is taking advantage of it. He wants us to see that the
Mayor Walsh of a minute ago has vanished. This is Gilbert
Walsh, once of Cobble Row, in a circle of his "new" neighbors,
in the town by which he is bound and thralled. He could move
out and away, as many not unlike him do, all over the land. But
we, who know all his greeds, have still elected him, maybe partly
because of them. He will give up the restaurant for more seemly
investment in the gambling casinos of New Jersey—but he cannot give up us.

"Well—" he says, "this is not the only porch in town." He is
pale, for him, but we can hear Walsh's Inn and Mayor Walsh
fuse. "I know Luray joins me. Whyn't you all come on over to
us?"

So—after all our goings-on, are we to see that porch again? On
the ride over, in the huge but homebred mayoral car, I am
frightened. *As it was, so shall it ever be*—surely I am still too
young for that text. In the back seat of this official car, which has
engulfed us all except for Tim, who is enviably tailing us in the
latest of his own getaway jobs, Luray leans over the front seat. "I
can't wait to show you-all what I've done to your house."

Mr. Evams and my father are on the jump seats, facing my

mother and me. My father says without turning, "Thanks, Luray. But tonight—just the porch."

Is Gilbert's nape a beefier red? The car is full of evasive summer light. My mother says: "Cross my heart, Luray, I'd love to. But tonight, let's just indle."

Luray sighs. "For thirty years I've heard her say that. And you know what? Tonight I get what she means."

Is the car so full of amity because it is the official limousine? Or because of those thirty years?

Tim is waiting for us at the bottom of our old front steps, now carpeted. I recall how he and I used to come out on those steps for our sibling revelations. I see that his car, though still a foreign brand, is now a sedate molasses-colored sedan. There have been changes; so there's nothing to fear. It might have been worse though, if we had come on foot.

"Some car."

He and Gilbert have said this at the same moment.

We go up the steps.

Our former house is now known around town as "the vault," on account of the Walsh's marblelike curtains, and the two wrought-iron cemetery chairs with high backs and low-curved legs, that flank the front door. Since Luray is a newcomer, she musn't be aware that in funeral-director circles here, which tend at times to include us all, those chairs, often rented for the occasion, are called "hired-girls on the pot." Otherwise the porch, though just as crammed as Nessa's, is now a Hawaiian paradise of chaises into which we sink modernly around one grand coffee table—plus one splayed-out pillowed affair that holds Gilbert in its center like a baseball glove.

"Won't fall backwards from this one," he says with a leer at me—and am I sorry or glad that his hand, once leaned for a minute on the knee of the girl I was, now squeezes the rump of the woman I am? "Ahrr, don't sit so far away," he says to me. But that place was always the best from which to hear.

"She always sat back," my father says. "She hasn't suffered from it."

So did you sit back, I want to say. But let's not tally up who has caused what suffering for whom. This is the present—because it hurts.

"Well, roll out the carpet, Luray," our host says. "Everybody —what'll it be? Tea? You don't mean it."

But we do—one neo-Bostonian choice, one Rio coffee-drinker who can no longer tolerate the American version, Mr. Evams who has always drunk tea, and my mother, who likes to pour it. I, fading into a wing-chair, have indicated nothing, have not been asked.

"Well, we're still for coffee," Luray says, but isn't sorry to be able to haul out her new twin-urned silver service.

"Why—it's almost exactly like Nessa's," my mother says.

Luray says, "M-mm."

"A reproduction," Gilbert says, twiddling his thumbs, "but we do our best. You know what intrigues me most about today?"

"What, Gil?" Mr. Evams says, almost tenderly.

"That that hoighty-toighty old gal—no disrespect—but that she would ever actually fall in with a jamboree like today's." Gilbert is squinting at the silver with some disdain. "Me—a mayor has to cater to all tastes. But that rip-roaring old aristocrat? . . . Excuse me—no disrespect."

"Age wilts the principles," my father says. "In favor of what's good for our muscle tone. Haven't you noticed that, Mayor? No disrespect."

Gilbert grunts. "Just like old times, this porch."

"No it's not—" I say from the rear. "For one thing, Tim is here. Not over at Pat Denby's." I hear my childish voice.

"Why—she can talk," Luray says. "Beginning to think she kept it all for her fans."

"Both senior Denbys are dead," her husband says. "Separately. And young Pat is in practice in New York. House up for sale."

The Walshes are more separate now, too, I think. Luray, although she still shimmies up to any man she talks to, is newly grim. Maybe she wanted a lover and didn't find one. Or maybe lost one. I should be ashamed of my diagnosis as not modern enough, but I am not.

"So what are you going to do with your house, Tim?" she says. "When your grandmother passes on. Going to keep it for weekends?"

"Simple. My grandmother is not going to die."

"Oh yes she is," my father says. "So she informed me, just this evening. People are beginning to bore her. She is planning to— 'Kick off for the trumpets,' were her actual words. She even has a due date. One hundred and four."

We can see Luray counting on her fingers.

"Dad—" Tim says. That's a new word, from him. "Let's tell them."

"You."

Tim turns to Luray. Every Christmas Luray writes on her card to each of us—as if her need is in some baffling way connected with the winter solstice: "Regards—and just remember, I have first refusal on the big house."

"I don't need the house or want it," Tim says. "Not ever." He hesitates, but I see he will save his own news until it is true and done. "So Nessa's sold it."

Luray says: "S-s-s—?" She can't get out the rest of it. "To who? Who could possibly—"

"Dare?" Tim has never liked her. I can predict the woman he's marrying. Small-boned, spirited, nice. But with a twee-twee voice, inborn or learned. I know certain actors still on the sexual fence who cleave to those, some happily.

"Who?" Luray wears dresses studded with nailheads or sequins, and lots of gold jewelry, but her true element is brass. I wonder whether, if playing her, I could convey that, and still keep the customers' sympathy.

"I can offer more," she's saying. "Whoever it is. Whatever the price is."

"I think not," my father says gently. He has always avoided her, but defended her, we never fathomed why. But now I see her stance, all pliant, swelling abdomen, as she rises toward him from her chaise. She wears false eyelashes, great curling ones that become her; she knows her element. And is pitiable in it.

Yes, I could do it. I could play her to the nines. If the audience were to see that she wants so much more than a house.

"Please—" she says, and I applaud. She hasn't chosen the right target, but how many can? And that rasp of hers has modulated like a veteran's. "Whoever it is—couldn't we work something out? Just tell me who."

"The Watanabes," my father says at last. "Knobby finds he doesn't really like Japan."

O Knobby Watanabe—how we have snared you.

Yet Knobby must know that, I think. That is what his obligation would be.

"It's my mother's bargain, Luray," my father is saying. "So I'm afraid it's a lost cause. She's going to live with them." He coughs, pulling in our attention eye by eye—and I am seeing where my talent comes from as well as my voice. He's going to play it for laughs. "Paying no rent, of course."

He gets his laughs, from all except me.

I am about to speak. To remind Luray of what is always more apparent from the rear, that even the most firmly lodged or recently acquired house is still mutable, to point out that Etsuko is willful, even that Watanabe is not young—when Gilbert Walsh leans forward, so much on the edge of his lush seat that he may tip it forward, if not back.

"If it's another house you want, Luray my old Dutch—"

That's Cobble Row talk, to call your wife that. It may have no etymology.

"If it's only the house you want to change," Gilbert says, "I know where there's one for sale. Craig Towle's."

So here we are, yes. I had forgotten the robins though, always here at this hour, and how they always looked to me—the bird nearest in drawing to the hieroglyph. It's not nearly the gloaming yet—did we have daylight saving time even back then?—but the dark is in the air. The robins stand to attention, looking just as stamped and Egyptian as they did then. They are eleven-o'clock-in-the morning birds, but they come to us twice.

My mother leans forward. "There are those robins again. What do you suppose they find on our lawn?"

If she still speaks of this lawn as her own, no one will dispute that just now, not even Luray—and I am no longer frightened. I am thinking that the children should not be in Maine but here with me on this porch, to listen from the rear as I did.

My father leans over to me there behind him, and shows me his watch. The only item he had kept out of a certain collection he inherited, it shows the calendar, not because it is one of those new electronic timepieces but because it is such an ancient one. When he enters the monastery, which he had last night told me he hopes to do if they will take him, he must dispose of all such goods, and will give me it. He whispers, this conspirator it so gladdens me to have, even at such cost. "What do you know. Listen to us. And it's not even a Monday night."

That name, of the native son who so aroused us and so blithely left us—are we going to pass it by?

Mr. Evams gets to his feet. "Time for my walk."

I get up too. "I need a walk too, after that meal. I'll come along."

The porch is silent as we go.

When we are a few paces away, I hear Tim's voice, and then my father's, answering him.

"Tim must be telling his news," I say. "There's no reason why I shouldn't tell you. He's going to marry."

Mr. Evams hesitates. "They all have their news." He hesitates again, then we walk on. Whatever it may be, he has decided not to tell me, or not yet. I am comfortable enough with that, hedged once again in the routine where he leads us, two musicians or even two actors, attending each other's stops and starts.

It's a short walk though a steep one—to the cemetery. "I drop by there most evenings," he tells me. "She wouldn't want me to come in rain." He hasn't yet dealt with the eventuality of snow.

We pass my grandmother's house.

"Confirm me something," I say. "Was Luray always—out for more than the house?" That's a hard way of saying it. But Luray would say it herself.

He slackens our pace, though not from need. A tireless walker, he knows the whole town's acreage. "I know a bona-fide real estate motive when I see one. Yes—it isn't just those turrets up there." He raises his face as if he can see them; perhaps he does. "She's always had the notion that the son of the house could somehow be bought with it. Of course the whole town knew."

I used to hate that phrase. Now the doorways we pass seem to me only easing, like muscles.

"We used to think it was Gilbert who so wanted it."

"He did once too. Now I find house property doesn't much interest him."

"That's how he knew about the Towle house! You're handling it."

"Towle's lawyers wrote me, yes. Towle wants a quick sale. And a pricey one. I told them this wasn't Hollywood but I'd give it a try."

"Why did you think Gilbert would want it then?"

"He—has a secretary."

"Oh? And as everybody has surmised?"

"We keep ourselves on the edge of knowing. That way, we can be tolerant."

I can tell he's smiling. I don't look up. "Cobble Row. Why does it always attract—the off-the-record in us? Or the lost."

"Old houses often do. Does yours—for you?"

"It did."

We are going the opposite way from the Row. The cemetery is on the first of those hills I used to call the autumn ones. The depot has the best view of them, for all the trains coming in.

"I know about my father, Edward," I say. "In case you weren't sure. He told me last night."

He checks his reply for a second, as always when I call him by name. "As he did me. And about your mother."

"Like—that there's a convent nearby—near that monastery?

An accessory one; where the nuns bake and sew? The monks brew only theology. . . . Like—that the two—forces—meet very congenially. In the most serene countryside?"

"He said an admirer wishes to marry her. Your father won't stand in her way. But hopes she will not."

What is sex but a question the body answers? In the end as in the beginning.

"It'll be the convent," I say. "All her life—she's expected to have only one affair. And—she will look just fine in a wimple."

That about does it. I can't remember when I last cried for real. It's much saltier. "No thanks. I've got a handkerchief somewhere." It's in my purse, next to a clip from a newspaper. "Let's change the subject. For instance—I can tell you what Towle wants all that money for. For that play."

How he lights up at theater talk. Some must find that strange. I know he comes to hear me in whatever I do in New York—though he never comes backstage afterward.

"Not a new one?"

"No. He was never able to get it produced. He's always rewriting it; it's always being announced. And he hasn't done so well out there lately. Nothing since that movie *The Troupe*."

"I heard that was very visual. So I didn't go."

"Very. The way a movie should be. I hated it at the time. For other reasons. I was wrong. It has—what I've always thought he meant his plays to have." Though the words for what it had are not mine but Knobby's.

"What was that?" Evams's voice is harsh, for him.

It's not an easy thing to say to a blind man. "Respect—for the moment that makes you see."

"Oh, I understand that," he says. "Perfectly."

I know this. Why else are we walking here, so in step?

He seems to survey me; he often does. "You still see Towle?"

"Only twice. Both a long time ago. He came back here for one night. The last time—the time of that lawsuit—the one that never came to trial. I—slept with him. That one night. I owed it —to both of us." I glance at the face climbing beside me. The

town would have known at once what I have just told him; the
morning lanes here are so clear. The face is broader than it used
to be and not so blunted or smooth—altogether more recognizable on its own. It no longer has a twin.

"Then I had a note from him, opening night of *The Troupe*,
saying he thought I'd want to be there. I did. But I didn't know
I was to sit next to him. Long enough to hear him comment—
cool as cool—that the young crowd in his film, that girl his wife
and her silly friends—would never have done for a play. 'I
couldn't have written it in a play,' he said. 'Goofy was their
favorite word.'

"So I got up and left him—though I stayed to the end of his
movie. And that was it. I see his son Tarquin now and then."

He nodded. Tarquin studies with him.

"Now—I'm being approached to be in the old play."

"Because with you in it—he might get a production."

"How did you know?"

"I know property. And will you?"

"I told them—that I'm too old for the part."

He stops in his tracks. To laugh. I've never seen him laugh like
that. "You always were. A bit too old for your position in life.
But you've improved."

"Have I?" I cry—but there are no witnessing porches here,
only a path. "I asked Tim last night—why are we all acquiescing
so? And Edward—why am I so—glad of it?"

"You're in control. You've come into your own—authority."

"Does that mean—that I'm not waiting anymore?"

He doesn't answer at once. The path gets steeper; many have
complained. Though he is not puffing. "No."

I stop on the slope. From here one can see the whole town
too, but differently from the way Knobby will see it from his new
tower, in leaf time or out of it. Up here one sees the town not so
much entrenched as hollowed out of hills that of themselves
aren't much. "Craig Towle asked to use the town for part of that
film. Not a year after that girl died. And the town let him."

"We did," he said. "I'm told the shots from up here were

wonderful. And of the old factory. They renovated it you know. And Mrs. Tite's bookshop and Hawvermale's hardware. All for four minutes of a film."

I'd forgotten he was on the town board, and that he serves there for love.

"Now—he wants to use *me*," I say. "Again."

"And night after night." Mr. Evams says, his face averted. "But not just for himself. And do I hear—I think I do hear— that you will let him?"

"He's—I haven't seen the script. But he's given out an interview. Heard about it?"

"In part."

"Which?"

"I heard—that when he was asked about the sexual oddity in his play he said: 'I tell them that there are no monsters. But that's not what people need to believe.' "

My companion doesn't use a cane, but he has a folding yardstick he uses in the classroom, to probe a subject with. He scratches the ground with it. "And I heard—that when he was asked about his private life he said that there he was as interested as any man, and as culpable."

"You didn't hear the rest?"

"That was all that caught Gilbert's eye."

Our hills are now looking at me. No hill is ever too trumpery to be a stage. Even if one hasn't seen the script. Even if the script itself turns out to be trumpery. Across this valley, for instance, in the same stone so rough here in the path but on the heights so serene, there could be carved a sort of monument, not a face, but a body, like those grave ornaments with phallus and female lingam mixed. I had one once from Peru.

I can't carve, nor can I paint, but there are other ways of handling the divisions in this world. Deferential as my own way has to be, always taking direction, it is mine. I think of Craig Towle, walking his gangplank of words, dreaming that he keeps this separate from what he does when on the ground. To him,

I'm only a geisha of words, speaking to please, and by rote. But the real gangplank, the riskiest—isn't that one's life?

I steal a look at Edward Evams. Sometimes one steals from the blind without meaning to. They in turn have expressions the sighted must watch for.

"Want to hear the rest of what he said?" I say.

He has turned aside, but I gather he does.

"I have the clip in my bag. I'll read it." I have carried it around with me for a week. I could cite it by heart, but it would be underhand not to do as I say. Besides—he would know. "It's headed: 'Towle Discusses Revival of Play Never Produced.' " My fingernail travels down the clip. "Here. He says—'I wrote a play about the haunted provincialism in American life. And about the habit of grandeur that has been lost. But they wanted the little sociologies of the day—and little wisecracks about them. Little daily hauntings—but without legend. I was brought up on legend.' "

I waited.

When he does turn around he is staring straight at me. "So that's why he's selling his house. Grandeur, indeed. The town did him in; it's daily too. I always thought it would. And you can shut your purse."

But walking on, I can't help looking back.

"What do you keep looking at?"

He seldom asks that of a student. It's an honor. "At a ghost town."

He takes my hand. "That's already here. Up top."

Shortly we are there. It's a fine plateau, but the parking is bad. As many local people have complained. And for strangers, collecting epitaphs is not the pastime it was. So we are alone.

"You ever been here?"

"There's one grave I used to visit."

I'm not sure he's heard me.

"Our plot is right along here," he says, and when we get to it lets go my hand.

"I don't hold with the afterlife," he says after a bit. "I come for the continuity."

Mrs. Evams's grave has only a plain marker on it.

"She doesn't need more," he says, as if I have commented. "She knew I would come. But her dog—I had to put him down."

Many of the nearby graves have paper flowers on them, rustling like talk.

"She loved color," he says. "She used to say that holding onto me she could feel I had once been sighted."

"I remember." The white cameo they made between them, on that chaise.

"Ah yes—the sweater you knitted her. She was the sighted one—inside," he says, bending to the grave but not touching. "When she was dying she said: 'My heart is beating—blue, white, blue, white.' "

They are dunning him to put up a stone, he says; perhaps he'll have that inscribed on it. "Because it doesn't matter. And that's why I can't decide." He straightens up. "We can go now."

I ask why some of the newer graves around us are marked simply *L'Envoi,* underneath which is the name and the date, but no text—and he says the current stonemason is a French-Canadian, and many families leave it to him.

The way out is by another gate, cannily leading one from the newer plots to the old. It is polite to falter, to halt at least now and then.

The Towle plot, one of the oldest, is in bad disrepair.

"He had it done up when he first came back here," Edward Evams says. "But not since he left. I suppose Hollywood is legendary enough."

I stamp my foot, luckily not on anyone. The old ground may be disheveled but it is crammed. "Some differences one copes with as one can. He did what he did. So did we. But on there being divisions in what one or another part of this country can give us—I don't hold with that. I've toured too much."

"You tour a lot, don't you?" he says. "For someone who can choose."

Sometimes running away, yes—if that's what he's hinting. Sometimes not.

There are plots here that have blank headstones waiting. If Craig Towle's were already here I would address it. "I never did agree with him—about the legends. I never did—about ours. But I didn't know how to say it."

I still don't—except that the legend never stops, or waits to huddle in one place in a country. Greyhound bus stations, cinder tracks. Or first-class lounges with the Chivas Regal being drunk like a prescription for the afterlife. Dried snot on the marijuana pipe tossed into the cowpool built with government subsidy on a Vermont commune. Or Daniel Webster on some lost village green, ten feet high among the trailer trucks and to most nameless—and still talking in stone.

It never stops. It's we who tour.

"There's one grave I want to see," I said.

He has been round them all. When we get to it, he says: "Yes —that one."

It's the largest up here, a full crypt with a door, inscribed above: *See the immortal faces go down, through that portal.*

My grandfather put up that inscription, taken from some Latin that we have never found. The door is opened only for the dead, but the names of those who have entered are on the outside, each in his or her space. I walk around the crypt to its far side; he follows. Our plot is as well kept as ever.

Until the children came, gripping the present in their strong, death-defying fists, I used often to come up here. Leo's inscription is next to the blank space on which will be Nessa's. Towle had said to look, and I faithfully had, studying the two chiseled lines, never satisfied. The top line says, *I live your life,* the one below, *Do you live mine.* Perhaps it was a stonecutter's mistake. An omission. Or an inversion. If it had declared *I lived,* or observed *Now you live mine;* if it had commanded, *Do Ye . . .* if it had said that. But it says what it says.

Today, on the flat ground below, there's a small nosegay of twigs and grasses mostly, which don't wither as quickly or as dolefully as blooms. Knobby used to do this at Nessa's instruction. Now that she is past it, he keeps up the practice as he can. He has harbored that obligation all the way from Japan. Who would not approve of his having her house?

I must bring the children up here. I grow tired of the separate time sense of those who live too much by their secrets. More than that, I've been warned. Of those many who like me straddle the city and the town, the town and the nation, or like Knobby, two nations. I will strain with all I have—to keep the connection here. I would sin for it—and possibly already have. Would I love for it?

"Maybe I've toured too much."

"And I've stayed here," he says. "Which grave are you looking at?"

"Only an inscription. Not really a grave."

"None of them is."

"That one on the left."

He doesn't like to be read out what he himself can touch. He bends to smooth the carved stone, with those fingertips that can map skin. "Oh yes. I knew Leo."

"You—you what? But how could you have?"

As we near the age of those whom we knew first as adults when we were adolescents, they begin to appear more equal to us, or we to them, as we approach. He is surely not that old—as I am now too old to play nineteen.

"I was seven. And losing my sight. A person named Leo often visited me. And ultimately found me the school where I was sent to be trained. Saved. And where I found—" He gestured back toward the grave with the marker on it, Mrs Evams's now lost to sight. The blind gesture has more circumference.

"What was Leo like?" I am canny, not saying "he" or "she." "Describe."

"That's curious." His face lifts, as it often does for the past, nosing it into being, in pictures of what kind? "Towle asked the same. So I told him. That the year I was seven, I was living in a mist. Half-blind, or near-blind as I then was, is the worst. One doesn't yet understand the growing keenness of one's other perceptions. Yet I had noticed that people seemed not to characterize by sex the person who visited me, who said to me often, 'You can hear. You can touch. You can walk. You can—love.' They always just said: *Leo.* So one day I asked. 'Are you a woman? Or a man?' The person took my hand and said: 'Half-blind is the hardest, isn't it? When you are blind, I may tell you.' No one had ever recognized that I was so fiercely waiting to be. But by the time I was, I was already away at the school. And Leo perhaps was dead. I wasn't visited again."

So Leo remains—Leo. No one now would ever know Leo better than Edward Evans. Except me. How quickly we lose the mysteries we solve; how beautiful the rest remain.

I bend to that inscription. We must touch as we can. If he can bring himself to put up a stone, he may in time be able to stop visiting—which is what stones are for.

When I straighten, I see how much taller I am than him. Still, we resemble. We are both waiting. We are both able to find that good.

"Would you like to read my face?"

"I don't need to," he says after a minute. "Your ears won't have changed."

It is beyond rudeness to ask to finger-learn a blind face. Very lightly, I touch his.

Down below are the porches. Descent is always easier, or so we are told. We stop in front of his house. The fanlight is not lit. No one is expected. I will go on to my own house. What a straddler I am. It was the hayloft I really bought, not the house. A hayloft can be a stage. That one was my first. Now I can sell.

Walsh's is dark. They haven't changed our yard; they are not concerned with gardens. Neither were we. In winter, the same stiff weeds will be knocked about and still come back to plumb. It's not only the wind, no matter what Knobby says. It's not always the wind.

"That porch tonight—" I say. "What an envoi."

"Ah—" he says, "—was it that?"

Up these few steps is a house where the foot must step most surely, even if one enters there only for a cup of tea—which if I ask him for he will give. I am thinking that if I do, must I wait until winter? Perhaps I haven't toured enough, haven't yet run far enough toward the running world. He is teaching Nessa at her age only what he teaches us all. He cannot vary what he is or says, and those are the lessons which are dangerous.

I look up at this house, which has not yet been vandalized, and at a curtained window or two that I see Brenda still leaves carelessly wide. Across the way, the porch that once was ours is dark, though the birds return. I am standing at the double knot of my own legend, as we all are, in every part of every nation, and most of all in the nation of the dead. All lives are legendary. I haven't yet gathered in all the threads of my own, nor will I ever. Others will do that for me. This is the cued house where I learned that the hours flow under the hand like holy braille. That we are all one flesh—and that the flesh has eyes until the end.

He says, "Will you read my face?"

FINIS